Atlan

'A strange, remote beauty, hinted at rather than described, haunts Jane Gaskell's other world of Atlantis . . . a lush and fast-moving romance from pre-history or legend . . . '
Yorkshire Post

'Packed with wolves, ravishings, and darkling forests . . . violent, disjointed, but vivid.'
Christopher Wordsworth,
The Guardian

' . . . a fantastic tale . . . and a brilliant adventure story . . . beautifully written, brimming with ideas and imagination.'
Stirling Journal

'The description and dialogue are equally fascinating and make "Atlan" a worthy successor to *The Serpent*.'
Chelsea News

Cija's earlier adventures are described in

THE SERPENT and THE DRAGON

also published in Tandem editions

Atlan

Jane Gaskell

TANDEM

First published in Great Britain by Hodder & Stoughton
Ltd, 1965

Published by Tandem Publishing Ltd, 1976

Although *Atlan* happens BC, the translation
Christening is used in preference to some phoney
word like Dedicating-to-God.

In addition to the books mentioned in *The
Serpent* bibliography, I've found it useful to read
Ignatius Donnelly's *Atlantis* edited by Egerton
Sykes, and *The Dawn of Magic* by Louis Pauwels
and Jacques Bergier.

J. G.

Tandem Books are published by Tandem Publishing Ltd,
14 Gloucester Road, London SW7
A Howard & Wyndham Company

Made and printed in Great Britain by
Hunt Barnard Printing Ltd, Aylesbury, Bucks.

He is the most vile man living.
You must make him marry you.

Her mother tells Cija this when Cija is seventeen. And so Cija is let out of the Tower in which she's spent her intense lonely childhood. She must travel as a hostage with the enemy General's Army. She must share its dangerous passage of the plains, the jungles and the mountains – and seduce him so that she can stab him to death.

The hostage Smahil wants Cija more than he's wanted anyone. He rapes her. She stays with him because there is nowhere else to stay.

Cija is never sure whether she and Smahil feel love for each other – or hate. She is filled with loathing when she discovers he is her half-brother.

Cija escapes from Smahil. She discovers that the enemy General's Army is intent on conquering Atlan – the fabled continent of the Atlantic Ocean – which for centuries has been lusted for by the civilised world because it is unobtainable – its scientists have surrounded it with an impenetrable vacuum withdrawing the air from over the sea for a mile all around it, and cutting off the entire continent from the world's greed.

Cija reluctantly feels she must do anything she can to save the continent Atlan from the enemy intrusion.

Cija is helped by the Atlan regent, Juzd, who is disguised as a Mainland pedlar. He shows her how to reach Atlan before the enemy – through a secret tunnel of glassy substance, which enables her to cross the mile below the airless sea.

But when Cija emerges in the savage beautiful Continent, she is followed almost at once by the enemy General, Zerd, and his army-horde. The boy Emperor of Atlan, threatened on all sides by the kingdoms of the outer world who have learnt the secret of injecting the vacuum with air, is convinced that only the warrior-might of the General Zerd can save Atlan – and he freely surrenders his throne to Zerd.

Zerd has been amused by Cija's attempts to assassinate him and sabotage his plans.

In a moment of tenderness, he offers to marry her.

He puts aside his two previous wives: one wife the daughter of the Northern King, his King, who sent him to conquer Atlan hoping the adventure would kill him – the other wife the daughter of a Forest chieftain whom he married in order to pass safely through her father's territory.

Now he makes Cija his Empress in Atlan.

But swiftly it proves a loveless marriage. And Atlan, the virgin Continent, is now in a more squalid danger from the occupation of its new rulers than ever it was from the fire and blood of invasion.

PROLOGUE

Told by Scar, deserter

The Road

I HEARD the rider behind me after I had trudged twenty lonely miles.

I saw him first by the cloud of dust his mount raised. If there are roads at all out there, they are raw new tracts of dust like chalk, where the forest our axes cleared has taken with it all the sense in the soil, the roots and all that held it together.

I had to turn to see him. We were travelling the same direction – he fast, I slow.

There was not much cover to the sides of the road, only stretches of stumps. The proper forest was just that far away, I'd've had to run to make sure of making cover in time. The sun was broiling down and my head pounding already.

'Sod him,' I muttered aloud. 'He won't try nothing on me if he's a lone traveller. And he can't be after me, or he wouldn't be alone.'

I plodded on, keeping to the side. The heavy cudgel I'd toted all these miles seemed lighter again.

I was spattered with white chalk as he overtook me. He careered to a stop just ahead.

I saw he was mounted. Not on one of the Southern Army's horses, but on a giant white bird, the steed of the Army I'd deserted from.

He *is* after me, I registered, and I hurled myself on him before he could dismount and get prepared.

I bashed with the cudgel. I couldn't get high enough, those birds are tall, and instead of smashing his head it glanced off his shoulder. He had been riding, I noticed, with his short sword clear of the sheath. He managed to get hold of this. I thought he was going to slash my head or cudgel-arm, but as I was getting in with another bash he sliced that sword right down the centre of my cudgel before it touched him. It fell apart in two

7

slivers, each toppling an opposite way to meet the road in a spurt of dust.

'Whew! What a sword!' I remarked.

Before I could get my dagger out, his pointed on my lung.

'You wouldn't have found me worth robbing after all that,' he said. 'Are you worth killing?'

'What a relief!' I said. 'I'm no robber. I just reckoned I'd attack first. Why did you draw up ahead of me if you didn't mean to set on me?'

'I've been planning to put a proposition to the first traveller I met on this bloody lonely road,' he said.

'I've hurt your shoulder, sir.'

'Of course you have. But nothing's broken. Only pulped. It'll be fine except for going black a few days.'

'Well, can I help you, sir?'

'Where are you making for? And from?'

He wore the uniform of an officer in the Northern Army so I didn't like to tell him I was from the coast where some of our regiments were based, even though I'd ditched my uniform and was wearing the old civvies I'd signed on in.

'I'm just drifting, here and there,' I said. 'Making my way to the Capital. That's the nearest place I should find some kind of livelihood.'

'There are hundreds of you,' he told me at once. 'You're Southern by birth, aren't you? Signed on in the first Army to take you over here, deserted immediately and want to get lost in the Capital over the hills. Its streets aren't really paved with gold, you know.'

'You're on some errand there,' I said, bolder. 'I am bound to hit it soon, aren't I?'

'Quicker, if you rode my bird,' he said.

I looked at him. I felt my mouth drop open. 'I told you, I wasn't thinking of robbing you,' I said.

'I'll sell you the bird.'

'You *must* be hard up. But all the cash I have makes less than a gold piece altogether.'

'I'll sell it to you, and my gear too – not for money: in return for what you're wearing.'

He looked down at me, his face livened into a sort of intense silent laugh.

'Now, if they're after you for something,' I said, 'what good is it to me to be caught in your uniform?'

'Don't take the jacket, then, you wouldn't pass for a leader

8

anyway. You don't look like you'd won these medals. I'll keep this under your poncho. With my other gear you'll get along fine. I'm not escaping justice, anyway, but I don't want to be recognised when I reach Court.'

He dismounted and held the rein to me. 'A deal?'

I looked at his bird. It looked good-tempered enough and would eat up those miles. I looked at his harness, which wasn't distinctive, not Army harness. He must be out on a jaunt of his own. I thought of resting the blisters inside my boots.

'A deal, guv,' I said.

He led the bird over nearer the dark trees. All his movements were swift and taut, as though he was controlling a big excitement. That made me uneasy, in case he was putting me in extra bother of his own. He sat on a stump and started pulling off his high glossy boots.

As soon as he had them off I had them on. They were a treat after my old things that were hardly there at all, any more. The heels, leather stacked on leather, bit into that dust instead of sucking it in.

Pretty soon we looked near enough like each other had been.

As I'd discovered when he got off his bird, he wasn't even as tall as me. He kept his smart jacket with its embossed straps and medals, but it was well hidden under my old poncho. He pulled my shabby hood down. His face was all in shadow now, even those eyes just a more intense part of the shadow, his hair well hidden. He must have been glad of that since he wanted to arrive incognito in the Capital. His was distinctive hair, lank, so naturally fair and addedly sun-bleached it was just about white.

'You must be sweating under there,' I said.

'Better than the sun you'll get beating down,' he said, almost smiling at me.

I approached his bird cautiously. As he'd guessed from my voice, I'm Southern. Though I'd joined the Northern Army in order to get here to Atlan, I'd been in a foot-regiment needless to say. We Southerners had never seen these big birds the Northerners use for riding, till they arrived just over a year ago. I'd never been close to one, let alone ridden one, and that was by choice I can tell you.

He strolled over to it – he looked odd from the back now in my poncho and ragged breeches and decomposing boots, like a separate version of myself only I was him now – and he held the brute's bridle.

'Come over and let it get a look at you,' he said. 'If it knows

9

you, it may not do anything drastic once you're on it. You can ride a horse, can you? This is about the same, only you must keep your weight well forward, slouch hard. It can be a strain if you're not used to it.'

I sidled up to the thing. It looked down at me from an eye longer than both mine together.

I couldn't exactly stroke his nose, seeing as how it was a horny great beak with nostrils behind it. I put my hand up at full-stretch, pulling my armpit, and ruffled at the feathers where there were rudimentary ears. A ruddy splotched crest shot up on his head.

'That's O.K.,' said my gentleman. 'It's considering you.'

Four minutes later I was setting my foot in the wrought-metal stirrup, and swinging up into the deep bucket of a saddle.

I wasn't prepared for my steed to set off at once as though propelled. Luckily it knew which direction we were using the road for. I looked back. My crazy benefactor was already small behind me, at the end of a line of splay-claw prints in dust still flurrying. One poncho-arm was raised. He became rapidly smaller yet.

I applied myself to staying on the monster. I only hoped he'd stop when we reached the Capital.

And I wished there'd been time to suggest a swop of weapon-belts as well. I don't suppose he'd've agreed to *that*. But now I was minus even my cudgel. All I had was a bluntish knife with a warped handle, that I'd used to cut my meat ration in the Army and brought along as a sort of souvenir.

The journey seemed to take no time now I was careering along on this lolloping huge fowl.

Pretty soon we were flashing past the Capital's little outlying hilly farms. Pretty they were, prettier than any I'd ever seen on what we called the Mainland, the continent we'd left when we came and took over this pretty Atlan. Lots of flowers, and those skinny little Atlan blondes in their flimsy draperies waving and beaming from gardens and yards. Mostly these farms were still owned by native Atlanteans, or at least run by them for Northern masters from my Mainland. Lots of these Northerners, aliens here of course – but so welcomed they could hardly be called conquerors – were still only sergeants and such in their Army occupying the Capital.

But owing to the native Atlanteans' hospitality and the way they fell over themselves to be duped into generous service of what they called the Brave New World, almost any Northerner

10

here had his Atlantean harem, household, easy-come property.

Soon, and at last, the suburbs grew up round my dashing mount. But he didn't slacken. Children scattered before him. All I saw was their big eyes, and a flash of gold as I passed their clear-voiced groups. Gods, that spun-gold hair all the natives had, it was good enough to pave the proverbial streets. Still, it's only a matter of time, a few centuries I suppose, before it's muted down to brown and dun by our inter-marrying.

Nice paving. No more dust-clouds.

The suburbs were just about exclusively Atlantean in architecture. After all, we'd only been in occupation here about a year. We'd been concentrating on putting the plains round about to some use, harnessing the nearest river, felling the splendid timber, doing some silting up in the cause of industry. We'd not yet enough of our own population here to do much building. In the Capital, we made do with what we found. Very happily.

The ghastly bird hardly slackened even when we came in sight of the Canal.

I was wondering if he'd ever stop, if he'd go on right through and beyond the Capital and on for ever.

The Canal shone like green marble as we approached and the houses drew back.

But when we got closer we saw the strength of the young wind. The marble was all veined with white foam scudding about here and there and chucking itself against the white crystalline rock on which the kernel of the city was reared.

It looked miles wide, but itself like a giant frozen wave-top, all spume and spurl. The rock was amazingly pure, a middle-sized mountain of what could really pass for raw crystal. Turrets and walls and towers and little windows flashed back the sunlight uncountable times. At mile-apart intervals, bridges crossed the Canal to it.

Our nearest bridge was some way off. But as we got nearer at our rapid lollop, it grew bigger, looked more realistic and less like a craftsman's toy bridge.

Some gold-haired children, fishing off its edge, looked up wide-gazing. Our claws hit the bridge and made it resound. It was wood, mighty but with a hollow reverberation. The railings weren't high – or so I felt, perched on the six-foot bird. The Atlanteans who'd engineered this bridge were used to gentler mounts even than the horses I was used to in my own Southern part of the Mainland. The Atlanteans did a lot on foot, or rode

11

ponies or unicorns, or sat in carriages pulled by thoroughbred mules – pedigree sires, dams.

There was new traffic on the bridge now, though. A few horses from Southernland, and lots of Northern cavalry. I began to feel I fitted in better, I and my mount. No one paid attention to us – except the birds who shied or had to be restrained from ogling. Their bad-temper is always ready, so their riders have to be always ready too, on the look-out to stop a fight with the mounts of passers-by. Blinkers do some good, but not much, because the birds don't want them to.

Above the bridge-traffic and noise the mountain rose nearer. Now I had to tip my head back to see anywhere near the top of it. Soon I gave up bothering, had enough to do with my bird in all this distraction without getting a rick in my neck. Now we reached the bridge-end. There were open gates in the wall falling sheer to the scudding Canal, but the open gates were manned by twelve sentries who were scrutinising everyone who passed through, no matter how thick the crowd, and stopping whoever they decided to pick on, crossing spears in front of them.

'What's the hurry, mate, what's the hurry then?' Two spears barred the way of the man, not particularly ragged, in front of me. He looked lean under his stubble, like anyone who's done an odd day's walking and is ready for a meal and a rest. My own breath thickened.

'Let me by,' he half-blustered, half-whined, obviously having a go at sounding 'reasonable' with 'a bit of dignity'. 'I've been on the silting scheme.'

'And sneaking back for fatter pickings?' said a guard. 'The huts on the plain not good enough, eh? The scheme's not over, you haven't earned your pay and your government's gratitude yet.'

I'd had to wait a bit, while this went on, finding it hard in the busy gateway to sidle past. I knew why they'd picked on the bloke. He was obviously Southern, just like myself, and it was these Northerners who were in possession.

A number of Northern soldiers clattered through, cavalry, mounted on birds like mine. Some raised their hands in greeting which the guard acknowledged. They weren't in formation, looked off-duty in spite of their proud uniforms. I swerved my mount to join them and raised my hand in the same careless salute.

I was inside the wall at last.

Now it was lamp-lighting time.

'F . . . me,' I muttered in awe. This was the most impressive city I'd ever been in, like a palace and a mountain as well as a city, and probably a few thousand years older than anything on the Mainland. If our Temple-city in Southernland had been all cut out of ancient crystal and snow-colour rock like this, it would have been something like the heart of a religion. But there wasn't much hint of religion here. The kernel of the Capital obviously centred round the Palace, especially now the Northern Dragon-General had become Emperor of Atlan. A military palace: music, rich clothes, ladies like legends in flowing veils and all clean in sumptuous uncreased materials, scurrying pages, blossom-trees, singing from balconies and coloured beaming windows, prosperous wine-shops, noisy taverns, barracks, stables, medals, uniforms everywhere. And ragamuffins with braziers larking round, street-corner to street-corner, lighting glass-covered torches to flare secure from the wind.

I tried to pick out a tavern that looked the kind where no questions are asked. And I hoped this mount of mine would stop when I asked him.

Anyway, he was going slow now, because of the crowds.

I was exploring alleys with the sort of inns I could afford when a girl started yowling.

I looked up one of those little arched side-entries. There she was, struggling with four laughing toughs. I was going to leave them to it, when I noticed how appetising she looked with her bodice torn like that, also that she wasn't yowling too desperately. She seemed just the sort of girl I enjoy meeting, and I was glad I hadn't sold my bird yet.

I yanked his head round, and kicked him a little in the side, and obediently he strode through the arch and uttered a short bark, right up out of his big breast. The four toughs gaped, panting. They were all bigger than me.

'Let the lady alone and gerrorfahtofit,' I said. I never checked the bird. It kept right on at them and they scattered and tumbled away, the half-laughs still on their amazed faces. It was easy as that. I felt a new power on that bird, I can tell you.

I reached down and heaved the girl up in front of me.

She was all breathing heavy and smelt of female exertion. She clutched her bodice round her and peeped at me through her tousled hair, wondering whether to up and run or give me a try.

'You all right?' I said polite and nice, to show what sort I am.

13

'Oo, thanks,' she said. 'You were just in time, they were ever so strong. I was fetching some sweetmeats when they jumped me and dragged me down here. There they are – ' she pointed. There were sweetmeats scattered all over the cobbles.

'You still want them?'

'I better, they're a special kind, for the Empress.'

'The Empress?' I nearly dropped the sweetmeats I was scooping up – I'd discovered if I leant down, the bird half-bent its legs. It really was a thorough-trained bird after all.

'Yes, she's my mistress.' She took the sweets, brushed the loose dirt off and tucked them back in her apron-folds. 'She's got a thing about sweets, Her Majestic Highness has, and sent me out for some more.'

I didn't know what to think – whether to hang on for some kind of perk, or to get away quick. I still liked her, though. She was Southern, like myself, I could tell by her voice and also by her figure. I've seen enough of these skinny Atlan girls, so delicate you would knock them down with a good kiss, so pale you feel you could see right through to the veins and pulses.

Her hair was perfumed, and when we passed a lamp-flare I saw it was red as new copper, the brightest thing in these alleys.

'I'm a stranger here, love,' I said. 'So I can't take you to your gate unless you tell me the way. And can you suggest a place for me to eat and sleep? I don't know what prices are like here, though I should get a good price for him.'

'Who?'

'Scabbyflanks here – my bird.'

'But she's a she-bird, stupid! And what do you want to sell a good bird for? You must be skint.'

'I am,' I admitted, keeping quiet about the gold and jewelled medals under my belt. They were the cause of all my fear about being chased by the Army I'd left, you see, but they weren't saleable yet, not till everyone had forgotten about their theft.

'You must come to Court with me,' she said. 'I'll get you a seat at one of the tables. And probably a bed tonight and all. Here we are, actually, we came round the back way. The sweetmeat-merchant isn't far from us, you see.'

A very high black wall, jetty metal, stretched beside us.

'Here's the postern-gate I use to slip in and out,' she said. 'Wait till I find the key. You better dismount and lead her in soft.'

She was fishing about between her breasts. 'Shall I help?' I said keeping up my polite act, and before I knew where I was

14

my finger was trapped between two fleshy globes while she had drawn out the little wrought key that had separated them. 'You meddling – ' she began. I withdrew and apologised and she opened the little gate that had been invisible till then, but for a tiny key-hole for those in the know.

We led the bird through.

'Wait here,' she murmured. 'I must slip up and give her the sweets, she'll wonder where I got to. I'll be back in a minute, to show you the hall, and the evening-feast's just beginning.'

'She won't need sweets now, then. Stay with me.'

'Oh, she's got to have something to keep her occupied of an evening. She sighs and nibbles, reads or scribbles.'

'She's got the Emperor.'

'You *are* a stranger here,' was all she said.

'Promise you'll be back?' I caught at her springy waist as she turned to run up a little creeper-covered stairway in the mass of masonry that towered over us.

'Don't worry – stranger.' Her whisper still perfumed the air while I waited. The brute I'd christened Scabbyflanks shuffled a bit, but stayed good and quiet.

Before I started to doubt her return, my little girl was back again, fixing her scarf round her bodice, apron empty.

'She didn't mind? Nose about why you were slipping out again?' I muttered.

'No, bless you. She's not like that. Hardly seems to realise she's our mistress at all. She even likes to arrange her own cushions, make up her own bed, tend her flowers.'

'She can't be of Royal blood, then,' I deduced. 'Where did she come from before she appeared on the Dragon-General's new throne as his important new bride?'

'Don't think I can tell you that. I'm no wiser than all the guessing gossips. This way.'

It got lighter and noisier as she led me round to the front. On the way we stopped off at a barracks of stables where she got a groom to lead my bird away for food and looking-after.

Presently we turned a very big corner and there was the vast front courtyard. It was like a frozen lake back home in winter. Only no one was skating – just walking, running, wrestling, hurrying in towards the smells of roast. This courtyard was a thick floor of rather dirty scratchy glass, over what I found was deep green *water* – because it moved when I stared down between my feet, and I could swear a large shape or two were swimming about down there. The grand hall faced us. Big

15

rocky pillars like open arms to either side welcomed us in. The hall stretched back a long way in warm mounting platforms, and tables were laid everywhere, and cooks were tending big cauldrons hissing like cats hung over flames. Spits were turning and pages running, getting in everyone's way.

'If I squeeze up at my usual place you can fit in,' said my girl. 'Not these tables here, come along, they're the low-level tables for grooms and servers and the odd tramp or priest. You have to serve yourself down here, fight for the best cuts or get the skin.'

We kept going, mounting occasional daïs, till we ended up on the highest level but one. Here it was much quieter, you could hear a fountain plashing behind the chatter and laughter. She pulled me on to a long bench at one of the tables and servers brought chilled wine and poured it into the line of goblets down the table. The others brought miniature spits and we chose our cuts and offal.

For a while I was too busy getting outside the best meal I'd had in weeks – ever since I reached Atlan's coast, in fact, with the effing Army – to notice my neighbours at table. Gradually I realised what nice gear they were wearing, and I thought I'm on to a good thing here.

'What do they call you, darling?' I asked my little hostess.

'Yula,' she said. 'What about you?'

'Scar,' I said and she said, 'I can see why' and touched my face that is quite smooth but for that one jagged blighter – and stubble. 'Can I shave presently?' I ask and she smiles and says, 'I'll see to everything.'

I give one of those gallant growling sighs that mean I'm grateful for contentment and I'm tucking in to gravy and sirloin and leeks, and keeping my eye on a whopping blushing fruit, when a little orchestra, strings and drums and a pipe, starts up on a balcony.

On the highest daïs, the single stretch of table filled up. There were some breathtakingly important bellies being filled up there. I picked out some of the bandits who were wanted for execution back in Southernland. Here they are very top brass indeed, as they helped the Dragon make the impact which won him the throne of Atlan just when everything seemed lost. They lord it in every way and wear magnificent gear. Their leader Ael wasn't here though, he spends most of his time organising martial outposts beyond the capital.

There were commanders of the Northern Army I remembered seeing when they were causing riots and troubles in

Southernland. Bluff yet autocratic men, war-men, who helped the Dragon hold together his inexperienced rabble of an Army.

There were fair men I recognised as the Atlan high-ups. They are still given great honour as, though they gave their Atlan over to the Dragon, they still have a hold over the Atlanteans. One or two of them, like Juzd who used to be regent or something, are even able men in their own right – just the ones who must already be realising that in return for a measure of martial power and a breathing-space for Atlan that was so imminently beleaguered, they have obtained a form of ruin for her by admitting us with our little ways.

But of course the ordinary Atlanteans are full of hero-worship for our 'primitive vital qualities'.

There was the former Emperor of Atlan, obviously, the youngest man at the table, still a kid and still vivid with hero-worship in his eyes as he looked at the Dragon, the 'hope of the new world' he'd given up his ancient crown for. Now he's possessor of some title or other that's just been invented for him. He's got hair like gold flame, that one, but the fire seems to have got into his head.

There was the ten-months-Emperor of Atlan, formerly the Dragon-General. It didn't need the gold band holding his black mane, the gold all toothed to show it was stand-in for a crown, to tell me this was the Emperor. I'd never seen him close as this, only as a strident rider always in the thick of things, scarlet cloak flaring from straight shoulders, always a flashing sword or gold flashing on a dark arm as he gave the swift deadly-craft orders for which he'd gained his fame.

This close he seemed even bigger, of course, and his hard hybrid's skin gleamed like leather. I've heard it's very sensitive, though, so he doesn't lose any fun in life. And he was taking care of that now. Though I couldn't hear any individual words in this hall, he was flirting with a little Atlantean lady who seemed part of the ex-Emperor's household.

'Look,' said my Yula, 'here comes the Empress. It's not often she eats here.'

I looked up with interest. A stream of ladies entered past the plashing fountain. The personal maids looked a bit of a cut above Yula, I admitted. Among them, not first, was a small figure in white spun-silk drifting from the diamonds on her head.

We'd all heard plenty of tales about the Empress, of course, even in my land South of the mountains across the sea. But only since she'd been Empress – that was about ten months, as I've said. No one seemed to know where she'd come from before that, though there were some nasty rumours. We knew all about him – the history of the Dragon-General was common knowledge ever since he was a half-grown boy a decade ago, a bit of a hybrid and bastard, at the Northern King's Court. Every hand had seemed against him in those early days, and nobody'd dreamed he'd ever grab so much power. But *her* – no one knew what or where she'd been till suddenly she sprung up on the Atlan throne beside him.

He must have been crazy about her to kick off with, unless there'd been politics or intrigues behind the scenes to explain this high marriage. So she must have something special. But rumour was emphatic about all his recent adultery and larking around, so I reckoned she must be a tragic sort of a queen now.

Well, she *was* a right little disappointment.

As her white silks stirred, you could tell she was skinny as an Atlan girl without even their peculiar delicacy. Ethereal, I reckon you'd call them. The Empress looked just an ordinary little girl, the sort who's gawky and awkward at times, hardly old enough to take to bed. And that's nonsense, she's supposed to be getting on for twenty. One of those mid-girls, if you get me – mid-brown hair, grey eyes, no outstanding colouring (or bosom) and no expression to speak of but a mild, childish discontent.

As she seated herself among her ladies, the commanders and bandits and Atlanteans bowed to her. She inclined her head as to the manner born, but smiled rather shyly at the Atlantean ex-regent Juzd.

Her husband, the Dragon-Emperor, took no perceptible notice of her coming but he started flirting much harder with the Atlan blondes near him. He might not have existed for all the sign she gave, her eyelids never flickered his way. She took quite an interest in the food, and chatted with her ladies. One of the Northern commanders, the big shaggy bully called Clor, leaned across to tell her a joke and suddenly she surprised me by bursting into hearty giggles I could hear over the hall's row.

She didn't stop giggling to look up at another bit of commotion lower down the hall, but her husband did glance up. I watched his dark glance become a dark gaze under a drawn-down bar of brow. I twisted to look back down the hall. I had a bit of a shock myself, though I'm sure it wasn't for the reason the Emperor was looking so thundercloud-ish.

18

At a table where I seemed to have squeezed in, I was fighting with some Northern soldiers! I could have sworn it was me at first, except for the obvious fact that here I was watching the scene – especially as I'd so often had nightmares about this very possibility.

Then I remembered that now I'm clad in the crimson cloak with gold tassels, the pale gold tights and the glossy high tasselled boots of a Northern leader (part of my success with Yula) and the poor devil down there was in my old rags they must have galloped a description of here to the Capital, while I was still trudging to the trap. But now I'd swopped fates as well as gear, by the look of it!

Poor effer, he'd guessed I was a deserter but not that my pilfering of medals would be discovered and the discovery catch up with him. He'd known they wouldn't send men after just a deserter. He was out of luck, wasn't he? But he was fighting his Northern corporals very competently and without much fuss (but rather dirtily, far as I could see). The blokes around were beginning to cheer him on and nobody made to help the soldiers. So I decided not to complicate things for myself by stepping in and clearing him. His (my) hood had fallen back as he kicked a corporal where it does most harm, and his lank pallid hair showed up in the fireglow.

The Dragon called a guard to him (there were various human impedimenta round the Royal table, guards and tasters and such) and said something private to him.

The guard beckoned another and they set off straight down the hall.

Suddenly the Dragon made his first move towards his wife all night. He filled a goblet and leaned to give it to her (they weren't sitting next to each other as evidently she hadn't been really expected). She looked at him in surprise, took the wine with a sort of distant absent-mindedness, and didn't bother to taste it. If he was trying to take her attention off the scene at the other end of the hall, he just missed it himself. Before the purposeful guards reached him, my efficient gentleman had his corporals backed away doubled up clutching themselves, and he jack-knifed away and was out into that big night-broody courtyard. The Dragon at the high table glared. The guards dashed out, reluctantly followed by the groaning arresters and I could only guess at the outcome.

'Ready to go?' asked Yula beside me.

I remembered that at least I was in luck. I nodded and she

19

got up and led me out – past the fountain, the way the Empress had entered.

Outside lights beckoned from the towers and turrets. Star-blanched lawns stretched endlessly away to hazy trees with a glint of lake. White shapes like ghosts drifted, and I started for my knife.

'Only albino peacocks,' Yula laughed.

All round us were heavy scented masses of blossoms. 'Now for your shave,' she said. 'Wait,' I said. I twitched out of the way in my new cloak-pocket the ivory-handled spoons I'd scooped off that table while she wasn't looking, and reached for her by her fabulous copper hair, and pulled her into the shadows with me.

The Empress' Diary

Cija tells the story through her Diary.

Born officially a minor Goddess in the small sleazy country ruled by her mother, CIJA at the age of 17 has never met a man and has been brought up to believe men extinct, and all women hatched from eggs. Enlightened in order that she may seduce and assassinate the enemy General, she is given as a hostage to . . .

Zerd, the General of the enemy Army from the North. Called the Dragon-General because of his race (his father was also a feared Northern General, but his mother was not quite human, a female of a blue-scaled hill tribe) ZERD is now Emperor of Atlan. He has married CIJA, having foiled all her attempts to sabotage his rape of the sacred continent Atlan.

But his supremacy is not secure. His former master . . .

The Northern King has joined forces with the Southern mainland to attack and topple ZERD.

The Northern Army arrives in Atlan, led by **Sedili,** who is the Northern KING's daughter – and was also once married to ZERD.

Later on, **Lara** and her father and his Army will also arrive from the Mainland. ZERD's second, middle wife – LARA was abandoned by him when he decided to tame and marry CIJA.

Resident at the Atlan Court of CIJA and ZERD:

The ex-Emperor – still a boy, the rightful Emperor of Atlan, who voluntarily ceded his Throne to ZERD in order to obtain ZERD's martial aid.

Juzd the previous Regent of Atlan.

Ael the bandit chief from the Mainland who joined forces with ZERD.

BOOK ONE

THE EMPRESS

The Throne

I STILL get a shock and thrill when I enter the room I sleep in.

I think it's so big and Atlantean and Royal that I would have taken a long time to make friends with it if I hadn't been forced into it by my loneliness in it. Anyway, I keep remembering it's loneliness I've chosen so I'm not giving in just because it gets me down sometimes.

'You can leave me to myself,' I said as usual.

'But Your Majestic Highness – ' they twittered and scolded as usual. 'It's not fitting, it's not right, we have prepared sweet oils for your bath, also a bedtime posset for you to drink – '

'Leave them. I know how to use oils, and how to drink curdled milk. By the way, I hope you put enough spice in it this time, it was insipid last night.'

'Yes, don't fuss, Your Majestic Highness. Now let me ease off your sandals – '

I kicked these across the mosaic floor.

'Where are the sweets Yula bought? Off you all go, how can I relax in all this niggling of women?'

'Let me turn down your sheets, Empress. And don't forget the guards are outside your door if you want them.'

'I can't forget, they make such a row dicing.'

'We'll tell them to shut up a bit, Majestic Highness. Good night. Sweet dreams.'

'And to you.'

They bustled and rustled out. I mooched round in all that space, swore at the lovebirds in their cage, munched a sweet or two, the ones with almonds in that only Yula's tame merchant seems capable of producing, leafed through my diary and looked without enthusiasm at the sweet oils left for me to wallow in. I was deciding whether to miss my bath when I became aware of a shadow on the mosaic at my feet – a shadow beside my shadow.

I turned fast and unexpected as I could, but the window-space was empty except for stars.

Shrugging at my imagination (for I know how high my window is) I started to loosen my robes when I thought I heard a sound only just outside.

I ran to the window, though my heart was knocking and my instinct was to run the other way. I leaned straight out. But all I could see in the fluctuating breath of the night's vasty maw was empty window-ledges, down the face of the palace and up it. Empty but for sunset-birds still coorooing and pecking up the crumbs put out for them, and shadows of flowering creepers weighty with scent. But anyway the ledges are only wide enough for birds. And my window is on a high storey, up among the breezes flickering the stars.

I was still uneasy somehow, though, as I went back; I doused the lamp. Then, as though hypothetical eyes were grazing my skin, I decided I'd undress in the circle of my ivory screen. I entered it and in its glimmer which eclipsed my own, I was presently bare. I chucked my silks over its edge and then, about to emerge, I realised I'd left my nightgown on my pillow.

I dithered crossly. I'd started this, and felt it was another bit of my typical muddling that I couldn't finish it. I'd undressed sheltered by the screen in case there was an assassin or a peeper or an autograph-hunter or a vampire at my window (probably a bird fluttering) and now I had to stop imagining things and march out mother-naked and wriggle between the bed-covers. Then my heart really did stop! I was sure I did hear a step outside. I reached out an arm, dragged a stool into the screen's curve, hopped up on it and balanced precariously over the edge of the screen to get my nightie. There was a crack as the stool's wicker bottom gave way under the ball of my foot. I fell against the screen. It overbalanced and suddenly went folding back on itself like a big noisy fan. I toppled and fell amongst a flurry of silks.

A male laugh right in the room terrified me.

I started to scream for my bodyguard and a hard hand clamped on my mouth.

Caught up in silk so I couldn't get my arms properly free, I tried to twist backwards against this hard body behind me and get him off-balance, but he swung me round, tossed me on to

24

the bed so all the breath was knocked out of me and stood over me, arms akimbo.

'S-Smahil?'

Yes, it was him, his mockery jeering from the filthy ragged poncho, the hood thrown back from the gleam of his head.

'Oh, Smahil, oh, Smahil.'

He stopped looking at me for an instant. There was a glitter on his lean cheek.

He brushed a casual hand across this lean cheek as though a fly had annoyed him.

'Why didn't you simply put one of your drapes back on, get your nightgown back into the screen and cope with Empressly dignity?' he asked.

'I was confused. I was scared. You scared me.'

'I wouldn't really have scared you by choice, Cija.' He took one step nearer, with a kind of tenderness.

'Yes, you would. You'd do it on purpose to watch me at a disadvantage.'

'Oh, Cija, really. That was always the root of the whole trouble. You never understood that when I was rough it was only a mistake and you never believed I was honestly – in fact I'll say frantically – sorry afterwards – because you never *wanted* to believe I was sorry.'

'I never much cared, to tell you the truth,' I informed him, making sure all my strategic points were covered in silk.

He spread his hands.

'Oh, what are we doing? An age apart from each other, five *minutes* together and we're quarrelling.'

He stepped forward and sat on the bed beside me, keeping a respectful distance.

'Cija, I've travelled scores of miles to see you again. I can't believe it's you here with me.'

'How are you, Smahil?'

'Quite well, thank you,' he answered politely.

'I mean – where have you come from, and why, and are you safe, and – '

'From the camp based on shore. Because I couldn't leave Atlan knowing you're here, without seeing you once again.' He stopped. ' – once again. I've thought of you every night for every month of this year we've been apart.'

'It's not a year yet, Smahil,' I couldn't help reminding him. 'That shows you haven't really kept a count from our parting.'

25

'Just about a year,' he said, impatient. 'It's made up in pain what it lacks in weeks. Let me look at you.'

'Let me get dressed.'

'No, you're all right. You're all little and snowy and Cija – '

'Why are you leaving Atlan?'

'No, I can't tell you that, or you'd tell your big bad General. And I'm only just balanced now on the precarious point of your hospitality. Also, I've got NCOs after me for a crime I'd scorn to accept as mine – and I can't shake them rigid by telling them who I am because it would get round – and back to your monster.'

'Oh, Smahil.'

'Are you glad to see me?'

Dimly I remembered, perhaps with one clear sharp pang, that last time we had met I had been in the throes of a deal of misery and anguish. But four seasons had drifted past since then, and my world had rolled to a new position under my feet. I shuffled my feet and kept my gaze on them as I had that near-year ago. Then they had been encased in a bandit-bitch's frayed-thong boar-hide sandals, and one leg had been bandaged from my encounter with the huge snake. Now my crystal-embroidered sandals lay across the mosaic, ribbons tangled, and my feet were much cleaner than they were used to, each toe-nail shaped and painted a different pale glowing colour. My insteps were scented and there was none of a traveller's hard skin on my heels. (Still, I don't know how long yet it will be before all the exotic ointments they're lavishing on me will caress away the scars of the snake-teeth below my knee.)

'You killed my priest then, Smahil.'

'Only to keep you with me,' he said, matter-of-fact.

'Well, it sent me off as quick as I could get away.'

'You wouldn't have stayed anyway,' he said bitterly.

'I had to get to Atlan, Smahil.'

'To meet your General?'

'I never dreamed he'd come here. It's his Atlan now – which seems a contradiction in terms.'

'And you're his Cija – which seems a contradiction of all sense anywhere in the world. But I always knew it would come.'

'I'm not his. In fact it's so long now since we said more than Good Morning to each other – '

'Not Good Night?'

'I don't think we've even kissed since the early months – when

26

we were still campaigning on the Mainland and having a sort of wild martial honeymoon – '

'I can't believe that, my Cija, so don't say it to me. Once he got you, he wouldn't easily lose his desire for you. If only to prove his mastery.'

'No, it's me. He started being unfaithful, you see – '

'Did you expect anything else?'

'I don't know,' I said vaguely. 'But it narked me, I mean we'd only been married a few months. So I just went sort of cold. Then he got more unfaithful – I think at first it was to get me jealous, to make me show reaction. I got rather wretched – not often angry, just lonely and sulky. I wouldn't have anything to do with him – not for revenge or anything wifely like that. Just distaste for us both and a kind of pretending nothing had ever put us together in the first place. There were big scenes for a while. But we both take the situation for granted now.'

'Cija. You can't go on like this.'

'Well, I don't see what else I can do.'

'Come with me.'

'Then you must tell me where you're going.'

'I'm – '

'No, Smahil, not if you don't want to say. I must tell you I wouldn't come anyway.'

'Then you do love him?'

'It's a case of not wanting to go with you, Smahil.'

He took my hands very calmly and firmly in case I tried a shudder at their once-familiar touch. 'Only because of what you found out about that bitch Ooldra – mucking everything up as usual, even from her dirty grave!'

'Smahil! Your mother!'

'Rot. She got rid of me – like a puppy – or excrement – and as for my side of it, I knew her only as a snidey serving-woman with that little girl Cija well under her thumb.'

'But we – Smahil – us – we share the same father – '

'I don't feel it, you don't feel it, neither of us knew, beyond a tugging of flesh and blood and bone – '

He looked at my face, and drew me gently towards him over the starlit sheets. The silk Empress'-robe in which I was tangled trailed with me.

Smahil drew a thumb round my face, re-finding the contours and bumps and soft places he used to trace and tease with his fingers.

'Smahil, cuddle me and keep me safe for a night. We'll just sit

27

like friends and remember our friendly times till dawn – and then you must get away quickly. I'll give you the key to my own stable, and a pass-ring for my groom.'

'Yes, my lonely little Empress, but we'll lie in each other's arms under the covers just like we used to. I'll be very good, I promise you truthful. Let me unwind you –'

'I'll do it. Don't look. Chuck off your jacket and those rotten old boots – Ssh. . . .'

'The bed doesn't creak. What a lovely bed, Empress. And so wide all for one girl. I could hardly believe my luck.'

'Ssh.'

'Yes, go to sleep, don't worry about anything. You're looked after. Smahil is with you again, if only for a night. And it might be for ever.'

'No, no. Oh! – I'd forgotten your scar there, sorry.'

'I'd forgotten your fingers,' he whispered very softly.

I nestled my head on the shoulder that seemed like a home after immeasurable absence. My whole self, my body and all the long old tears inside my mind, ached in an ecstasy of un-expected refinding. How often I had forbidden even the curves of my body to long for the angles of his. I found I was trem-bling uncontrollably against them, like a cat that's been up on a branch too long, and his unique arms with a tremor of their own gripped me against those same angles.

I tried to say in my head, This is my dear big brother, but it sounded like a line in a play, or something meaningless appliquéd on top of rich tapestry, and my precious leader's lips clamped down on mine as though they would never leave ever again, and became a world.

I lay a long time in the morning after I'd frantically harassed him to leave, and then to go alone, and then again to go, to get away, till I was hating him again. My nerves felt like blisters, and in the dawn-light he'd strained up from the climbing creeper and I'd bent down till we could have fallen melted into one form – and again his mouth became a world, a lost world, the dawn-birds patterned the sky, and at last with my eyes wary to the stirring horizon, I'd pushed him away, shoved him till I thought he'd never go, not safe, and I shook afterwards alone in this emptiest of rooms.

Then I cried, and slept, and made up for lost sleep, and woke still with prickling eyelids and drooling.

It was only after a few hours that the loathing took me, and long shudders shook me while I bathed as though that meant something.

The women bustled in at their usual time and took one look and said the Court must be informed I should stay abed because obviously I'd got myself feverish.

Ael arrived three days later. He and his bandits hurled themselves through the gateway and pulled up in the courtyard like a patchwork hurricane. They waved their spears in their fierce salute to the Dragon. All the other bandits we've kept here to aid our commanders looking after military matters in the Capital, leaped over balconies and even out of windows and raced across to the new arrivals, leaped two on a pony and they all embraced each other and clapped each other on the back and swore and yelled with laughter.

Zerd dashed down the steps like a bandit. He and Ael embraced as Ael dismounted, and then started punching each other.

Ael and Zerd came across to me together.

'Greetings, Empress.' Ael bowed.

'Greetings, Ael. I hope I see you well?'

'Of course, but all the better for your interest.' He always said these things as though he were very proud of knowing the correct civilised things to say. 'And your own August person?'

'My Empress has been abed all pale the last days,' Zerd said. He mounted the steps beside me. In case he put his possessive arm round me, I moved off down the gallery. They followed me.

'I'm desolated to hear that. But I trust you are recovered?' the bandit lord said in his light voice. I looked at his blue deep eyes. He knew I had never told Zerd he'd offered once to hide me from Zerd, and to teach me the two arts of war and 'love'. There were a few things I'd never told Zerd, even in those first burning nights when we talked as hard as we loved.

'What news?' Zerd asked.

'We fought hard to keep 'em with us,' Ael sniggered. 'We explained we'd sooner have them dead than let them go to swell their old King's big head. A few sneaked off, though, while we butchered the rest of their mates. Then we pursued those. We caught up a few in the tunnel, and did them there. Not many got away in the end.'

'I hope you didn't leave bodies to rot in the tunnel?' Zerd rubbed at his lip.

'No fear. We were tired by then, but we hauled them back with us.'

'We can't intercept them – we can't flood the vacuum with air and sail that small stretch of sea till my erstwhile sovereign gets his scientists ready and does it himself. It might benefit both sides, but I'm not helping him, he can wait till he does it to get at me. There's only one thing for it – we must erect barricades and steel traps with secret locks in the tunnel itself. And a strong guard of men to be ready there night and day. And get our spies and sentries through quick to the other side.'

Zerd and Ael strode on past me to the terrace, talking intently. Zerd suddenly stamped beside a group of doves picking up the bits left them. They rose in hysteria, unused to rough treatment. Some left token splashes on the marble. Zerd and Ael rocked with laughter.

Our troops, which have been dispersed to outposts here and there in an attempt to colonise this hardly-explored island-continent, are called to return to the fold. All day and every day the Capital and its surrounding hills resound to the marching of my husband's armies. The barracks here overflow. There are towns of tents outside, and the Canal is busy under a flotilla of business-like boats. The bridges are usually jammed, manned by wardens shouting themselves hoarse to get things moving.

On the terrace, I leaned against the balustrade. I felt tired. The sun was too hot and I had a headache from the clamour and glare on the Canal which was all hit into waves because of the boats, as though it was not a clear day when the water should have been placid as a millpond.

But I kept on watching the scene, though I had to narrow my eyes. A kernel of the Court was messing about on the terrace behind me – there was a girl singing to my husband and Ael, and another strumming a ghirza – the commanders were talking hard over wine and their eternal dice; I'm sure they play left hand against right in their sleep, and the click and curses are an absent-minded background to any conversation even if it's serious. My ladies were chatting with some of Juzd's nobles.

I didn't want to join in. Looking out over the Canal bustle was really an excuse to keep my back turned.

'Shut up,' I whispered when the singer sustained a high note with some tremolo. 'Belt up,' I muttered to the parrot squawking beside me. I tickled its breast feathers for something to do. 'Oh, *shut up*,' I hissed as I heard my husband give his

30

umpteenth shout of laughter, joined by Ael's rather ghastly giggle.

Suddenly all the traffic on the nearest bridge was disrupted. Traffic wardens and uniformed Army leaders bounded to the scene. A phalanx of tired marching soldiers was thrown back on itself. A mule, so covered in foam and lather and chalk-dust that it looked albino, charged snorting across the bridge. Slumped in the saddle, its rider looked asleep – or dead.

As he disappeared under the arch which led him into our city, I recognised the travel-stained uniform he wore. Sickly pink and green – the uniform of my mother's country!

I pushed the parrot away. 'Page! Page!'

None of the lazy brats realised they were being called. They're not used to me calling them. I grabbed my nearest maid.

'Yula! Quick as you can – down to the gates. There's a rider from my mother's land. Get him passed in – get him here.'

I waited impatiently now. My elbows on the stone cooled. A shadow passed before the sun, a breeze whipped the Canal, goose-pimples ran like fly-feet up and down my arms.

Someone stood beside me.

My heart lurched ten miles and I gripped on the stone before I turned. But though I'd been able to sense it was a big man, it was only dear old Clor. My body slackened with relief and disappointment.

'Chilly, Goddess – ' he stated. He has never been able to get used to call me Empress. 'Here's my cloak, if you're going to insist on standing here.'

'Oh, Clor, what about you?'

'I'm well enough, we're keeping warm with wine and company.' He tucked it round my shoulder with his heavy soldier-hand. I felt like crying.

'You're a love, Clor.'

'Don't want you sniffling and sneezing, do we,' he growled and padded away. I did hope Zerd had seen his commander look after me but I don't expect he could spare a glance from the entertainment.

A curtain gusted inwards over the archway, and scattered dice. Someone stumbled in, escorted by guards. Yula ran behind.

It was the messenger from my mother, his right arm limp and bloody. He knelt before Zerd and then had to be helped to rise.

31

'Emperor – Immense One – ridden hard with a weeks-old message from the Dictatress – '

I had half-turned and watched without staring.

'The Northern King has laid us to waste,' the messenger cried, and stopped, gasping.

A stab went through me.

A guard had to support the mesenger. 'The Dictatress – begs you to honour your alliance – she defended our land in your name, and claims its vengeance.'

Zerd laughed.

'It doesn't take much to deal with that proud little slag-heap. I've done it myself with a stamp of my boot, and my men grumbled about the loot. The vengeance is a mightier matter. But you can tell her it's already under way. What's up with your arm?'

'Not a new wound – the King's Northerners got me last week – though your own men tried the same, at first – ' the messenger added with a hint of resentment.

'They do well to be wary. Take him away and tend him,' Zerd said.

I hurried past Zerd and touched the messenger's good shoulder.

'Tell me – the Dictatress, is she hurt – will it take long to build the country up again?'

He turned and recognised me. 'Goddess!' he stammered, and tried to fall to his knees. I put my hands on his shoulders and kept him standing. 'Your mother,' he said, 'is aged in the months since you saw her. The priests have incited the religious populace to anger at the way she and your husband allied to put the High Priest in prison. She dare not kill him till it can be kept secret. She mentions you more often than she used to. Now the third devastation of the country she has poured her heart's blood into has her in a frenzy of rehabilitation already, but she is like a woman in a fever with it. She sleeps a couple of hours here or there, and orders slaves executed all over the place if they don't jump to it.'

'My poor little country – her life – ' I said. I felt as though I were choking. 'Once again it is ruined, and once again the blame must be laid at Zerd's door. This time it was to get at him, to throw a challenge and a threat in his face, that my mother and her people had to suffer. If she hadn't given in, for- given him and submitted her old hate, she would never have found herself in his enemy's way.'

32

'The city still stands – to some extent,' he said. 'But the country about has been razed by fire, and the farms put to the sword.'

'And worse,' I guessed, bitterly.

He nodded mutely. 'Go and let them see to your arm,' I said. 'We'll meet again at the meal after sunset.'

I turned back to return to the balustrade. Dusk was gathering and the sun was making a spectacular dive into the Canal. Vaguely I noticed that the singing had stopped. The singer and ghirza-strummer were lolling beside Zerd and Ael. Ael and the strummer were giggling softly together. Zerd was pushing grapes into the little pink pouted O of the singer's mouth.

In the dim, dying light I saw him shove her aside and stride across. I didn't realise he was coming to me till he stopped in front of me. Even then I kept walking. He stopped me with a hand on my arm, then took it away again quickly. I could feel the others trying not to look as though they were looking.

'You're crying,' he said in a hushed voice.

'Am I?'

He touched a finger to my face, and brought it away tipped with a pear-rounded glitter of tear.

'That was neat,' I said in spite of myself. 'You didn't break it.'

'What are you crying about?'

'What do you think?'

'Sit next to me tonight. You mustn't stay so on your own. I'm not interested in that little slut.'

'Nor am I,' I said quite violently. 'You don't think I'm moping, that I'm lonely or something? My mother's country – will you send her men and moneys to help her put it on its feet again?'

'I'm tired of your mother's country,' he said. 'Don't you ever stop talking about it?'

My parrot fluttered past, squawking 'Shutupshutup' and in the garish lilac light of the dying sun every pair of eyes I met seemed to be staring in a lilac insanity.

I opened my eyes. My women were bending over me, exclaiming and clucking. 'What's the matter, you sound like a coop of hens,' I said. I had to fall back on the pillow. My eyes seemed to split my head and my belly was a melting-pot of pain.

'We *told* you you got up too soon after that fever,' they said, their eyes all big and worried. 'And you've been sleeping so badly, and getting up so early to do nothing. We told you you needed more sleep.'

'I feel dead –'

'You nearly were,' they scolded. 'We just came and found you in your bath – either asleep or fainted, hard to tell, you've been so wan lately. You *must* let us tend you to bath and bed in future. You must have slipped off while it was still hot and just lain like that without noticing – your body looks quite burnt, but you'll be all right now we've salved it.'

I winced. I remembered forcing myself to lie there while the heat scalded me and yet I shivered as I forced down more and more of that revolting drink and wouldn't let myself retch it up again, while the steam added to my drunken dizziness. Couldn't they smell my breath? – Too bad I'd spoiled everything by fainting before I'd finished.

'We got some hot wine between your teeth, I think that brought you round,' said my chief lady who is just like an elegant nurse. 'But don't let your husband get a whiff,' she added gaily. 'Now, lie straight and drift off to a healthy sleep this time. We must take care of ourself in future, mustn't we? No more dashing up and down stairs, no more hard riding in the hills.'

'Why . . . ?' I mumbled.

'Didn't you know?' Her eyes were all lit up, she was delighted to be first even to tell me, and the others listened all ears. 'Didn't you *realise*, you silly dear Majestic Highness? You're going to be a mummy.'

'I feel like one already,' I moaned, but they didn't understand and they patted my queasy stomach and beamed and smoothed my brow.

Now that my women have found out, the news will infest the Court. I had better inform the father so that he isn't the last to know. Oh, dear, the timing is a bit difficult. I'm sure he's at least kept *some* count, he must be aware I haven't slept with him for well over three months. He'll think it's a bit unpremature when it's born, won't he?

Well, I must face up to things. I practically invited this monster into my inside, this corrupt blossoming of a double sin, and as I can't get rid of it I must face another monstrous intimacy. Who am I to wail about being unclean – now?

I really was scared. I daren't work out a plan for cornering

34

Zerd. But I couldn't put it off till, say, tomorrow, and just wait for an opportunity to present itself.

I always used to feel shy of him, and now after a long estrangement I am terribly shy.

I had not missed his bed as I'd missed Smahil's, partly because we'd never had much chance to *sleep* together anyway on campaign, always off to some new place and snatching moments together. But mainly because I'd never really begun to think of that fierce famous body as *mine*.

In those old days, when my mother had ordered me to seduce him, I'd had more confidence. But now I knew what was involved. I also knew what deceits were involved, multiple deceits, some seemed unfair even to a bastard like my Zerd.

As I set out to look for my lord and master, I realised in confusion I didn't know where he'd be at certain times. The evening meal was over. I had been unconscious then. I looked in the main hall but he wasn't among the courtiers courting and dicing. I looked on the terrace, cold in the naked night. There was a couple whispering at the balustrade, but the man was short and thick-set.

I began to fear a nasty hollow fear. I began to wander like some legend of an Empress-ghost, looking everywhere, carrying the knowledge and the uncleanness heavy in me. I would look in that red bedroom last.

I kept trying to think of *other* places to look, even when his bedroom seemed the only place left. Finally I ventured out into the night on the bare lawns.

Perhaps he wasn't even *in* the Capital? I remembered I hadn't been to evening meal for over a fortnight again now. For all I knew, he and Ael had left again and were away on another of their little jaunts getting everything ready for the coming war that was nearly certain now from the Northern King on the Mainland.

A little I myself had gathered, of the threat from the King, from Smahil's dawn-bleak entreaties to me to go with him and perpetuate sin. What an age, a world ago that night breathing heaven and hell seemed now, and how much more ghastly than I had expected it to seem.

I leaned against a big solid tree. The bark smelt wonderful and very real and yet clean, and here and there its harsh friendly texture was softened by a tiny parasite moss more like silk than velvet. The leaves muttered and poured through the wind's fingers above me.

35

Oh, Gods, my lips formed the words in a moan too painful not to be silent. If I'd known this would come of that unclean night, I would have gone with him. Oh, Gods. I would have, I would have gone with him.

I'd be with Smahil now. We'd look after each other. He'd see I didn't suffer all alone. He'd bully me into thinking things are normal and fine. He's like Zerd in that way, they neither of them believe in sin because they believe in nothing but what they taste and bite, smell and smite, see and hear. But I am tasting sin now. I can hardly touch it more, for close on a year it will be within me, and after that for a lifetime I shall never be able to forget it.

Perhaps it is better that, carrying sin, I should know sin. Perhaps Smahil lulling me to complacence would be added evil. Perhaps it is a blessing I didn't know, didn't go.

I blundered among a grove of dark blossoms. I disturbed little birds (or big insects) drowsing amongst the perfume. They whirred away. I pushed forward, using my hands like a blind beggar. I was begging for something, too.

When I came to the end of the grove there was still only blackness. I couldn't see the gleam of a statue or a fountain to guide me. I was rather glad, in a way, I hate being near statues at night. Now I realised I'd be lucky if I came across any nits locked in each other's throbbing arms out here. I'd have to stumble across them to find them, but they might show me the way back to the Palace. As for finding Zerd, he could have been yards away without either of us realising it.

A knee-high white shape drifted to me, its snake-like head ducking and jerking. I knelt. 'Hello, ice-peacock. Stay with me. Be tame. I'm so alone, much more alone than you realise. I need a guide through the night. I'm not used to the night in my own gardens.'

The peacock pecked at my hand as though it hoped for crumbs. I caressed its throat. Its pulse struck at my fingers. It stalked round me and, as I thought it was about to leave me, it adopted me and followed me as I wandered on.

A dear little drizzle began to fall. It was like a living mist, it borrowed the tiny glitter from the stars and magnified it into a single shimmer over everything. It struck like needles on my bare shoulders, then melted instantly.

Something started up from under the foliage under my feet. 'Oh, it's raining! Come on!'

I made towards the shapes. I made too fast and I cannoned

36

into a girl. Her flesh was slippery and fragrant in the rain.

'Oh – oh – oh!' she gave a series of shrieks.

'I'm sorry,' I said, overcome with shame. 'I meant to – ' I tried to explain but her shrieks continued.

She was trying to move away from me and her legs and hem had got entangled with the peacock. It was starting to get huffy. 'Calm down,' I said. 'It'll bite.'

That sent her off again.

'What is it?' asked the man who'd strolled up behind her.

'A peacock,' I said.

He reached for her I thought, and his hands found me. Once on me they travelled immediately, strongly. 'I knew the voice of the wandering girl with the peacock,' he murmured, 'even through those squeals. And I know this shape.'

I knew his hands at once because of the tingle that went over me. I hadn't known his voice through his companion's hysteria. He picked me up and strode on into the rain and the scent of the dark. The sound rose, yet it was diminished by distance. I found my head was capably cradled against his shoulder-swell.

'Zerd – that poor girl –'

'She and your peacock'll make friends in no time.'

'She'll be lost in the dark –'

'She knows the gardens well, I'm told.'

I also recognised the timbre and tremolo of her high notes. Why had he said he wasn't interested in that singer? And why call her a slut, the other night, as though he wasn't glad she was, as though he had the calm right to be contemptuous of anything but pristine purity? And why had her flesh when I stumbled against her been so fragrant? How could I invite his attentions after he had been with her out in the night under the stars and the flowers?

'Put me down, Zerd.'

He put me down at once.

'You want to be taken back,' he said flatly.

'Why should I?' I said, sweetly. 'It's a long time since we've been quite alone with each other.'

'Don't get sarcastic,' he told me. 'Give me your hand – please, Cija. It's just so that you won't get lost.'

This was difficult. For once I didn't mean to sound sarcastic. I'd never been good at seducing him in the old days, never really got anywhere till I'd interested him by giving up, and he'd decided to have me and done something about it at once. In other words, I still had no experience of making love, only of

37

being made love to. 'Zerd,' I said and then I could think of nothing at all to add. All I wanted really was to be friends, but at once my pride rejected that yearning too.

'Say what you were going to say,' he said from the steadying heavying rain.

'I don't know what I was going to say.'

'Come under my cloak, darling. You needn't touch me. You mustn't catch cold.'

I hoped to my Gods he hadn't already heard rumours. But he wouldn't have mentioned it like that, even in his coldest most suspicious mood. And I'd never given him cause for jealous suspicion.

He drew me with him, in the bar of his arm, into the shelter of his cloak.

'Tell me, Cija, do you often walk alone in the gardens?'

'Are you afraid I'll interrupt you another night?'

He was silent. At last he said, 'Each speaks more sweetly than you do.'

My heart gave a leap, though I bade it be wary. He was moody, and trying to make me jealous and realise what a shrew I am to knock back friendliness and groping concern. If he'd started assuring me he was trying to find me in each of these girls, or that he could never forget me in their embraces, I'd've run and escaped from him.

'Shall I tell you something?' he said presently in a bit of a mumble, strange from his resonant voice. 'None of them has your sweetness to touch, not one of them.'

And I found that, after all, I couldn't run. His arm was like fire around me.

I must stick it out, I thought.

'Don't make me laugh my head off, I have a headache already,' I said.

'I'd like to shake you sick,' he said savagely.

'Go ahead,' I said. 'You're my Emperor as well as my lord.'

The cloak dropped and the rain slashed and splashed on me as he gripped me and turned me. His hand glanced on the edge of a blow across my jaw. My eyes stang. His fingers tightened round my neck and he drew me so against him and then at my shoulder's nearness he put his head down to my shoulder and the swell of my breast and was wracked by gasping shudders that shook me and he remembered to loose his fingers round my neck. My neck started pounding immediately. It felt swollen.

38

'Raining on my breasts – ' I said. 'I'm sore there, let me alone – '

He raised his head to kiss me as I've never been kissed before. I felt as though a storm had caught me up. His ferocious mouth tasted salt. Salt rain.

I was limp when he let me go. I felt electric, I was tingling as though all my nerves had received a separate live shock.

'Zerd – '

'Cija – '

Now my pride pushed up its miserable head. If I must stay with him tonight, it must not be as if he overwhelmed me and I was wooed like a romantic child, a spinsterish wife who was only too glad to accept embraces which had just come from a little singer in these very gardens.

It must be at least my conquest. I would remain deliberate and cold, aware of each caress that was in a style new from the months with me, aware of the smell of her. I knew I would be disgusted afterwards, so I would not be fooled now.

I was about to sit up and place my arms round his neck – I was so marvellously aware of everything that till now I had not even realised we'd sunk together on to the sopping wet grass – when suddenly he hauled me up, picked up the cloak and tucked it round me as I tottered.

We walked on through the downpour. The grass squelched at our sandals.

We arrived at the white glimmer of the terrace. The rain bounced like silver flame on the marble.

'Good night to you,' Zerd said. He turned towards his rooms.

I scurried after him. I seized his now trailing sodden red cloak. 'Zerd – ' He looked down at me, we stood together in the beat of the rain. 'I'm pregnant.'

He picked me up and gave a whoop that in any other less noisy weather would have had every window full of faces.

Holding me tight, he strode into his flickery torch-lit rooms and past the startled saluting guards and through the heavy studded doors. He laid me as though I were porcelain or a basket of eggs on the big red bed. He kicked the doors to, yanked a leather curtain across them, and came and kissed my hair. 'Oh, Cija.' He laid his hand over my fairly flat stomach.

'Has he kicked yet?' he asked.

'I don't think so.' I had meant to confess everything. It was impossible. I was terrified of the reaction the confession might draw. In order to soothe my shame, I said 'What number of children will he become youngest brother to?'

'I don't know, my own little Goddess. In Northkingdom they used to point blue brats out to me, but they never showed a scrap of proof. There are so many – of that race – there. Lara's pregnancy miscarried. That mustn't happen to you, it was probably just as well in her case. You must have our baby. Oh, Cija, everything will be different then.'

He kissed my eyelids very tenderly and very lingeringly till they had stopped fluttering nervously.

'Zerd, don't make love to me – ' I said anxiously. Now that he had accepted my pregnancy as all his own work, without any arguments at all, I no longer needed to force myself to the further ordeal.

'Of course I won't. Only four months or so to go! Why didn't you tell me sooner?'

He laid me in his bed and held me strong and gentle.

Autumn is making its presence felt. My second autumn in Atlan. The first season that I am meeting for the second time, here in the reality of this long-mythical continent who has condoned her rape, on whose ancient crystal throne I sit.

Zerd's troops are being made ready for winter campaigning – or winter fighting.

Sleds, extra boot supplies, pontoon bridges for swollen rivers are being rushed ready.

I still go riding every day. But Zerd keeps a watch on me these days – a strict watch. I am no longer allowed out alone – nor even beyond the Canal. I must stay in the city itself. And he scolds me to ride my tamest steed, not a bird but a milky mare with a single white horn spiking from her forehead. These are rare but beloved steeds for the Atlan nobility. They don't breed in captivity but seem happy enough, so I don't know how they are trained from the wild state to such docility after they are captured. Also, I have to have my ladies with me. They are very glad and 'I told you so'-ish about this, but it makes me feel all hampered.

Before, I used to dash on a poorly-harnessed bird – through the city, over a bridge and up into the hills before anyone recognised me.

Now, cheering crowds fellow me. The women give my ladies posies and fruit for me. They shout good wishes to myself and my embryo heir. I feel I should wear fuller clothes, though I don't yet need to.

40

The mark of his strangling fingers that night has faded, and at least I don't still have to wear that high collar to hide the lurid bruise.

Whenever I pass the barracks – there are more barracks than anything else in the city, all sorts of magnificent crumbling old council chambers and palaces have been hastily converted to barracks – there are parades and exhaustive drill going on in the vast yards.

Poor things, they always have to stop and salute in mid-step when I go past, I am so recognisable now with my special robes and caparisoned unicorn and entourage of women, with four guards bringing up the rear and two theoretically pushing the way ahead.

Each evening Zerd and I sit side by side at the long glittering table. I think all the Atlanteans and commanders, not to mention my own ladies, feel easier now that we are sort of officially man and wife again as well as their separate Emperor and Empress. Everyone is more like a family-household, my ladies feel more comfortable about laughing and gossiping with Zerd's commanders.

Zerd fills my goblet before the server can reach it. He peels and pips fruit for me as though I were the baby. He never touches my hand if he can help it, certainly not under the table in a not-particularly-furtive long complicated clasp, as he used to when we were very newly married. I am beginning to wonder if I am just the vessel in which his heir must not be ill-housed.

After the last wine, we gather on the terrace and the torches are brought. With more wine, Zerd and the top men, and Ael with his nastiest-looking bandits if he is here, retire to a corner and argue and make maps with dice and goblets and knives on the marble. But there are no singers and wine-girls now, and presently Zerd comes to me and his hard arm gathers me into a swirl of his cloak. Like the rustling of a corn-meadow in wind, the kernel of our Court bows and bids us farewell for this day.

The guards' spurs ring and spark as they spring to attention. They salute and fling open the first of the doors leading to the bedroom which is no longer Zerd's, but ours.

We undress decorously, myself within a screen, and the little pigtailed girl who folds my clothes and puts me into my linen shift bobs her head and glides out.

We get into the bed from opposite sides, and if he doesn't take me in his arms at first, when I wake in the night his arms will be round me, or he will move to kiss my hair in his sleep.

41

As far as I can tell, he has not even glanced at anyone else since I told him I am carrying a child, yet he has not made any move towards me, not of what you could call desire. At first I was rather touched, but now I think I was wrong. He is being a model husband, and sovereign father-to-be, but to sleep with me night after night and not feel desire is abnormally unlike him. Sometimes, in spite of myself, so close to him, so cared for by him and remembering what I thought at the time was our delirious love, I long to snuggle really close and put my lips to the hollow at his collar-bone, feel his hard mouth on mine. But I dig my nails into my palms and lie rigid in case I make a move I can't recall, and repeat to myself, 'It was delirium, yes, for me. And habit for him' in a tiny clear cold voice like a spike in my brain.

I was bending by the rock-pool, chucking seed and insect-eggs to the fishes, when Juzd's reflection appeared beside mine.

'Hello, Juzd,' I said.

'Empress,' he bowed.

'Talk soft,' I shushed him. 'I managed to slip away. They haven't found me yet.'

'Somehow you don't seem to have been fashioned for a crown,' he smiled. 'How shall I put it so that you understand I mean no offence – You would say, you don't seem cut out to be a Queen.'

'I don't feel like an Empress, particularly of Atlan,' I agreed.

'Hardly Empress in anything but name. I said Queen.'

'How do you mean?'

'Neither North nor Southkingdom can really be said to be part, any longer, of your possessions.'

'You mean because they're conspiring to get together against us?'

A silver fish flashed like a blade beneath the water-gush.

'Because they never considered themselves possessions. They are simply great kingdoms which retired for a space to lick their wounds and re-build their power. They have dealt easily with such border-guards as your mother's land.'

'Zerd is famed throughout the known world for his general-ship,' I said rather defensively.

'Even in Atlan we had heard the echoes of Dragon-fear,' he smiled somewhat dryly. 'But it is also undisputed fact, Beloved, that he was given rabble to make into an army as he marched. He has accomplished miracles with the gutter-scrapings his

42

King hoped would defeat his skill. But even my people are beginning to realise that but for their whole-hearted welcome, and the generosity and sacrifice of our former ruler, your General would be crushed by now between sea and war.'

'He might not have pulled through against such enmity, such numbers and such crowns. But by now our Army is drilled and trained to splendour. And it has been through a lot with him.'

'It is still infinitesimal in comparison with the weight of the combined Mainland powers towering ready. And he is not the Northern King of his North-born troops, even if he is their Emperor in Atlan.'

'He is their warrior-lord!' I said, surprised to feel angry with Juzd. 'Those whose loyalty was doubtful have fled now, back through the tunnel, and most of them were killed under the sea by Ael and his bandits.'

'The Northern King has no need to worry about the air-injection of our ancient wall of vacuum,' Juzd said. He put his hand under the water and one by one silver fish gathered to caress his fingers with the nibbling and bubbling of their busy mouths. 'Don't forget, he has for a long time held the secret of the air-injection-formula his scientists discovered. Now the Southkingdom, whose confidence he sent Zerd to gain (or Zerd's own death and defeat, if overtures of peace failed) is only too ready to ally with him, swollen as it is with the fever of its hate for Zerd, its lust for vengeance after his snatched victory.'

'You mean the Northern King could make the vacuum into air again any time now?'

'And it's only three days' sail over the sea, then, and a beach with breathable atmosphere for landing operations. You galloped our under-sea tunnel in less than three days, didn't you, on your long-legged bird?'

'He was an exceptional bird,' I said expressionlessly.

'I am sure he was. But I am sure the first ships to beach here in quite a presentable number of centuries wouldn't take much longer to get to us, once there is no more vacuum.'

'But we have sentries posted – and a strong coast-guard – '

'Even your army, let alone your coast-guard, is smaller than the forces that either of your enemy-kingdoms will muster.' Juzd's long fingers tickled the pulsing belly of a big silver fish, which goggled in contentment.

'You say *your*, not *our*, Juzd.'

'I am aware, Beloved.'

'But Atlan's army would be behind us.'

'What army?'

'Oh, come, Juzd. Atlan has an army. It was all ready to defy us before it decided to embrace us and ask for our famous aid – '

'*Our* army is thin in numbers, far-spread to gather all together from the Continent's corners, and un-enthusiastic,' Juzd said.

'What do you mean, un-enthusiastic?'

'You are frowning, Beloved.' Juzd sighed. 'Yet how recently, I remember, you were a frightened child determined to keep your freedom, and if possible to keep Atlan clean of the power-symbol which now shares your bed.'

'He doesn't really share it,' I said inconsequently.

Juzd made circles in the water and the fish circled with his long honey-colour fingers.

'Juzd. Atlan's men with their sting-ray spears and their memories of science will be behind us, won't they?'

'We determined to forget our science.'

'But the people love us.'

'The gold people – ' he said. 'The gold-bodied, gold-hearted people can see no evil, their eyes are the wrong colour to perceive it, it will not filter through their vision. But Atlan hates you.'

'Atlan . . . ?' I whispered.

'Ancient Atlan, the world that has been enclosed from the world. Her forests breathe hatred, her heart beats hatred of the filth of the invader, her streams run hatred, her very rocks sweat hatred.'

'Tell her – tell her, Juzd – if we had not come, war would still have come. The airless ocean would still have been rent in this century. Zerd is protecting her – as he was asked.'

'I can tell her nothing. He is protecting nothing. He is power-crazy, he lusts for the scent of death, all around him.'

'It is only that he has been bred a soldier.'

'But we have no – *bred* soldiers.' He spoke the phrase as if it soiled his lips.

'Juzd. My heart beats with the child's. See me back to the terrace.'

We walked silently through the blossoms still foaming amongst the red, lankly-blazing leaves. There was a smell of rottenness more than of ripeness. The path and sward were coruscating stale rain to the pale ringed sun.

Zerd saw us from the terrace. The ladies darted forward to

44

exclaim that *here* I was, after all, but he strode forward and they fell back.

'You've been alone a long time,' he said as he reached me.

'Oh no. I've been with Juzd.'

'That's what I meant,' he said.

Juzd bowed gravely and without hurry to each of us and paced to rejoin his nobles.

'What does he mean with those bows?' scowled my husband.

'He always bows like that.'

'That's just the trouble,' he said. 'If I'm not too hard-pressed, I shall not place too much trust in that quarter.'

'Juzd has always been our loyal friend, Zerd.'

'Yours, maybe,' he said.

A lean white hound wandered past, an Atlan albino, not many of our animals are here. Zerd picked up a bone Isad had finished gnawing away from the table, and hurled it at the animal. His aim was as good as it always is, so I don't know why he had to prove it, unless he wanted to hurt the beast. It didn't yelp, or make any sound, but turned its great azure albino eyes on him and slunk away like a shadow.

'It's like you,' he said.

'Me?'

He reached and ruffled my hair. 'You never make any sign if you are hurt. You make a big mistake with it. You incite people to try and try till they force you to react.'

'Certain kinds of people, maybe.'

'I have always liked watching you, wondering when you would show your breaking-point. But not now. Now you are my infant. There must be no breaking-point.'

'That's what you think,' I said, lightly and briskly. 'I must collect my things tonight.'

'Where from?'

'From your room, of course.'

He stared.

'I am getting too big,' I explained as though to one of life's illiterates who needed things spelt out. 'I'm not sharing a bed when I need all a bed's space to myself. It's not dignified, nor is it comfortable.'

'I tried to make you very comfortable.'

'I have been,' I said politely. 'But now time is moving on.'

'Nonsense. You are not half the size you should be. You're probably not thriving.'

'I am perfectly healthy. But I must feel comfortable – and

45

perhaps a little more royal now. After all, I am not the baby.'

His expression deepened and he made a move to me, but I went on, 'I shall send a maid for my combs and shifts. You will find the shirt I borrowed the – first night – has been washed and folded on your weapon-chest.'

He cursed violently and turned on his heel.

The Court, surreptitiously, stared.

So tonight at the table Zerd was unpleasantly moody. He didn't take any notice of any other woman, which surprised me, but he gloomed and glowered and didn't speak much to anyone but Ael, and cast a pall and even a certain dread over the company. I was quite bright and happy but they all had to make an effort to keep up with me, you could tell.

Presently, at the far end of the hall, I could see a group of jugglers enter. I sent a guard down to summon them up to our end.

They trooped up and stood bowing. Our table brightened up. They started doing wonderful things with little glass balls. I grew dizzy watching – I get dizzy easily now.

While everyone was exclaiming and clapping and demanding more, I noticed an old woman huddled in a hooded raggy mantle, sitting apart.

'Come over here, old mother,' I said.

'Your good Highness,' she mumbled – she didn't have many teeth. 'We of Ancient Atlan wish you well. How is the little pet of an embryo? Is he going to be blue-scaled, or half-and-half?'

Other people have surmised on this. I am afraid the child, when he does arrive months late, will have no chance even of being dark-haired. Both myself and my brother Smahil are fair.

As I thanked her for her well-wishing, I scrutinised her. 'Ancient Atlan' she claimed to speak for, or be part of. I knew the phrase referred to the inner reaches of this continent we hardly know – to the villages and the hamlets, even the forests and their inmates.

'Your troupe are marvellous,' I said.

'Most of 'em my flesh,' she grinned.

'Their instruments seem to have an understanding with them. They share an instinct –'

She cackled in appreciation of my compliment. I was fascinated by the one yellow fang clinging precariously to her wan

46

upper gum. She smelt very strong, a smell of wood-smoke, long-ripe womanhood, like an old forest beast.

'Have you eaten?' I asked.

'I'll eat with my boys later, thankee, Highness. If your good nobles leave us a little something.'

'You shall have plenty.'

One of the jugglers produced an opalescent egg from Juzd's ear. He cracked it. A little bird dashed out of it, fluttered away cheeping frantically.

The juggler inclined his head to his applause, and the shadow of his hood lengthened his nose oddly. I stole a glance at Zerd. He was clapping.

The juggler sat down cross-legged and the others sat to form a semi-circle round him. He produced a long thin green pipe. The sounds he produced wailed out through the hall with immediately recognisable magic. Within minutes almost the entire upper end of the hall was silent. This juggler's music-making had an authority, a potency like old strong wine.

Suddenly, beside the crone, I leaned forward intent. The music was striking chords behind my breasts. I tried to remember what this combination of wails and low notes meant to me. You couldn't call it a tune. But there was a thread of melody in it, and a high leaping ululation pulsing like the keening of a marsh-bird calling rain.

I looked aside at the crone.

She was watching me.

'Tell him to stop,' I panted beneath the music. 'That music is bad magic. He knows that perfectly well.'

'That be earth-magic,' she intoned. 'There be nothing wrong with earth-magic.'

'This is the dancing-music of the Forest,' I said. 'My bird was torn to pieces to this music, when I first entered Atlan.'

'It's having no effect on your Court, only making 'em slit-eyed with waking dreams. It's your own memory puts the harm in it.'

'He's the same man, isn't he, under the hood.'

'My boy? I don't know what man you'm talking of, Empress, bless you.'

'He was with the animals – that night – when Zerd entered Atlan in the great storm.'

'Not my boy, Empress. He's good with animals, if that's what you mean. But he mainly plays for hall-folks, to get our food.'

'You're being deliberately obtuse,' I said. 'I'd know that ghastly pipe anywhere. And his yellow fingers dancing their own dance on it.'

The pipe allowed silence to tremble in the hall. Then there was a shout, and they were throwing tribute to him. The ex-boy-Emperor threw an agate-headed pin from his cloak, Clor and Isad and Eng flung gauds and my ladies tossed flowers from their hair, Zerd a chain of heavy links. Ael gave the man coins. From Juzd's hand flashed a little knife which stuck quivering in the marquetry floor. The piper pulled it out, kissed the blade as a note of honour and gratitude, and thrust it out of sight in his cloak. There was clamour for more music, but he shook his head and pointed to his mouth to show he was dry, and the troupe followed him down to the odorous spits.

Beside me, the old woman creaked to her feet.

'I'll tell them to see you are well fed, and given a byre with warm hay by the stables if you need a roof tonight,' I said.

'We sleep under stars and a wind,' she said.

The pains lasted three days and three nights. I gripped on the bedclothes, and on the midwife's arm. Anxious faces floated above me. I thought I had split and was bleeding to death, and they wouldn't tell me.

I was delirious. Two scenes re-enacted themselves mercilessly in the murk, trapping me in with my pain. Zerd's dark angular face bedevilled me.

'*Why* didn't you tell me sooner? Answer me, tell me. Did you think I wouldn't be glad?'

'Oh – I didn't think you'd be interested.'

'*Interested!*'

'Zerd – I honestly think I've longer to wait than you say. I've – worked it out, and –'

'Cija, your arithmetic is pathetic. Do you think I haven't remembered exactly how many days it is since our last time?'

And then the scorching interview with Juzd.

'Juzd, you know that man, don't you?'

'Empress?'

'Don't hedge. I am speaking only for myself. The man with the pipe.'

And when we had agreed on the fact – 'Juzd, I want to see that old woman who was with him. If ever I saw a wise-witch, she was one.'

'What shall I tell her you want?'

48

'Tell her to bring a potion for hurrying the child. He is too long on his way.'

'You may harm the child.'

'Juzd, I more than half hope I will kill him.'

The old woman, stinking as an old forest beast. 'He will be puny. And sickly.'

'Don't you realise, he's already overdue?'

'I've seen mothers-to-be at a few months showing the signs bolder than you do.'

'Give me the potion.'

'Odd to hear an Empress plead, oh, yes. Here it is, black and strong as night and twice as wicked. It's a lawless brew, outside the rules of nature, and the very plants and bitsies that went to make it up are resentful of the way they've been used, so there's added hate in the brew. Anything that sups this inside you will fight to get out. And it's a strong sooterkin if it lives at all.'

The first look of the stuff in the dirty earthenware-banded phial was enough to tell me she had not fobbed me off with a harmless mess. It still bubbled in its vessel. The mere smell was enough to make me retch. Yet it was sweetish too.

I thought the child was turning in me, turning and turning because he didn't know how to come out. I was swollen to a mountain, and he was a volcano. I hated that woman screaming, every scream seared my ears, head, throat.

There was commotion at the door. They wouldn't let Zerd enter. He strode among them, his red cloak blurring my light.

'Cija.'

His voice was so hard and urgent it pierced my pain. I tossed my head on the pillows. They burnt, they were sore. He caught my hand.

'My mother had a hard time with me,' he said. 'They are too strong, our race. I hope his skin is not already rougher than an ordinary babe's. Hold my hand. Grip.' I could feel my nails digging into him.

But there was another day yet.

'Is he a girl?'

'Bless him, an heir, fair as dawn.'

'You mean pale, or beautiful?'

'Both, Highness.'

'Has Zerd seen him?'

'He could not wait. Now you look, we'll prop you up –'

'I don't want to see it. Is it deformed? How many limbs?'

'He is perfect. A little pet, a little beauty. Tiny, he's good as gold, hardly knows he's born yet. He thinks he's still in the dark in his mother, and he's curled up like a rose-petal. His arms are like fingers, but he's perfect.'

'What did Zerd say about it?'

'Nothing.'

'Smahil! *Smahil!*'

But no hand came from the darkness to reassure me, to pet me out of nightmare. I remembered for the thousandth time that all I have of Smahil is his absence.

I started up in bed as though I could fling off that heavy weight of dread. But it remained, yawning avid around me.

The bed-curtains, great thin swathes of silks and gossamer with metallic tassels, quivered as if from the touch of a tangible malignance.

I must get out, or any minute I'd be crushed.

I swung out. The mosaic struck like ice on my soles. It is nearly winter now.

I grabbed up the fur-lined sheepskin I keep by my bed as a wrap. I ran through the big dark chamber. The lovebirds woke, and I could hear them begin to coo and nibble each other. I heard the child, that I will not have in my room, wake in his nursery-annexe. He began to wail as a matter of course. Sleepily but at once, a woman's voice tried to soothe him.

The corridor was awake with guards. They gleamed under the guttering torches in the wrought wall-brackets. Their weapons and breastplates sent out sparks. When I pattered out alone, the nearest involuntarily made a move to intercept me. Recognising me, three followed me at a respectful but wary distance.

You could feel the unrest in the palace. The building's distances, far and near, resounded with hurry and a wonder – a disturbance, that wondered why it wondered.

There was something thrumming the air.

Out on the terrace flares flamed to the odd wavelike-wind. My ladies and women from the kitchens, nobles and grooms mingled, jostling for a better view. In all, over a dozen people were gathered here at the balustrade. Other terraces were similarly burdened by the restless sleepers, or the members of the Palace's night-life, who had somehow sensed an imminence.

They fell back before me. I went to the balustrade, clutching the pelt round my pleated linen bed-shift, followed by my soldiers.

'What is all this?' I demanded. 'Why are so many people night-walking?'

'We don't know, Your Majestic Highness, not really. But the air seems odd, doesn't it? Not everyone has noticed. But some of us couldn't sleep.'

I stared across at the hills. Dark and quiet as the curves of some vast voluptuous sleeper, they seemed to be throbbing.

'It's an earthquake coming on,' I said, not liking my own shrill voice that had meant to sound calm, knowledgeable. 'I remember the ghastly earthquakes on the Mainland –'

'There have been no earthquakes in Atlan for centuries on centuries,' said the boy ex-Emperor in a silk wrap behind me.

'That's no earthquake,' Juzd said intently. 'The air is pulsing. Atlan's heart-beat is quickening.'

Suddenly, beyond the hills where the sea lies two days' ride away, the sky erupted. You could tell it wasn't any mountain erupting. It was just as though the sky itself had split. My son in the nursery behind gave the first screams he has ever given though he couldn't have seen anything, and there was no sound. The stars started flashing like mad.

Then the sound did come. A thin intermittent scream piercing our eardrums. Icy cold fingers squeezed my heart.

'Oh, what is it?' I asked.

One of my soldiers (looking a bit ill) said, 'Don't worry, Your Majestic Highness. Look, it's beyond the hills. We're all right here.'

The nasty flashes were dying now, anyway, and it was harder to see the dead-calm Canal.

Then suddenly there was a tremendous explosion-sound. The air trembled against our skin.

Everything was normal again. Only my maid Yula had fainted, but was being revived by a small red-haired young man with a scar that was a horrid livid colour in the starlight.

That really upset me, somehow, because I remembered Smahil's bit of scar. Is he still safe out there, wherever he's gone, I thought, or is he – what?

'Gods!' I pulled the sheepskin round me. My arms prickled as though the fur lining were gritty – or full of electricity. 'What was it?'

51

The next day we gathered again. Near twilight, a messenger panted up the steps four at a time.

'A messenger from the General by the shore – ' He was a Northern soldier, and in the heat of the moment forgot that Zerd is now a 'foreign' ruler – 'They've injected the vacuum – '

'Who? Who?'

'Our King, I mean our King that was – sailed up to it and got the scientists to inject the atmosphere right into it – but no sign of their sailing through it, over the sea-tunnel to us, yet. Their ships were bowled right over by the explosion, they miscalculated or some such thing, and the ships somersaulted and landed up in a shocking mess.'

'Was our Boy Blue hurt then? And our gallant lads by the beaches?' The soldiers on the terrace crowded him, half-forgetting my presence.

'No, no, but the atmosphere didn't half take a funny turn and he spared me to make sure nothing had happened here, and to give a few messages to the garrison leaders here, to make all ready for the public Christening and the Procession as he's returning soon.'

I suppose Zerd knows what he's doing, I thought. Sounds careless to me, though, coming back now.

'Do you hear, Empress dear?' rustled my ladies. 'He's coming back.'

They are all half in love with him.

I stretched my mouth to a sickly smile.

When Nal was safe to go into daylight and fresh air, the Christening Procession erupted through the City. In an open carriage, Zerd riding alongside, I brushed the thrown blossoms from the little face. It was just about the first time I had held him in my arms. He was wrapped in a long shawl banded with pearls and white fur, but he mewed in it like an angry kitten and hit the sunlight with his minute clenched fists. He was already very strong and self-willed, and I had to make an effort to hold him so he wouldn't fall.

I felt weaker and more feeble than he.

The populace roared and waved. Every few minutes I raised Nal a little so that his future subjects could see him, and my arms ached. Before we had reached the Procession's half-way mark, Nal opened his mouth and began his high yell. His eyes – azure like a soft evening and sliding about as he tried to focus – closed up and disappeared into a red angry little crumpled face that was all toothless yell like an ancient woman's.

I tried to smile aside at Zerd, but he rode the bucking curveting black bird with a hand and legs of iron, and never looked at me or his heir.

His eyes are the only part of Nal that is the colour his skin should have been if he were Zerd's son.

The platoons before and behind us shone like a variegated river, all rapids and whirlpools of colour and massed blare.

Then came a roar quite different from the crowd's cheering. The crowd swayed to look.

What happened next was quite the opposite of chaotic, but I was so confused, so totally bewildered, I thought the City or myself – or both – had gone quite insane. I only pieced it together later.

I looked to my side – and Zerd wasn't there. He had thrust his spur into the bird's black side, and ridden off into the roar. He'd gone without a word. But four officers, as though by previous arrangement, spurred up and flanked the carriage as the driver on the front turned smartly up the little side-street we'd that moment reached.

'What is this? Stop, stop! Zerd!' I cried, afraid of dropping Nal or I'd've sprung out, royal robes and all, sure it was a kidnapping.

'All right, Empress, don't fret, Your Majestic Highness,' said an efficient leader. 'The City is now being attacked. At this moment, we are under siege. By order of His Momentity, we're getting you and the Prince to safety.'

'Nonsense, Zerd never said a word to you.'

'Correct, Empress. Neither he did. Just now, that is. But this is not the surprise to us our enemy smugly thinks it is.'

'Not only the enemy,' I said sharply, 'were smugly under the *silly* impression that this was a peaceful procession for the introduction of the heir presumptive to his future subjects. I am afraid that I, and the baby Prince, and the populace who have turned out to be butchered, were all trusting enough to think –'

'Oh, we don't mind that some of the Atlanteans may possibly get slaughtered, or get panicky,' said the leader. 'After all, they refused to keep up their Army to back us. Oh, war is evil and no longer necessary, they said. They'll soon see how necessary it is. If no one fights, no one will be able to make wars, they said –' The leader gave a crack of laughter as he pointed an extravagantly gauntleted hand and the driver belted into a deserted alley. I held Nal tight.

'Ha,' cried my leader, the promise of battle after he'd escorted me to safety had made his eyes glitter and his tongue run light. 'If we hadn't made believe we could be taken by surprise today, they'd *never* have attacked.'

'That *would* have been terrible,' I murmured.

'Indeed,' he agreed. 'We'd have wasted so much time, temper, supplies. They can afford to wait – we, under siege, can't. We knew from our spies that they were just out of sight among the hills, that we were in effect under siege, and that they knew of the little Prince's birth, bless him,' he added perfunctorily, 'and were waiting for the Christening Day when they could storm the bridges while our attention was elsewhere. But a sharp look-out was kept, and we knew just when to draw the bridges in over the Canal.'

'Draw them in – ?'

'Perhaps no one thought to trouble you by telling you, Empress, the bridges can be slid into the City, leaving the Canal naked. Our Zerd found this out early on, and has had them repaired and kept well-oiled.'

'But – Gods – up there, on the walls, silhouettes – I can see fighting, that's fighting, isn't it – '

'Oh, yes, Empress, that's fighting. We couldn't shoot all their boatsmen down with our javelins, could we? They've boated over the Canal, thrown ladders against our walls. Again, we can't toss down all the scalers. There are two armies out there – Northern, Southern. As many of each as could agree to coalesce in time to come across on the Southern fleet that's got itself ready, after the Northern flagships had their little mishap at the injection. Still, they were wary of us. Too wary to attack without an element of surprise, of sneaking up. We're a city of soldiers, after all, and *his* soldiers at that.'

Half-a-dozen men came running, clattering down the alley. The men in Southern uniform outnumbered those in Zerd's. But Zerd's cut down the Southerners as we watched at the alley's other end, and blood spurted to the brick walls and coloured the little lichens. One Southerner, his face set in a snarl, came crouching dodging down the alley. He hadn't seen us at its angle. Casually our leader cut him down, and his bird daintily clawed the body out of the way.

'They've got in,' he said with distaste. 'Scaling-ladders, catapults, they've got all the equipment. Bully for them. Still, that procession broke up pretty smart into fighting units with all their orders well drilled, and the "spectators" in all the Barracks were armed to the teeth and itching-ready too. The milling panicky crowds of Atlan civilians will get in their own and the enemy's way, but not ours. We've rehearsed the lot.'

'Did we have to welcome the battle right here? Why couldn't we cut them down on shore?'

'What, as a whole big-headed Fleet beached, outnumbering us over three to one? Now, Empress, you're forgetting they aerated the Vacuum, aren't you?' he reproved me. 'I expect the few traitors, the bastards, I do beg your pardon Ma'am, I mean the turncoats, who got away to our ex-King – I expect they gave away the means of entering our under-sea Tunnel from their Mainland end. But this wasn't a question of waiting at our end of the Tunnel and cutting down each little helpless head as it emerged. This was the landing of a giant enemy force. They would have beaten us back perhaps slowly – but surely. Into the interior of Atlan – they'd've scattered us. Probably cut us off from our Capital. Entered it in our absence, only a few sentries here to defend you then, Your Highness. Here we are! Hey!'

We had reached the nearest barracks. Sure enough, the gate-guards were ready. They passed us in at once, no passwords demanded, only haste. The big high thick iron gates clanged shut behind us – shut out a little of the poor City's clamour.

But the leader of my escort couldn't wait to see me into the barracks-building beyond the parade ground.

'Empress,' he bowed in his stirrups. 'Your servant, to death. My service to the Prince.' He saluted. Before I could summon any answering gesture, any grudging benediction, he turned his barking bird. He rushed at the gates as though he'd've jumped them if they hadn't opened in time. Two of his number followed, yelling their Regiment's war-yell. One remained.

Nobody came out from the barracks. There was a skeleton-staff of door-sentries here. I was helped down from the carriage by the remaining officer. He'd dismounted. There was no one to take Nal from me. He was hiccupping and kicking in his shawl. It had got entangled with his furious tiny legs. The driver took away the carriage and bird in the direction of the stables, probably also empty.

Under the arched spears of the saluting door-sentries, the Golds Cavalry officer led me up an echoing bleak stone stairway with javelin-slit-windows letting in red slivers of the early winter sunset.

'I want a warm room,' I said, forestalling any idea he too had of leaving me. 'His Highness seems to need changing.'

'Uh – of course, your Majestic – I mean, you'll be wanting the Mess.'

Resigned to the fact that I'd get nothing better, I followed him into the big bare room. It was as horribly hygienically tidy as only an Army room can be just before an attack is expected. Recently scrubbed, and all that.

'I want a fire in that hearth,' I said.

'Of course, Majestic Highness. We knew you were coming – but we didn't leave one – just in case of sparks, while it was unattended, you know – '

I stood still till he stammered, and hurried to get a glow going. He puffed and blew. When there were flames crackling the laid wood, I sat down on a leather-padded stool. He stood up. His face was red, especially his ears, and he brushed at the marks on the knees of his uniform.

'Are you longing to get out to the fighting?' I said.

'I'll mull you some wine, Your Majestic Highness.'

'Do you know how to change babies?'

'I'm a bachelor, Highness,' he said in terror.

'Oh, all right,' I said crossly and started to experiment. 'I think you'll have to leave the wine on the hob. Can you just hold him still, without suffocating him if possible, while I – '

He got redder than the hissing wine. You'd've thought it was him, not me, whose blushes should have been spared.

Nal screamed and tugged at the demeaning grip on his limbs and got redder than anything. He had been warm and comfortable before this rush of cold air and enforced cleanliness.

'I need fresh napkins – ' I said.

'Yes, Your Majestic Highness.'

'Don't just agree with me. Aren't there any here?'

'Bandages – ?' he suggested.

'That'll have to do. Hurry, while I hold him and burn these.'

I regarded my offspring now we were alone. He sensed a steady regard, and quieted, and stared gravely up, trying to focus on me. A sort of bloom was laid over his eyes, like the bloom over ripe grapes, or over the eyes of the blind. Is he blind? I wondered suddenly. I won't know till he's at least a year older, whether he's deformed in some dodgy way like being stone-deaf. Or insane.

They say the fruit of incest is often unbalanced.

Incest. I haven't said that, even to myself, since this birth.

You little unspeakable monster.

Presently I became aware of the shuffling and scraping sound cautious from the rafters above my head.

I looked up, frozen with alarm, hardly daring to breathe, not able to move and hide myself. All the time the back of my mind was thinking. It must be only rats.

Then a square of red sky opened, and feet appeared.

I screamed.

The soldier came rushing back. He took one look and had out his big black blade. Three newcomers dropped lightly on their feet in a neat circle surrounding him.

Clash clash – immediately there was blood on his poor arm, and he was parrying three strokes at once. His back was against the wall except there was no wall behind him – only another enemy.

I laid the bare baby down hoping he wouldn't roll off. The intruders wore the uniform of the Northern King, so like our own uniform I had to look hard to make sure they weren't wearing the scarlet bars Zerd uses. I snatched up the wine mulling on the hearth. I chucked it in the face of the man farthest from my defender. He yowled and clutched at his eyes. They were awful yowls. I know it was a rotten thing to do. But it was the only weapon handy. My soldier got under his relaxed guard, no time for a cleanly judged kill, he stuck him in the stomach. The man writhed on the floor, that was quickly a pool of thick red spreading across the boards, moaning about his sight and his life's blood together. I flurried to him and knelt. 'Oh, Gods,' I said. 'Oh, I'm sorry, I'm sorry. I had to.' I raised his greasy moustached head, that I'd thought so repulsive and such a threat a moment before, and tried to soothe some of the pain and despair out of his face. 'I'm *sorry*,' I said. He rolled his eyes and gurgled. Blood bubbled out of his mouth and stained my dress.

I rose. My soldier was fighting, a little more evenly matched, with the two men left. He was getting the worst of it and looked awfully wild-eyed. This time I got a burning brand out of the fire. But I couldn't make up my mind to hit anybody with it till it started scorching my finger-nails. Then, as my soldier's breathing got hoarser and jerkier, I dropped the brand back on the hearthstone. I took the baby off the stool and laid him in a corner, praying no one would kick him, and hit the nearest man as hard as I could with the stool. It was *ghastly*. His head seemed to crack. I gritted my teeth in case I'd brained him, but he bumped to the floor, stunned but intact.

'Well!' grunted my soldier, sensing the end of his own despair.

Just then his assailant struck up his knife, and pierced his gullet. I thought I'd be sick, but at least it was quick. I ran and picked up the baby and faced the remaining man.

He staggered to the stool I'd stunned his friend with, set it upright and sat groaning. I stayed silent. Nal sucked his thumb with a squelchy sound.

Presently the man coughed and sagged forward. There was blood all over his jerkin.

I crept closer. I touched him. He toppled sideways. His eyes glazed.

It was the child's genuine wailing that soon reminded me there was nothing below his robe to swaddle him in, no milk for him. I tucked him under one arm and ran out of the room. I hoped I could find my way back to the stairway and then to the sentries.

The first stairway I hastened down seemed to wind for ever and ever, and to get colder and darker. By the time I realised it was the wrong stairway, there were big spiders examining me from web-mazes on the stone, and damp trickling beneath my sandals.

I started to hurry up again. But I heard heavy boots and accoutrement-clanks up there now. Was it sentries – or the enemy? The man I'd stunned – had he woken and was he still looking for me, for whatever unholy reason he and his fellows had arrived in the first place?

Perhaps it was a blessing in disguise I'd come down here. I put my hand over Nal's damp mouth. This time he didn't try to struggle – he was only an uncomfortable, cold, empty premature baby who should still have been in a womb.

There was the flicker of torchlight in some turning behind me. I backed down here. Here the drip of damp down the walls was audible. The pervading smell was nasty, musty and stale. It wasn't just one man up there. There were several. I backed down the narrow black stinking passage. There were puddles, and moisture entered my sandals. I glanced down aside – and saw a faint reflection on the wet ground, and the shadow of a barred grille across it. And as I looked, the silhouette of a man's head was superimposed on the bars.

Slowly, I looked up. There, in the wall across from me, was the little grilled opening with the light faint behind it, and the man's head regarding me. It was too dark to make out his features, or even his gaze, till a scimitar of white flashed out and I knew he grinned.

I moved closer, clasping Nal.

'Juzd,' I muttered. 'Holy Gods, what are you doing behind bars? I missed you in the procession today, but I was talking to you on the terrace yesterday.'

'The keys are hanging from the wall-hook in that niche over there, little alien Empress,' he said.

'The niche has a gate, and it's locked,' I reported.

'We shall have to do something about that, Beloved,' he said. 'See that decorative centre panel of the gate? Push that carved point to one side.'

I did so and the gate snicked open. I got down the big iron key-ring and hurried back to Juzd's cell.

'But there's a lock on that niche-gate,' I whispered.

'Yes, Beloved. Your soldiers don't know much about our old City. That big key on the right will do the trick.'

'Tell me why on earth you're here, Juzd. Who had the nerve to go this far? Zerd will have him executed.'

'I very much doubt it,' Juzd said dryly. He pushed the door I'd unlocked and stepped out beside me. I had a glimpse of the cell with its mouldy straw, its scabrous walls and the scuttle of what must have been a rat.

'What are *you* doing here?' Juzd asked. He pulled his cloak around him. 'I'm going this way – at the back of this niche there's another little panel your husband's bright boys don't know of. I'll come out the other side of the Canal. Coming? You're very welcome – we'll take fine care of you.'

'Who will?'

'Ancient Atlan and myself,' said Juzd. But I knew I wasn't going. He seemed already to have receded from me as he stood there in the fleering murk, his bright hair and his Atlan-deep gaze all I could see.

'I'm in no position to set out on more travels,' I said. 'I'm a mother – ' I fell silent, hoping Juzd would never find out how.

'And your husband expects you to be safe here,' Juzd nodded. 'Very well, Beloved. We shall not meet for a while now, you and I.'

I felt my sanity was leaving me, my conscience and my balance, the touchstone by which I judged all my thoughts and actions (would I like Juzd to know this? Would I be proud of this before Juzd?) as, wrapped in the blank triangular cloak, he bent into the niche and the panel at the back slid open on an eye-defying yawn of blackness. 'Juzd! Take a light with you!' I cried frantically. He chuckled as if amused, and the last I saw

59

of him was the very dim glimmer of a strong narrow hand raised in farewell – or blessing. The panel slid back into place.

Nal began to toss and sob as if his entrails were being torn out. Yes, those were real tears glistening on his screwed-up face. He wasn't just dry-crying for attention. He doubled up as if all his instinctive little being could be aware of was agony. He only knew he needed something. I knew he needed milk, but there wasn't any.

I wandered in perplexity to the stairway again.

It was hard to tell through Nal's cries, but I could still hear hasty movements up there now, over the steady roar of the suffering City beyond the gates. I decided not to risk going up there yet. I sat down on the lowest step, and hesitantly opened the front of my dress. I put Nal's face to my breast. I felt a sort of repugnance at letting him touch me this close, which I don't think I'd've felt quite so strongly if he'd been a little girl. At least, I thought, this should be a good thing for me too – I've been aware of a soreness in my breasts for a long time, which of course is the heavy ready milk. I wondered if he'd know what to do now. As soon as his mouth touched my nipple, he knew all right. He stopped gurning. His mouth took a tight sucking grip and pain shot right through me. Oh, it really did hurt at first, I could feel it going out of me like a strength or a virtue, but presently it became an exquisite rhythm. Nal's face was smooth and ecstatic. His crumpled rose-petal hands no longer wrenched the air, they lay and moved like lily-blossoms on gentle deep water. His toes twitched in perfect animal contentment.

Looking at him, my ears closed. I was not aware of Zerd till he passed me on the steps, his cloak swirling, and turned and stood over me.

I looked up, my eyes clearing of some dream or other. Nal, aware only of fulfilling the first instinct he'd been born with, sucked on with his eyelids half-closed over his bloom-blue focus-less eyes. Zerd's fingers tapped like a reflex of impatience against his dagger-hilt. Yet in the gloom I realised that his gaze was a compound of thoughts which cancelled each other out so that I could not guess his mood.

'A very unexpectedly domestic picture of my Queen,' he said. 'Or shall I say a slattern-picture. Your royal robes must be ruined on this dungeon-step, Madam.'

'Ssh,' I said after a pause.

'You are very unconcerned,' he said after a pause which was quicker and tighter. 'Yet you know I must have seen that cell-door is swung open.' He bent down and stared into my face. His eyes were angry-hot as coals. I felt scorched and yet the helpless child at my exposed breast seemed a protection and a courage. 'Where is he?' Zerd said.

'Zerd, someone must have thought him guilty of treason against you because he wasn't keen to help with Atlan's army, and then suddenly your enemies turned up! But it's all right, he's not in danger or anything. I got him a key and he's gone.'

'Are you really so innocent – or do you think that I am as ingenuous as you sound?'

Nal's mouth fell away. He was almost asleep. I pulled the lace and then the velvet back over myself.

'He's waiting near for you, isn't he?' Zerd said between his teeth. 'Is he still in the building? Answer.'

'Zerd, please – '

The baby had a moment of complete contentment. Then his tiny body was racked by hiccups. But he didn't look bewildered. Too young even to have all his senses yet, still he is already somewhat inured to the knowledge and the expectation of pain in this newest of worlds.

'What do I do?' I said. 'Take me to the Palace and my women, if it's at all safe. Do you suppose I pat his back?'

Zerd took him in one hand, by the slack of his Christening gown, and evened his breath while he continued to glare at me. But somehow I couldn't feel so scared any more.

'Don't tell me,' he said, 'that you expected me to return for you so soon.'

'I didn't think you'd ever come back,' I remembered how lost I'd felt. 'I thought you'd decided that if I was killed in the attack no one could blame you – after all, you'd spared four whole men to get me to a dubious safety.'

'Gods, I should have left you,' he said after a deep intake of breath as if he were controlling himself. 'I was sure you *were* gone, already, when we found it empty up there – except for corpses. What happened up there? Was that Juzd's doing?'

'I wish it had been,' I retorted. 'No, it had to be mine.'

He looked blank and angry at the same time.

'All those men but one – *one*,' I said, 'were brutes who clambered in through the roof-trapdoor. I've an idea they knew I was here, and had come for a kidnapping – or assassination.'

'They weren't from me,' he said at once.

'Why do you think I might have supposed they were from you, Zerd?'

61

He sat down on the step beside me.

'What did *he* say to you?' I was confused, and he added, 'Where did he go?'

'Honestly, he didn't tell me.'

Nal interrupted with a kittten-burp.

'Our men will soon find him within our walls,' he said. He went back to another tack. 'Did you say you dealt with those brutes?'

I nodded.

'Well, tell me. How?'

'Oh – I blinded one with hot wine and the soldier who stayed with me was able to kill him and another before he died. Another I stunned with a stool – he's not dead, perhaps he's gone now.'

'My men told me he was dead. He's lying in a pool of blood. We saw it dripping through the boards of the ceiling below. We wondered what before Hell had happened to you.'

'That's the other's blood.'

'Come on up. We'll beat him to consciousness. We'll get out of him who sent him here – and if he knew you'd be here.'

He stood up, and held down rather a brusque hand for me. He became aware he was still holding the baby tucked under one arm, and offered him at me.

I took Nal. He was wearing a blissful expression and was fast asleep. His toes were curled under his trailing pearl-hung robe. We walked up the stairs, Zerd's stride not adapting itself for me so I had to hurry to keep up.

'Is everything in the City under control now?' I panted. 'Is the battle over?'

'We're incredibly outnumbered but they've had to retire. We've taken so many important prisoners in our little enclosed space which we know and have rehearsed this day in, they've had to agree to a truce. We parley tomorrow.'

'Well, at least you found some use for your heir.'

'He's off to a good start, then. Let's hope he remains useful.' He added sourly, 'His father may live to be proud of him yet.'

'Zerd, what do you mean? *Tell* me, Zerd, tell me what you mean –'

'You know.' He sounded brutal. I was scurrying up the dank steps, burdened by Nal, and couldn't see his face. 'Did he like him? Was he overjoyed or dismayed to see his pallid hair, his subterranean flesh?'

My heart beat again as I realised he meant Juzd.

62

'Oh, Zerd!' I laughed, I was so relieved and so surprised at that idea. 'Zerd! Please turn and look at me. I'm fair. I have pale skin – ' I'd been going to say normal skin, and stopped myself in time. 'He's taken after me – to start with, anyway.'

He had turned.

'Cija. Tell me, truthfully – ' and he didn't quite say, For the sake of whatever honesty has ever chanced to be with us, but we both knew that was how he asked – 'Is that Juzd's son?'

'By my own Gods, I swear he is not.'

He took another deep breath. Then, a little awkwardly, he came two steps down and leaned me against his side with a strong arm. 'Give him to me. He's heavy for you. You are white.'

He half-carried me up the flight, I was so weak.

Smoke billowed down. It was acrid. I coughed. Nal woke. He stayed silent, but tears stood out from his eyes.

'What – ?' Zerd cursed.

Two sentries dashed past, heads down, cloaks over their mouths and nostrils.

'Have you fired the place?' Zerd asked.

At that voice, they turned. 'Momentity? Thank Gods. We thought you'd left and were outside, as we couldn't find you anywhere – but then you weren't outside either. We don't think the place'll stand long – not the wooden galleries and rooms. It's too old, too much wood.'

'What was it?'

'Sparks from a brand half-out of the hearth – no one noticed, till the North wall shot up in flame – '

An officer hurried to me. 'Give me the Prince, Empress. Would you deign to take my hand? I think you'd go faster.'

We rushed past the room from which gusted hungry tongues of fire lusting for something else to fasten on. I thought of that poor soldier in his funeral pyre. I loathed myself for the glad way I'd humiliated him, just because he was part of the plan in which Zerd had used me as a pawn.

'Wait – ' Zerd ordered a leader. 'There's a man lying in there, senseless, probably nearly suffocated. But I want him alive. I have a few queries to put to him.'

Like shadows in a fog, Zerd and the leader disappeared into the burning room.

The officer, Nal and I emerged in the barracks yard. The hurrying sentries saluted. My clothes were smoke-blackened,

63

my face smudged and my elaborate hairstyle all over the place.

With a crash and a menagerie-roar, half of the old barracks disintegrated and flames shot out over the unresponsive stone, leaped untrammelled and at liberty high in the sunset.

I couldn't see any figures moving amongst that ancient wrought stone, now splintered so low.

As though from a passion purging the clouds, without warning a downpour descended.

The flames fought, hissed and spat like maniac tigers gold and malignant, and were quenched.

Lightning savaged Atlan's sky.

We had gathered on the terrace, myself and the Court, and stared out over the Canal in spite of the rain which had steadied in the night but still fell as if a bottomless well had been tipped over above the Continent. Slaves held canopies above us. We could hardly hear ourselves talking, under the sound of the drumming on the sodden canvas. But we didn't want to say much.

The Canal looked like a green boiling cauldron. One solitary bridge had been replaced, and stretched like an eager-spined serpent arching to the beleagured suburbs – where the enemy had encamped just out of sight in the multiple bosoms of the hills, where just out of sight the parley took a course we could only imagine.

The night before, Zerd had at last re-appeared from the smouldering ruins. Smoke-sootened, ragged as tramps, he and the leader had trod out of the chaos – little lines of blue, white or scarlet flames still running up and down edges of beam, rafter or carved panel among the lurching stone debris while the rain teemed down – dragging with them a blubbering Northern-royalist. I had heard no more all evening, all night. All morning.

A sigh went up from the Court. The canopies trembled, and rain spat in my face, as the slaves' grip faltered. I was shocked to find I'd been biting my nails. The bridge-guards, little shiny-armoured menikin down in the wet distance, sounded strident horns. I could make out individuals in the returning troop. The standard-bearer, the one-armed bandit who was chief in Ael's absence, Zerd in his gold cloak, Clor and Isad and Eng, even the boy ex-Emperor who was taken along for show.

They were a long time in the City streets. The Atlantean citizens had turned out in the rain. Slow to turn from a hero-worship that had been so dedicated, they cheered and wanted to know their future, their fate. They still trust their chosen war-lord. But many of them brought out newly-maimed, or were newly in mourning, and their summer-colour gazes must have reproached him.

They joined us in the Black Gallery where big fires had been tended. The ex-Emperor kept coughing and sounded croupy. The bandit vice-chief complained of rheumatism in the arm he no longer has.

The Court clustered round. The ladies questioned the commanders. I intercepted a server bringing hot ale to Zerd.

'Zerd, ale. What happened?'

'Thank you.'

He tipped up the bowl and his throat was all I could watch, the dark adam's apple moving galvanically.

'Zerd?' Patiently I tried again.

He put down the empty bowl and conversationally said, 'Aagh', as he pulled the back of his hand across his mouth.

Once I would have sat down on his knee and waited for his arm to fold me against his chest, whether further information had to be coaxed or nagged out of him. Now I sat down closer to him than for a long time, on the foot-stool which happened to be near his chair, and fixed my concentration on his face.

Clor came over and they talked. I still couldn't catch much. Zerd met my eyes, and laughed, and ruffled my newly-done hair as if I were a favourite bitch.

'I'll tell *you*,' he said, 'you can't stay here any longer.'

'No indeed,' rumbled Clor. 'We must get her away before many more sunsets.'

'I'll ask the sun-head-lad' (that's about their kindest name for Atlan's ex-Emperor) 'where there's a safe retreat.'

'What's all this?' I pulled a face. 'I can take a hint. Sounds as though you want to get rid of me.'

'If I don't,' Zerd said rather over-dramatically, 'Sedili will.'

'What's Sedili?'

'Don't say,' he was surprised, 'you never knew the name of my first wife?'

I took care my mouth shouldn't fall open.

'But you divorced her by proxy –'

'That doesn't trouble her. She's here ahead of her father, my erstwhile King whom she claims is still my father-in-law. It only needs Lara to turn up. The family party would be cosily complete.'

'Poor Lara, that little princess would have no claim,' laughed

5   65

Clor. 'She's not the third wife, crowned Empress, nor the first, legally married – ' he stopped in confusion and tried to disappear into his beard.

'So you'd prefer troublesome claimants out of the way, to leave you both alone,' I said in what I expect failed to be a casual tone.

'Sedili would,' Zerd laughed loudly. He sounded pleased with himself. 'She's accusing me of treachery and revolt – not only against my King, but my father-by-marriage. I pointed out my King deserted me while I was still trustingly carrying out my duty to his orders. But she came back with the fact I'm using my King's troops against their allegiance-oath to their sovereign.'

'What is this Sedili,' I said, 'a sort of warrior-maid?'

Clor and Zerd rocked with laughter till they had to clasp each other's shoulders.

'Wouldn't describe her so myself,' Zerd was actually wheezing. He slapped his hard thigh. 'What a bit of luck, though, that she turned up, eh, Clor? She'll complicate things for her new Southern allies.'

'Well, never let it be said your third wife tangled things,' I rose. 'When do I leave?'

'You're a good child, I knew you'd see sense at once,' he approved. 'Now, where were we, Clor? Call Isad and Eng. I'll want the bulk of bandits just here, supposing this crack was the red canyon – '

We have been allocated only three carriages 'for the sake of safety, secrecy'.

'You can only take three women,' Zerd told me. 'For the rest, you'll need gear and a bodyguard.'

My ladies wept. They protested at length that each wanted to come. Now I discovered which I was fondest of, which I shall miss.

'I must have the wet-nurse. And you, Lady Frellis. But who shall be my third?'

They all talked at once.

'So many of you have husbands or families here. You are part of the original Atlantean Court, or have become a part of the garrison.'

My red-headed maid Yula bustled up.

'Strikes me you need someone practical and capable, Highness, going to a draughty old foreign castle in the middle of nowhere, with a little son and all. Me, I can cook and sew and cosset and do everything but look haughty like the rest of these high-nosed dames – in fact, come to think of it, I'm good at that too at times. What's more, I've not one tie to keep me here – only my man Scar, who's a fine groom and would make up your bodyguard.'

'Yes, all right, Yula, all right. Go and pack then. And you packing for me – keep in mind what are necessities and what, out there, will be useless trappings of pomp. I can only carry so much in three carriages.'

'We don't know *what* you're going to do, Highness. Suppose there's hardly any furniture? Suppose the roof leaks and there is no wine-cellar? I wonder if there are hens – and if they lay?'

Mounted on his black bird less black than the night, Zerd drew a little apart from his commanders and leaned his arms on the edge of my carriage. It was more a chariot, open but hooded.

'Well,' he said. 'This is farewell for a while, my little Empress.'

'I wonder you dare to call me that, in case there are spies about. I've heard that she insists she is the rightful Empress (till you relinquish the title to your own rightful King) because I was crowned only as your consort, which legally she is – '

'I do see,' he said, 'that you have some idea in your head. You must have found out that little trio who dropped in on you the day of the attack were from her and sent for you – '

'I'm not afraid,' I said bracingly.

'You shouldn't be,' he said seriously. 'I'm sending you away for your own safety.'

'All the same, I hope my absence will prove useful.'

'Let's say, Sedili's presence may. What on earth is all that drab baggage?'

'Mostly rugs and blankets. And medicaments and salves.'

'Do you expect so many wounds and illnesses?'

'Must be on the safe side, especially with a child and women. And we expect to be freezing cold. Couldn't we have had closed carriages?'

'Just keep your hoods up. These racing chariots are built for speed. That's urgent, once you start, and so is secrecy. Why do you think I was so glad of a starless night?'

'It's horrid. Like a vast tomb.'

'You won't get lost. Your drivers are faithful devoted Atlanteans with brains like maps.'

'Well, we can't keep them waiting for ever. Good-bye, Zerd.'

I felt his stare. I held out my hand to him. Only when he took it in his hard hot one did I realise mine was like ice.

'You're like ice,' he said. 'Are you wrapped up enough? Are you wearing those high boots? Did they bring the fur I ordered?'

'Zerd, you sound like an elderly fussy husband. Tell the drivers to start.'

He gave a signal and sat astride the saddle regarding me. I wasn't truthful. He looked younger than usual, though I already know he is younger than any of his commanders. The chariots creaked, swayed into efficient motion. On an impulse I held out Nal to him.

'Bid your heir farewell.'

As though with a reflex action, he half-took the furry bundle in his arms. Surprising me, he buried his face for a moment in it.

'Hai! Hai!' the drivers cried urgently, mutedly, and whips cracked as though muffled.

Zerd straightened. His hands tightened on his rein.

The chariots leaped forward. The Forest on the yonder-side of the City spread, seeped towards us. The Canal, the frozen stalagmite of City in its centre diminished. The escort-commanders diminished. Zerd diminished.

White flakes flurried noiselessly at us.

'The snow, the first snow of the year, will muffle our passing and, if it keeps up, cover our track too,' Yula sang softly from the adjacent chariot.

Nal's nose turned to a blue blob.

The Dark Forest

WE were well into the Forest by morning and thought it safe as well as imperative to stop for a rest and food. Actually, most of the females in the party had dozed during the ride, and we woke very cold. Though I didn't *feel* hungry, I knew I must have some food.

We rested the birds which drew the chariots (they are more bad-tempered but more adapted for long distances at a time than horses are, and though they're bigger and taller than horses they take up less room with only two legs instead of four) and posted look-outs while the drivers changed with their deputies and sat apart ready for sleep. The escort started fires in mounds of earth like home-made ovens (hard to dig in this frozen ground) till the snow ran in rivulets but there was no smoke. We roasted some of the dried meat we'd brought to last the days of the journey, and the salted vegetables, and placed our mugs on the oven-mounds to take the chill off the ale.

One of the bodyguard, the small man who is Yula's friend and has hair as red as hers, wandered poking in the snowy bushes. He went to Yula with a couple of handfuls of gorgeous-looking black berries. They ate and laughed, and squabbled over the fattest ones.

My Lady Frellis, the Atlantean widow who had been my head lady-in-waiting and is now the only one, murmured, 'I'm going across to remind him his Empress is present, and might just conceivably be glad of a little fruit.'

'Oh, leave them,' I said. 'He had to scrabble amongst the snow to search each berry out. I didn't.'

Suddenly a hare lolloped across the glade. The nearest bird stopped browsing in his nose-bag, shot forward an attenuated neck downwards, a spread claw up – and the hare's dainty tracks ended in a gout of blood red on the snow, steaming a little. A squeak, and the fresh carcase was being shoved into the bird's beak.

I made a mental note never to leave Nal near these birds.

The other birds near, all tethered leg by leg to the first who was tethered to a tree, began to push their big heads at their fellow, hoping to get some of the hare before it all went. He barked to warn them off, and crests rose on the heads of two resentful males.

'Someone shut them up!' I said. 'We must stay quieter!'

The nearest groom was Yula's Scar. But he backed away from them. An Atlantean ran up. He put a hand on each crest – he had to stretch from tiptoe – and smoothed them, and gazed into the big red eyes, and breathed on the beaks which grew less restive.

I went near the man Scar as we all prepared to set off again. I didn't want to humiliate him for small reason, so I said quietly, 'You must be quicker with the birds next time.'

'He's Southern, like me, not used to those brutes,' Yula spoke up for him.

'But you promised me he was a fine groom,' I said in an extremely chilly voice.

Yula went red. 'I meant for horses – didn't realise we'd take birds –' She began stuttering. Of course she had known we were using birds for this journey. We'd all discussed it.

Scar helped Yula into the chariot next to mine. He glanced at the wet-nurse already seated in mine. She had been quietly looking after Nal. In spite of the cold, her sallow breast was matter-of-factly bared for the child. Scar made a grimace, and then found he'd caught my eye. I actually began to feel sorry for him, he must be so embarrassed after two almost-simultaneous brushes with the Empress. But he quite deliberately winked one bold eye, as though he were pretending to commiserate with the female-ness of myself and the wet nurse, bound to our functions, but didn't really feel anything but a sort of contempt from the height of his male superiority.

'What a cocksure little lout,' I said to Lady Frellis, though she hadn't seen the wink.

'I don't think Yula, or he, should have been allowed to come,' she said. She had kept saying I should choose someone more 'suitable' than Yula.

'But they are more suited than we to this kind of excursion,' I said.

'I expect we'll find them quite incompetent,' she guessed.

'They were so eager to come along, according to Yula.'

'From devotion and loyalty? Or to stay out of the way of their fellow-Southerners who might start attacking again any minute and call these two turncoats and deal as hard with them as most people do with their own folk who've turned traitor?'

'Ah, well,' I said indulgently, 'it's too late now to fret. We're all in this together.'

'I wish more snow would fall,' fidgeted the nurse. 'We've left a fine trail now.'

'Just look at the bare boughs and the rimey sun like a huge teardrop,' I said. 'We're away from the buildings and streets – and walls – after close on a year imprisoned there. We're amazingly free now – the horizon is as wide as the Continent!'

'Or as near as spying enemies,' the nurse grunted.

Well, it looks to *me* as though that gloomy foreboding of the nurse may well have been prophecy. I haven't said so to anyone but one of the Atlantean couriers.

'When we made our last stop yesterday,' I said in a low voice, 'wasn't that smoke, where the trees were lowest behind us?'

'Perhaps a puff of your own breath obscured your vision a moment, Majestic Highness.'

'Don't baby me, I shan't start a panic. And wasn't that the sound of riders behind us when we stopped suddenly – just before the pursuing sound had time to stop? That was why you ordered us to stop so unexpectedly, wasn't it – so you could disconcert our pursuit in its efforts at silence?'

'That was why, Empress. But I can't state that we're being pursued. There are our own people in these forests. Trappers, nomads. After all, if there were enemies so near, they could have fallen on us by now. Or picked us off by javelin from the trees.'

'They're stalking us, to see where we're going.'

The Atlantean just looked at me, showing no alarm, no surprise, no attempt to reassure me. No thoughtful gesture, like the teeth-picking of Ael, the fingers across the chin of Zerd. They are a very difficult race to read the eyes of, though not to gaze into the eyes of.

'How many more days away is this crumbling castle we're evacuating to?' I demanded.

'Three or four at top speed.'

I signed that we should set off again immediately.

He handed me into the carriage with the right reverence but so competently that I was nearly swung up into it. I sat back

71

beside the nurse, with Nal, and Lady Frellis. I pulled the heavy
fur hood more round my face. It is the long thick fur of white
snow-fox, and I hadn't at first realised that part of the numb-
ness in my face was due to the ice formed on the long fur
tendrilling against my skin.

'Maximum speed then,' I said as he arched into the saddle.
'All day. All night. We can sleep at dawn.'

The baby is getting nasty-looking skin, for it really is the consistency of a flower-petal, and is chapped and even bruised by
the raw wind and the potency of the cold alone. I advise him
completely covered with a shawl, just so ventilation can get
through the stitches. He nose-dribbles more than he mouth-
dribbles, and seems very weak again, too feeble even to cry or
cough or hiccup or vomit much.

Except for our own haste, the forest is so silent it seems devoid
of life – at first. But each glade as we enter it is full of little
patterns, tracks in the snow, weasel and rabbit and raccoon and
probably other creatures, indigenous to the long-enclosed Continent, which stay out in the winter. Once, for instance, there
were tracks I nearly got heart-attack from – 'Horse!' I pointed.
'No, wild unicorn,' said the Atlanteans. 'Can't you see the light-
ness, even less weight than from a riderless horse? And the fine
cleft?'

When we leave the glade, there are all the marks of our own
passing.

But there is also the snake coiled under snow and leaves – the
hibernating rodent glimpsed in a hollow log, curtained in by a
dew-jewelled spiderweb whorling the log's open end – silky
cocoons of insects clinging in anaesthesia to twigs, cocoon and
seed-knobbed twig alike an arid outer casing for the force of life
to come.

I am beginning to forget there were ever walls and roofs and
nights at a time when I never saw stars. The palaces and
bridges seem here a dream, an illusion of grandeur. Here I am
out on the old trail again, bound down the trail of my wandering, journeying of a life – I don't know what I'm going to do, or
if we'll ever get there anyway – there is danger behind us, I am
certain of it and so is the Atlantean leader of the escort even if
he won't say so, and the Forest seems to breathe icy hostility
around us. I am all alone, even if there are people and animals
alone with me, all alone just as I always was. It *was* an illusion,
all that silly business of getting married and muttering endear-

ments and romantic scorching promises under beaming heavens – and here we are, out in the snow and the cold and the dread with my marriage behind me, my illusions at last finally behind me, the world I almost knew behind me.

I am glad as anything when the snow falls, of course, because it obliterates most sign (and sound) of our passing in the Forest. But it is nice, as an extra, when it starts falling at dusk. It seems all white and violet in turn as it spins a little as it falls as it flurries slightly around something which turns out to be a big owl that gives a couple of satisfied mournful hoots, as though it alone of all creatures is boasting that it is perfectly at home with mournfulness.

They are ghastly gaunt black flapping birds too. 'What are they?' I ask the Atlantean riding beside me as I hand him a swig from the leather bottle of young sour wine.

'We call them hrafen,' he says.

They caw like a very unused old gate. They give a very nasty impression, as though they were harsh careless grave-cloths or something, flapping through the drifting snow, at home in the presence of the ominous as the owl is with the mournful.

'Look, raven,' says Lady Frellis. We lurch over what must be a sprawling root camouflaged by drift. The carriage is almost tumbled before the driver copes. I am thrown against the nurse. She is clutching Nal, but the child, though cruelly jerked, does not whimper. He is losing the strong-willed personality he had begun to show even through his prematurity and weakness, and now sometimes I wonder suddenly if he is lying there in the nurse's arms dead. His face has no colour beyond a tinge of blue like a snow-reflection. As when he was born, he seems to be trapped between life and death, more liable to slide down to the left than to be tilted up to the right.

Would I miss him if he succumbed and became as empty a little shape as he looks? Of course. It would be terrible as that little form that had at one time (though not so recently) been full of life was shovelled under the blank snow somewhere out in a huge numb forest in a land alien to the parents. But the parents created a hideous double, quadruple sin of which this infant body is the blossoming, the visible fruit, a sick rarity like some unhealthy pallid carnivorous orchid pulsating deep in jungle. He seems now part of my entourage, for which I, as the cause of the whole expedition away from home and safety, am more responsible than the armed escort. I'd miss him as I'd miss the blue-squinting driver with whom I've never spoken, or the superstitious grumbling nurse. Do I love him? No, he makes my flesh creep. I feel ill when I know that he issued from deep in my own body, that I was the deep jungle which first spawned him, and why.

I disentangled myself from the nurse's rusty shawl.

'Raven,' juddered the nurse. 'They are an ill omen.'

'Harbingers of evil?' I asked Frellis.

'They are fierce, but mainly birds for carrion,' she answered coolly. 'They usually follow the wolves, and then fight for the wolves' kill.'

After midnight when the first howl reverberated through the silver boughs, the silver silence sent shivering against itself.

'And now wolf,' I said to the leader of the escort.

'Calling to his mate.'

'He was near.'

'Calling to the pack,' said the nurse.

I said to the Atlantean, 'Faster.'

'They are immense wolves, in these forests, fast as ghosts,' the nurse said quite smugly.

'Not swift as our birds,' I said.

'Swifter than a load of carriages, women and baggage,' the Atlantean said.

'Oh, Gods,' somehow I'd expected him at least to remain reassuring to the end. 'Do you think they'll attack?'

'If they do,' he said without any sign of concern, 'we won't have much chance. They run in packs of twenty or thirty, like devils when they smell flesh, berserk, ready to rend when they're already half-killed.'

'I don't want Nal to die that way,' I said.

They appeared like un-faked phantoms. You looked hard at the white tufted bark about, and you thought you saw the usual glimmering of snow-shapes back there behind in the tangling of gloom, and then you realised the same glow was keeping pace with the chariots, a twin glow, staring straight into yours, a pair of eyes. And a loping, tireless, phantom-grey body, very big, shoulders nearly high as a horse's from the ground. 'Look –' you tried to say. But the words stuttered thick in your throat. And the people whose attention you wanted to draw were also pointing and stammering. And the chariots were accompanied by long lean loping tireless wolves, all with eyes burning in our direction.

The drivers shouted, 'Hai! Hai!' and lashed the birds. The birds crashed through the snow and undergrowth, crests up, eyes smouldering un-focused.

The snow flurried fiercer. I looked up, my teeth chattering. We were all being shaken against each other in this rush. The ravens were skimming along just at the level of our heads. Swart and smug, wings beating with a rasping swish to send them skimming forward amongst the big gliding furry flakes.

The leader of the Atlantean escort held his mount beside us, though it could have sped far ahead of the chariot. It kept trying to. His knees gripped it hard and his knuckles ridged the leather gauntlets.

The first wolf sprang and immediately three others followed. From the corner of my eye I could see the others circling, alert, waiting. The birds became demented. The slap of a wolf's paw dealt with one great crested spine, rearing prisoned in harness. The lean wolf-head, eyes like oblong torches under the sloping brow, sank and there was more blood than I could believe in, and an utterly bestial growling, gurgling. The lifeless body in the shafts, and our chariot behind it, were swayed this way and that by the teeth sunk in the jugular vein.

The other bird, beside the part-eaten one in the chariot shafts, stood stock-still trembling in every limb, glaring sideways.

Should I get out (but hardly away), or stay here so close to the kill and terrible killer? I shook Frellis when she wouldn't answer me. I realised she'd fainted. The only bet, I thought, was to clamber into the snowy branches above me before the other wolves turned their attention this way. Some others had already, in this five minutes, killed two of the drivers. But the Atlantean beside me had risen in the stirrups of his frantic mount.

The remaining wolves came so thick they themselves were like a flurry of ghastly snow.

'Yulven, stay your lust, Yulven of Ancient Atlan,' the escort-leader said in a quiet voice. The tone made no impact under the terrible sounds hurting our ears, but a little later the words seemed to echo (still quietly).

A wolf which had reared at his throat dropped again like a bouncing flame. The other wolves, except for those worrying at the freshly dead, fell silent and remained staring at the Atlantean.

'Death waits differently for the Ancient,' he said in a voice

75

which remained quiet even with a vibration behind it — not of fear, from its sound, more a controlled hypnotic thrumming.

The greatest wolf, an albino with pale eyes like the green flames from burning driftwood, dipped his paw, talons sheathed in the pad, in the snow and sent up a little ice-spray. An odd mark remained in the snow, a scratch like a cross half-closed on itself.

The wolves bayed. The boughs shook. The wolves turned and disappeared amongst the trees. Those who had killed, dragged steaming corpse-chunks with them.

Yula and the nurse were hysterical. I desperately wanted them to shut up, I thought the row might incite the wolves after all. Frellis had recovered unnoticed, and lay pale as a ghost with her navy eyes all sunken, fixed on the Forest, tremors shaking her from head to toe. I took Nal from the nurse. I was afraid she might drop him. He mewed and stirred in his shawl.

One man, a tawny-headed Atlantean soldier, had a terribly savaged arm. He had tried to beat off a wolf with his dagger, and would have been killed at once if the leader hadn't spoken just then. He was laid in a chariot and his arm bathed in melted snow. It was hanging, badly torn, only just still attached to him. Rather luckily he went into a sort of fever and muttered and snored together while his arm was smeared with a heavy salve to deaden its sensation.

The Atlantean in his saddle bowed to me and began to re-organise things so that each chariot had a driver and team, in spite of the dead.

'We must bury them,' I said.

'What is left? — yes,' he said. I got out and helped them dig the bodies under the snow and even a thin stiffening of frozen earth. 'You are their liege-lady,' he said. 'No, it is only to keep myself occupied and a little warmer,' I said. 'I couldn't hope to atone, anyway, for bringing men to such a grave.'

He didn't reply with the little speech I'd expected, about their coming only to obey orders, and probably thus avoiding death at the hands of the besiegers back at the Capital. Actually, my conscience felt quite clear really.

Scar dug well, and even took off his cloak to it, so you could see the muscles rippling like a bigger man's under his jerkin. He looked sour and impatient when I started working, but when they began to drag the bodies over to the shallow graves, he said 'Not for you, Your Highness' and handed me up into the chariot without being impertinent or particularly smarmy

76

about it, which by now came as a surprise to me.

We moved on, raggedly now. The graves had been marked by stones, which is really all we could do in a forest of such potential trackers.

The ravens perched on branches and squatly watched us leave.

'They won't claw – anything up, will they?' I asked nervously.

'Too deep and stiff for them,' answered Scar, who was now our chariot's driver.

'How lucky we were our escort-leader turned out to be one of the rare nobles who share knowledge with Ancient Atlan,' Frellis said. 'I'm sure your husband didn't realise he had chosen such a valuable man to send with you!'

Suddenly I thought this might have more implications than she meant.

Scar wasn't such a good driver as the man now dead behind us. He was competent enough, and went at the job vigorously. But it was very rough, jerky handling, with corners and obstacles always taken a fraction too late, and a lot of cursing.

'Oh, *quieter*,' I said at last. 'I'm sure we're nearing a camp of some kind. There's a big gusty glow between the trees – must be a fire.'

'We are only nearer than I thought to the inn,' the leader said.

'An inn? Out *here*?' I said. 'Oh, you're joking.'

'Oh, no, there is, indeed,' said the know-all nurse. 'For travellers, and the roamers of the Forest often stay there all winter. For they're rich, the Forest nomads, after their singing and tumbling in great halls, after their begging, their pilfering. And their waylaying of travellers upon the highway.'

'Then it's addedly an inn to stay away from,' I said. 'A den of thieves, murderers.'

'Perhaps someone could go there to get help for our sick man,' the leader mused. 'He needs a doctor.'

'They won't have a doctor in that place,' Lady Frellis said.

'Every man who lives and dies in the wild must be a practised doctor,' her fellow-Atlantean said with a touch of impatience.

'This man,' I said and I looked at the delirious soldier, 'will die in the wild if he is not well tended.'

It was agreed that two riders (we couldn't spare more) should take the wounded man to the inn. The rest of us would

77

wait out of sight till near dawn. If the others hadn't returned by then, nor given any sign, we would make our way on without them. Actually, I thought this would be quite a good excuse for them to leave this perilous party and stay on at the inn, but the man groaned and moaned so we felt like murderers for every moment we kept him from a doctor.

In spite of my rather Empressly reaction about dens of thieves, I began to think – while they gently lifted the man out of the chariot and laid him over a saddle – that it would be rather nice to stop off for a while at a warm noisy shabby inn in the snow-bound Forest. We have had no vestige of cosiness for a long time now – no songs, no warmth, not enough food and never hot enough, only haste and dread, and the icicles forming in the corners of our wind-lashed eyes.

Little inns, and the sort of people who frequent them, were for so long so much more my own climate than enormous palaces and nobles. I always thought the palaces (and especially the nobles) were what I was waiting for, but they've been striking cold on me ever since I got myself amongst them.

I wandered a little nearer the direction the men had taken to the inn's glow. Our chariots were preparing for the move-off at dawn. Biscuits and very dried figs were handed round, also the same old wine. It's good wine, but I'm tired of it.

At first I thought I could hear, through the trees, a rough sound of song from the inn. Then I realised it was shouting, on a note of urgency. I stepped aside as a man crashed out of the gloom and undergrowth beside me. Our Atlantean escort-leader dashed over, but the man was one of our own soldiers who'd gone to take the sick man to the inn.

'Empress – they're coming – pursuers from Sedili to capture the Empress – thought we'd been killed by the wolves – so they went off to the Inn to celebrate but recognised us as we entered – killed Teld – coming – ' He flung himself into a chariot and seized the reins. The leader had lifted me and chucked me absolutely without ceremony into another chariot, not my own. But we were too late. Through the murk and the glow poured seven or eight riders. They were yelling but grim. They rushed on us without using their spears, though that put them at a disadvantage when our men loosed their javelins. A couple of pursuers toppled off their mounts, one screaming with a javelin-point in his throat, but they waited till they were close enough for hand-to-hand in-fighting till they attacked us bodily.

Our leader drove his chariot at them, swerving and scattering their formation on their birds, and loosed another javelin. But they closed in on him. They forced him to reach for his sword.

I wanted to get out of this chariot, to the one where Nal had begun to cry against the nurse's nipple. As I tried to stand up in the lurching carriage I realised how bruised I'd been when the leader tossed me here. A couple of newcomers suddenly vaulted over that other chariot-side and began tugging at Frellis: she looked astonished and then tried to hit them with the heavy gold medallion on the end of her necklace.

'Now, now, Empresses should behave more ladylike,' one of them grunted as he lugged her on to his mount.

It clicked in my mind. Sedili had given orders that I must be captured alive, even if only so she could watch me die herself. That was why they hadn't risked javelin-casts, or spear-thrusts. And now they'd mistaken Frellis for me – she looked quite an Empress, tall in her furs and necklaces, with her straight back and her haughty, open face. Whereas (by accident or design) the leader had tossed me into a plain carriage without any embossed rugs, and I was as scruffy as I usually manage to get, my hood-fur and hair entangled, snow brushed from the branches I'd wandered through all over my cloak.

Another soldier was reaching for Nal, who obviously was the Prince! Not much good trying to disguise him as a bundle of figs, or a pillow – he was now roaring his head off and turning mauve. I fell out of this chariot and jumped for the soldier picking up Nal by the scruff of his shawl while the nurses threatened to curse them if they attempted rape.

An arm snaked round my waist. I turned and bashed with my fist for my assailant's crotch before I saw him. It was the Atlantean. 'Use your sense,' he said through his teeth.

'Let me get to Nal,' I hissed.

'Who's this, then?' the man holding Nal turned and stared straight into my face.

I made a lunge for the child. The man and two others grabbed my arms and twisted them, hard enough to only just avoid breaking them. I screamed as much with fury as pain. The Atlantean's hand sliced to my assailant's throat, the knife glittering clean for the split-second before the blood spurted.

Two others of Sedili's Northerners converged and matter-of-factly battered him to the snow.

But before their spears could at last make their fatal stabs, a new element shocked the battle. A great grey shape hurled itself on the prostrate Atlantean and straddled him, eyes glaring and

79

fangs grinding, and a series of howls rose and belled against each other in blood-curdling disharmony as about a score of wolves leaped for the throats of Sedili's men – who had trailed us so carefully only to come to this when they threatened the life of the Atlan noble.

In the chaos which now broke loose, the screams of women and men too, the awful growling of the beasts which our men didn't realise were our allies and tried to kill, it was only a reflex action which still enabled me to grab the baby into my own arms before a wolf, inches from me, dived past me on to the man who'd held Nal, and I looked round me in bewilderment and choking panic.

Where to go? Not one chariot, not one saddle was now safe or even get-at-able.

I was too near the ground this time to leap for the boughs above, even if I could have reached them hampered by the baby.

The sounds and sights were nightmare. I was the only non-fighter on the ground. I kept edging towards the deeper undergrowth. Miraculously, and after a lifetime, I had nearly reached it when a wolf turned and saw me. Its head was nearly on a level with mine, and its pupils were like crosses fleering out of the green irises so alien in the sloping face of fur, so wide apart to be looking at me both together, that I felt giddy.

It paced towards me. I remained as though rooted in the snow. To have turned and run would have been useless with four powerful legs like that behind me. The wolf came right up to me, never taking its blaze of gaze from mine. I knew that its hot breath would stink, that its teeth would be incredible agony before I became part of its mouth, but I quite consciously thought, This is a terror and a glory. It is a fierce finality to be torn apart by a blazing master of the elemental Forest. This is not the humiliation of old age, not the treachery of poison.

The wolf was so close I could see the glistening of the pore-dots in the texture of the nose-pad, the sloping hairs each like tough silk, the dribbeted red blood glutinous on the hairs by the lift of the lip, the sickle-point of the fang behind the puff of wolf-breath on the frozen air.

I had no desire to close my eyes at this death. I didn't want to miss any of it. I felt a ridiculous spineless submission, a fascination of surrender since no defiance could be the slightest use.

The wolf lifted one lean paw, tapered and elegant as a

thoroughbred horse-hoof, and brought it down like a touch of grey-fur-thistledown on Nal's forehead.

Tears like diamonds sprang out in the corners of the child's eyes, the blue of snow-shadows.

The wolf stayed so, its breath coming in visible wafts against my throat. Nal in my arms seemed to gather warmth and heaviness and calm. The calm of the wolf itself, in all its alienity, seemed to enclose me from the turmoil and the slaughter in the glade.

The wolf dropped to all fours and trotted back into the battle, where men shrank from it and a killing-howl ululated from its mouth.

I dashed into the undergrowth, pressing to me the child in its calm like a talisman against the Forest.

The Red Inn

IT was long past dawn when I came to the Inn.

I had wandered in a wide circle, dreading re-finding the glade with the necessary recognition of bodies – or, once again, of my own death.

The Inn did not front directly on the Forest. It is a thatched and shingled log-walled square, long and two-storeyed, that encloses its own yard with the hen-coops, little cow-pasture and stables – for the animals, meat, udders and eggs need to be kept farther than the humans from the Forest.

It is surrounded by a garden where so many herbs and veg-etables grow among the flowers and rose-trees that the foraging of the occasional bold rabbit or fox in vegetarian mood can't make much difference. But now they were all under a white muffling that showed only bumps and hollows as sketchy clues to shape.

I stopped by the gate and rung the bell that hung there. The jangling sounded deafening to me, the white silent Forest watching and listening behind me, but it can hardly have im-pinged on the early-morning clatter of that long log square – the clang of pails, the lowing of kine, the bustle of bed-banging and mattress-shaking, the creak of the pump, the splashing at the well, the cross clucking of chooks and the brazen defiance of a cockerel, and over all the singing and swearing.

I jangled again and Nal whimpered.

One of the shutters was thrust open in the snowy log wall overlooking the snow-humpy garden. A face in a white winged cap squinted at me.

'Want to come in, do you? On your own, are you?'

'Hurry,' I called. 'I've been out in the Forest, in peril from the wolves, all night.'

There was a momentary pang at the consciousness of

treachery to the wolves. But now in the cold bleak morning it was very hard to remember that the wolves had actually meant to spare us.

Nal set up a thin wail.

'Ah, the poor bitsy,' cried the woman. 'I'll be down in a moment. Don't go away.' She banged the shutter.

I had no intention of wandering a step from that high withy gate.

The woman was so long I thought she'd been waylaid by some household ruckus and forgotten all about me. I jangled the bell a couple more times. Nothing happened. I considered climbing the gate, but it was high and I had to hold Nal, and though it was of very thin wood to front on such a dangerous Forest, its very suppleness would make it a dodgy proposition for climbing.

Finally the woman led a small procession down the snow-cleared path from the enclosed yard. There were three men with pitchforks over their shoulders.

'You're sure you're alone?' she called over the fence.

'I don't *think* I'm mistaken on the point. Except for my baby,' I replied. I was so numb I was afraid I'd drop him.

'When I open the gate, slip inside,' she ordered, brandishing enormous clumsy keys. 'I'm not having any more sneaking out of the trees.'

'If they fancied, they could easily bash through your gate if not the paling fence,' I said conversationally as I slipped through. 'You ought to have it made tougher.'

'It's tough enough,' she shrilled. 'Like a spider's web of elastic wood. Take a sennight to hack through. You talk of what you know, my fine madam.'

I still thought an axe or cudgel would make short work of it, and I eyed the crudely-armed men.

'Do you always greet patrons like this?' I inquired.

'None of your lip,' she said. 'We've had trouble enough the last night. Commotion, a sick soldier from heaven knows where, and a beastly killing that started the cows off mooing.'

I hoped the soldier would say nothing in his delirium.

'Why, have you a doctor here?' I asked, hoping to find out how he was being tended.

'Doctor be tending him now,' she said. 'But it's a fever, hard to stay its course. Never much you can do for a fury of a fever.'

The silent men shouldered their pitchforks behind us all the way up the shovelled path. We turned a corner of the long house that formed nearly a complete square. Here we were in the yard that was so big it included a well, stables and a frozen duck-pond in the bit of grazing where the three cows and a muscular rust-toned bull poked their nostrils amongst the hummocky snow. The farther sides of the house, the logs puffy as a face cut in shaving and doctored with cotton-wool, showed through the haze of the morning.

My feet incapable of sensation in my boots, I followed the woman over the cobbles, avoiding the yelling playing brats, the slatterns fighting the well-handle, the dizzily darting hens which were determined to obstruct human movement.

I realised that I felt a little light-headed when smells of frying coiled out from the house.

The woman led me up a rickety wooden step-ladder and we were in a low-beamed red cubby-hole, any light and warmth flickering from the charcoal in the wrought-iron brazier swinging from the beam over my head. As I was to discover throughout the entire Inn, the walls were of rough red clay, which gives the entire building a rich dark atmosphere.

She sat down at a scarred desk.

'How long do you want to stay?'

A nasty thought occurred to me for the very first time. I put my free hand in my cloak pockets. Nothing except a few soggy hankies. No pouch or purse.

'I think till a thaw – ' I said uncertainly. 'But I'll have to pay you for everything right at the end of my stay, not weekly.'

'Indeed you'll do nothing of the sort,' she said. 'We don't manage on trust and pretty promises here. How much can you afford? What sort of roòm, how many meals? Will you be wanting water? Will you want a fire, a brazier, a candle or the plain dark?'

'Gods,' I said, 'I want everything of the best. But I shall have to pay you when I can get word to my household. I was in the Forest on my way to – ' but I must give nothing away. 'On my way to my country house. But we were attacked by wolves and wild men. I'd appreciate it if later someone could go out to the glade and find if anyone is still alive. But I have no money on me, nothing, not even napkins for the baby.'

'The cheapest rags we have here,' she said, 'are a brass-coin each. If you give me the money, I'll tend to the lovely.'

'I haven't even one brass-coin,' I said.

She snorted. 'Then what are we wasting time for? The Forest will provide a roof and nuts.'

84

'In this cold? With every animal among those trillion trees raging with hunger?'

'What about your fur hood? I'd take that for half a golden piece.'

'It's worth far more than that. How much would that buy me?'

'A night for yourself and the infant in a heated room, two in an unheated.'

'Can't someone go out to the glade?' I pleaded. 'I have goods and chariots there.'

'A fine tale,' she muttered. 'If you had chariots, why did the wild men dare to attack? More likely you are a dishonest serving-girl and you thought you'd make it here with a cheating tale of woe and get a stay for nothing instead of a flogging, yes, you and your bastard.'

She made me so angry with her hostility and stupidity and the stubbornness of her big mammal-femaleness, her position as mistress of the only household for miles and miles, her plump hands akimbo on her formidable hips. Then I suddenly remembered that the mauve mewing in my arms really is a bastard, and Gods grant he were only that! Nonsense, I said to myself, he's a little prince.

'You annoy me, my good woman,' I said. 'Send men to the Forest and then doubt me.'

'And why can't you go yourself?' she said. 'You've legs.'

'I'll go with the others,' I said. 'I'm not going back there on my own. And of your charity, surely you could give me something for my stomach – even if it's only a cup of hot water?'

She did just that. She boiled me an earthenware mug of water over the brazier.

I drank it and felt a little more alive. Then I went out to meet the same three surly fellows with the pitchforks. I carried Nal, though she tried to bully me to leave him in her care. He'd be colder with me, but Gods knew what might happen to him otherwise.

Almost without speaking, we trailed back into the Forest. The glade was quite easy to find. Tracks of men, birds, wheels and wolves ran everywhere in and out of it. The Inn-men's knuckles whitened on their pitchfork-grip as they saw the light wide-stride wolf tracks.

'Yulven,' they said in low pale voices.

The glade was a mangled chaos. The dead birds were the messiest sight, feathers and blood everywhere on the snow. The wolves had stripped them to the bones, and the skeletons had been tossed and split. Scores of little feeding rodents and wild-cat looked up with blood-stained teeth bared as we approached. There were plenty of dead men, or parts of dead men, and the ravens were having their way here. Under the squawking and swart flapping, we could also make out wheel-hubs, harness-poles, bloodied saddle-cloths – all the wreckage of what certainly looked like three chariots.

'Ugly, bad place,' mumbled one of the men who was extra-ordinarily thick-necked and either taciturn or a bit of an idiot.

'I can't even tell how many dead, or who,' I said, listless with despair.

'You'll never be able to tell now,' nodded another of my newest escort.

'Bury them,' I said.

'What?' he said in horror. 'We've work enough waiting back at the inn. Who wants a job like this, burying bits of innumer-able strangers all together in ground frozen solid?'

'Burn them, then.'

'And fire the Forest with them?'

'This Forest needs destroying,' I muttered.

'Leave them,' he said wisely. 'The creatures will have their fill, and not prey so much on our vegetables. Then, under a few more snowfalls, what's left will moulder and rot into the forest-floor, and by spring the ground will be that much richer.

We left the crawling, squeaking, crackling, barking, pullulat-ing glade and went back to the inn.

The inn-woman demanded, 'Couldn't you salvage anything from the chariot-remains?' but even her men laughed at that.

She scowled. She was still resentful that I hadn't left Nal for her to fuss.

'Well, what bright idea have you cooked up now for trading on strangers' trust?' she asked.

'You'll have to take me on as a maidservant,' I said. 'Give me my meals and bed as wages.'

'Oh, I'll have to, will I?' she said, her big red lip curling up so that I suddenly realised she was cruel as well as in a position of power. 'And what if I don't need a scullery-maid?'

'I said maidservant. I'm doing no rough work. The rest of my household will arrive looking for me with the thaw,' I lied hollowly.

'They can thank me then, for keeping you alive,' she grinned.

I sneak a few hours' sleep every night on a pile of rugs in a cupboard – a shut-bed like the one in which I used to sleep with Smahil in the Southern Capital on the Mainland – and Gods, that's not yet three years ago – but this is smaller, and has no window, and no sheets.

The cupboard is under the stairs. As it's dark throughout the house by the time I get to bed, I leave the bed-doors a little ajar. This is partly for fear of claustrophobia, partly to get a little air – I sleep with Nal, and sometimes I am terrified of rolling over and suffocating him, or of us both suffocating anyway. I try to keep him in a nest that includes my fur hood which I've refused to sell (so far).

Under the stairs, rather a noisy place to put him to sleep in. I worried at first.

I wondered whether it were only harmful pride, my refusing to give him over to the care of the inn-woman. She says she only took me on for his sake (though I really do suspect it was mainly to have a very good go at humbling me into the state of a wet dish-rag). But owing to her meanness, all the lights in the house go out very early in the evening, unless guests pay extra, so no one uses the stairs much in the dark, and we underneath them are not too disturbed.

Sometimes, though, I'd almost sooner the reassuring sound of footsteps, human bustle. I lie in the stuffy cupboard, unable to sleep though I'm aching after my scrubbing and ladling and serving, and I stare out where I know the door-crack is, though it's hard to distinguish the outside-dark from the inside-black. I imagine reasons for little creaks that seem to get steadily nearer: I strain my eyes to see movement, and only see hallucinatory white spots whirling round my eyeballs. Sometimes I almost wake Nal just for companionship. It quite worries me when he sleeps soundly all night: it seems unnatural for a baby. On his fretful, noisy nights I am glad to hold him, to curse and soothe and shush him, though in the morning my eyes are ringed with shadows dark as bruises, which never completely disappear, probably never will.

I feed him now myself, of course. My breasts are globular with continuing milk, and even the skin looks creamy except for the nipples rosy with use, so I must suppose I am still healthy and the meals I get and steal (kitchen leftovers) are enough for us both. But my hands are red and cracked, they seem never to be out of greasy water. And it is hard to remember not to stoop when I'm walking.

Now and then, after nightmares, I steal some embers. I light the brazier with them after it has been officially doused. But I have to remember to get up in time to put it out again before she comes down.

The last time she came padding heavily down with her candle after midnight, looking for an ale night-cap 'to settle her belly', she saw the brazier I'd lit outside my cupboard. I was wakened by a ringing clout across the side of my head.

When Nal woke too, and wailed, she picked him up, crooned and rocked him.

Some nights I'm grateful for the faint sounds of roistering from the rooms of the richer guests in the farthest wing of the long red house.

Some are beggars and buskers who have made a tidy pile in their wandering year, and are living it up till the winter has eaten it up in more than comfort, and they are ready to take to the road with the spring thaws.

Others are bandits, I'd swear it. Not ours: but bandits native to Atlan's forests and the rock glens. I think I ought to be able to recognise the type by now.

Naturally, I thought I'd soon be sent to take a bowl of gruel, or fresh lint or splint to my own sick soldier – the start of all this disruption of Zerd's plan for my disposal.

But I am beginning to wonder if he has died, or been told to stagger off because he costs too much to keep.

I've asked the other servants. But most of them are very dim, and say, 'Oh, we've heard something about that. But we can't say for certain. Oh, here comes the Mistress. Ssh.'

There is a Master too, a squat man with a ferocious moustache under a shiny red-veined nose. But though he sometimes lays about him with a knobby stick, he doesn't inspire us with the sick panic that is always her fore-runner.

As far as I can gather, the 'doctor' is one of the prosperous beggars resident in the farthest wing, the opposite side of the great big yard. Each wing has its own servants – or slaves.

It occurs to me to wonder how the war – my husband's war – is going out there beyond the muffling of acres of Forest brooding and ready to burgeon under snow. Is the world, too, out there, is it bursting? We get no echo here. This is old Atlan, inner Atlan if not Ancient Atlan, and we are not interested here by

88

the foreigners' wars on the periphery of the vast busy Continent.

Now the snow drifts softly over the besieged City – is it still besieged? – as it drifts over the tall grim trees watching immediately outside our bit of garden here. There, the ice and crystal of the great courtyard are marked with blue tracks. Is Zerd riding out on his savage black thoroughbred, his scarlet cloak or his gold-sheepskin mantle the only bright spot under a lowering sky and a threat that is lower still? Has he been buried with wounds as scarlet, with spears as sparkling in that hard chest that I knew a brief while?

Has he ever thought of me since he saw me off to 'safety' with my ill-fated escort in the chilly void of that night?

Perhaps it is snowing, too, in the winter out over the grey writhen sea, above which the dolphins can leap and breathe the virile sea-surface oxygen for the first time in uncounted centuries?

It must be snowing in the Southern Capital, the children playing in the streets, little bundles of furs and leather, the lamplight glittering on the icicles that hang in rows, quaint-shaped as candle-drippings, from all the eaves.

It is snowing in the mountains and the bandit-hills. The big bears sleep and stink in their caves. The snow builds in drifts around the enclosed gnarled roots, just as it grows and grows here.

It is snowing on the ghastly plains, tortured storms of snow endlessly driven by the malignant, pathological unrest of the winds.

Is it snowing in my Mother's little kingdom?

Snow, yellow on the canals and the sleazy tenements, green ice, perhaps covering some of the new scars and sores my husband's first royal father-in-law has once again inflicted on her small hopeless land? Is she still gathering together the tattered remnants of our traditions, our pride and our intrinsic divinity? Does she look out over the troubled seas, that I used to watch from the years of my childhood in the tower that watched the deserted end of the bay? Has she given up hope of help from her son-in-law – rather illegally in-law? So many of us have had to give up hope of that help.

Reenah bent over me, dripping cold water drop by drop on my face from a hand-mop.

I sat up the instant I woke. As I grasped her by the throat,

89

she stopped in mid-giggle and managed to squeak, '*Cija!*'

'Oh, *sorry*, Reenah,' I said. 'I didn't realise who it was. Did you want me?'

She sat on my bed and spoke quietly. Nal still slept in his nest in my hood, near my feet. In the half-light, always white because of the snow outside, her profile had a look of her mother the inn-woman's, except that she hasn't yet a triple chin or pendulant cheeks, and she plucks her brows in a thin arch.

'Look, I really feel dodgy,' she said. 'It's the curse. I usually change with one of the other girls over in the guests' wing where I've got to serve the breakfasts – but she's got her eye on some-one I'm going with, know what I mean, Cija? and she's a randy bitch I wouldn't trust as far as I could – and on my life, I can't see you bothering to double-cross me, you're always so sharp and get-on-with-your-work-ish – so do me a favour, love, and get over there with the breakfasts. Eh?'

I swung out of bed in my shift. She helped me put my arms into my jerkin. I slid my feet into my boots.

'You'd never think these were the clothes I arrived in,' I grumbled. 'Stained with kitchen-grease and been slept in for a good part of a whole Winter.'

'You can tell they were good once,' she said. 'Only rich people wear white and pale colours, only they can afford all that changing and keeping clean. And only they aren't afraid of showing up in dark places.'

'You can't be too ill to show me to your wing,' I said. 'I'm not sure of the passages and stairways.'

'Come on, then,' she said, groaning.

I had to knock on the crudely un-symmetrical, nail-studded doors and give pitchers of mulled ale, mugs, and bowls of meat-soup to the idle guests who eventually roused themselves to answer. This meant long trips back and forwards to the kitchen, for I could only carry so much at one time.

The guests' wing is less draughty than ours. There are curtains (I had to shoulder these aside, with both my hands full) across the passageways. The small many-paned windows over-looking the courtyard are well-glazed. No cracks left.

You could tell it is an abode of casual luxury. There were sounds of snores all along the corridor.

I kicked on one door which opened at once and I found myself lifted right off the ground in two effortless arms, while I was roughly kissed.

Being seized like that, I'd dropped an ale-jug. I clung like mad to the covered tureen full of rare pork-stew. 'Let go, you damn lunatic,' I said as I bit that rough mouth, 'or so help me I'll tip this stew down your hulking neck.'

He let me slide to the floor so suddenly I lost balance and nearly fell. He seemed to have done this on purpose, because only then did he notice I was a stranger.

'Well, f . . . me,' he said, 'you're not Reenah.'

'Look what you've done with all that exuberance,' I said levelly. 'Ale all gone – and all stained over the carpet. Who's supposed to pay for more ale? – and probably a new carpet too?'

'You, if I complain I didn't get my morning drink,' he grinned.

'Tell me now if you want another drink brought,' I said. He annoyed me, a big rich important beggar-rat throwing his weight about for the season in which he could share servants. He was tall and lean and scruffy, stubbly jaw, a mane of unkempt hair. And flash, with tarnished tassels jostling each other from a wide tattered-silk cummerbund and all sorts of jewels clashing colours in his ears, chained round his neck, on his fingers.

'Of course I want my effing ale,' he said, raising his brows over a hawk-nose and somehow looking intimidatingly autocratic.

I shan't bother trying to reproduce all his conversation word by word. Every second or third word is so filthy I'm reeling as I listen to him. (Before I'd managed to get acclimatised to our bandits' speech, I'd become an Empress, and they mute their language as much as they can remember when I'm present, though of course it's mostly second-nature, they aren't aware they're swearing at all, and when they really want to curse they're hard put to it to find something unusually horrible to mouth.)

But it stung me – the whole situation as much as his attitude.

I felt like shrugging the whole burden of servility and responsibility for myself and Nal and our tepid warmth and scrappy food right off my bowing back.

'For your information,' I said stupidly, murmuring it because I was tired but also because I wasn't quite sure I meant to say it, 'I am a servant, for whose service you are paying as long as you're a patron of this inn. But I'm not a slave.'

He didn't look amused. I'd known this defiance could only antagonise the brigand-bully, bent on living like a lord while his foul-gotten gains lasted. Dirty, tired and unkempt, I am too unattractive to do anything but antagonise him.

'Get that ale, slut,' he roared, 'or I'll knock your greasy head through that wall and then see how much use you are to our hostess.'

With that subtle threat echoing down the snow-lit corridor, I went back to fetch more ale. Reenah's little fancy was certainly safe in my care.

But as soon as I sneaked a moment free – hours later – I found a bit of cracked fly-spotty mirror.

I looked at myself properly for the first time in months.

Reenah, being the inn-woman's daughter, and some of her girl-friends are allowed to heat water for a wash. I have managed, painfully, to keep fairly clean in icy water. It has had a drying, flaking effect on my face, though. But my hair has not been washed for a very long time. And I have worked and slept in the same shift for an equally long while. It makes me sick to look at it, let alone touch it and have it around me, but it's that or go bare! All the weaknesses of my body are apparent again. The snake-dents in my leg, for instance, are blemishes now that I've no slave.

My hands have roughened so that they are unrecognisable, and my little slim wrists have gone all puffy.

I picked Nal up and rocked him, for he is all that I have of my own though he's another symbol of uncleanliness as well as an effective burden for holding me back.

'As soon as the thaw breaks,' I promised him, 'we'll get away, out into the trees and streams and chilly sunbeams. There's peril out there, but at least it's clean peril.'

His little face puckered. He belched and then was feebly sick over his smock. I sponged him with my hem. He is very sickly and always looks a little blue.

I was scrubbing the kitchen floor next. It isn't stone, but old wood, knotted and seamed with dips in front of oven, flagged hearth and pump, and big cracks through which the rats scramble up in the evening – they aren't scared of us, and can't be bothered to wait till night.

We have cats, of course. Fat and sleek if they are personal pets of the inn-owning family. But *they* have to keep out of the way of all the others, lean and very fierce. Even the kittens hardly let you touch them.

The dogs live mostly outside in the yard and stables (thank heavens). They are all very bouncy and un-house-trained.

Some are big, some small, but all have enormous yellow teeth.

There are sometimes pitched kitchen-battles between rats and cats. The cats are rarely bitten dangerously, and rats are sometimes killed. But it is usually the cats who retire, ostensibly in disgust but really in defeat.

I was feeling a bit more at peace with myself. I had stripped in a wooden tub – so old it is growing moss – and washed thoroughly all over, in water I'd managed to heat in a cauldron while everybody thought it was for the pots. Already crumbs of grease were clinging in rings round my wrists again, and couldn't be got rid of, only shifted. I had soaped the worst stains on my shift, and sponged them, and then heated the dress near a stolen brazier to dry it. It looked better, fresher. But there are no such things as aprons here except for the family, and it was already sodden again around my knees.

But greatest triumph of all, I had done something to my hair. In the same warm water I'd washed in, I'd soaked and soaped my hair, then scrubbed and scrubbed at it with an under-rug from my bed till it was quite dry – and quite clean! It had gone fluffy now, instead of hanging in lank lifeless strips, and the curl had sprung back into the ends.

It had been quite a problem deciding whether to bathe in the water I'd washed my hair in, or vice versa, but finally I'd decided I was cleaner than my hair, and I'd bathed first. I'd got into trouble for remaining hidden so long. They'd called and called me for various tasks, and knew I must be malingering. The woman gave me three sharp slaps across and across my head as soon as I reappeared. My head still rang and throbbed, and there was a high whistle in my ears, because I'm not strong enough any more to take that sort of thing.

She noticed my hair.

'*I* see what you've been at on your own,' she leered. 'You must have used our soap for titivating yourself. Well, you've made the choice! If titivating is more important than nourishment – you shall pay for our soap with your meal.'

As I eat once a day, this means I've been working empty since yesterday morning and shall till tomorrow morning.

A pair of good leather boots, that showed signs of rough treatment and hard wear, paused beside my brush.

'A conscientious *servant*, I see. Sometimes she deigns to work.'

But I wouldn't look up.

93

'Do you bring your grudging service to me tomorrow, or will Reenah be well enough?'

My shoulders and arms ached so that even their extension, the brush, seemed to me to be aching.

'Don't worry,' I said kindly. 'I'll beg Reenah to be well enough.'

But apparently he thought I was trying to insult him.

'Slattern,' he said with other words before and after, and he casually kicked over my bucket as he walked on.

I am glad that I didn't give him the satisfaction of calling after him or even making an exclamation. For all he knew, perhaps I hardly noticed.

But the filthy cold water splashed all over my tortured floor, my freshened dress, and dripped amongst my soft clean new hair and into my eyes.

I rubbed a forearm across my eyes, that were full of dirty water and tears, and it came away black-splodged.

As I bent over the floor all over again, my head seemed to contain little red-hot iron balls all rolling into the forehead. My eardrums sang a high keening song to themselves.

Because I had to do the floor all over again, and had already been a long time before that, getting myself easier to live with for a whole half-hour, I was very late indeed for my next job.

The gong was banged. There was a general rush. Everyone dashed for the eating-hall. But the inn-woman appeared in the kitchen, to make certain that though I'd banged the gong I went without supper.

'Don't try to forget you've taken on Reenah's jobs as well as your own,' she said. 'The sick soldier needs a tray taken in to him. I'll check with him later, don't you worry. If I find there's been any snitched, you'll really get it my fine miss and no mistake. If he's been sick or anything, empty that too.'

'I don't know which room he's in,' I said. 'I don't think I saw him when I took the breakfasts.'

'Well, it stands to reason not, if he's ill in bed, doesn't it?' she jeered. Her gay sense of humour peeps out every now and then.

'How do I find him?'

'Fourth door from this end of the first-floor corridor – in the guests' wing. Door with a panel kicked in. And don't linger. Don't say anything you don't have to. Your tongue's a little too long, for all your vowels are so careful.'

The tray of supper was on the table behind her.

She crooked her finger at me.

'Over here, dear,' she said.

I went over to her. I thought she was going to put the tray into my arms. As soon as I was close to her, she transformed the coy beckon to a fist. She hit me again and again, in amazement and with my head reeling I lost count of the times, but it was over six.

She really has taken a dislike to me, I registered.

She's glad when I do wrong, because then she has more excuse to get at me.

'Perhaps that'll teach you to finish important jobs, like scrubbing, in good time,' she grunted up between big spikes of clenched teeth.

'Here, here, you'll strain your arm, good woman,' a man said. The big lean bandit stepped forward and caught her wrist before she could bash me yet again.

I think only the blows had been holding me up. I staggered back against the kitchen table. There were whirling spots in front of my eyes. I had to gulp down the taste of nausea in my mouth.

'You let me go, Madfist,' she gasped. 'I'll not rest till she's black and blue, otherwise she'll have nothing to remember this by. I'm not one to let my servants go untrained, even if they do come to me with no more training than a cuckoo.'

'She's black and blue already,' interposed another voice after an apologetic cough.

A hand, a man's hand but cool and full of sense and understanding, felt my forehead.

'There's a contusion here,' said the new voice, interested. 'Are you wearing a ring, by any chance? Not right to slap a girl with a ring on your hand, unless you want to blind her.'

I tried to clear my senses, and saw the man bending over me. He stood between me and the window-dusk, but I could just make out a gentle bearded face. Actually, because of the slant of the eyes and mouth, it should have seemed a roguish sort of face. But I suppose it was the momentary gravity of the eyes, and the way he was touching me, that made me think him gentle.

'What in Eff's name did she do to you?' the big bandit demanded of the woman he was still holding back from me.

'She took nearly all afternoon over scrubbing this floor,' she exploded.

There was a pause, then both men burst out laughing. Even I

95

thought rather sourly, They just don't realise what a business scrubbing is, nor how it matters in a household.

'Well, if that's all, set me to finishing it, good grandmother,' said the big one. 'It was I who spilt her filthy bucket, and made her start again.'

'She's finished now, at last, Madfist,' the woman glowered. She just might be a grandmother, but a fairly young one.

The first time she'd called him that, I thought she'd been calling him names from temper. Now I realised this must be what he was usually called.

'She needs salve on that cut,' the bearded one said. 'I think I'll take her back to our room, Madfist.'

'That,' the big bandit said gaily, 'is quite all right by me.'

The bearded one put an arm round my shoulders, to show me the right direction. But he must have felt my uncontrollable trembling. 'Here, you've taken a bit too much,' he said. 'Don't be afraid to lean against me.'

I said in a low urgent voice, 'Please don't take me to your room.'

'You'll be safe as a crone, little slattern,' the big bandit said rather unkindly.

'I'll only get into worse trouble from her tomorrow. She'll resent your looking after me,' I whispered.

I was sincere inasmuch as this was true, and if they'd left me to stumble on with my tasks, I'd expect less rancour from my mistress the next day. But I also rather hoped this would throw a new light on their smarmy motherly landlady, so if they did decide to take my part they'd know what they were doing.

They literally had to half-carry me over to their wing, and up the stairs to their corridor and door. I felt rotten, sort of drugged and not really interested in living. All my weakness seemed to have culminated at once.

They kicked open their door and hauled me inside.

'Down you lay, on the nice soft cushions,' the bearded one said. 'I'll salve you till you won't know you ever had a knock – after the first bit of stinging.'

His salve did sting, too. I was still shuddering, and felt very sick.

'You haven't been eating enough, have you?' he reproached me.

'I doubt she gets much chance,' Madfist said with amusement. 'The merry harridan would see to that. But look at those shadows under her eyes. And she's white as a clean sheet – and

96

you can see her little cheekbones and jaw so clearly it's indecent, she looks all exposed.'

'Not a pretty picture,' I murmured. 'Thank you. I'm grateful for such detailed concern.'

'Give her some cheese and bread,' said the bearded one.

Madfist thrust something between my teeth, but when I swallowed as a reflex, I found it was fiery spirit. 'Get this in your guts,' he ordered. 'This'll do you more good.'

'She'll only get drunk if she doesn't have food too,' the other said severely. 'Here, little one, sit up in my arm and I'll feed you.'

At first I felt like laughing, they were treating me as such an invalid when only a couple of hours earlier I'd been doing heavy housework. But I found I really had gone under – I was almost too tired to swallow. Finally I could only rest my head on the flashy-cloaked shoulder. 'No more, thank you,' I pleaded. 'I'd better get back now.'

Madfist strode up and down, regarding us. The tarnished threadbare tassels of his ostentatious cloth-of-gold sash swung in brisk arcs and hypnotised me.

'What she needs is sleep,' he said over my head.

'We'll hurry her back to her own room while no one's noticing,' said the one who held me.

'No, oh no we won't,' Madfist corrected him. 'They'll know just where to find her then. She'll have a proper sleep here, and then she'll be ready to face the morning.'

'Face the morning is right,' I muttered. 'No, thank you, gentlemen, but I can't. You are very kind and have indeed made me feel better. But, unappetising as I may be, I know better than to sleep with two brigands in a house where I have no friends.'

My hand flew to my mouth as soon as I'd said this. No one had ever told me they are brigands.

But Madfist laughed.

'Someone's been talking out of turn,' he said. I thought he meant me, till I realised he must mean Reenah or someone. 'I've never met you before, I'll swear, and don't tell me we're *obviously* unrespectable.'

'You can sleep in the other room, the one that used to be mine before I gave it over to strays and lost causes,' said the bandit with the beard – as opposed to stubble, for neither could exactly be called clean-shaven.

'And you can put the key under your pillow.'

They helped me across the fringed home-cured sheep-pelt rugs, to the door that led into an adjoining room.

'My baby,' I murmured. 'I can't, really. My baby can't be left on its own.'

'So you're a parent?' Madfist said. 'Goat shall fetch your offspring to you, never fear. No wonder you're now wary of sleeping with strange gentlemen.'

'I'm surprised you don't think I must love it,' I said. He annoyed me.

'Ah, no,' he said benignly. 'Those who know what they're about, and do it for practised pleasure or profit, know better than to get caught even if the prospective father doesn't care one way or the other – eh, Goat?'

'Tell me where to go, and I'll fetch your little baby,' said Goat.

I still felt a great revulsion about sleeping here, in spite of their various reassurances, and the luxurious comfort of their tatty surroundings, and the promise of an evening as well as half-a-night in bed.

But I straightened up in amazement as I stepped into the other room.

Lying on a bed, looking bright and flushed against the pillows, was the soldier of the Atlan guard who'd nearly lost an arm to the wolves, and had to be invalided here.

'My lady – !' he stammered in even more surprise.

Then he looked at my awful clothes, and my two companions, and closed his mouth but not his eyes.

Madfist's eyes narrowed. But he only said, 'Yes, a lady, you're quite right, in spite of the state of her. She's sleeping here tonight. We've assured her you're in no fit state to attack her.'

The soldier looked worried. He knew I was probably incognito, yet he felt he should treat me with honour. For my part, I was wondering how much, sober or in delirium, he'd told his two benefactors about how he came to be near the inn in the first place, and who he'd been taking where, and why soldiers in a different uniform had arrived to kill one of his companions, and chase the other into the bitter Forest again.

'I'll sleep on the floor,' he said. 'The – lady must have my bed. I'll turn the sheets back to front –'

I wished he'd be less dutiful and solicitous.

'Oh, that's all right,' I shrugged in a very un-Empress way. 'Let the lad keep his bed, he needs it more than I do. I'll curl up on these pelts.'

'This is the girl who was supposed to bring your supper you never got, Laran,' Madfist said. I'd never before even heard the poor soldier's name.

'Oh, that's all right, I wasn't hungry anyway,' he said at once.

'That wasn't what you were saying earlier when we decided to go out and hurry it along,' Madfist said with a wink. 'Very polite where young ladies' feelings are concerned, these lads in uniform.'

But he was no longer really uniformed, I noted with relief. He wore only a shirt, that no longer much resembled an Army shirt. And though his jacket lay on the rush-bottom chair beside him, someone had thoughtfully or greedily stripped off all the medals.

'So you're the doctor?' I asked Madfist in surprise.

'I can carve a man up as well as anyone,' he boasted. 'No, it's my friend Goat here is the sawbones.'

'Thank you for everything, Goat,' I said.

'I'd think shame not to help anyone in distress,' this bandit said earnestly and apparently with sincerity. 'Now, little one, tell me where your baby is and I'll get him for you.'

'In the cupboard under the stairs in the office-wing,' I said. 'You may not notice him at first, he'll be lying in a fur hood.'

He belted off. Madfist started to drag a couch in from the other room and pile it with things like cushions and shabby once-grand cloaks.

'You'll kip down here, Laran,' he said. 'Can you get over here on your own? Your little lady shall have a proper bed for a night. Cursed cupboard under stairs be – !' (But I won't repeat what he said.)

Even Laran, who must be nearly better now but for a splintered arm, helped me to the bed.

'Pull your shift off over your head,' Madfist ordered. 'Here's one night you needn't sleep in it. We've plenty more logs to pile on that blaze in the hearth.'

Laran blushed and I glared mutinously at Madfist, who was already glaring at me in anticipation of my refusal. Then suddenly I thought, All this is absolutely marvellous, and I have no need to be suspicious. I discreetly wriggled out of the thing, for the first night in ages, and Madfist with a most ungallant but quite funny show of repugnance flung it on the chair, and then confused me by tucking the covers round my shoulders.

Goat ran in. Nal was hiccuping, he must have been carried so fast.

'Here he is, the ducky,' Goat cried like a right nit.

'Is this your hood he's in?' demanded Madfist.

'Well, yes,' I had to admit.

'Pretty good once, wasn't it? But I don't know the fur at all. This is foreign fur,' he said slowly. He looked slyly at me. I felt relieved rather than insulted when he said, 'I wonder who you had this away from?'

But he didn't press questions, howcomes and wherefores. I thought I was lucky. Or perhaps I should be suspicious.

'Sleep tight, watch the fleas don't bite,' crooned Madfist. 'And sweet dreams all night long, little slattern.'

At first when I woke I had no idea where I was. The fire had burned low in the night. The embers were glowing and crackling, and spitting a bit, like an ill-mannered but companionable old animal.

The shadows flickered a bit, but in the unevenly-plastered red corners of the room they brooded motionless and very big.

I hadn't got to sleep as easily as I'd expected. The wind had gurned and belly-ached around outside the log walls. I get more peace in my shut-bed, I thought, after all. Then the wind began to whoosh. Finally it wailed and howled. It sounded heart-rending, a child lost in the Forest, and blood-chilling – a soulless spirit avid for souls.

I expected to see fresh snow driven high by the window. I sat up in bed. There was a new sound, that I haven't heard for so long I had to search my mind to remember what it was. Steady rain was drooling down the panes like an idiot child.

The dark was murky. But the morning *felt* advanced. There was no crowing from the cock, but the cows were making short moops and the billy-goat was restless.

I got out of bed, then remembered my shift and got into it quick.

In spite of the gale, Nal had not cried since he was brought here. I got the usual catch in my throat – half-hope, half-sick dread – as I wondered if he had died.

But no, the little mouth was only just disturbed by his very faint breath. Look at his eyelashes, I thought in wonder. Aren't they long. Resting on his little thin grey-tinged face like something alien to him – beautiful curving plant-life. If he lives, he may be a pretty child.

I gathered him up. I padded to the door that would open on the corridor. I hoped Laran on his couch would wake, so I could ask him how much the bandits might guess, but he snored so peacefully I hadn't the heart even to make a bit of accidental noise.

The rain stopped in the late morning, long enough for us to see a big round sparkle-splashed red sun floating up through the mists and big as any mythical moon.

It was doing crazy light-jiggered trick-things with the myriad-million leaves of the Forest – with the yard-cobbles – with the cows' brand-new emerald-green pasture – for the snow was left only in little grubby-white floes spinning here and there on the dimpled puddles and the tempestuous gutters and swirling drains – every puddle full of smug-billed paddling ducks, happy at last.

'I've lived here so many months. But I never knew there is moss on the well-head,' I said as I paused to lean on my broom.

'And you never knew there's a certain code. Any self-respecting bitch keeps away from a friend's male,' said Reenah coming up behind me.

'Don't get silly, Reenah. Your Madfist doesn't appeal to me at all. He's a big swaggering lout. What's more important to you, I don't appeal at all to him.'

'Don't try to smooth me with niggly lies. It'll soon show if he's dividing his time with anyone else.'

'It wouldn't be me, love. He says I look white as a clean sheet – better than a used one, I suppose, but not madly seductive.'

'Then you were with Goat when you were missing out of your own bed last night? Best of luck, then, Cija. But I better warn you, love, Mira's got her eye on him. Had some luck, too, and liable to act possessive.'

'Oh, Reenah!' I sighed. 'Listen, for your interest as well as Mira's, all I did was *sleep* last night. In the soldier's room – and he snored,' I added hastily. 'Madfist and Goat have hearts of gold and they told me to sleep in the warm for once.'

She stared at me, which was impossible till she'd brushed the strips of sun-yellow hair out of her eyes.

'No one would make *up* such a daft story. But don't you believe it, either. Those lads! Hearts of –' She spat.

'Haven't they looked after the soldier for nothing?' I demanded.

'That keeps Goat amused,' she shrugged. 'He always likes to have something to try out his leechcraft on. It would be a pesky lame hare, or a raven with a broken wing, if it wasn't a sick

101

man. And *he* was glad enough when I broke the joyous tidings I was going to be a mother – even if the father wasn't.' She took a quick look sideways, through the hair, for my reaction. She still wasn't sure of me. 'Goat saw his chance of playing midwife.'

'My little Reenah!' I said, touched, and hugged her, though she is bigger than I am. 'Does your mother know? When is it due?'

She rested her brow on my breast. 'I lost it,' she said pathetically. 'All my hopes gone – gone! I was sure he'd be a boy, a son, like your little love. Oh, Cija, my little pet gone. He would have married me if it had've been born, to help me face Ma. Madfist was the father, you understand that?'

I knew she was most interested in warning me off, in staking her claim. But I felt awfully sorry for her.

'Were you in great pain?' I said.

She nodded. 'But the grief was worst.'

I patted her. 'But, Reenah, he's probably gone through a form of marriage quite a few times already.'

She sat up, hair swinging. 'Oh, I know that!' she said. 'But it would have made a difference, and he might have taken me off with him. He only visits occasionally in the summer, and you never know where they'll choose to spend their winter.'

Her last words were drowned (literally) as great torrents of rain swashed down, dousing the sun, putting out the light, shimmying silver reflections troubling the red clay walls.

Rather unfortunately, just as I'd managed to convince her the brigands couldn't care less about me, dear old Goat hurtled in and pounced on me.

'Why did you sneak off this morning?' he demanded. 'We were going to give you some of our breakfast when our pretty Reenah here turned up with it! Now I'll swear you haven't had any, you look so peaky! Come now and get something inside you. You won't tell on us, will you, Reeney?'

'I'll be missed, Goat –' I protested.

But he ignored that and went on, 'Oh, and bring the little fellow along. I must see to him. He's hardly happy with his little self, is he? You don't want to see him develop rickets or something, do you?'

I ran to get Nal, in spite of all Reenah had just flatteringly said about a pathological need for lame ravens, etc.

'He just must have more light and air,' he pronounced once in his rain-flickery room while Madfist pushed me down by the fire and grilled bread and sausage for me. 'You're still feeding him milk? Yes, he's still very young, isn't he? Do they let you have the top off the cream, ever?'

'I feed him myself,' I said. I was glad the soldier was in the other room, where Madfist had left off dicing with him to come in here. Somehow this seemed sorry state for an Empress in her own land, not even to have the buffer of a wet-nurse between self and all the humiliations of reality. Worse than work-cracked finger-nails instead of my long gilded ones, and a grubby shift instead of silk flowing from a knot of diamonds.

'That explains some,' Goat said with a grunt of satisfaction. 'You've hardly enough nourishment in you for yourself. This is absurd. Tell Reenah, she seems to be a friend of yours.'

'I'll tell our Reen.' Madfist turned the sausage with a finger, and let out an oath as he sucked the finger.

'No, I think I'd better,' I said. 'Thank you.'

'Don't want complications,' Goat said knowingly. 'Now, what are we going to do about Baby?' He flipped Nal's chin, trying to raise a smile or gurgle.

'Well, I'm leaving soon,' I said. 'He'll get a change of air then.'

'Oh, are you?' Madfist thrust the sausage at me. 'Where?'

'I've no idea. I'll make out. I'll manage somehow. I only know I can't stay here a moment longer than's necessary.'

'We're getting a bit browned off, ourselves. And we're not existing under your conditions. But you haven't any ideas on where you're off to?'

'None.'

'We're back on the road again before the end of the week – '

'Oh, does Reenah know?' I said before I thought.

'Why should she?' Madfist stared.

'It's none of my business,' I looked straight back at him, recovering myself. 'Only that she leads such a boring life in summer when everyone's gone.'

Madfist slapped his thighs and hooted. 'Is that the sob-story she's been spinning you? I *knew* you were new to inn-life! There's no end of life here in summer! Compared to summer, the Long Snow is a coffin! There are new guests putting up every night, drinking, dicing, fights and off to a friendly bed! What are you on about, girl? Our Reenah has a *very* full time summertime, eh, Goat?'

'It wasn't a sob-story about ordinary loneliness,' I said sharply. 'Use your sense. (If any.) She misses you.'

'I'm sure,' Madfist said derisively. 'But she keeps very busy

103

trying to forget me. Don't worry about her. Did you know she's spent this winter with three others in this wing, as well as your humble servant? And then she tries to tell me the brat's mine!'

I hadn't been going to mention that in spite of the fact I knew they each knew. But at that I said, 'Well, she ought to know!'

'How? You don't know what you're on about,' Madfist scowled. 'So shut up and use your mouth for eating.'

'Perhaps she wanted your child,' I tried to jog his sympathy for Reenah.

'Then why did she tell all the others it was theirs, too? And we all checked with each other and never let on to her.'

'She told you first,' I rejoined lamely.

'No, she didn't, she told Blacksquint first!' Madfist said triumphantly.

'She must have been half out of her mind in any case,' I insisted, speaking for Reenah of whom I'm fond and for vulnerable womanhood in general. 'Scared of when her mother found out – with a mother like that, of course she had to try to get married till she found she'd lost it –'

'Oh, where were you brought up?' Madfist said in disgust. 'The old harridan doesn't let a chance go of charging extra for the extra services of Reenah and her friends – and Reenah keeps count, never lets a free night slip by for friendliness' sake! The old cow was the same till we started going to inns with younger staff and she had to stop treating her daughter as a rival to be squashed out of the way, and start making use of her talents. As for Reenah "finding she'd lost her lambkin" – Gods we don't even know if there was one! Unusually careless of her, if so. Anyway, Goat gave her one of his brews and within the fortnight we heard the first and last of it.'

I stood up, almost snatching Nal from Goat's arms.

'You don't prove a thing with your clever world-weary lectures,' I said. 'Then why does Reenah bother to make a friend of me as soon as she finds I'm sort of conventional in outlook, and try to keep you away from other girls, and go to the trouble of making up a long story about her tragic bereavement as if she was a normal girl led astray by love? Even if all your story is true, and none of hers, which has yet to be completely proved in spite of things which are beginning to piece together in my memory, she's obviously keener on you than on anyone else, and she's also never had a chance to be anything but a – a confused, mixed up sort of girl because she's never lived anywhere else!'

'You're not walking out like that,' Madfist stated. He yanked me back by my hem so that all my dignity went rather zero.

'Sit down and try to look pleasant. We were going to invite you to leave here with us – we're taking Laran and moving back into the world. But I suppose now you think we can't be trusted to take care of an innocent young mother?'

'I never was under many illusions where you were concerned.'

'Didn't we look after you nicely last night?'

'You were probably lulling me,' I said sulkily and feeling very inexperienced and awkward. 'I don't suppose I'm giving you any new ideas, but I'd be crazy not to take into account all the probabilities of being as useful to you as say Reenah is to her mother, or even of my child's limbs being permanently twisted while he's still weak and malleable, so that he can make an effective professional beggar later in life. I don't know much about life on the road, I admit. But I do know a bit.'

'We won't take offence at these unworthy suspicions – ' Goat said nobly.

'Ingratitude,' murmured Madfist who was grilling more sausage.

'But what will you meet up with once you've burned your bridges behind you and got away from this admittedly unsavoury set-up?' Goat reasoned, as he matter-of-factly removed Nal once more from my clutches. 'You'll meet robbers, rapists, killers, perverts and just plain brutes, all on the rampage again after being penned up all the prison-months of the Long Snow. Even if we are all you suspect, you must admit we'd steer you into trouble more pleasantly and in a far more civilised way than some of the appallingly uncouth types you might meet up with?'

'Don't listen too much to him,' interposed Madfist. 'He's so innocent in his own well-meaning way, he doesn't realise you might take him quite seriously in your own innocence. We'd simply take you along with us till you felt you wanted to throw down roots somewhere else. No strings – no ties – just the pleasure of your conversation, the triumph of seeing you, perhaps, *smile* once or twice.'

I looked quickly into his eyes.

They were so wide, so clear and sincere and honest that I just couldn't believe there is no ulterior motive for the invitation.

'You're very kind indeed,' I said. 'You know that. But I feel I must stay on a little longer here. Something more than the offer of drifting may turn up.'

I took Nal from Goat again. But I found I couldn't meet Goat's hurt look.

'Well, the thaw is here. But not your fine friends,' the inn-woman smiled pleasantly.

We were shovelling away the last of the grubby packed ice which had been the bottom layer of the drifts in the courtyard – I and two of the men, while she pegged out clothes to flap in the first dry breeze of the year, no more of the stuffy scorching beside braziers.

I was happier doing the shovelling than she'd've liked. Sheer hard work and malnutrition have made very brittle my finger-nails that I used to be able to grow so long. Several of them are torn off below the quick, others are bruised black and tender. So it is less irritating to hold a shovel than a cloth or scrubbing-brush.

'Perhaps they got lost? I'm sure they wouldn't mean to leave you without word,' she chattered with an innocent look. 'You were so sure of their promises.'

The clothes flapped with a rending sound, her shifts pregnant with air, the Master's yellowing under-tights galloping out from the line. The linen seemed delighted to be out on the wind again; to be longing for *complete* liberty. But none of it flapped back and hit her in the face, though she didn't trouble to stand out of its way. It wouldn't dare.

The wind was like a knife of ice right through my single shift and jerkin, in which I shiver even in the red house. But I was glad to be out here. I could even smell the Forest, which is no longer senses of sight, sound and smell buried under snow.

I could even hear the streams breaking the ice and carolling with youth's triumph right in there under the branches bursting and surging with potential foliage.

In a good mood, also invigorated by the air of the new young year, my hostess continued to try to get a rise out of me.

'Poor Lady Cija, it *is* a crying shame. Don't you feel *most* indignant? I feel sure nobody would blame you if you did. I should give them a piece of my mind and no mistake, when they do make up theirs to turn up. I only hope they don't take all this year – and next Snow too – about it.'

As I smiled, I could feel how thin and pale the smile must look. But it was clamped tight against gritted teeth, or it wouldn't have existed at all.

106

'Keep your courage up,' I said. 'You may have to put up with me a while yet.'

She beamed as though she could imagine nothing more exciting.

She has won, it is obvious to us both. In one winter she has done a good, thorough job in beating me down into something much more contemptible than the exiled Empress who arrived expecting lodging.

'*Here*'s a sign of spring,' said the man with the hook-nose, who had taken the opportunity to lean on his shovel while she concentrated on me. 'Guests arriving.'

The woman looked up at the sound of shouting riders pushing towards us through the Forest. Now that the white is melting, you can hear the crackle of undergrowth too, and the birds are here again.

The riders were still some distance off. At times you couldn't hear them at all, the wind blanked them out.

But the woman sniffed this wind, her eyes glazed but the poise of her head all awareness, like a dog pricking its ears.

'I swear I know those lads,' she said. 'I know that song, those crazy laughs. It can only be the kine-thieves up from the Bluedowns. Bustle, bustle, you fools! Bar the gate, Goitre, and Cija set the girls to the shutters!'

I splashed back to the red house.

'Reenah! Sylna! She says to bolt everything up, the kine-thieves from the Bluedowns are on us!'

'The kine-thieves are up from the Bluedowns!'

'The thaw has released the kine-thieves!'

The girls ran to shutters and cupboards. They were pink and big-eyed, not sure whether to wail or giggle.

'Now we'll see something!'

Reenah tumbled out of Madfist's and Goat's room, still laughing, pulling her tunic back on one shoulder.

'They've been pretending to use me as a ball – devils they are, straight – but what's this everyone's yelling? The boys from the Bluedowns? Gods have mercy!' she cried, and then laughed, and then clapped her hand to her mouth in genuine consternation.

'We'd better keep them out, if we can.'

'If you can,' Madfist echoed as he followed her.

'It doesn't matter to *you*, of course,' Reenah flashed. 'If our inn is wrecked, our men end up with broken heads –'

'And you provide a little free pleasure, for once, to our merry

107

mates,' chortled the customer with long black mustachios, and he and Goat seized each other in a tender embrace and danced round the room knocking down sausage-strings from the beams with their flailing arms.

'You'd better stuff the baby up the chimney,' Reenah said to me.

A stab of shame. I had forgotten Nal entirely.

As I ran for his cupboard, Goat whirled out of the dance, leaving his partner to stagger into the hearth, and caught me.

'Not the chimney, love, not the chimney. They poke their swords and spears up the chimneys first – they know everything of value is stuffed up there among the soot and jackdaws' nests. Give the pet to me.'

'To you?'

'The lamb is safest of all right in the wolf's den,' Reenah said with quite an edge to her voice. 'The only place the pack would never think to hunt for him.'

Goat took Nal from me with a show almost of reverence. He smoothed the unkempt fur back from my son's wisp-veiled forehead.

'What will you do with him?' I said. 'Where can you possibly put him where he'll be safe?'

'I'll hold him,' he said simply. 'Don't fret, I shan't drop him, I shan't let anyone snatch him or bang him.'

I wasn't too certain this was wise. But the inn-woman came bustling up and shook me by the shoulder. I looked into Goat's eyes, and he smiled back reassuringly and showed me how watchful his care was by pretending to drop Nal and then catching him just in time while I gasped.

'Never fear,' he said, 'I know I'm holding the most precious of all things to your heart, the little bundle in which all your hopes and fears are wrapped up.'

'Get on with it,' screamed the woman. 'Hide the hams up the chimney, lift the trap-door and drop Reenah's bracelets down there, push a heavy skewer through that broken catch where there's no bolt!'

A confused yelling, very loud and long, burst on our ears.

'They're on us!' screamed Sylna.

'Not quite yet, dear,' smirked Madfist. 'Don't be so eager.'

The inn-woman aimed a blow at his chest. 'Ah,' she said savagely. 'You can joke. It's nothing to you that my house will be a shambles, my ale squandered, my men all with broken

108

bones to be set while I try to get the place in order after your fine fellows have ridden gaily off again.'

'No wonder they call you mean,' I said with sudden sympathy. 'You have to collect all the money you can, if your goods are broken up like this before every spring-cleaning becomes really *necessary!*'

But she gave me a clip across the ear for my impertinence and Madfist chuckled.

Reenah opened the shutters she'd just been frantically bolting. On tiptoe, we crowded round her shoulders.

The men at the fence were making only a token resistance, and I don't blame them. The woman squalled, but from what I'd heard it was obvious you could never keep these hooligans out. A holocaust of yelling devils with fair hair in plaits or in flowing manes, some leaped the high fence on their lean rangy ponies (they were marvellous ponies, my heart glowed to watch them) and others beat on the fence with cudgels, kicked it with iron-studded leather boots. The woman had been right. It was tough stuff, and didn't give easily. Frayed and bent more than broken, they beat it low enough, here and there in its length, to trample through.

Reenah banged the shutter again.

'Did you see what they did to Stuttering Gwil?' she was wide-eyed. 'He'll be abed a fair while now, and we shan't fairly be able to call it shirking. And the Idiot? He'll be babbling *now!*' She herself stuttered. 'For Gods' sakes, come and help me keep the chests and closets pushed against the office door.'

The Bluedownsmen didn't bother with the main doors when they found the weight of all our heaviest furniture against them.

Vaulting off their ponies, leaving them to trample and browse on their elegant long legs through the cabbages and herbs in the kitchen garden, the Bluedownsmen hammered on the shutters and the little back doors up steps we hadn't time to defend. They took time off only to bat their hands against their mouths and produce a horrible ululating howling. The shutters couldn't hold out, the wood splintered and the hinges squealed, and pretty soon the Bluedowners were pouring through.

They poked through business-like boots and cross-gartered leggings, they scrambled over the sills, they landed on the floor in neat squats and as they leaped up yelling they seized a struggling girl, or bounded for all the places they knew we'd hidden our hams, ale, goldsacks and valuables.

The girls were genuinely having a go at defending their

home. They screamed and clawed, again and again rescued their friends by coming at the attacker from behind with a swung poker or something heavy.

But I just tried to look invisible in a corner, and tried to look out for Goat.

The inn's men broke in after the robbers (though not Stuttering Gwil or the Idiot). They tried to do a bit of shooing out, but it was hopeless of course. The Master, moustaches bristling, and the man with the thick neck lifted one robber bodily and threw him out of the window, but he appeared again through another window a few minutes later.

'Help us, you scum! We've been your hosts a whole Snow – don't just stand there!' growled the Inn-man. But Squint and Goat and Madfist and the man with black mustachios, and the rest of the paying guests, just stood slapping each other on the shoulder and doubling up with laughter.

I tried to dodge safely across to Goat – I was sure he'd forgotten that bundle he held was a live baby – but the 'safely' bit was a tall order.

Over and over, I had to zigzag back again from a rough hand or a whole line of toughs blocking my way and shifting like a living net to tangle me in their outspread arms. I had a few sharp struggles, but in the confusion I was lucky enough to get away each time by wriggling like an eel – I am so skinny and bony now that I am hard to keep hold of and not very inviting anyway – and once I had to bite a grubby hairy wrist very hard and that did the trick, though I really had to spit afterwards.

I tried to keep an eye on Goat, across the milling rooms into which I followed him as the confusion surged, swayed. But I could only do so at a distance. I kept losing him.

I was sure he'd lose his sense and gaily hit somebody with Nal. Or chuck Nal at someone to make them laugh.

But I had to admit our resident bandits were the only people the newcomers didn't lay a hand on – except now and then in boisterous recognition or ecstatic greeting.

The whole thing became more out-of-hand. Girls really were dragged off. A small fire flared. Sobbing with fury, the inn-woman got her family to help beat out the sparks. Curtains were slashed down for no reason, and numberless window-panes broken for the fun of it. Originally, we'd taken care to fold the windows back open behind the bolted shutters. It's no easy matter getting glass replacements in the middle of a gigantic

Forest – even tiny thick wimpled panes the size of a child's palm.

A man with red plaits and wearing a fortune in jewellery rode his pony up the wooden stairs till they broke and wood and hooves crashed through on to the bed I've slept so many dark winter hours in.

They found where we'd stashed the ale casks, and dragged them out with noisy gleeful pride. Even before they were all happily drunk, they pierced the casks and the ale spurted out in honey-brown fountains. This waste enraged the inn-woman more than their drinking of it.

I was in a state of heightened awareness. I'd decided I might not reach twilight un-maimed, nor even alive. I was prepared to kick ruthlessly the instant any arm grabbed me – from any direction – but I wasn't prepared for a big stifling cloak suddenly pulled dark tight over my head and shoulders. Struggling desperately but uselessly, I was hauled along I didn't know where.

Knocked and bruised, dragged through things and over things, at one point I reached an obstruction I thought must be an up-ended table. I didn't want to manoeuvre it, I had no idea where I was being dragged off. I blundered, bleakly miserable amongst all the noise and movement. I realised the obstruction must be a row of casks with men squirming over them, their mouths to the spouting holes, fighting each other off. Hands trapped my ankles, fumbled up under my hem. I lost any will to help my captors. I sat down in the enveloping cloak, that someone's arm wouldn't loosen round me. I was picked right up, someone had my arms all tangled in that cloak, someone else gripped my ankles together, and I was carried right over the casks as though I was flying.

I made a violent hump of my body and succeeded in kicking my head free, but not my ankles. I landed *hard* on the plank floor. Wrestling savagely with the cloak-folds, I at last emerged in the smoky dull-red air of the inn.

Unable to grapple me properly again, they were laughing so hard, were several of the Bluedownsers. Also Madfist who had the grip on my ankles and now decided to send me really crazy by wrenching off my dilapidated boots and tickling the soles of my feet.

I twisted across the planks and managed to get near enough to him to bang him about the shoulders and chin with my fists. I tried to hit him hard but he hardly noticed.

111

'I'll claw your eyes out, Madfist,' I managed. 'In Gods' names tell me, where's Goat? I *know* he wouldn't leave me like this!'

Madfist roared. 'Hey, you're pined for, lover-boy!'

Goat wandered into my line of vision. He still toted Nal. 'I've still got our pet, never fear,' he burbled in a syrupy sort of voice. 'Don't take any notice of these lads' unfortunate manner. They mean you nothing but good.'

'It's all to your advantage, I swear,' Madfist assured me.

'You never do anything else,' I glowered. 'Give me those boots.'

Madfist released my feet, leaped up, and disappeared in the chaos, and came back with a pair of fur-lined shoes – not as good as mine had been, but ten times better than they are now.

He hunkered down on his heels to ease my feet into these.

'Where on earth – ?'

'Don't ask silly questions,' scolded Goat. 'You'll only get awkward attacks of conscience if you're answered.'

'They're Sylna's!' I struggled up. 'Why isn't she wearing them – what's happened to her –'

Madfist cuffed me, not all that good naturedly. 'Give over,' he growled. 'Shut up. Come along.'

'Where are you taking me? Gods! Goat, please – please ask them not to –'

'We're *not going to hurt you,*' Madfist hissed, glaring at me in the least reassuring way possible.

The back door was swinging on broken hinges and a drizzly draught.

Out on the cobbles the hens clucked and darted. They suspiciously examined the men sitting round, slumped against the log walls, groaning – Stuttering Gwil with what looked like a broken collar-bone, among sick-drunk robbers. There were pools of vomit.

'Goat – can't you see to Gwil?' I stared in horror at the man's lolling head. Tears were running down his face.

'We're in no mood for waiting around.'

'It was your friends hurt him for his bravery.'

'His cowardice, you mean. He was more afraid of the old woman than of the Blueboys,' Madfist said.

Goat looked at me, at Gwil, and hesitated. He gave Nal to me. I smiled gratefully at him. He loped across to Gwil. Madfist cursed.

Goat set Gwil's collar-bone and I helped where I could. Gwil was unconscious and swollen. Goat improvised a splint and an

112

awfully complicated bandage – he always has useful bits of old rag and phials of this and that amongst his clothing. I began to feel quite queasy at the sound and looseness of dislocated bone. Someone else came over to us from the group of impatient, swearing brigands. It was Laran, my soldier, thin and pale but walking, with his arm in a flowered sling that looked like a bit of the bedspread under which he's lain all winter.

He smiled at me as he helped hold Gwil straight for Goat's sensitive, probing fingers. He couldn't address me correctly so he didn't speak at all till I did.

'I presume we're all off and away, Laran?'

'I think it's as good a time as any – Lady. But I don't think we'll come to harm.'

'Guard you with our lives,' Goat promised extravagantly.

He and Laran lifted me on to the pony before Madfist.

'At least we've left pleasant memories with that trussed-up fool there,' Madfist sneered. 'They'll know that can only have been your work, my gallant Goat. It may make them think kinder of us for leaving without paying our last month's rent.'

He kicked both heels at once into the pony's flanks. It strode forward, its shaggy muscles swelling effortless against my own weary dangling legs.

A Forest camp after dusk, and I'm still alive. The wood-smoke writhes blue against the foliage. Sleepy birds cooing and crooning above us. Fire-hatched crickets, creaking. Frogs, burping. A smell of the inn-woman's cherished stolen spiced boar-hams grilling over the fresh-wood flames.

Madfist yanked me back against him. I stiffened.

'Oh, for blanksake,' he grated. 'Lean against my shoulder and try to look as if you like it. Or at least look pleasant. If you look unattached you'll find you'll belong to everybody – whether you look as if you like it or not.'

'Thanks for your thoughtfulness,' I said reluctantly. 'But I have to see to Nal. Could you sit with your back to me so I'm more or less screened?'

Goat bounded up, all beams.

'My Gran says she'll be only too pleased to feed the pet,' he announced.

'Your Gran must be dry long ago,' Madfist hooted.

'I'll look after him myself, thank her.' I was unwilling to let Nal out of my sight in this company.

'No, she really is my Gran, believe it or not,' Goat smiled

at me. 'I knew she'd be waiting at the Blueboys' camp. And as she is nursing her own last year's brat now, I don't see why the other side shouldn't do Nal.'

'Promise he'll be O.K.?'

'You'd believe anything this bastard chose to tell you, wouldn't you?' sneered Madfist.

'My Gran is a fount of fertility. She adores babies,' Goat told me.

'Likes the *taste*,' Madfist said ferociously.

I spluttered my head out of the ale-mug that was being passed round, full of my late Mistress' property, into which Madfist had forcibly ducked me.

'I'll come and have a few words with her, if I may, Goat.'

'She'll be delighted.'

Madfist tagged along, grumbling foully.

Goat's Gran was suckling her young under a tree. She is not at all like the old woman who helped Nal get born. She is as fat as a woman always on the move can be, and freckled, with glossy faded braids as long as mine used to be.

'So this is the honey,' she said in a dark guttural voice. 'Sickly little ape, eh. Do him good to draw some *rich* milk – ' she looked sharply at me. 'Can't think of weaning *this* yet, can we?'

'If you hurt him, you'll never suckle another ape,' Madfist promised, playing with his knife.

She snarled at him as she took Nal from me and straightway set him to her other breast.

Goat hurled himself on Madfist. 'My Gran is no monster – '

'Then it must have been your father's side – '

They rolled in the spring undergrowth till the fierce exertion dissipated their ill-temper.

Two greedy limpets, the babies clung to the splendid sun-splotched woman. I stared, trying to gauge her kind, till my intentness drew her eyes and she stared back at me, defensively, and would not smile.

'Your sort isn't fit for motherhood,' she said from her throat.

I liked this, perhaps just because it is a change from the inn-woman's sugary attitude. I don't see why I shouldn't trust her, I thought. If she hurts Nal now, it's something I didn't expect, and I can hardly blame myself. After all, she *is* healthier, he'll never get any nourishment from me till I get stronger. I've done my best for him.

As I trailed without enthusiasm back to Madfist, I wondered how everything would turn out. I have been an exile a long time. But I was respectable. I had a home, a place in life, an employer to whom I was responsible. It's another step farther into exile – exile from myself as I have always struggled to see myself – if I become a straggling vagrant.

Always, before this, I have managed not to get drawn into the vortex of the lawless. Sometimes it's meant quite an effort. I've even been absurd in my refusal to trade danger and uncertainty for the safety of the criminal society. But I wouldn't stay with the black priest Kaselm in his subterranean labyrinth. I was only a handful of days with the bandits of the Mainland mountains.

I looked at the brown whipcord-and-steel boys chasing each other and wrestling so magnificently you wanted to watch and pick up a few tips. I looked at the camp children swinging and somersaulting through the chilly branches above us, using filth and agile back-answers in an indiscriminate vocabulary that is such a happy change after the coy confidences of a gaggle of well-bred ladies-in-waiting. Of course I'd love Nal to grow up like that. It's the way a boy should grow up – except that it means an ultimate maturity resembling Madfist's or Squint's.

Obviously I'm on my own as a parent now. Nal will have only a mother. Women are pitiful at bringing up boys. Either they spoil them into horrible sops incapable of taking their place in any world full of danger and the demand for initiative. Or they just somehow mould them in their own image, simply because they are the only mature model around. Or they try desperately to counter-effect their own natural influence, and keep pushing and shoving the child into virility and masculinity and overcoming cowardice-obstacles and all the rest of it, till masculinity is poisoned for him even when he woodenly achieves it. I expect that as a mother I shall be a mixture of the last two.

But only if I'm on my own, or surrounded by women and servants. And yet how awful to bring up a little Prince among lice-ridden brigands and whining beggars, so that before he's reached puberty he can't get the nits out of his hair, he despises cleanliness and honesty, he's a natural rapist-sneak-murderer without a conscience, and is probably riddled with unimaginable diseases. I wouldn't be happy ever again, even if I had also ensured that he could fight and climb and bully like a superman.

And am I really to become the drab-drag I already look?

'Are you going to sleep with me tonight?' Madfist asked abruptly.

'Why, Madfist. How unexpected. It is courteous of you to *ask*.'

'Don't try to be funny,' he growled.

'I'm sincere about this. Listen. It's still not too late to double back and get Reenah. She'd be thrilled to be smuggled out. I'd like it better with her to talk to, too.'

'You think I'm in a desperate state or something? There are a dozen willing darlings here prettier than you. Don't flatter yourself you attract me at all. There isn't even much of a challenge in your unwelcoming personality – I'll swear you'd be just as sullen and sarcastic no matter how much pleasure I'd prove I could give you. I'll admit to a curiosity as to what you're like – probably milk-and-water with bones in. Mainly, it's pure good-heartedness. You'll be bothered far worse if you don't take advantage of my kind offer.'

He had paused in his pacing and when I glanced up at his eyes he was looking down at mine. Not just his words but even his face still annoyed me just as it had when I'd first met him. Still, he's not just handsome. Even while he gets on my nerves, I have to admit he's attractive.

'Go on, little lady-slattern,' he invited, his lip curling back from large square teeth. 'Tell me you find me disgusting.'

'I could tell you I am under oath to be faithful to a memory. Or that I am too weak after that Snow to do more than sleep. But actually I do feel a real revulsion. Technically you're attractive – but I'd loathe having to get involved, to find out about your body, to be so *close* to anyone, especially someone of an alien sex –'

'You prissy-talk as though you were still a dear little virgin,' he jeered loudly.

Various eyes flicked at me.

'No, the child's very much mine,' I said levelly, though under the clean trees the words tasted like bile.

'And a frigid virgin at that. Or a lesbian,' he tried to sting me.

I wouldn't even ask him to lower his voice. I stood sullenly and kept my head low so my unkempt hair might hide the blush I'd felt scorch me.

116

'You can lie under my blanket, then,' he said after breaking a silence by spitting. 'I won't touch you. I'm not panting for you, lovely, believe me.'

'Can't I have a blanket of my own? Plenty were brought from the inn.'

He stared at me so that his eyes bulged out and he looked distinctly unappetising. His big fist clenched. I was sure he was about to knock me reeling. He spat with sizzling deliberation and slouched off fast to the fires.

I found Goat had sidled to my shoulder.

'You shouldn't have done that,' he said reproachfully. 'You've upset Madfist. You'll have a miserable violent night of it if you seem all on your ownsome. I haven't a blanket of my own, so I can't do anything about offering you a bed.'

I wouldn't have minded sharing a blanket with dear Goat, even though his bottles might prove a bit uncomfortable.

'I'm fine, Goat,' I smiled. 'It's not even very chilly tonight. Look, there's an angle between these roots. Just my size, and the wind can only get at me from two sides, and one side there's a fire only yards away. I've spent many less luxurious nights.'

He patted me into the gnarled trunk-niche. 'Sleepies,' he crooned. 'Take a swig of this and curl up as though you mean it.'

It was hard to sleep. Fires, dogs, bawling and brawling. Not even the children seemed to intend sleeping before dawn. The flames leaped on my eyeballs even under closed lids.

But the worst of the night soon started. I lost count of how many times I woke with a terrified jolt and had to fight or argue with one, two or three red-black rough-handed silhouettes.

Their drunkenness was a help in that if you could argue tenaciously with a sound of logic, or pretend someone *was* just on their way back to you, *yes*, they *are*, they got tired and lurched away shaking their heads clearer again. But otherwise the ale had got them brutishly difficult to control.

Every time I got to sleep it happened again. This time there were about half a dozen. Judging by the fumes of their beer-heavy breathing, there was no hope in even trying to argue.

'Please – please let me go – ' was all I could say. They were guffawing and getting in each other's way but any moment they'd remember to be purposeful.

'I'm *with* someone – ' I managed to shout into the nearest eardrum.

'He won't grudge us twenty minutes,' he assured me. I was so tired and so sick with revulsion I was no longer clear or neat who and where it was best to hit or claw – fighting, I've found, is like dancing – when you're tired you get untidy, lose your sense and precision. I could only struggle, not keep still for an instant, and sob prayers. 'Perhaps if I heave I can manage to be sick all over them,' I thought with new hope.

Before they got irritated enough to stun me and be done, two bullet-heads were slammed together with a heavenly melodic ringing sound.

But the others didn't combine to launch themselves on the single newcomer.

Not another word was said. The big new silhouette just stood before the flamelight, legs astride, ready and so menacing, but quite casual as though there were no need for further threat.

One of them turned to me. He was big and bulgy, but he whined, 'Why didn't you *tell* us it was Madfist you're with? That's sluts all over. Love to see fights started over them, any excuse.'

'I love what there's been of this one,' I gasped, muttering anything that came into my head to see if I were still human.

They shambled up and away, pausing only to slide an ingratiating hand over Madfist's lean shoulder. 'No hard feelings, eh, feller, eh?'

As I smoothed my shift as discreetly as I could, sort of as if I wasn't doing it at all, I noticed the girl standing behind Madfist.

She was twisting her weight from hip to hip, sulky and bored.

As the last gallant sidled past him, Madfist seized his wrist.

'Skullbar, aren't you?'

'Didn't mean a thing by it, Madfist, straight, straight up, Madfist. Didn't know she's yours. Just a bit of a giggle.'

'You can have this instead. There's plenty of life left for the night.'

He joined the wrists of the man and girl in his own grip, laying his fingers winsomely against her lips when she started a shrill of puzzled protest.

Formally he introduced them.

'Swelpet, Skullbar, Skullbar, Swelpet. Shush, my dove. My blessings on you both.'

'Gosh, you're a real friend, Madfist,' enthused my attacker.

Madfist benignly watched them out of sight. He sat beside me, inches from me, back against the bark, his knees drawn up. I was aware from the corner of my eye that he wasn't looking at me, but in case he'd be aware from the corner of his if I looked at him, I kept my eyes on the sturdy battered fire-flickered leather of his nearest high boot.

'Enjoy your freedom? Your independence?' he asked viciously.

'Thank you for coming back, Madfist.'

'You realise I could turn this to my advantage and not a soul, not even you, could blame me. I'll stay with you if you're friendly, I could say. Not unless. I'd have you begging me on your knees.'

At first I didn't know what to say. The silence lengthened till it sounded like my agreement.

'I could go to Goat,' I said.

He pointed. When I was slow to see, he pulled my head round by a grip on my neck. Goat was lying not far off, a big fur blanket straggling farther and farther off himself and a girl with a pool of flaxen hair.

I looked at my hands as if they interested me. It wasn't Goat's deceit that put me off balance.

It's only last year that I stopped believing sex *is* a very private rare sort of thing. In my first year out of the Tower of my childhood, when I was seventeen about three crowded surging years ago, I knew that the General Zerd and the Governor of the Southern town bordering the plains were both monsters. They were the only people I knew who seriously behaved as though sex were something not *just* for producing babies. The talk and the coquetry in the Beauty's entourage, at HQ in the Southern Capital and of course in the Temple-city among the hills up-river were quite excessive, but I thought that was only because they were sophisticated haunts of vice. Until I learnt through my poor little Lel what people really meant by perversion. I thought the word 'pervert' invariably applied to people (like Zerd and the Governor) who used sex for more than seeing that the population of the world didn't disappear.

Smahil, and later my marriage, and most of all the simple accumulation of time and experience, have shown me that

119

it really and truly is something that happens quite often, not just a half-horned half-haloed much-fabled much-rumoured kernel of rarity.

But every now and then the reality hits me – not as indecent – I've never in all my life had real moral training, because till I was seventeen I wasn't even told that there were things called men walking the world outside the Tower (so I've no conscience-inhibitions to throw off) – but as unreal, a nightmare, a fantasy, impossible.

'You're not one of us at all,' Madfist said beside me.

I looked austerely at him.

'I thought that went without saying.'

'I mean,' he thoughtfully began to shred the wings off a fire-hatched cricket he'd caught and I was even more steeled in my repugnance, 'You don't even belong in this *country*.'

'In this Continent.' I watched him.

'You're not amazing the juices out of me,' he replied. 'I'm not jumping out of my skin with amazement. We know the foreign Army paid us the honour of a visit, and there's a foreign Emperor now. We even know there's air for boats and fishing over the sea now.'

'News gets around in your profession,' I said politely.

'On the road, that's the life. But you couldn't have fooled us in any case. Not with that mud-colour hair.'

'It's lighter when properly washed, with clean water and frothing soap.'

'And you're plumper when you're well-fed, I suppose,' he said with what seemed an air of civil disbelief.

'May I go to sleep, Madfist?'

'You can lean on my shoulder.'

'You'll get pins-and-needles.'

'Then I'll tip you off, won't I? Rest till then.'

Somehow each episode of my acquaintance with Madfist, when I'd thought each one was scraping him more on my annoyed nerves, had built up in me a truly unshakeable belief in his confidence and his power of protection. I noticed this as the instant I touched my forehead carefully to his hard shoulder a great wave of luxurious security swashed over me. It was a wonderful feeling, a physical feeling. My eyes closed to sweet darkness. There was no prickling and fluttering of the eyelids, no leaping of flames yet in the darkness. My headache might never have been, I couldn't remember what it was like to have a headache, yet a moment before my head had been throbbing. My spine and arms relaxed. The blood didn't bang my pulses. He folded his arms round me. I could smell him. But it was the sweat of a man, a strong man who wouldn't let anything hurt me until *he* decided it should be allowed to. As long as he decided to look after me, I was safe.

I was so close to him, impersonally close and yet inquisitively so, that I wondered if I listened hard enough I might hear the bristles pushing through his chin as the time of his last shave receded in the distance.

The beat of his heart swung me into sleep.

They took so long, Goat and Madfist and Goat's Gran and Goat's Gran's two brats and one baby and Nal still in his hood, saying good-bye to the encampment as we struck off on the road, that I wandered on ahead into the morning.

Laran lingered with them, not noticing my gradual recession.

Their feet all pounded the snow-bared gravel above me.

'Where the – ?'

'She's slipped away, given us the go-by –'

'She'll come to harm –' that was Laran.

I hadn't meant to disappear. I'd only slid down into the hollow below the roadside to examine what looked like red berries already oozy. But their reaction made me *think* of escape, and real freedom, and getting rid of even the encumbrance and responsibility of Nal on to a woman full of milk and instinct, and being just myself again – no longer a mother, nor Laran's Empress, nor Madfist's debtor, just myself in the swelling spring with the clothes I stood up in.

'Here I am, if you've finished your uproar,' I said.

Laran gave me a hand as I scrambled up again.

Gran snorted. Madfist stared at me as if I were a ghost already. In spite of the bristles dark-blond like a bar of shadow, it took some moments before he stopped looking white about the gills.

As we walked on, I thought, What's up with him?

He's not in love with you, Cija, don't kid your little self. I believe him, even, when he says he's not exactly obsessed with the idea of carnally possessing you either, as my nurse Glurbia would have put it had she put it at all –

'Have some berries,' I invited my companions.

The oldest child grabbed the lot and stained its mouth royal purple.

No, I don't really want Nal to grow like that, I thought as we straggled on.

I was surprised to find I could keep up well. I may have been getting run-down all winter, but I've also developed stamina – my muscles run easily, they're used to work, and there's not much flesh to hold them back. But Gran kept up fine, hugging Nal to her as she strode, her big open-work sandals striking the gravel, Goat and Laran taking turns at carrying her own baby.

Both she and Goat's parent must have started off thirteen at the latest, I thought. She's hardly older than my own Mother.

'I'll carry Nal,' I offered. 'I'm well able.'

'*I'm* sure,' she growled disdainfully.

How quickly Atlan threw off her sleep. She had made use of it only so that she could burgeon in a concentration of peace. Sunbeams slant between the trees, stripe the path which becomes just a track; new grass is a lighter sweeter green, of more clarity than I've seen ever; a starring of flowers, like something scattered till you realise they're simply growing up out of Atlan herself, adorable shapes and delicious colours. Huge trunks, gnarled, probably contemporaries of the initial vacuum-creation, have now outlasted it. Ferns quivering on still air. A hum, a vibration of insects breaking from chrysalis, waking nests in hollow trees. Roots like tentacles grasping the beloved fecund earth, glossy with moss, moss of nap like velvet or rich fruit and starred with minute pinprick blossoms.

Ebony twigs, creamy constellations, pendulant catkins, busy birds – the Forest sunned itself in a grateful glow of life, surging to the tiniest thread of detail.

'Soon it should be quite warm,' I muttered, humping the checkered shawl full of cheese and meat and bread I'd been given to carry.

I was still glad we'd had to leave the Bluedownsers' ponies that had carried us to the campment-fires last night.

As the sinews behind my knees started their first nagging, Madfist said, 'Here we'll eat', and fell like a log into a swathe of tall young grass. The glade received him.

We lowered ourselves beside his abandoned relaxation. The toddler unwound its stranglehold-legs from round Goat's neck. We unpacked the food. The wineskin was passed round: each of us in turn arched our throat to the arching gush of the sour ruby liquid. The oldest child tickled the underside of Madfist's jaw with a plume of feather-tipped grass. Madfist sensuously

122

suffered this till, without warning, he bounded up and tripped the child who became breathless with laughter.

I felt fidgety and guilty watching Goat's Gran's magnificent sun-splotched breast meaning everything to my son. I felt inadequate and inferior. I also felt I was wicked to be so glad to hand him over to her. Yet he couldn't know the difference between her and the thin, impatient girl who had seen to him all winter – or if he sensed difference, this must be better.

I tried to look as if I weren't watching, but my eyes would keep sliding sideways under my lashes.

At last I said as though I'd just noticed, 'Isn't that a stream-sound?'

'A dainty sparkly rill just ahint of the glade,' Goat burbled. He was making finger-nail slits in flower-stalks. Already the youngest boy had a chain of flowers casting transparent shadows on the tan of his neck.

The stream beyond the trees moved fast.

It was quite wide, and here and there became big pools, still mobile, instinct with cross-currents and whirlypools.

I knelt on the slope, my face closer and closer to the fascination of motion. But I could see no reflection of myself, no acknowledgement of my existence.

After the months of snow, after the dull red clay, endless walls, the dark wood and the interior-smells and all the stifling fug-laced-with-draughts that make winter in mean exile, this water was the most beautiful thing I'd seen.

It was even more vivid with movement than with colour. It swung and hit itself on the curve of a cross-current, and exploded in bright ripples, and swayed into a rhythm. It was dance. It was galloping horses, it was wind through jungle. The colour itself was shocking. Blue, green, violet, haloes and threads of white-yellow. But this jewel denied existence to me. Like almost all the nature of Atlan I had ever met, it ignored me. I became less than invisible – a zero, or a blot, a bubble round which Atlan's atmosphere closed and flowed, resolutely pretending not to notice. The water was too busy with itself to reflect me.

I thought I saw fish coruscating under there – an eye staring, a tail flickering. The hard wind left over from winter, in its fight with the spring-surge, had knocked some of the new-born ivory flowerlets right off their ebony twigs. On the water they became part of a corpse-dance. They floated, then flew into a vortex, swam like blizzard-driven snow. At first they seemed

123

suspended several feet above water. Only the floor of the pool, not on its surface, lay the dizzy violet shadows. And shadow-ink spread under the bending trees.

I put my finger in the water. Instantly it was enclosed in a gold sealing. I dipped in my feet. The water seemed very live: there was a strong tug. It was not too cool, under the sun almost warm.

I pulled my shift up and up till I was shoulder-high in the tugging. I chucked it and the jerkin over to the bank, and almost overbalanced, and hoped they wouldn't slide down the slope.

Among the lilting blossoms – which were lustrous as sentient satin, not corpses at all, just little independent intensities – I felt grimy and unworthy, as if I polluted the pool.

Even since my last bath, there had accrued to me weeks of sweat, the sweat of unwilling work, of fear.

In spite of its speed and glow, the pool was not glad. Or rather, it was alive with its own joyousness, but it was not glad to accept me. It did not reject me, as it had rejected my reflection. It just didn't notice me. It continued to swirl and scintillate on its own wave-length. Technically I would be clean when I came out. But I wouldn't feel cleansed and kissed as I would have felt emerged from un-Atlan water.

Surrounded by light and carrilons of colour, I yet began to feel isolated, dimmed. I was about to clamber out, wondering for the first time how the slope-bank would reject me, when Madfist's boots came deliberately along the grass-line.

He lounged on the bank and grinned down at me.

You're just a big cliché, Madfist, I thought in amusement. When girls are bathing, legends and epic-lays always admit the grinning male stalking to the bank.

But I looked down at the water and was glad of the conflict of motion and colour. Only a pallid foreshortened glimmer was me. He confused me more than I meant him to. He was out of my control even in relation to myself.

'Nice you're here, Madfist,' I said to unnerve him too. 'Have you any fairly clean scarf or sash, say, that I could dry myself with instead of my only jerkin?'

'Nymph surprised,' he archly leered, because that's what he'd prepared to say and wasn't going to waste it.

'Have you . . . ?'

'I've an idea about hiding your clothes anyway. What would you do then?'

'Stay where I am, it's lovely and warm,' I lied briskly.

'Maybe, till I carry you out,' he conceded.

'Madfist, I wasn't telling the truth. I'm getting sort of numb. Please hand me a scarf or something, or my jerkin. And then go away,' I added.

How grateful, nevertheless, I was for his appearance. He was solid and real on the bank. He talked to me, teased me, accepted without question that I existed. And the pool hardly reflected him. It took his colours, brown and maroon, and broke them up. Away they darted in slivers.

He unwound his multi-striped sash.

'Here, hang on. I'll help you out.'

'I can manage,' I scowled.

He began to annoy me a lot again.

I stood there pallidly glimmering till I realised how far my lower lip must be out. I unobtrusively withdrew it and tried to look impressive.

At last Madfist stood up, stretched his arms till his biceps strained his rather tatty jerkin, yawned till his chest became magnificent so I felt incredibly skinny and female, rose and ambled over to my clothes. He picked them up under his arm and disappeared among the trees.

I *wasn't* going to come out of this water. They could go on and leave me if they wished. They'd undermined my responsibility, I could no longer help it if Nal passed out of my hands. I'd stay here till summer and warmth if need be.

I waded round in my new home, hit the water once or twice, plucked a pebble from the overhang and skimmed it across, realising I'd narrowly missed a round-eyed fish.

Madfist was squatting on the highest point of the bank where he hadn't been a minute ago.

He looked as if he'd been settled there months. Without a glance in my direction, he was examining my clothes like a pawnbroker or prospective buyer. He whistled between his teeth.

'Give them to me, Madfist.'

'Did you know, you were beginning to ooze tears when you thought you were all alone.'

'Give me my clothes.'

'What will you give *me* then?'

I tried to sound prim and unafraid. 'There's no question of that, that's no element of the conversation. They're my clothes already, I don't have to buy them back.'

125

'Don't you?' He swung my shift by one shoulder. 'This is threadbare, rotting away.'

'Then it's no good to you.'

He looked at me in aggravation, tired of the verbal dead-ends, and tossed my clothes at me. They spread on the water, spread on the ripples which spread from them. I rescued them before they dipped.

I pulled them on at awkward angles. I waded ashore and had difficulties with the overhang. Eventually Madfist hauled me up, settling the matter with one swing of his competence-strength after all my scrambling and worry.

Dripping wet, I shook my hair and spattered him with drops. I had intended studious silence, but he leaned forward and kissed me. My heart lurched and thudded like a drunk.

It wasn't the rapacious kiss I'd expected. His mouth was closed, his lips firm and dry. They throbbed against mine. I drew away, panicky, and found he had not touched a finger to me. He was lulling me, I decided.

'Which direction is the glade?' I asked. I felt humiliated when my voice came out husky.

'I'll rub you with my sash. Don't worry, our sun's penetrating. You'll dry quite soon. You won't catch pneumonia.'

'If I did, Goat'd look after me.'

'He won't have to.'

He rubbed me impersonally till my teeth chattered more from his roughness than from chill.

'How come Atlan gets such a swift sudden spring?'

'It doesn't seem so quick to us. How new are you?'

'I didn't expect to find bandits in Atlan,' I said inconsequentially.

'Atlan has *everything*,' he boasted.

Back with the wayfarers, Madfist walked by me as though naturally, swinging my stolen shoes by their thongs. I was still rather soaked. Laran looked a bit startled, as though he were wondering when to step in and announce my true status.

So far I'd never yet had a chance to be alone with Laran. As soon as Goat and Madfist got to insulting each other, I beckoned to Laran.

'*Empress* –'

'Oh, Laran, *please* don't. That's what I keep meaning to tell you. For Gods' sakes, don't tell these men who I am. It would alter their whole attitude to myself and Prince Nal.'

126

'That's what I hope –'

'No, no, it might even be dangerous. Please.'

Laran drew stiffly closer to me as Goat turned to say, 'By the way, love, sorry about not getting a blanket sooner to you last night. I found a girl with a fur one, and I was going to bring it to you, but she wouldn't give it to me straight away – and, well, then Madfist came back to you, bless his heart of gold in his rough exterior –'

'That's all right, Goat.'

'It's sweet you are.'

I was now warier of admiring the scene. I had been ready to adore the peculiar brightness of Atlan. But I sensed, just as I had when I first landed, that the land felt me to be indecent. I had been the very first prick of the spearhead, the forerunner of the invasion. For centuries and centuries before mine, no alien foot had trod Atlan's crystal shore, pressed her flowers. Hours after mine, the animals and the Army came, the foreign Emperor took his advantage and in a snap of his primitive-scaled fingers overthrew the ancient dynasty, pollution came, artificial manure poisoned the very soil, war came.

I suppose my admiration is an insult. I am a sycophantic germ, marvelling at what I destroy. Or so Atlan sees it.

I looked at the Forest with less wonder, more analytically. But I couldn't help admiring it, though it isn't interested in drawing a foreigner's interest. It is more than a flora and fauna different from that I'm used to. It is more than a sunny day in novel surroundings. What would be yellow on the Mainland is gold here. Even the rot smells sweeter.

'Didn't we pass this way last night, on the ponies?' Laran asked.

'We're making back in a wide circle,' Goat said matter-of-factly.

'To where?'

'The inn. We want to use it next year. I've decided we must pay the rent we owe, to keep their good-will, their trust,' Madfist said.

'In the uproar,' I said in surprise, 'she can't have noticed what was taken and what left.'

'Besides, one should always be reliable where one can,' Goat agreed with Madfist.

I felt chastened. These weren't my ideas of men 'on the road', even in Atlan. I hadn't worried overmuch about the denuded inn-woman.

The sunset was blood on all the spikes of broken panes as we neared the inn. We had not seen that glade which had been so terrible in the snow. I wondered if anyone would ever see it, wonder about the wheels and shafts with their fading gilt, and the disarranged skeletons.

A deep gloom, even melancholia, came over me as I saw the place again. It looked so long, so low, so black and yet avid. I was sure it was waiting to welcome me back in.

'Will you be long in there?' I asked Madfist.

'We'll all stay the night under a roof now we're here,' he said. 'We shan't get another chance for a while.'

'I can't go in there,' I said. 'I'm a runaway servant.'

Madfist rubbed his stubble. He looked over my head at Goat, his tawny brows jerked query.

'You'll look after her out here while we pop in, won't you, Laran?' Goat asked.

'With my life,' Laran said promptly.

'No,' said Madfist. 'Not just Cija and the soldier. I mean, neither is of full strength. Goat's Gran, you stay with them.'

'Not for no one,' she grunted. 'The kids need warmth and roast potatoes.'

'Come in, Cija,' Madfist said. 'You're with us now. But stay out of the old bitch's sight if you're nervous. You're only a kid yourself. If she starts anything, we'll deal with her. But you stay with Gran and the kids and get warm.'

We entered without being challenged. The gate and fence were still down, the kitchen-garden ravaged, the goats untethered and bleating the pain of their sagging udders.

I followed under the shadow of the eaves. My heart dropped.

Big horses were in the stable. Their harness lay on the stable benches. Scuffed and plain, but the more impressive of real service for that. An influx of the visitors the spring always ushered in must be complicating the rehabilitation of my long home.

Inside, there was utter confusion. It was pathetic. Everything seemed in exactly the mess the Bluedownsers must have left it. Everyone was running round in circles, picking things up and putting them down again somewhere equally useless, or just slumped staring vacantly.

Reenah darted forward, hugged us all, kissed Madfist, kissed Nal.

'Oh, what a lovely, lovely surprise! Into the dining-room with you. Cija, you and the other lady and the pets must have

128

the little room. I'll get a fire built in there. Oh, how delightful!'

She lingered, her hips wavering towards Madfist.

'Show the others in,' he said. 'I must have a word with Cija a moment. See you, Laran, Goat-my-boy.'

She swung away.

Madfist waited pointedly till Goat's Gran and the brats got the message that they were to go on into the little room. I tried to follow but Madfist put an arm either side of my shoulders.

'You're sleeping with me tonight.'

'Thanks, Madfist, but it'll be even greater luxury to have a bed to myself in the little room –'

'I'm not asking you. I'm telling you.'

'You have changed your mind.'

'Yes. Haven't I a right to change my mind?' He then said something crude.

I think I must have turned white. I hadn't expected to be told he felt like that. There was a pause in which I couldn't think what to do, where to run.

Then I said in exactly the same voice as before, 'I wonder what we're eating? I must go in and help Goat's Gran with the –'

'Did you hear me?' He wouldn't let me gloss it over. 'I said –' He repeated it several times. I felt he only wanted to hurt me.

'Let me go!' I whispered, choking. 'I said, let me go, you gutter-rat.'

The filthy phrase stopped. I could breathe again. He stepped back from me. I would have bet on the certainty he'd hit me. But all he did was say very quietly, 'You can never do anything to please a snob-nose who fancies herself a lady. You're too crude, or else you're so subtle she can pretend not to understand.'

'You go onwards tomorrow,' I said. 'I'll stay here with my employer, if it's come to this sort of impasse.'

I meant to keep Laran with me as my own protector, but I didn't say so to Madfist in case he made trouble with Laran.

Madfist cleared his throat, which wasn't like him. Then he said, 'It has. It's up to you,' and slouched away.

Reenah joined me in the room with the Gran and children. She quickly laid a fire while we picked over the packed savoury tray she'd brought.

'Reenah –' I said, nervous of her jealousy, 'I'm not with Madfist, if you know what I mean –'

'I know,' she smiled. 'But don't mope or feel down, dear, I

wouldn't mind if you was. Not tonight! I'm hoping to catch the eye of one of our guests – and since you're my friend, don't *you* tell Madfist *that*!'

'Does your mother know we're back?'

'She never knew you left.'

'Was the chaos that bad?'

'She's been drunk since midnight, only just come out of her daze,' Reenah said.

'*Drunk?* They forced it down her – ?'

'No, bless you. By the time everything was smashed up and there was no hope of saving it, we just relaxed like we always do and made a fine party of it, the gayest maddest party of the year.'

The little boys were thrilled with the food. They can't be used to eating as well as last night anyway. Between raids and all that roast meat and spear-stuck cheese, I suppose they make do on what they can pick or trap, or steal from occasional hen-houses.

But the actual prepared meal of a household is a different matter again. Just as she always does for a customer's meal, Reenah had spiced the meat and garnished it with herbs and a single silly-looking bay leaf. The steak had been rolled in fried breadcrumbs and a chestnut and mushroom sauce poured over, though owing to the ravages of the boys' own mentors, the boiling in old ale had had to be omitted. Slabs of Inn butter were melting to a golden sizzly grease. There were crushed juniper berries and thyme and soft chunks of big scarlet carrot. And beakers of the frothy dark-creamed milk which I don't really like – it's so sort of musky, such *female* milk, you can't forget it's come out of a cow, still warm from her ruminative steamy-grass inside, and as I know personally each of the inn cows and don't like them at all this doesn't fill me with enthusiasm.

Still, as I've hardly ever before in my whole life at this place had the cream on the milk, I glubbed it up just for the sake of it.

While the children poked about with their fingers, sucking the blisters, enchanted by their first taste of real home-cooking which they'd never imagined exists, I huddled to the hearth.

Goat had pulled off one of his woolly jumpers, only a little too big for me, and made me wear it under my shift while the sun dried it on me. It was now rather bleached, because of the peculiarly penetrating spring sun, but I kept the jumper on underneath. The cuffs, unravelling scratchy wool, wandered down over my knuckles. I spread my jerkin before the fire and tried to check the sneezes tickling the membranes of my nose.

Gran suckled the two infants while she yelled at the boys and fed herself. She took no notice of me.

The boys started with wonder on the curd pudding under a sticky pall of bramble jelly.

Suffering the first explosive sneezes of what I am sure will be a horrible cold, I struggled out to the lavatory.

The back corridors were just as nauseous, and about as slimy, as the draughty nasty lean-to lavatory itself. You had to watch where you put your feet. None of the braziers or oil-lamps had been lit, and a horde of men had got rid of their drunkenness here. Under all the other smells lay one almost more depressing, the staleness of the unlit oil-lamps.

The spring seemed to have ended immediately it began.

The circle we'd trodden had been more than the circle in which Madfist led us in clean hope from the raiders' fires and back again to these miserable clutching walls enfolding their fug and drudgery. It had been the old trap-circle of negation.

The dim saffron light at the end of the corridor was murked by a large shape.

She trod forward groaning, one hand swinging a lantern so that the knuckles and podge of her hand and the soiled front of her apron which her other hand kept massaging were in light, her face above and behind only boding silhouette.

'Ech, ech, my belly, my guts,' she was crooning to herself. I suppose I should have felt sorry for her. I cowered to the cold clay wall, afraid of her discovering me as though she were some monstrous obscenity. When her irresponsible light did find me, the worst had come. All she did was peer, squint, make a grimace of distaste, as though I was the worst of all to find in a corridor she always keeps scrubbed (by other people) and in which she was meeting so many horrid things, as though I were the capping nasty optical illusion she'd suffered from her hangover. But I felt a nightmare had culminated in her finding of me.

'You, you sloven,' she said energetically, but still touching her apron-front as though it were delicate glass, 'into the tap-room with you. We've five guests need attention, and too many girls malingering. Out of your hole and into the light. Comb your greasy ratstails first.'

Now had come the table-turning. But I couldn't see it making impact.

'I am with Madfist and Goat. I am one of your paying guests now,' I said.

131

'*They* may have told you that,' she gave a leering laugh. 'But I know them. When they leave, they'll no longer have use for a whey-cheeked whine with a millstone-bastard. Into the tap-room, I said.'

She didn't even know we'd ever been away!

At her last roar, and the giant shadow of her raised fist running up the wall, I hurried for the tap-room.

She followed, grunting.

The tap-room didn't seem itself. It was in almost jet dark. The beam-hung braziers had been slashed from their chains just as the hams, the cheeses, the turnips, the strings of onions and herbs had been cut down. The couple remaining hung lopsided, so that any coals lit in them would slide out at once.

A few candles dripped baroque icicles of tallow over the bottles in which they'd been stuck.

I couldn't see Goat, Madfist or Laran among the strangers at the benches and trestle tables, though it was rather dark to make anyone out. I expect they were in the dining-room, having a good stodge before they joined the company for dice and story-swopping.

'Get serving,' the woman hissed. She was my mistress as if the day in the sunshine had never existed.

Sylna and the bent grey woman Phla were moving listlessly among the tables.

'What we need is a fire,' I went forward. 'That would make up for the braziers, give light and heat. Why hasn't anyone thought of that?'

'Smart cat,' said Phla. '*Some* people don't enjoy raids, you know. They have to recover from them. They don't enjoy them, like *some* sprightly people seem to. We're tired enough. Do it yourself.'

'I am,' I remarked. I was trying to find wood in the scuttle, but there were only residue sticks, twigs too weather-damp to burn.

'Here,' demanded one of the new customers. 'We're not cold, if you are, inn-girl. Let's have some service round here.'

They didn't look as if they should be cold. Each wore real travelling clothes, shabby and knocked-about but professionally thought-out – low hoods, big cloaks to wrap round you several times, high boots with sun-ray spurs.

Sneezing, I collected up the glasses and took them behind the bar for refilling.

This unfamiliar work – for I'm officially a scullion, a scrubber and a dweller in grime and grease and backstairs slime – the clinking of glass and pewter and the brisk movement, got me feeling more alive and less melancholic. So perhaps even more did the virile smells of beer and the fantastically potent cider the inn has brewed for centuries, and the fact I was surrounded by men even less indigenous to this trap of a place than Goat and Madfist.

Professionally tilting the tankards so I could control the amount of head on each drink, and then plonking them down before the customers so the froth overspilled, I felt pride in my imitation of a barmaid.

'Aren't you eating more than those old grilled sausages?' I demanded of the man at the head of the table.

'We've ordered a meal,' he answered. 'It's being prepared now. Thank you for your concern, pretty.'

I felt warmer at that, though in this light no one could tell whether I was pretty or not.

'I'll mind the bar, with Sylna. Phla, go out and find some wood for a fire,' I said.

'I'm taking no orders from a scullery-sloven,' Phla sniffed with a haughty nasal gurgling.

The men all laughed at the wrangling women.

'Don't fuss, scullery-sloven,' said one. 'We aren't pining for a fire.'

'No, but I am,' I snapped.

The nearest man peered at me. At least, I couldn't make out his eyes in the shadow of his hood, but he seemed intent on me.

As Phla passed, Sylna gave her a poke in the back.

'She's no sloven, she's something better than your sort.' I don't think Sylna's one of my loyal friends or anything. It's merely that there's a rivalry between the different wings, and Phla belongs to the garden wing.

The nearest man reached for my wrist. 'Your top-sleeve is damp right through,' he said in a dark resonant voice. His grip was strong and I didn't at first realise why it seemed odd. Then I noticed his fingers were trembling. I thought he was cold or neurotic, and anyway he was trying to draw me into the nimbus of the candle.

'Yes, I'm ravishing but thin,' I said sharply. 'Now you don't need to see for yourself. I've things to get on with.'

Goat, Madfist and Laran clattered in.

The strangers gazed narrowly at them, Reenah popped her sunny head round the door. 'The second dinner is ready for

133

your pleasure, gentlemen.' 'What are you doing here, Cija?'
Goat cried. 'She hasn't bullied you back into service, has she?
Shoo, love, back to the little –' Madfist motioned him to silence.
He wouldn't look at me, beyond an involuntary sideways
smouldering glare, and suggested a night of gambling with the
newcomers after the meal. Laran stayed silent. 'Before we eat,
drinks all round!' said the low dark voice of the leading
stranger. Sylna and I brought the drinks. As the leader took his,
his fingers groped to the tips of mine. His shoulders were wide
and straight, the folds falling like black stone, the alert head an
oblong of command obvious in spite of the anonymous features
over the shadowed bas-relief jaw briefly edged by a black bar of
beard – but his fingers trembled.

'Here's to a sociable evening – win or lose!' he said, pushing
his arm and glass high.

The nearest candle plucked amber from the liquid.

There was an answering shout from all assembled. Only
Laran remained silent.

'Let's have lights here!' Madfist roared. 'Phla, you slut, can't
you get a fire going!'

Laran suddenly made towards me.

But two people forestalled him. Sylna rushed on me first.

'Cija! I didn't see before! You've got my second-best shoes
on! I never thought you were such a hussy!'

Madfist slapped her away. 'I gave them to her,' he said as
though that settled any point of ethics. 'Cija, no one wants you
here. Get back to your room. Go to bed, enjoy your cursed freedom, *don't* choke on it merely because *I'd* love you to.'

Gran snored placidly. The boys whispered and jerked out
muffled snorts of laughter. Gradually, they paused for longer at
a time and presently their breathing had deepened and they
were asleep.

The room was also full of that whiffling and whuffling and
that milky smell of sleeping infants.

The starlight fingered the spring frost against the panes. The
edge of one pane sparkled like a moveless perpetual *stab* of light,
where it had been broken the night before. But under the cow-
skin rugs I was not cold.

Only I had to keep wiping my nose with the hanky under the
pillow.

I knew that out there the spring was swelling, swelling, like a
flood to erupt all over the land. The balmy breeze told of seeds

134

thrusting up under the window, of the black soil panting in labour, the gold boughs in an ecstasy of conceiving. The breeze bore the hoots of owls, the bark of a badger, the death-squeal of a mouse. Insects ticked.

The night rolled on. I had wakened again after midnight.

The shouting and cursing and laughter from the tap-room, which had risen louder and louder, had now died as the fire must have. At one time someone had produced a ghirza, and strummed while everyone joined in a ragged chorus and stamped on the floor. But now the house lay silent and you could almost hear the wings of the night-moths which had the silence to themselves.

I wondered if Madfist in his bed were conscious of my nearness in the house.

I wondered if Reenah shared his bed or the stranger-leader's.

After one evening back here, I knew I couldn't stand it. I'd often heard people speak of 'a living death'. But I felt the inn was a living grave. It stank, it clutched. Better that Nal grew up swearing, stealing and climbing green trees with the bandit-brats, than milking the cows and listening to the slow stupid views of the half-witted hired-hands filtered through a straw twisting in dirty teeth, the inn-woman alternately kicking him and smothering him in sentimentality. There would not even be any people his own age here. The girls must be good at managing that. I suppose they even thought of making the right preventive preparations when the Bluedownsers hove in sight.

Anyway, as soon as Nal was a boy he'd run off of course with the first bandit-gang to fire his imagination.

My conscience pricked me. Who did I think I was, to get a better offer than Madfist's, more disinterested friendship than Goat's? And loyal Laran, too, would be with me.

I might go off with people like the dark strangers, and find they really were a case of stiller waters running deep, end up with my throat slit or something.

Who did I think I was? Because once by accident I'd got myself on to a throne – because the divine blood of a royal house thousands of miles away slunk through my arteries – I supposed I must always hang on, wait about for something better, something 'worthy of me' – and thereby wait away my life and my son's and my duty – my debt to Madfist.

He was all bitter now. He was hurt. He knows I consider myself too good for him. He has done his best for me because he

135

found me wretched, yet I can hardly say a pleasant syllable to him.

The bed creaked when I got up. But the snores continued unruffled.

I wriggled my feet into Sylna's second-best shoes which are tight on me. I touched my jerkin, still stretched on a line before the embers. It was a bit moist even now. I left it.

I padded the corridors.

My ear to the studded door. More snores. No kissing, no bed-springs. The handle turned. I held my breath. I felt desperately noble.

Madfist sat up in mid-snore and the nearest bed. Starlight glinted on a knife-blade.

'It's only me,' I breathed through Goat's self-advertised slumber.

Then I thought this dim female figure breathing a dim female phrase could be anyone – Reenah, Sylna, Mira, anyone. I was about to add my name when Madfist on a long breath said ' – Cija . . . ?'

'Yes, Madfist. Are you – alone tonight? I've – I mean, I've come to you.'

The starlight struck blue sparks from the blade he didn't even put away. He sprang to me. I was glad to note he was wearing his voluminous ragged striped shirt, if nothing else.

'Madfist, you're squashing the breath out of me – your knife's in my side –'

He apologised muttering, sheathed it. Suddenly gentle, he took my hand, led me to his bed, picked me up and swung us both under the pelts, pressing me tenderly to his chest.

Lying stretched against each other, our kiss was just a flickering feather.

'You're shuddering,' he said under his breath. 'Tell me the truth. You've come to me out of gratitude. You do loathe me, don't you?'

I kissed his cheekbone of my own accord. 'No, Madfist. You're strong and you seem to own safety, to be able to toss it around and juggle it with danger. That's why I can't stop shuddering. It seems an enormity, the step I've taken, coming to you.'

His fingers twined in my hair. We might not have been in bed together but feet apart, for all the advantage he took.

'I think I'd sooner you didn't require it of me, after all,' I added because I thought he couldn't.

136

'No, no.' His hand strained on my shoulder. 'But you're frightened. You're not pretending. There are plenty of nights ahead of us – and days to talk in. You'll get to know me, you'll find what a decent fellow I am at heart. You won't be frightened, and you'll come to me because you want *me*, not because you were grateful and I grabbed you in your fear.

'Here, I'm going to fix you a swig of good fire, stop you looking so woebegone. There's time ahead, little pigeon, trust Madfist. I'll keep you somehow, I'll manage it someway.'

I wondered if his last words referred to some claim of the woman's about my breaking contract, or something. But I was content to trust him as he said. I closed my eyes as he put the mulled mead to my mouth.

Footsteps up the passage outside.

Madfist's mouth drew down as he cursed his memory. He just had time to grab on his trousers and buckle his belt. He kicked Goat who was awake instantly like a trained Forest-man.

Two of the hooded strangers came in without knocking.

'You weren't expecting us so early?'

Though the leader's face above his beard-edged jaw was shadowed, I could imagine the lift of his brows when he said this. It jolted me. I stared at him. But there was nothing familiar about the half-seen face.

'We were just having a little conference. Don't consider yourselves in the way,' Goat at a glance took in the situation.

Although Madfist's bed was rumpled, I sat decorously on it, my feet on the floor, and enjoyed the mead.

'It completely slipped my memory that I'd asked you along,' Madfist said airily to the strangers. There seemed a false note somewhere, and it struck me that Madfist was proud to be found with a girl. That must be nonsense.

'I thought Gran was going to see she didn't stray,' Goat muttered.

'Gran is snoring,' I said.

Goat took me by the arm. 'Into Laran's room with you, lovely. We've business to discuss that won't interest you.'

'Keep her here,' said the stranger-leader. 'We know who she is.'

But he didn't bow to me, or treat me with reverence.

I wondered if he really did know who I was. Then I remembered Madfist's phrase about 'keeping me somehow'. They must be discussing selling me.

'I'm involved in this?' I couldn't give anything away by

mentioning the obvious. 'Could I have things explained?'

'No, no,' Madfist said. 'This is serious. Remember what I said earlier about trusting me? I'll find a way, but you must obey. Into the other room.'

The stranger-leader made a swift movement towards me, but the room separated us. I was glad – I was afraid he'd meant to grab me. I would certainly sooner stay with Madfist and Goat, and Gran with her useful attributes too, than be dragged off by these strangers who were probably emissaries from Sedili.

Goat unlocked the adjoining door – odd that it should be locked already – and instantly Laran rushed forward into this room. He must have been listening on the other side of the door.

'Why were you locked in, Laran?' I began – but he was a startling sight, very wild-eyed indeed, and cried, 'Empress, you can't wish to remain with these men?'

'Yes, yes, Laran, I do.'

Goat said in a brisk gabble, 'You're overwrought, friend, you need a tranquilliser,' and tried to push Laran back into his room. Laran cried to me – 'Do you *know* who –' and Goat went, 'Tsk, tsk,' and drew back his arm and slashed across Laran's throat.

Laran slumped to the floor. Blood had splashed the walls and darkened their red.

I tried to run to Laran. Madfist and the strangers sprang forward. The second stranger pulled me behind him.

'Empress,' he said. 'Do not grieve for your soldier. We shall avenge him, and all the ill you have suffered.'

I couldn't take my eyes off Goat. Nausea gobbled behind my breasts. I still couldn't believe my friendly little doctor could kill as eagerly as he healed.

Goat and Madfist, knives drawn, faced the bright steel of the strangers' swords.

'There is no longer any question of ransom,' said the leader in the cold low voice that only grazed his bearded lips. 'She is here. You have done more than show you have her – you have made her available. We have only to take her.'

'We lied to you,' cried Madfist. 'She is not the foreign Empress.'

'Dear Gods, so that's what it's been all about?' I simpered. 'No, I should think not indeed. Rather a nice notion, though.'

'We recognise her,' the leader with a touch of a grim smile continued, 'and also her soldier that you have murdered.'

'You can have her without a blow struck,' Goat said. 'You are in a nasty weak position if you break your faith as parley-messengers. You may call on your three mates, but we have an inn full of bull-necked fighters with pitchforks behind us. And they will fight for us, never fear. Our little Reen bless her, daughter to the lady of the house, will see to that if any violence blows up. So just hand over your ransom money and be done.'

The leader stepped forward and would have rammed his sword through Goat, but Goat's long knife parried, held him engaged. Goat was good with a blade, and it was moments later that the two steels slithered apart. Goat cursed in rage, and died. The red walls dripped new blood.

I recognised the leader from that killing blow even before his hood slipped back. He and Madfist were promised to each other now. Madfist had not been content to stun the other man, who hardly had time to let out his piercing whistle. The blue knife had stabbed him through and through.

'Reen-ah!' Madfist roared.

The three other newcomers, tangled with half a dozen inn-men including the puffing puzzled Master, rushed through the door.

Zerd's blade confused Madfist, drew blood from his knife-arm, cut the knife away. Bounding straight for me through the mêlée, Zerd caught me up. I was half-pulled, half-carried for the corridor. He didn't glance at me as he wielded his sword among the thick bemused vicious inn-men with their ghastly axes and hammers. But I couldn't look away from him, his dark beard-edged profile foreshortened above me, his sinewy snake-texture arm around me, the miraculous flash and parry and stab of his lean-hilted sword.

Other inn-denizens sprang up around us. They shouted hoarse, they flailed their incredible weapons, their eyes gleamed small and red in the reflection from the few red braziers, the red clay walls with their sliding globules, their wet red splashes.

'Into this room here!' I had to yell twice before he paid me attention. 'Nal's in here!'

'Nal?' He looked blank.

'Our son!'

'We'll have to leave him.'

'We can't!'

I flung myself aside out of his unwary grasp. I dashed into the little room. Gran was in the process of pushing a cabinet against the door. I just got past, jarring my hip. She snarled at me, baring big gleaming teeth. The babies were clutched to the mountainous breasts, Nal more securely than her own.

139

The boys, not knowing what to expect, stood big-eyed at her knees.

'Quick, give him to me! He *is* mine!' I cried –

'My grandson said, Hang on to him. I never disobey my grandson,' she said.

Even at such need for urgency, I couldn't say, 'Goat is dead.' I was afraid she'd cry or something, and I'd be floating on the gale of her grief.

The cabinet crashed, splintered on the floor. Zerd and his three remaining men advanced. The last disabled two pursuers and set to shoving two beds against the door in the ruin of the cabinet.

'She's got Nal – ' I cried as Zerd dragged me to the window.

'Which is he?'

'In the hood – '

Gran didn't struggle, but surrendered him quite meekly to the male with an air of authority.

We plunged through the window, glass flying and skinkling at the swipe of Zerd's arm. Zerd dropped to the ground, landed matter-of-factly on his feet. I clung petrified to the broad sill eleven or twelve feet above him. Men poured out of the inn door towards him.

'Jump,' he ordered.

'Oh, Zerd – '

'Throw me the brat.'

'Promise to catch him!'

He nodded. Nal and his hood spun through the air, parted company. Zerd fielded the right one. I leaped and found that I too had been caught. Zerd stooped, picked up Nal again from the ground, pulled me racing across the loam and cobbles. The geese scattered, hissing, snake necks stretched.

The three companions once more with us, we reached the stables. Nal and I were swung into the saddle. Hitching girths, we were confronted by a large shape with a rake raised like a javelin. The rusty prongs were aimed for my eyes.

Reenah behind her mother jerked her aside. The rake clattered harmless among hooves. 'Let her go, for Gods' sakes,' Reenah screamed. 'Have you no sense at all, you old bitch! Let her go, we don't *want* her here!'

We galloped out. We flew the fence. Madfist bounded after. For a space he was beside us, sobbing with the effort of panting. He was trying to stab the horse I rode before Zerd. His hazel eyes rolled, no longer handsome, foam flecked his mouth. The

140

strain was too much. The knife wouldn't answer his wrist. Zerd reached down to chop at him. I hit up Zerd's arm.

Madfist fell away. We sped between the trees.

'I had to leave my bloody saddle behind,' grumbled one man. Zerd pulled roughly at my shoulder.

'Well, explain yourself.'

'You didn't come to find *me*?'

'We had the news of your death, days ago, from a scarecrow survivor of your Atlan guard, who limped to us through the winter and many delays. I am out on other business. I ordered a detour to the Inn of your reported death, to make inquiries as to whom I must hunt for revenge.'

The wind sang in my hair.

'But you are Emperor. Is the War over? Or are you in flight, that you leave the Capital?'

'I had to leave it.'

'For more than my revenge, I'll warrant. I'm lucky. You came yourself – I don't think it would have turned out so well with just your messengers.'

'Without me to haul you about, you'd have stayed with your own tattered hero.'

'No, Zerd. No. I just didn't realise it was you. I thought you were Northerners from Sedili. Why didn't you make yourself known to me?'

'I couldn't risk your making me known to *them* – by startled accident – or design.'

'Gods, how you trust me.'

'If this mission fails, our War is lost.'

He held me close.

'I thought you were dead, Cija, as I'd been told. And still I recognised you in the dark as you served us. Couldn't you recognise me without my saying to you, "I am your husband"? Had you forgotten what I look like?'

'Your hood – that beard – ' I touched it, shyly. It was strong and coarser than his mane of hair.

'Why were you with that robber you didn't let me scar?'

'I wasn't exactly *with* him, Zerd.' Through no virtue of my own, I reflected. It had not been pure conscience-stricken nobility that had sent me padding to Madfist to say, 'Here I am. It's up to you.' It had been a growing curiosity about him, a way of using his strength without feeling guilt. I had kidded myself, and I'd been blessed indeed that things had not gone too far, that (helped by a little concentration and a certain loss of

141

memory) I could look at my husband with clean eyes.

'Tell me how they contacted you,' I begged. 'Who did they think you were? Messenger from yourself?'

'Evidently your soldier Whatzisname babbled in his delirium. They twigged you were his Empress. They told no one at the inn except your little blonde friend. They took you and the heir away intent on sending to the Capital for ransom. But on their first night away, we arrived asking for news of the fight and the soldier with the wolf-torn arm. She sent a fast messenger to them and told us to wait.'

His arm was tighter and tighter.

'And you're not a corpse at all,' he said. 'You're breathing, breathing and breathing. You're still yourself. They haven't buried you under this foreign earth. You're still Cija, every inch of you Cija, every hair on your head.'

I was glad I'd washed today.

'Oh, my jerkin. It's still in front of the fire at the Inn.'

He wrapped me and his heir in his travelling cloak.

The wind flows around us. The horse's mane, plaited for extra warmth, sings like a sword.

The baby stirs, sleeps again, back in my arms which are his flesh, his blood is a doubling of my blood. Does he know he is with his kin, he who is my son and my nephew?

I trace with my eyes every scale, every skin-grain, every muscle, every ripple of movement in the hands and arms that enclose me and guide the reins, all that I can see of the half-man whose chest and shoulders shelter me, whose heart I can feel throbbing into my clavicle.

I wonder how he thinks of me. What am I to him? Has he ever felt the thrill down the spine, the *melting* of the heart, the scorching gush of tears to the eye-corners, that I get when I think of certain aspects of him?

Do other people get those feelings about the people they're in love with? Am I the only person in the whole wide world who does?

Am I in love with him? I get these physical sensations, physical yet as far as I know completely detached from sexual yearnings, when I think of Smahil sometimes, too. I know I'm not in love with Smahil. It's just that he taught me about living with a member of that sex I used to believe extinct. In the bleak Southland, he was all I had so I got very used to him so my life misses him, all sorts of nostalgia are tied up with him –

But I used to hate Zerd.

To my Mother, Zerd is the most important person in the world. But she hardly thinks of individuals. Her country, that I have hardly seen, is everything to her. Yet all I have done, too, has been done originally for her country.

How touched was he to find I'm still alive? How suspicious of me? He used to know about Smahil, in Southern City. He convinced himself Juzd was the father of the child I say is ours. He must suspect Madfist. He has only used me to watch, to gain amusement from, all the time he has known me. There must be some tenderness. But I'm sure Goat felt tender about me while he gave me his jumper while he planned to sell me, and he felt tender pride in his healing of Laran too, before he ran him through just to stay his loyal tongue.

I used to think, when I was a bride, that Zerd knew the same ecstasy of passion and confused, half-doubting love he surprised in me.

But he is so experienced. I suppose every girl has felt something of that in his arms. What does *he* think about while he skilfully, instinctively gives the right impressions? Can he tell us apart? Does he now and then forget if this worshipful submission is Cija or someone else, so to save coming back to reality to think about it, he just mutters, 'My darling', in a tone of adoration?

Madfist must have been getting gradually keener on the picture of himself in bed with a young Empress.

He'd've done better to bring more bandits back with him. But then I suppose he didn't want to share the ransom with them.

If I twist my tongue in my mouth I can just about feel that there are new teeth jutting through at the back of my gum. Wisdom teeth, I suppose. Well, it's about time, isn't it? That's something – teething when my son does. But I won't get much idea of how he's feeling when he starts, he'll have a whole mouth full of it and no ready-made explanation for this explosive *new* sensation.

Isn't he good with a horse. But I bet he'd have preferred birds except for the necessity of disguise.

The beard suits him. But then anything suits him.

War, power, conquest mean more to him than her country to my Mother. Am I at least second-best? Or do I come a long way down in the list of his amusements?

But what splendid arms. What a marvellous heart-beat. What vitality. I could never ride and dice and drink and fight and

143

leap and fight and ride without any sleep as he is doing. I suppose conquest is the only possible passion for such a man.

What Zerd fingers. They're strong, fairly shapely but such an impression of strength. Yet though I think they're beautiful I can't find a more analytical adjective than Zerd.

My fine friends did come, after all, and carry me off, you see, fat inn-woman.

Oh my Gods, Oh my own little Divine cousin who knows exactly the feel of the blood running in my veins, isn't it leaping beautifully now?

Still searching for the quick adjective, which is a habit that must grow on Diary-keepers, an Atlan morning is as obviously 'a gold morning' as mornings watched from my Tower used to be blue mornings – till you think, no, look at the light, *look* at the light, it's 'a silver morning'.

Anyway, an Atlan morning is a morning lucent with light.

Zerd dismounted, led the horse by its bridle.

He put a clump of primroses and trembling cool fern into my hands, a rippled feather in my hair.

He kept up with his men a running badinage too complicated to reproduce, but it was full of wit and provoked wit and had unexpected turnings, and was all nonsense, and everyone was laughing till their jaws hurt happily, and there was horseplay mixed in with it, and lots of good old honest showing-off. The other men are young and fun, they're lovely. They seemed to feel very bad last night about their comrade stabbed by Madfist, but they have been hand-picked for this mission whatever it is, and they are high-spirited in courage.

It is easy yet surprising to remember, at times like this, that Zerd is not much older than I am.

When I was born and soothsayers and silver-eyed wise-women were making a to-do about the old prophecies, Zerd was a small boy of seven, a bastard with a mother the Court his father lived in considered close to animal.

He saw the other bastards of his famous father, honoured even by the King for his war-craft and the victories he brought home. The other bastards would be judged according to their looks or intelligence or personality. But he had to have all of these before anyone would even look at him without jeering, or laughing, or shuddering.

The legitimate children were like beings on another plane, far above him without question. And what did he think of the little princess, the King's daughter, when he saw her pass? Did she ever jeer at the lean energetic narrow-eyed boy with the dull-shining skin the colour of a thundercloud? Did he decide even then to dazzle her and own her, to hook himself up to her level and level her down to his?

What is Sedili *like*?

The Dark Castle

WE came through the butterflies and foliage.

'There is a white star on the horizon,' I said.

'No. That is your castle,' he said.

It was the evening of a hard day's riding.

Like a mirage, a mythical moon in mists, the little castle glimmered on the horizon. I was sure it would disappear before we reached it. I had spent a good chunk of a year trying to get to this promised haven 'only a stiff ride' from my throne.

As we neared it, as it became more and more constant in our sight, not just a flash frequently lost behind boles and creepers, it blazed up.

'It's on fire.'

'That's the sun dying on all the windows.'

And next time it appeared from behind the grizzled trunks, the ferocious foliage, it was itself dead. The light had left it. It was diminished, hard to pick out, a grey point on a dark hill.

It was hard to tell when the jungle of the Forest proper ended, when the savage secondary growth sprang up. But presently it was obvious we were cantering through the grounds of the Castle. Up the steep hill, the dark ilex, the ivy and cypress and yew had succeeded in partially smothering the weather-chipped, scabrously naked statues, chalk-white forearms hirsute with patches of fungus, broken fingers clutching outwards in a symbolic-statuesque gesture, grasping the drizzly breeze.

'You'll soon be home.'

'This has taken you a long way, Zerd, and a long time, out of your way. Whatever your way is.'

'It's worth it to see you to your door. If I left you within an inch of it, I'd not sleep sound wondering what monsters had abducted you, what pits you'd fallen in. But here you are at last, chatelaine of your new domain.'

146

'I don't like it.'

We continued to ride into the gathering dusk, which seemed to me to be growing out of the dark vegetation of the slope. The trees had been planted long decades ago for their decorative qualities. They were therefore, now they were wild, treacherous-looking trees. They were slim and bending, weighed to one side by a massed curve of creeper-like awful expensive heavy drippy filigree jewellery. Retrogressed willows are the worst I think, willows that were planted for scenic display and have become part of the scenery, look so sinister as though they were sneering and laughing at we humans who innocently put them there.

Even our escort had fallen silent. It is a steep hill. The horses climbed doggedly.

When I looked back I caught my breath. How high we'd risen! The slope shot away below us, patched with leering white stone nymphs and heroes amongst the dark, and from way down there where the valley joined the Forest, a haze of mist seemed to be rising after us.

'But you will be safe here,' Zerd said.

I had thought he'd hardly heard my last remark, which had fallen flat minutes ago. I wondered if perhaps he were troubled, obscurely, by the rotting yet alive atmosphere of the place.

But the whole idea of the supernatural is unthinkable to him. He doesn't even jeer much at the superstitious. He just can't make head nor tail of it, unreality being real.

'Is it fortified?' I asked.

'Well enough. I asked for a place with a moat and good walls. But don't get nervous. I shouldn't think any force will come against you. Just as well, since most of the original guard I sent to you fell to wolves and Sedili's Northerners, and I can't spare these. I shall send more to you as soon as I'm free.'

'Who especially recommended this to you?'

'Your friend Juzd,' Zerd said without any expression beyond a lift of his lip from his teeth. 'I fancied that however *I* might distrust him, he'd not lay you open to danger. We discussed it months before the actual invasion of the Northern King's force.'

My spirits lifted slightly. I hoped Juzd knew the place a little, beyond its attributes of moat and strong walls. It might prove less unfriendly than its grounds in the dusk.

When we reached the summit – which we did involved in a blown spray from the head of a waterfall – the castle reared mammoth grey walls. No hint now of the glimmer sunset lent

147

the stone. Lizards flickered among the creeper. The drawbridge was up.

Candlelight fleered from a couple of arrow-slits in the keep. 'Dogs,' Zerd growled. 'Fools.' He stood in his stirrups and roared, 'Gate!' before one of his men could forestall him and act as herald.

A bit unfair. Not one of us could have been recognised.

You could almost feel the disbelief waxing, wavering and waning in the building.

Then, with a squealing and shrieking like the wanton slaughter of a large number of pigs, the chains unreeled. Dripping with water-weed and slime, the underside of the drawbridge majestically descended.

We clattered over the planks. Our hooves made a hollow sound, suggesting we were not very corporeal.

As I glanced back, I saw the mist had risen right to our heels.

It seemed that the entire population of the place converged on us at our entry. There was Nal's nurse, whom I was half-glad half-resentful could now take him over for me, and my exquisite high-nosed lady-in-waiting Frellis, and my red-haired maid Yula, and four members of the Atlan guard. Though it had been praiseworthy of these to get the remnants of my household in the last broken chariot through the Snow, through the howling winter of the Forest, to their unwelcoming destination, they looked with a kind of dread at their bearded Emperor (so unexpectedly away from his Capital).

'You expect court-martialling for not making more certain whether or not your Empress did die in that last flurry, don't you?' Zerd said jovially as they saluted. 'Well, you shall get it, but not yet a while. You're needed here, now that we have recovered her august person, and the way you guard her henceforth may have something to do with the verdict at your trial.'

The captain of the Guard was not here. Either he had been killed by the Northern attackers, or it was he who had adventured back with the news to Zerd.

'Oh, come in, come in,' quavered the brown nurse, quite overcome at Zerd's presence and my reappearance. (And at my appearance too, I expect.) 'There is a meal, there is a fire, and the sheets have always been kept aired. We have made quite a home here, but till this blessed moment it has been a home without a mistress, a wheel without a hub.'

The candle splattered hot tallow at me as she swung it in her efforts to seem poised. She swooped to dab the grease from my

148

limp servant's-shift (as though it were priceless robes) and the flame dipped.

'Here,' I pushed Nal at her, 'take your charge. I'll carry the candle.'

'Oh – no, no – ' she was horrified. She dithered, but Frellis took the candle. The nurse and Yula gazed at Nal, touched him as if he might be a vision.

'Oh, the angel, the little hero, the blessed blessed pet! What he's been through, what he's survived! Look at him lying in a hood like an infant cherub!'

Disturbed, Nal woke and started to cry.

The Castle room they had chosen as a living-room is huge as a hall. Vast vaults disappeared in gloom and shrouds of spiders-webs above the little corner where the fire had been lit, and settles grouped about it.

At the gusting of the spring wind in the chimney, the fire roared and turned blue, then crimson. The draughts bellied forward. The spiders-webs swung in the vaulting.

'I'm sorry this is all the welcome there is,' the nurse continued. 'There's not much of what you'd call state, I'm afraid – '

She peeked at Zerd, afraid she'd said too much about his choice of a retreat for me.

He dropped to a settle, thrust his legs out before him, pulled me down to his knee. 'Where's the meal?' he asked. His arm folded me in such a way that I could only rest my head to his chest, unless I wanted a rick in my neck. He rubbed his chin in my hair.

'There's so little – ' the nurse said, looking at all our new men. 'Oh! But by that I don't mean – what there is, of course, Your Momentity shall not have to go without.'

'Is *this* the housekeeper I sent with you?' Zerd asked as she bustled away.

'She's the Nurse,' I said. 'It should more properly be Yula doing this, and will be now Nal is here. But we don't have a housekeeper. The major-domo was among those killed.'

'Don't sit on the bare wood, Highness,' suggested Frellis. I was coughing. 'There's a pelt on this settle here. And we have found half-embroidered cushions in the attics, which we are finishing.'

Nal, in Frellis' arms, was still crying. She shushed and rocked him. He wailed.

To a background of Nal's cries, the gusting of the flames and the comfortable comments of Zerd's men (not overawed at eating with their rulers) the Nurse brought in duck and sauce.

'There are no vegetables,' Zerd said. 'Why?'

'Oh, Your Momentity – ' she didn't know what to do. 'That is all we have. Now that you are here, we have set more poultry in the oven. But there are no vegetables up yet in the garden – '

'This is lovely duck,' I said to calm her. 'You find meat easy to come by?'

'The guard throw-spear duck from the battlements sometimes,' she said. 'We are using up the stock in the courtyard pond so fast!'

'They must go hunting,' Zerd said. 'There is plenty in the Forest, young and tender and easy to trap in this season. I shall send hawks and falconers later on. And gardeners to see there are at least the elementaries of diet here.'

'We are so sorry – we hadn't expected – '

Zerd cut her short. 'Esal,' he commanded one of his men, 'see what is needed most in this huge hole, and present me with a list in the morning.'

'Can no one quiet your child?'

I murmured. Nal's wails penetrating the bedroom walls meant nothing to me. It was a miracle to wake in Zerd's arms.

The sun splashed rose on the floor, the tumbled patchwork coverlet. It was a rosy morning.

Something scuttled across the floor.

I thought of rats, and cried out in disgust. Zerd sat up, pulling me with him, and laughed and pointed.

'Hens! What state is this for my Empress!'

'They roost under the bed,' I said in wonder. 'The sheets *are* aired, but they haven't been able to keep the hens from roosting under the bed!'

'It's all the enclosure of oak and corner-posts and long stiff curtains,' he rubbed noses with me. 'Very conducive to brooding. Brood with me, Cija.'

But I was beginning to feel claustrophobic. I crawled to the end of the bed, past its curtains, and tried the old marble floor with my toes as though it were a pool I was reluctant to bathe in.

'I must have a rug put by the bed. Or they must at least ferret out a mat from somewhere. I wonder which of my clothes, if any, survived the fight and the flight?'

Trailing sunbeams, tangled in whirling streams of dust-motes, I trod marble to the window.

'*Zerd!*'

'What's up?'

'The *sea*! Did you know? There's *sea* outside the window!'

'Yes. The hill is on the point of a deep bay. Now that there's atmosphere over the sea, and the breezes don't have to reach the land above a vacuum, you'll be able to eat fish if your household knows how to bait a rod. And teach my heir to swim. He may need every means there is of a quick escape.'

Only half-listening, I caught my breath at the dazzling shifting expanse, so *big*, a giant crocodile twitching his skin.

I couldn't see where the waves hit the shore. A curve of the castle wall, of the ilex-grown hill, hid the beach. But I could hear the boom of breakers, the surge of surf. I knew that the moaning in my ears all night had not been just the winds.

'You are so right, standing just like that.'

Zerd, dark against the pillows, lounged back and watched from half-closed eyes.

'A gauche girl in a shift, watching waves from a tower.'

I looked at him, startled. I wasn't sure that I liked the gleam in his heavy-lidded eyes. He seemed to be considering me, more than that, to have summed me up and poked me into the right pigeon-hole in his mind.

'When I first saw you, when I was the first man you ever saw. When all your eyes had ever looked out on was waves and sky. Stars and a wind. When you believed yourself a goddess, and I was not even the evil alien General, because you didn't know your little sex had not conquered the world.

'A skinny brat, with temper-lines already round your mouth. Your toes poking out over space. The lichens and the dawn colouring the crumbling stone leprosy-shades of green and pink. Ancient white chalk new on your soles. Your bed-shift and trousers crumpled and not at all transparent, round-necked like a child's, with a spider inching up your smock. The haughty look to end all haughty looks masking the child-bitch's face, till I startled it, till I made the eyes fall, and life would never again be quite the unquestioned little circle for you, your own Divinity disturbed only by the adoration of your nurses agitating for your own good, your Mother in all her incomparable splendour of muddle-headedness, and the sea and the sky.'

'You've never seen me as anything else,' I said.

'What else are you? The amateurish posturing hostage with her little heart in her throat, the brave runaway, the servant masquerading in boy's clothes and sure of a desperation of

151

anonymity while all the time I knew and overlooked – the pouting Empress – so easily metamorphosed to the slattern at the inn – all these have happened because I released you from the Tower. You are my creation.' He grinned.

I knew he thought it was all funny, he was mocking me. But it must be there, for him to bring it out, especially that last phrase.

'Even your wife? She's still the silly deluded clouds-in-the-air girl you tricked out of the Tower?'

'Tricked?'

His brows were quizzical, the first thing that had ever fascinated me in him.

'Wasn't it time the bird spread its wings? You have a very modest idea of my picture of you. I couldn't get the girl with the chalky toes out of my head. You were the most unreal thing I had ever seen. I told your Mother her daughter might make a valuable hostage. I had no idea she would let you out to tutor you to seduce and assassinate me!'

'Oh, yes, *awfully* funny,' I agreed, glowering.

I wished I had not slept with him last night. I wished I had not loved him so much. Better Madfist than for the destroyer-General, laughing, to be my lord and master.

'So you'll send on to me all that Esal tells you we need here?'

When I looked back at him, after the pause, his eyes had darkened and blanked out.

Disarmed by our candid night, he seemed suddenly vulnerable.

'You sound as if you're dismissing me,' he said.

'Oh, no. Don't be silly.' I tapped my foot on the marble. 'Can you go to your own room now – I have to dress.'

'I'll dress you. Come here.'

He held his arms out to me.

I flung myself into them, sobbing.

'Zerd, Zerd, I love you. Honestly I do. I suppose it's only right I should belong to you.'

'I love you,' he said into my hair. Only the seventh time he has ever said it.

'Where are you going? Will you come back? Are you safe? Where is it you're –'

'To look for Lara,' he said.

The first split second, the name seemed sweet and sad. It reminded me of the soldier Laran. Then I remembered the pretty plump pink princess.

152

I shot away from him as if I'd been stung.

'For *Lara*? You mean you're leaving Atlan altogether?'

'No, no. I'm not that mad. She and her father are here – her father the Mainland Jungle Lord, with all his men still un-numbered as the leaves of his kingdom, have crossed the sea and are even now marching on me (as they suppose) in my Capital.'

'So –'

'So my only chance of deflecting him is Lara. If his men join Sedili, we are lost. We go under completely. There is no help in the native Army, the Atlanteans are pacifists. They would sooner create any excuse, than train themselves into an Army. They have the skill in arms, but there's no heart in them. I have only my few thousand renegade Northerners between the might of their former King – and the threat of my other father-in-law, the Jungle Chief.'

'But he has brought his numbers all this way simply to re-venge his only daughter. He would have been your rabid ally if you hadn't put her aside.'

'She is with him, I am informed. So I must see her.'

My heart was moaning. But I kept my back straight.

'But, Zerd, you won't find it easy to dupe her again. She has been humiliated. You left her without a word in the Temple-city, and when you became Emperor of the new-found Con-tinent, you never sent for her.'

'That's why I must see her myself. Before his might reaches the Capital and instantly destroys us. No messengers will work the trick. It can only be between her and me.'

'She will order you killed from virulent hate, or her father will before she has a chance to set eyes on you.'

'I think I know Lara better than that,' said her former husband.

I didn't know which I wished most to hear – that Zerd must fail getting back her favour (and be trapped in imminent danger) or that all his dreams of hanging on to his dodgily-gained Empire were safe, and he able to build himself into the mightiest monarch of the known world.

'With her father's lethal force on *my* side –'

'You will tell her she is your rightful Empress because you married her before me?'

'Something of the sort, yes, Cija. I only hope she hasn't heard of claims prior to *hers*. I hope she never meets up with Sedili. Of course, no claims of my former wives legally hold water. You were crowned my consort.'

'But neither were divorced.' I sneezed and pulled the covers round me, ignoring his arm.

'Listen, Zerd. If she's made an offer of Empress-ship, *she'll* jump at *that*, all she needs to have is a letter from you, delivered to her by one of the men she knows is trusted by you – a high commander to give the occasion honour, Clor or someone.'

'It was I she fancied she was marrying, not any of my commanders or messengers. It was I who humiliated her by dumping her with the Temple and jaunting off to the hills with you, Army, brigands and all. It was I, she later heard, who had put her aside for you. And you of all people, her former slave. It is only I, no commander or messenger, who can coax her to subjection again.

'Her father's favour will veer to her interests.'

'But you may be killed. Zerd. They know how to torture, those Jungle men.'

'We fail anyway if Forest and coast both besiege us,' Zerd said. *Fail* is the nearest he has ever come to mentioning death in connection with himself.

'How lucky,' I said in a nasty voice, 'that I've been reported as dead to dear Sedili. Lara may have got to hear that little rumour, too.'

'Yes, it's fortunate I found this place for you,' he said. 'Just the time you need to be safe.'

'Safely out of the way.'

'I shall send more men to you, though, immediately I am able. *You* are here at last, and that's the main thing. But you need your own garrison.'

'Is Lara going to find out I'm still alive somewhere?'

'You are my Empress,' he said. 'Nothing can alter that. I shall simply play Lara along for a while.'

'How will Sedili like that? I thought you were considering some game with her too.'

'That's why Lara can only be gentle-baited,' he said simply.

'Well, the best of luck. Meanwhile, I'll try to make the best of things out here on my own.'

'I shall make sure none of your new garrison is even remotely attractive,' he said.

I actually managed to hit him pretty hard before he got that snide judo-lock on me.

'You'll be late setting out. I must dress,' I said presently.

I threw open the tall cupboard. Yes, here hung my clothes. In delight I ruffled my hands through the silks, the net-fine linens, the furs, mossy velvets, a fabulous fragrance clinging to each. But after the months in rags I felt I'd be inhibited in something long and flowing and precious, I'd have to be so careful. In the end I shrugged into a lace shirt, a big belt with a big swash-buckle of a fastening, and a long gathered skirt of knubbly black wool.

Zerd didn't say anything about how I looked. I expect he thought it was no good making servant-girls into Empresses, they could hardly be expected to effect the grade.

Tactfully, no one had brought us a breakfast. It was nearly noon. Zerd draped himself over one of the fireside settles in the web-fluttery hall. The Nurse and Scar (I'd forgotten all about him) served us with scrambled eggs, tomatoes, toasted ham and good red wine.

'The cellars are marvellously stocked, Momentity,' Scar said in a chatty way as soon as he saw that Zerd liked the wine.

'So I see,' Zerd answered, and to my annoyance started quite a discussion. I was sure that when Zerd left, Scar would be even more insufferable and smarmy-yet-full-of-*equality* than ever.

The entire household, all ten of it, turned out to watch our Emperor and his merry men off.

There was now no hint of mist, even when I peered down the hill at the valley. The ilex glowed like jade. An arm or a hip like a diamond scintillated here and there as a statue emerged from a grove. In this seclusion, the dew was still thick as massed mirror. Hoof-pocks remained in it when Zerd and his men had gone.

The guard staying with me stood straight at the salute. The Nurse dabbed her eyes with a disreputable apron she should not have been wearing. Nal, quiet at last, waved his fists and grabbed a sunbeam.

When he had disappeared from our sight quite over the edge, Zerd reappeared and returned to me and bent from his saddle and kissed me again.

'I love you,' he said, the eighth time ever and twice in one morning.

Once more he galloped beyond the ridge.

We trailed back over the drawbridge. I could see the moat in the bosky light this morning, and very stagnant it looked too.

As I have known this place for barely twenty-four hours, but that being mostly a time for which it was housing lots more big men than it is, already it seems pretty empty.

I have a plethora of time on my hands.

There is no longer a baby to look after. There is no longer any routine. I can stay in bed as long as I like, drift off to bed when I like, order a meal when I feel hungry (and get it), disappear on the beach or exploring the building for any length of time and have to answer to no one. I needn't even overlook the supervision of the household.

But with all this alternately aching and beckoning void of freedom, I have done hardly anything.

The castle yawns ahead of me. Rooms and rooms, great halls and galleries and attics. We have settled in the merest corner of it. It is dark and rotting. I don't want to penetrate it.

As for the beach the other side, where the hill faces the unknown across the blinding ocean, the Ocean no one has ever found out about the other side of, nor even if there *is* another side – I've had enough of yearning out over windy old waves.

The women between them are trying, with cunning probing subtle queries, to find out where I have spent the winter. I might as well let them gradually winkle out references to the inn, which they can cleverly put together and compare with each others' notes, but I'm not letting out that I was a servant. That sort of thing can impair one's image.

I don't like sleeping alone in the big curtained bed. There are shadows and webs I never noticed when Zerd was casting some of the shadows. It's better in the dark than with a candle – a candle-flame chucks crazy shadows. The hens are company. I'm grateful for them. Even if a ghost creaked the floorboards, I might only think it was a hen.

At first there seemed nothing at all wrong with the smoke. It seemed a natural extension of the stone griffin's head from which it was belching like a swarm of bees. But as I drew nearer across the drawbridge, and less absent-minded, I realised what exceptional smoke it was. How thick, how oily, how full of bubbles, as though as much liquid as vapour. What scintillant colours shot through it at unexpected moments, licking it from within before they sprang through it into the faint, faint pearlised haze which was half-distinguishable just above the smoke. But surely that griffin-head chimney, avid profile gulping sky, outcropped of a part of the hoof far away from that over the inhabited portion of this castle.

156

By slow degrees, the place is becoming a home. But it's surprising how any place is less likely to seem home if you haven't worked in it. The inn with all its squalor and degradation seemed nearer to my bones than this great shell in which I wander aimlessly. Even in the Tower of my childhood, I would often have to help my nurses keep the place clean, rinse the plates in the fountain, feed Sneede's turtle.

Yesterday I untangled an armful of wild roses from their thorns by the moat. Then I had no idea what to do with them. I took them inside and in a corner of the kichen-ramifications (only a segment of which we have civilised) I found an old earthenware jar. It was less cracked than the others lying in unwieldy mounds, infested with earwigs and crawling buzzing things like chips of lapis lazuli. I rubbed the dust off with the hem of my petticoat, because that was all I had handy, and it became very black indeed and I hardly felt like wearing it so I had to slip out of it. I filled the jar with roses and water from the pump. Now it is leaking all over my bedroom table (a handsome hunk of oak-log, carved, with a levelled top), but though the Nurse pops in several times a day to wipe up the mess, she has in an excess of reverence to my whims not even put the jar in a shallow bowl to catch the leak. If they're going to pay such deference to my aesthetic tastes, let them.

Bored with the known and tamed shadows of this crumbling hugeness, reluctant to adventure into the unknown shadows, somehow sickened by the three landward sides of the hill which seem to me to be its rotting sides, I am driven down the remaining side, sliding on the spume-wet rocks, clinging to the shrill grass.

It is certain that here at least they would not let me have my way. Frellis and the present Captain of the Guard have each earnestly warned me, on separate occasions.

'I beg you not to explore the seaward slope,' Frellis revealed urgency in her well-modulated voice. 'Take the roundabout walk to the beach, by all means. But not the cliff. That is far more dangerous, don't doubt me, than your former habit of riding alone beyond the gates of our Capital.'

'Madam,' the Captain felt he must point out, 'I must advise against the shore, at least till the calm tides of summer.'

He expounded his warning, getting even stiffer as he spoke of treacherous tides rising before you thought it possible, taking you by surprise from behind when you thought you couldn't possibly get cut off.

But here the air is clean. In continuous motion, virile with the sea-salt, it admits no suggestion of the dank sweetness stealthy on the hinter side.

I perched on a boulder, invisible from the Castle.

I clasp my arms round my knees, my chin on them. The air shivers against my flesh, my spine. The seabirds mew, learning to trust the strong air which for centuries has been absent over the sea (except for *very* high above it, of course). Their instinct to fish has survived the centuries for which they have had to deteriorate to shore-scavengers. Crabs don't sham dead any more when I'm here, I stay so still.

I think about nothing, on purpose. I just drown my eyes in the horizon which may never have known a sail, never once since the time slimy serpents as big as villages were the only masters of the waves.

But after a while visions sneak into my mind. Pictures of a man nailed to a wheel revolving into and out of a pit of flames. His flesh is no longer indigo, and the defiance of his face is unrecognisable. The pink princess stands smirking. There in the grim silence of the victor stands her father, his metal ornaments reflecting the licking of flames gleaming from his dun skin garments, behind him the dun warriors, numberless as the leaves of the Forest.

I see the cavernous red bedroom in the Palace. There is movement in the great bed. The maid with a face as impassive as a piece of furniture folds the clothes over the screen. But it is not I in our bed, and the clothes over the screen are all frills and pink net.

My face is wet with salt water. But I'm under no illusions, I'm perfectly well aware which is brine and which my self-pity. Because I'm afraid it's the second picture which makes me cry most. Perhaps that's only because it seems more real.

The grey water swashes over my feet, and recedes, leaving an inorganic-looking strand of seaweed, still swaying, sucking my toes. I know it is about time to go, and I climb the rocks while the grey belly of the sky sags down to my head, the winds whistle and the sprays lash me.

The smoke, already acrid, already tightening the insides of my nostrils, was obviously wrong. It should not have been there at all. Not in the middle of the night it shouldn't.

I was possessed, by a sort of cold fever. I thought I should not rest till I knew what caused the smoke. I was horribly afraid of what might be causing it.

I pulled a wrap round me and trod star-beams and hard cold shadows. I groped for the door. I never quite trust doors in rooms at night, no matter how well I know them by day. Often I'm dead certain they've shifted a bit.

It was the first time in my entire three weeks here that I have entered the corridor outside my marble and old-wood room after dark. I have never been to the end of this corridor, either way, because I always enter it from the head of a rusty-railed staircase nearly opposite my door, and leading up from the room we've appropriated as a living-room.

In this fusty musty echo-ridden hollow hill of a place I simply don't feel like exploring, perhaps because the place almost seems to expect it of me – can hardly believe that, with nothing to do all day, I'm not all rabid to kid myself believing I've come to 'possess' the dust-snowed vistas, the rafter-gloomed aisles. But when odd smoke is hinting fire in an unoccupied fastness, I suppose something must be done. For moments I believed the castle had combusted the smoke in order to lure me into traversing the endless corridor.

At least it did not turn, I thought. It stretched long but limp, devoid of corners. But I found, when I looked back, that it curved. It was a snake of a corridor.

The one lamp in the socket outside my door (I now carried its twin) threw a sheen on the whorl-veined marble. But the flame itself had vanished behind me.

Presently my sandals struck a note less staccato from the marble. Once or twice I nearly tripped. The smoke was disgusting, and obviously in urgent need of dousing. I took time off to swing my lamp at the floor instead of just the walls in which I hoped to detect the opening which must be responsible for the smoke, stench.

The floor was chipped here. Toadstools were grinning up from between the broken pavings.

I stopped. In all this length of hall, there had so far been no door. Suddenly I wondered what is behind these stretches of wall with their long cold arms about me?

The smoke was thicker here. It stank. Colours flicked it. But they were not flames.

If I found the fire causing it (and at the *thought* of *finding* it, the tiny hairs on my neck-vertebrae all rose like a dog's hackles) how could I beat it out? I had no water, nothing heavier than my hands, only the lamp containing yet more flame.

It must be put out. But I must rouse help.

I wasn't sure where the soldiers slept, not exactly. Nor Scar – with Yula probably. But I'd tell Frellis and she'd see to it. I could even go straight back to bed.

In the pallor thrown by my lamp through its greenish glass, my toes and the toadstools were sharp, like little white teeth. There was a thick bubbling sound in the smoke ahead of me.

I pelted down the way I'd come. My breath hurt. I fell against Frellis' door, it seemed three or four hours later.

'Frellis, it's me, for Sweet Gods' Sakes unbolt your door –'

The bolt shrilled. I nearly fell into Frellis' arms. But I swayed, remained upright. For a moment I could hardly speak, my lungs erupting, my heart hurting, but I realised my terror was far in excess of what I had to tell. She stared in alarm.

I mastered myself and was able to say with controlled inflexion, 'There's very thick smoke farther up the corridor. A fire must have broken out – please see that the men put it out.'

'A fire – ? How could it have started – up there? . . . ' But she gently led me to her couch and patted me down before she dashed for the other doors.

Bored alone, I wandered after her.

From Yula's door, as I'd guessed, both Yula and Scar emerged dishevelled. Frellis, her own face expressionless with distaste, made a jerky movement with her arm as though to shield my eyes from the sight of the red-haired woman and man in night-gear.

'There's fire up the passage –'

Scar, apparently unconscious of the nervy way Yula looked at me and tugged the darned wrap across part of the swell of her flesh, looked out. There was no smell here, but far up the deeper murk bubbled in the narrowing perspectives.

'So there is,' he agreed. He leaped up the stairs behind him, four at a time. 'Fire! Fire!' he yelled loud but without worry. The soldiers, pulling jerkins over their heads, clattered out.

They saluted, some while still headless, and gathered to stare up the corridor.

'It's gone –' Frellis said sharply.

Scar's mouth fell open. The lamp-pallor glinted on his teeth, wet and shiny as he slid his tongue across them. His eyes took on a glazy lustre, startled at last.

160

The soldiers swayed shoulder to shoulder. They had seen nothing but they realised we had.

Frellis recollected herself, pulled the cloth tighter over her tall stately form. Her eyelids flickered at the opulent untidy Yula.

'Someone must go up there and look in the rooms – ' I said.

'The passage comes to an end in a blank wall,' said my knowledgeable lady-in-waiting. 'There are no doors opening off.'

Birds – barking and clawing their way up the dank hill between the statues and the ilex who faded before the stridency of Northern cavalry.

Thinking at first that we were faced by an enemy force, we raised the drawbridge and waited behind the window-slits, sharpest weapons ready, while the somnolent flies buzzed about our ears.

But the leader carried a flappy flag on which the royal arms of Atlan glittered, the gold threads only a little tarnished. As they advanced, as they beat the steeps, we saw the carts of provisions they trundled with them. Oxen and fruit-like bunches of live duck added cacophony to the ugly resonance of the birds.

So he is safe!

My first thought. He's done it. He's got her father on his side, he can afford to send men and provisions openly through the land. He's with her now.

But he had sent munificence, even for an Empress to receive. Poultry, grain, potted baby fruit-trees to be planted, gardening and farming implements.

Oxen and a hundred and fifty mounts for the stables.

'Where shall we put them all?' I muttered to the Captain of the miniscule Atlan Guard as we took the salutes of the glittering scintillant horn-blaring procession parading for approval through the courtyard which in the morning seemed vast, by evening was only just large enough.

'We shall rehabilitate the barracks behind the stables. They are roomy enough, though in bad repair.'

'That will soon be dealt with.'

The Atlan captain was itching to get going with proper sentry duty and all the thousand and one other things that are possible with the glory of a proper Castle-garrison.

But he wasn't sure what his new position would be. And sure enough, he is of course quite inferior in rank to the Northern major in charge of the new company.

Suddenly I laughed. I couldn't possibly explain why. Frellis thought I was a little light-headed from relief at the change in our position and the realisation that my husband is assured enough of his to send this expedition openly.

'He would have sent more men if he'd feared seriously for you – ' she murmured.

But they seemed so many, many men, I couldn't imagine having been sent any more.

I continued laughing. They were indeed, almost every one, hand-picked for their lack of physical attraction. My heart flooded with warmth. This was Zerd's completely private joke to me.

The major, rather squat with bristling ginger whiskers, rode up to me. He indicated the men who followed him with a great crate.

'Personal, for Your Majestic Highness' gracious acceptance,' his finger-tips were glued to his salute.

'We thank you.' I inclined my gracious head.

The crate was lifted to the balcony on which Frellis and the Atlan Guard stood with me for show. It was lurched into the room behind, where the Nurse and Scar began to rip away the plank-covering for me.

'His Momentity directs me to convey to you news of the monument which he has commissioned to be erected in the White Square.'

'He must be relaxed in his attitude to the King's siege if he can trouble himself with statues.'

'The siege is lifted, Highness. His Momentity issued forth and took the besiegers by storm while his new allies from the Mainland Forests took them by surprise, by tempest if I may coin a phrase, Your Majestic Highness, from behind. The King's forces are routed, scattered to the beaches and cut off there from their ships the Emperor's bandits have sunk. Many prisoners are taken, many more already executed.'

'This is great news.'

'The monument, Highness, represents Your Majestic Highness's gracious self with the little Prince. He is an infant in Your Majestic Highness's arms, clutching with one tiny royal fist on a fold of Your Majestic Highness's long gown. The inscription – I have here the full inscription which perhaps I may beg leave to read to Your Majestic Highness – but it tells of Your Majestic Highness's bravery, and Your Majestic Highness's devotion to the heir of the realm.'

I was so surprised and touched I could hardly trust myself to speak in case the whiskery Major heard the tremor of my voice.

'The statue is made of stone or marble?' Frellis asked, which seemed to me rather out of place, rather looking gift-horses in their teeth.

'In clear crystal, Your Majestic Highness,' the Major addressed himself to me. 'With crowns of toothed gold upon the heads of Your Majestic Highness and His Highness. Lovely it will look, if I may say so, sparkling in Your Majestic Highness' Capital City's sunlight.'

I pictured its sparkle and liquid lines and happiness melted my breasts.

'It is thirty feet high,' the Major continued proudly.

Oh, Gods, that's a bit much, isn't it, I thought with a shudder. Thirty feet of jelly-opaque giantess clasping the symbol of her fertility. But how vulgar, how thoughtful, how darling of my General.

The planks fell apart in the room beyond.

I complimented and dismissed the Major who backed cere-moniously away below the balcony.

The Nurse held up for me the pleated chiffons, the spider-laces, ear-rings like chandeliers.

I knelt on my own royal knees by the crate. I scrabbled through the extravagant Empress-gear (for whom was I to wear this stuff?) while the others exclaimed and drew hissing breath. There was a note in the neck-ribbon of a useless flow of wild-rose yellow. 'FOR MY LITTLE GODDESS IN HER TOWIR.'

Sentimental, brief. No news, just something calculated to bowl me over. Had he written it himself, or told a secretary to send it and choose an array of expensive stuff? He himself is not too quick at forming his letters. I have watched him signing despatches in the old days, or signing orders he has dictated in the later campaign, but I have hardly ever seen his writing to recognise it. In any case, *this* has been written in a black bold scrawl, but there is a mis-spelling.

So thirty-foot of crystal public homage is being erected in the Capital. So much for Sedili. So much for the pink pearl.

I must inquire very carefully, very tactfully, what position the new ally, the Jungle Lord's daughter is occupying at Court.

Now I come to think of it, it's distinctly odd that now of all times he should slight her for me.

The East slope, the overgrown fields, are being reclaimed. The whole place is noisy. It has come alive out here – the barracks, courtyard, slope. I shouldn't walk alone now, and I suppose I must wear clothes more like Zerd has sent.

It seems that now only the cliff and the vasty seaward maw of the horizon, these only are now left to me.

But walking reluctantly, though for the third time, to the end of the corridor in which the smoke appeared and disappeared, and still finding nothing farther than a blank wall aspired to by the converging perspectives of two other blank walls, I looked up at the sky (for the roof has fallen away over the broken flagstones, the enamel of lichen, the thrusting toadstools).

A deep pale-blue, that blue the sky takes to itself only in early spring. Some traily transparent taglets of cloud going pretty fast.

I jumped and hooked my fingers on the edge of broken roof. Something hurt, a nail or a sliver of sharp granite. The pretty-pace breeze chilled my teeth as they stayed bare in a smile I couldn't shut off. I felt great. I promised myself I'd stay on the roofs till twilight, till after supper, I'd ruin my velvet and lose my ribbons. I levered myself through the sky-blue opening, scrambled for footing amongst shards of debris. The blue lifted to thousands of miles above me and I stood upright in a fluctuating fragrance of manure and sun-concentration and ozone and kitchen-smoke (bacon, burnt cabbage) and stables and stale gutters and bleached stone and space. The waves on the other side of the hill could be suddenly clearly heard, liquid wallops on the cliff. Blood dribbled down my hand. My ribbons fluttered demented. I took a sadistic pleasure in their bewilderment. I wiped my hand on the velvet.

Pacing from gutter to gutter, I disturbed flocks of doves. The roofs were silver with centuries' layers of droppings, they stretched like a tumbled stone sea to every side of me. The blood-spot trail behind me ceased as the wind closed the cut. My hair razored my face, spat in my eyes.

I jumped an eight-foot drop to the next level, waded some way through ground-ivy. Spiteful stuff.

Splashing through a gutter full of old rain and corroded rust, I saw a red blot far to my right and on yet another level.

Inquisitive, certain he could be up to no good, I came nearer, my sandals off and tied by their thongs to my waist-ribbon. My soles savoured the coolness, the heat, the tepidity, the grittiness or tickle or slide of each texture beneath. It didn't occur to me I might be scared, alone with a man and acres of space. I felt, as I stalked at him, that he should be afraid of me. Not because I held rank, but because I was high above the world. As far as possible, I kept chimneys and gargoyles and copings and eaves and roof-stacks between him and myself so that he should not get warning of my approach and evade me.

By the time I was close enough to recognise him, he had risen. He bowed to me. This annoyed me, as though he were mocking me, because though I hadn't made a really big thing of stealth, I'd have bet he couldn't hear or see my approach.

'Empress.'

'What are you doing, Scar?'

'Fishing, Empress.'

I nearly told him to stop taking the – when I saw the man was telling the truth. He had been lying belly-down beside a pool with a crumble-carved edge. His fingers were wet, and of the dozen or so pool-fish one he'd successfully tickled lay palpitating on the stone.

'It's dying,' I said.

'They do, out of water.'

I looked sharply at him, but his face was so earnest I could only know he was laughing at me.

'They're only golden ornamental fish,' I said. 'We don't need them to eat. Put the thing back.'

'They're good to eat, Empress. We need food.'

I picked the wet trembling body up and let it slide from my palm into its element. It had just strength to rebegin breathing. It stayed gathering itself, unbelieving, and the others came and drew it away out of sight beneath the scum of lily-pads.

I glanced at the red-haired man. His face was taut with anger. His scar was a jagged livid weal. He didn't bother to restrain his glare. He looked a nasty little animal, in two minds whether or not to hurt me.

'You will walk with us to the opening,' I said.

I rose and began walking. With a look of superior amusement, almost a shrug, he humoured me for a while and accompanied me, strolling not behind but beside me.

'Wouldn't Your Majestic Highness be more comfortable with Your Majestic Highness's sandals on?' he suggested respectfully after I turned my ankle on a flint spike. They were still slung dangling round my waist. I ignored him.

I wanted to forbid him ever to come up on the roof again. But it would be an order I couldn't possibly see always enforced, and

165

he could laugh at me at his leisure while he disobeyed it, so I couldn't give it.

'How often do you come up here?' I said remotely.

'Frequently. I am flattered that you want a long talk with me, Empress.'

'It is not far to the opening,' I said in a perfectly icy voice.

'No,' he agreed. 'But we are going a roundabout way.'

'Where do you climb from?'

'Why, from the broken staircase over there.'

Though I was annoyed he knew of a staircase I knew nothing of, I was glad he didn't get up the way I had.

'Lead us to your staircase, then,' I said.

He turned and held up his hand to help me over a fence of toppled stone which I manoeuvred myself in three upright steps.

'You know another way, Highness?'

I inclined my head. The nasty little mercenary, for that was all he'd been when he got himself in my Guard, is a disruptive ripple in the present lake of my servitors. Their presence annoys me but not as much as his.

Perhaps he's a spy of Sedili's. It would be easy to insinuate himself with Yula.

'How did an ornamental pool get up here?'

'I suppose this was once an airy terrace. Your predecessors as owners here took light refreshments while feasting on the view.'

That he should attempt polished flippancy with me irritated me most of all.

'Scar, what do you do all day? Apart from tickling little golden fish.'

'I guard your sacred person, Empress.'

'The Atlan Guard, the Northern Company are doing that, Scar. But they seem to do it with set hours of sentry-duty, with drawn swords, and a salute here and there.'

'You miss the salutes, Ma'am?'

'When we report you to the Major, you will receive lashes for insolence.'

'And I'll deserve my name even more.'

I gathered he was now working on the system of being hung for a sheep instead of for a lamb. But he'd get more than he bargained for, I silently promised him.

It occurred to me that I'd like to know if he'd ever seen any more of that odd smoke up here. But I couldn't very well ask now, nor expect a reliable answer if I did.

'You can see for miles here, can't you,' he said in a conversational way. And so we could. His impertinence was so dead-pan I kept doubting whether it really were impertinence, or simply a thick skin. Our pace seemed to slow as we walked. The air breathed crisp on us. I kept thinking this was the last time I could ever come up here – because I really couldn't run into him again up here, not after ordering him whipped.

Athwart a bastion of masonry that seemed designed more to push the roof down than to buttress it, Scar stopped. He turned to me, his boot scraping a screech from the osseous stone.

'Empress,' he said abruptly, measuring me with a greenish gaze, one eye cocked higher than the other, 'You want to ask me if I ever saw more of the shy smoke, don't you?'

'Have you?'

'Yes.' He straddled a cloud, it seemed to float past between his legs. On such a slight man, the simultaneous impression of being a colossus was grotesque. I felt unnerved. 'I know what makes it,' he said.

'What makes it?'

'You didn't ask me before I mentioned it, because you felt it wasn't the thing to ask a man for information just before you had him tortured.'

'Tortured is a ridiculously strong – and insolent – word for a routine punishment.'

'If you had ever been whipped, Empress –'

I was about to say yes we had, and we'd got over it like anyone else, but thought better of it. Instead I said nothing, so that the onus of getting to his point still lay all on him.

'Empress,' he said, spreading his hands in a frank open way, wind riffling through his fingers, 'You go right ahead, ask me that question you want to ask without any embarrassment. I tell you what makes that smoke, and as a sign of your gracious gratitude, you give me nothing, put yourself out in no way – merely change your august mind about reporting me to His Excellency the Major.'

Automatically my fingers curled, my hand clenched. I think I was just about to hit him myself. Then suddenly it did seem very simple. After all, there were many difficulties attendant on having him whipped, rippling repercussions for myself and my comfort here that he hadn't even thought of.

Am I balanced on a hypothetical throne for nothing? I can change my mind if I wish. In this way I had signified my

167

extreme displeasure with his earlier words, yet now could repeal my awkward severity.

'You're lying,' I said.

'Well, you don't *know* I am, Highness. And I know I'm not. Most interesting it is, the source of the elusive smoke.'

'Why didn't you speak of your knowledge before this?'

His hair seemed an indecent red, an uncontrolled unadulterated colour. Everything else up here was muted, misted, ossified. Even my fluttery garments were less spectacular than the sky.

Again his hands spread, his shoulders lifted. But it was a pose. He was in charge of the conversation.

'Empress, I have only just discovered the source. I would have told you tonight.'

'You found time to fish for your personal amusement.'

'I had not been told the smoke was a matter of urgency.'

'Not in so many words, no,' I agreed. I muttered like a disgruntled girl beaten in an argument, and nearly kicked at a stone before I remembered a sense of rank. 'Well,' I said, 'it remains for you to fulfil your part of the bargain. You will show us this source.'

'Thank you for instigating your side of the bargain, Empress, your generosity is – ' Momentarily lost for words, he bowed very low and swirled his short cloak in what I suppose he thought was a courtly manner. 'But as for *showing* you the source – I shall gladly *tell* you of it – but I think it hardly wise nor safe to visit it again in case we – and especially Your Majestic Highness – are discovered – '

'You are whipped, Scar,' I said levelly, 'unless you show me this source and I see it with my own eyes.'

There was a sharp hiss of intaken breath. Surfacing from his bow, his face was blotched, but it was from anger. He swung on his heel and set off rapidly. 'This way, Your Majestic Highness,' he said. But he hadn't got more than seven paces before he turned and waited to make sure I wasn't left behind.

Well, I thought. Is he going to dredge up some wonder to present to me? Or is his brain searching frantically for a convincing lie?

The going became rougher. Scar led effortlessly, not hesitating at divergencies. How often, I wondered, had this least appetising of my subjects explored the open lanes and byways up here, almost till they were his own?

I refused to touch his hand, I kept back from the busy swish of his cloak. In places the way became difficult. I climbed and balanced for myself, ignoring proffered help.

A stone battlement crumbled as my grip found it. It toppled into boulder balls. One of these hit my foot. Another bounded to within an inch of my naked toes – and split the plaster I'd been treading. A hole gaped between revealed rafters. A little smoke rose, and I flinched quite violently till I realised it was a spiral fume of dust.

'Empress,' Scar said in alarm, 'let me help you. I beg you, do me the signal honour of accepting my arm – or my shoulder. If any harm comes to you or the baby while you're under my aegis – '

'Baby?' I said sharply. My voice cut like an alarum into his satisfaction with his vocabulary.

'Come, Empress,' Scar said. 'You're pouting a little under the waist, that's a secret no female can keep however Royal, so why bother yourself trying – '

But he was before even myself in mentioning this. Till now, it has been a vague doubt at the back of my mind. I had no wish to find myself quite so laughable. A wife who lives like a spinster, yet spends all her time pregnant. Pathetic.

'I'm not delicate,' I said, deciding in the circumstances to drop the Royal 'we'. 'I can manage fine. Just carry on.'

Scar knelt by the hole and peered into the well-shaft of gloom.

'We must be quiet,' he sighed. 'Can you keep that in mind, Highness? Or we may land ourselves in a spot of trouble.'

'Keep leading.' I added, 'Stop fussing', and watched smugly as his jaunty-stiff neck stiffened.

When I opened my eyes, no such corny remark as 'W-where am I?' escaped my lips.

I knew where I was. Back home, in my shut-bed, Smahil somewhere near, or even if he were a mile away, he was homing to me, his only instinct to get the work done so he could leap astride a home-bound me-bound bird.

If anyone says *home* to me, I always think first of the Tower, then of the sleazy lodgings I shared with Smahil in Southerncity – the two places in which I've been most emotionally excoriated, most moonily bored.

I lay quite content for a while. But my eyes couldn't find the right knot-holes and warping in the oak-beams above me. Then it struck me that the blankets were surely extraordinarily heavy. Lastly, it struck me that I was peculiarly drowsy. Even if I'd wanted to wake up, I'd find it awfully hard.

I *couldn't* be at home. I'd been somewhere else since. Several somewhere elses.

I couldn't be in my bed in that gloomy castle I seemed to remember having lately occupied. Because it had curtains. There were no curtains here. Perhaps they'd been pulled down. Perhaps some female had decided to launder them. But there were no chook-clucks under the bed. Perhaps I'd put my arm under the bed, if there were no maternal beaks to brave, and see if there were any fresh eggs.

I couldn't move my arm.

'Get off my arm, Ooldra,' I muttered. 'Can't you ever leave me alone?'

'You're awake?' said a voice.

It was a peculiar gravelly voice, yet seemed unaware of its own odd ugliness. Oh, yes, of course – a man's voice. There are men in the world. Men aren't extinct. People happen like they did in my ancient books, they don't break out of large eggs.

He was a face. Above it was hair the colour of garnets. Below it, a long box of wooden laths, sloping at a back-angle, a cross between a coffin and a cage.

A silver-edged scar dodged his eye and nicked his nose.

I said, 'Scar.'

'No good blaming me, Empress. You asked me to lead on. You wouldn't listen when I said there was danger. You wouldn't –'

'You didn't say there was danger of capture.'

'I didn't know,' Scar muttered. 'He was only an old man, living all alone. I've often spied on him. I'd swear he is alone. He seemed a weak old effer –'

We were speaking in whispers, though throaty with emotion. We watched each other's restless eyes, which would not meet, and the beams above us. I couldn't move hand or foot, arm or leg. I was in my coffin. I could see very little else of the room. Lots of wood, faint erubescent or jaundiced glints which might be reflections off shaded glass. We didn't even know if we were alone, but the room had a stillness like under water, and was silent except for a steady ticking, a rhythmic bubbling.

'Everything about our approach would have been different, nevertheless,' I stated, 'if you had warned me we were approaching a living person. How long has he been hidden, buried here? Even the people who recommended this castle said it was decades-deserted.'

'I would have said. But you needled me.'

There was use neither for recriminations nor for this frankness. We would have nothing to say to each other till we could whisper something constructive.

Time passed, the reflections blinked at the overlapping ticking.

'Scar. How long have we been here?'

'I don't think long, Empress. I don't feel hungry, nor thirsty, I'm not conscious of my bladder.'

'We've been drugged though, haven't we. Perhaps our whole bodies are still asleep inside these framework things.'

'We were drugged after being bopped on the head from behind, Empress.'

'Scar.'

'Yes?'

'Are we in our coffins, Scar?'

His mouth drew down in a grimace like a snarl. He thought I should have the restraint and taste not to ask a question both uncertain and morbid.

'If we are both missing, Empress, after the evening meal of the day we were on the roofs – there'll be a full-scale search. Word will eventually be sent to your husband.'

'The Major will be reluctant to confess mislaying what he was set to guard. Whatever your old maniac means to do secretly to us in these boxes, he'll have done it by the time my husband hears we're missing.'

'And then he'll only think you've run off with me, eh, Empress?'

'I doubt it,' I said cold and mendacious.

'In any case, he'll be after us. Perhaps he'll find us,' Scar said with a good imitation of nonchalance. 'From what gossip I've gleaned, without wishing to give Your Majestic Highness the impression that I've been chatting about Your Majestic Highness's private affairs as you might call them, I gather he'll be more upset at the idea of your leaving him than at your death. Even more upset, I *should* say.'

I could tell Scar thought we had no hope. Otherwise even he wouldn't speak to me so.

'Your information is off-centre,' I said dryly. 'My husband's previous wife is with him now – the daughter of a strong ally he needs desperately.'

'Don't they gossip to you, Empress? The Major's lads are full

171

of city-news. Doesn't His Momentity have room to mention these dull politics in his letters to you?'

'What dull politics, man? Don't smug-talk in riddles.'

'Your pardon, Highness. But your husband's previous wife, Princess Lara, isn't it, and her father the Chief-Lord of the Mainland Jungles, are busy conciliating His Momentity.'

'Explain, Scar. I don't know anything, as you know. What hold has my husband over them? Is he blackmailing them into being his allies?'

'But, Empress, they came to be his allies. They set sail as soon as the vacuum was filled – simply to come to his aid.'

'You mean – they wanted pickings from the new continent? And they thought Zerd more likely to be the winning side than his former King?'

'No, no, Empress, no, they knew he was losing. They knew he was in dire straits, threatened with annihilation by the might of his first father-in-law.'

Scar's eyes slid sideways to me at this mention of yet another wife before myself.

Lying there, facing the roof-beams, the tale of my husband's fortunes seemed as unreal as our situation.

'Go on talking, Scar.'

'It's all truth, Empress,' he said as though I'd suggested it was a bed-time story. 'His Momentity expected, am I not correct, that his second father-in-law had followed him here for revenge after His Momentity deserted Princess Lara for yourself. But in the Mainland Temple-city, where the desertion took place, Princess Lara had apparently been misbehaving herself – before your husband, then officially her husband, forgive me if it all sounds confusing to a mere commoner of an outsider, left her.'

'You mean she was unfaithful to Zerd in Southernland?'

'And he neither knew nor cared. But her conscience was heavy with this. In her father's jungle-kingdom, it is a law thousands of years old that an unfaithful wife is killed, that her crime has blotted her soul and her husband's honour. She believed it was in righteous disgust that His Momentity left her, and in indignation took unto himself a new wife.'

'Poor little Lara!' I exclaimed. I thought, She must have been unfaithful only in a bid to gain his jealousy.

'She confessed her fault to her father. As we all know, she is the darling of her father's heart. He could not have her publicly denounced and execution invited by the elders. He snatched at a chance to cheat the law. If her people could expiate her sin against her great husband, she would have made up to him for the sullying of their marriage contract, and he might renew it – and make her Queen, her father General – but not till then.'

'You mean that Lara really thought there'd been some sort of divorce – simply because she was unfaithful and he left her?'

'I humbly suppose,' said this nasty shrewd little sneak, 'that she saw the life about her in the Army and at the Southern Court – and while I'm not suggesting it was in any way licentious, it must have seemed to Princess Lara that such things were not held in quite the horror which her people held them – but when she tried it, and coincidentally her husband left her, all her people's beliefs rose again in her. Her guilt supplied for her an all-too adequate reason for his repudiation of her. When battles and earthquakes, and your husband's conquering campaign, wrecked the South, the only place she had to go was her father's kingdom, where she had to explain why she was a cast-off wife. Coming to offer his services to Zerd, I mean His Momentity, is the only way Lara's father knows to reinstate Lara with a claim to the Throne of Atlan – himself with a claim to the pickings the Northern King would be less generous with. But he comes humbly.'

And my generous-hearted Zerd would take full advantage. He would squeeze every drop of humility from the Forest Chief – the Jungle Lord as this Southern Scar called him.

Recovering immediately from his amazement that he was not after all on his knees, begging for air, he would keep the Jungle army in suspense for his favour even while he used its force.

That was why a thirty-foot monument to the faithful fertility of his present-though-absent Empress is rearing its glossy head in the Capital. To make Lara hang her burning blushing head. To make her father redouble his powerful efforts to show goodwill. To make them crawl for Zerd's forgiveness.

And at the time, I'm sure he never even noticed his pink princess had dared take a lover.

'The gossiping Armies have provided some interest, then,' I said, 'for our last hours.'

'Keep your chin up, Empress,' he said bracingly. 'We'll laugh at all this tomorrow. What can the poor old bastard want of us? He probably just wanted to know if we'd do him harm. He was afraid of newcomers so close to his private suite.'

'Afraid?' wheezed an unpleasant whine. 'Not afraid, my young friends, not *afraid*, of that I assure you.'

The old man shuffled round so that he faced us.

173

I wondered how long he'd been listening, but my memory provided the click of the door by which he'd just entered behind us.

He smelt as though he hadn't washed for several years, so I suppose he hadn't.

He was pretty old, though the long draggle of spittle-smeared beard made him look older. He wore a threadbare velvet smock, embroidered with signs I knew, from my adolescence with Ooldra, as signs of particularly abstruse potency. His frayed-rope sandals exposed toes with nails like twisted talons.

His eyes were slugs, poking probosci, magnified behind two thick monocles with black cords twined in his beard.

'We didn't mean to trespass,' I said. 'We were under the impression this castle was empty. To be candid with you, we moved in here some couple of months ago.'

'I know that,' the old man wheezed. 'But I couldn't come to get you, could I? So many of you. Milling around. I could only wait till you came to me. You'll admit that.'

'Why do you want us at all?'

'I don't know that I do,' he said fretfully.

I was too keyed-up to disaster to feel any relief. He continued, 'But there, one mustn't be wasteful. One must use the resources at one's disposal.'

'We aren't at your disposal. We have lives, friends, avengers of our own.'

'You aren't at my disposal, eh?' He peered, removed a monocle, snapped it back in the flesh-folds that had become its socket. 'You aren't, eh?'

And there seemed suddenly no answer.

The wood behind my nape was hard. I hoped it was at least as hard for Scar.

The old man came to me. He put his fingers on my face. My nostrils flared and flinched. He pulled down my lower eyelid. 'Not red enough,' he said. A gob of saliva hit my cheek. I couldn't wipe it off. 'You're not too healthy.'

'Hardly surprising. I expect my blood has paled with apprehension.'

'Apprehensive, heh?' He laughed like rusty hinges. 'You'd be elated if you knew what you are about to become part of. Yet I don't know. You can't be a very important part. It's nearly complete as it is.'

'You're one of these mad-scientists one hears about, I take it.'

174

'Mad?' A shower of drool struck my face, into my eyes, 'Little fool, little cretin female . . . '

'This lady is the Empress of Atlan,' Scar spoke for the first time since our captor's appearance.

'Empress of Atlan?' The old man grabbed a handful of my hair. 'Dun hair, dun hair.' He wrenched it and spat 'Indeterminate eyes' and I thought he'd shove his long nails in my eyeballs.

'There is a new House,' Scar said, as I was wondering whether to say my hair was only ready for a shampoo.

'There'd have to be,' the old man giggled. 'There's no Mark on her face. Not the Mark of the Emperors. Yes, yes, there is a Mark. An alien Mark.' He looked at me in loathing.

'At least tell us what great experiment we're to have the honour of helping along,' I said.

Scar swallowed audibly.

'I don't know that I want you as any part of it,' the mad-scientist repeated. 'Besides, it's really complete already. You might even topple it off-balance.' He looked malevolently at us, as if he knew that's just what we'd like to do. 'I'd do better simply to kill you. I don't want your crapulous "friends and avengers" rushing along to find out all my –'

'You can raise great ransom from us,' Scar said, his tongue lizard-licking his lips.

'Have you – ?' the old man, obviously a pure soul un-interested by money, reeled off a list of words running into each other, glutinous consonants and minor-key vowels, probably the names of chemicals.

'Full supplies,' Scar answered.

'I shall make you write to ask for them. When they are delivered, you are free.' The old man accompanied his galvanic decision with jerky gestures, plucking at the gigantic jewel round his neck.

Scar and I did not need to exchange despairing glances. I was sure we hadn't one of these things. Also, it would be a painful job spelling out such a letter, even with the madman's help.

'Why not let us go to take the letter?' I said foolishly. 'After all, you can trust us just as much now as later. We're stuck here as much as you. Why should we want to harm you? Why should we even want to invade your privacy? What harm have we ever done you?'

'What harm? What harm?' At first I thought he'd start gobbling and spluttering again. But a crafty gleam enlivened the monocles. 'You think you're both in the right, don't you? Think I haven't a rheumy leg to stand on if I shut your blabber the best way there is?' Like an albatross, his claw-fingered hand swooped for an embroidered pocket. He drew out four glittery fish, now slightly disintegrating, and with fluff and green capsules coalescing to the scales.

I stared blankly.

'There, these I drew from your bony bosom – ' the old man shrilled. Scar's face was irrigated.

'My little fish! My little fish that I pet and eat! On what am I supposed to live if even my little secret roof-pool is plundered? Mushrooms from my cellar, watercress from my dish-flannel, and no good protein at all I suppose. Why, if that's the way my visitors behave, it's about time I *had* some visitors isn't it? Not that either of you is toothsome. Stringy, both, and full of ill humours I'll warrant.'

'We could give you food.'

'Very well. Food and – ' again the barbarous list.

'So that's settled. Let us out.'

'Only one of you. The other remains as hostage. Which do I trust least?' The monocles fleered in our eyes. 'The man's eyes are cocked at different heights, and besides, it was he on whom I found my little poached fish.'

The old man applied chiselled keys to my coffin. When I tumbled out he had to support me while the blood returned like white-hot needles to my limbs.

The room widened suddenly to my vision.

There were no windows. A stuffed alligator stretched close under the ceiling. Vivid liquids hubble-bubbled in twirling tubes. A network of instruments like shiny insects ticked and over-ticked. A skeleton leaned gaunt in a corner, a skull suffered rictus on a pole of the screen that enfolded one far corner. But craziest of all, a small old woman stood submissively behind the coffins in one of which Scar still lay. Her hands were folded across her apron. She was very quiet, but her eyes were bright as sparrows'.

'I didn't realise you weren't alone – ' I said.

The old man shuffled forward and hit the old woman across the face. She rocked on her heels and righted herself without lifting a hand.

'She's stuffed!' He wheezed and spat his giggles, peering at my reaction.

'She was one that really was too stringy. I couldn't bring

myself to it. Unreasonable, I know. It's all the same once it goes down. Still, I don't think she'd've been especially nourishing. She's better as company.'

'They're wonderful eyes,' I said.

'I'm glad you like them.' He pulled at her eyelids as he'd pulled at mine, and showed me an eye winking on the palm of his hand. It was exquisitely-tinted crystal and vaguely magnified the racing lines of his palm. He seemed gratified at my appreciation.

'You write the letter,' I said. 'And you'll have to show me the way back to civilisation – I don't know it.'

'That's mainly why you've been released,' he grumbled. 'I don't want to go near them all. It's your domain – *Empress* – '

'Write your letter,' I said. 'We'll discuss the route later.'

Scar's pale eyes, from his coffin, considered me. He was wondering if I'd be soft enough to come back for him after all he'd said. We were both wondering if the old man would really be trusting enough to let me go when I could easily bring back a force to destroy him and his laboratory.

But he sat mildly down, reached me a chair, and began scribbling with a tatty quill pen that spluttered more than he.

I didn't like my chair. At first I just didn't like the horsehair scratchily overflowing the decomposed leather. Then I disliked the wild life busy in the rents and slits.

Beetles I could stand.

'Did you know there are maggot-things in your chair?' I inquired politely as I rose.

'Oh, this place isn't dead, you know, not dead at all,' he said. 'It's quite live. I'm not just the old hermit I appear to be, existing in solitude, oh dear me no.'

'I shouldn't have thought maggots are much company for an intellectual.'

'That's just it, they're fine, like my old lady, they don't *natter*,' he snapped, which put me in my place didn't it.

He wrote the letter and sealed it with a sizzle of hot wax. He handed it sternly to me. 'The people who look after your stores will know if you have broken the seal of this private missive,' he reminded me. He didn't believe for one instant that I was any sort of Empress. He probably thought Scar was far more valuable, and that if he'd left a chit of a girl in her coffin, nobody would have bothered with a ransom.

I could still hardly believe it when he gave me a map back to the inhabited corner of the castle, and let me go. I did not look at Scar in case his gaze was too full of hope or hate, but I kept expecting to walk into a trap as I raced back the way the map bade.

I kept overshooting corridor-openings and having to turn back again. I strained my eyes and ears and the back of my neck which might tell by a prickle if danger were near.

The corridors were ankle-deep in dust and fluff-balls. Here and there footprints had left deep-edged pocks. Swathes of curtain mooped, more velvet with dust than their original material. Rats chirruped and twittered in the murky folds. Ivy tap-tapped like a restless visitor on gloomed panes.

When we approached the dust-choked passages once more, I stopped.

'Here,' I pointed. 'Here is where I noticed the roof had fallen in. Half of you follow us on the roof – to the stone gargoyle with a broken horn. There's a trap-door there which leads down into the room behind his laboratory. The rest of you follow me, but stay behind till I call.'

Since I had insisted on going back myself, Frellis had insisted on accompanying me and the four members of the Atlan Guard.

I hadn't wanted to let the Major's men in on this, which seemed too private an incident, and neither my Atlantean lady nor my Atlan captain had urged me to get the help of the Northerners in dealing with one old man secretly resident in my retreat.

'Yula was hysterical,' Frellis said in a taut-nostrilled voice.

'I hope she's not proved to have reason,' I said.

'Of course you must say that,' I could tell that in the darkness, Frellis was permitting herself a smile.

The door looked ominous from the outside. It had a leering look, too, because it had warped slightly awry on its desiccated hinges. I made a sign to the guard who piled carefully into my arms the big baskets of cheese, hams, eggs and deadly acids.

I scraped my sandal on the door. The tension of Frellis and the guard could be felt above me, round the corner from me. The hinges howled. The spittle-stippled beard, the twin Cija-reflections of the monocles peered at me round the lean of the door-jamb. Cija's four reflected eyes were startlingly fish-stares of fear. With an effort I tried to feel calm and look human.

'You hadn't given me up? You haven't done anything to him yet?' I asked.

178

'Not yet, not yet. This is your ransom? And you came your own little self – to prove to me you've told no one how to reach me, which of course you have.'

'Oh, no, no, I haven't.'

'It makes no jot of difference whether you have or not.' Jauntily he flipped his beard as he ushered me in like an errand-boy, showed me where to set down the baskets on a large marble slab.

From his coffin Scar's eyes watched me the same way they'd watched me an hour and a half earlier.

The old man fingered the food, shook the acids as if he were sharing a joke with them. '*Now*,' he mouthed in glee. Suddenly the embroidered rags swirled, he turned on me. The old hands gnarled as tree-roots but as vegetable as weasel-paws had me in a lock I'd never met.

'And you'll be just as useful, Empress-female. In spite of the live swell of your innards.'

'You can't hurt us now. I *have* told the castle where to find you. They'll avenge us – '

'I can deal with them.'

Before the dry hand closed my lips, I got out a sound that had been meant as a call but came out a most unregal scream with a panic-sob in it.

The Guard and Frellis raced in even before I'd made it. The rest of the Guard dropped through the rotten framework of ceiling. The old man shook with laughter. 'Just the suspicion and treachery I expected,' he crowed. 'Oh, no, you can't trust a soul, can you? But I'm prepared, believe me, no skin off my nose.' He plucked at the gigantic jewels of his necklace and drew from the clicked-open rubies and onyx pinches of yellow salt. He threw this at the Guard who reeled back choking.

Everyone in the room, even Scar, gasping, strangulated. Only our host, who'd clipped a polished mask over his lower face, remained cool and efficient.

Within minutes we were all bound. Still we strained against the bonds, not to free ourselves but to open our lungs. Frellis was in the coffin I'd occupied. Others of the Guard were in similar slanting cages. The rest of us slumped against the wall, our hand-chains hooked to staples behind us. The sound of coughing cacophonised the air, gradually subsided. From the coffins, Scar's pale eyes, now expressionless indeed, and my lady's navy gaze, and the azure eyes of the other Atlanteans found a focus in me.

179

'All! All here!' The old man's gloat was muffled. He didn't unclip his mask. Our breathing still wracked us, sharp yellow vapour still darted, wreathed the room.

'All except a brown woman with pendulant dugs and a puling man-infant. Eh?' He smiled at our gasps. 'Those I can get any time, now all the other birds have been trapped into one trap with one stone. All easy, it's been, couldn't have been easier. You all *walked* into my welcome, eh my dears? With cheeses, eggs and acid as bonus.'

'You've spied well,' I said painfully. 'But not for some time. Didn't you know an entire Army company has arrived here since apparently you last numbered us?'

'Quiet,' he snapped. Mercifully his still-necessary mask shut off the shower of drool from my face. 'You've lied enough. Now save your last breaths – you're no good to me choked blue, and as for your unborn child, I want it live.'

My throat dried, died. Zerd's child budded in my womb.

The old man advanced on the captain of my Guard. From yet another pocket he'd pulled out a scalpel. The scalpel shone in the bubbling beam of the test-tubes.

The captain's eyes dilated. His jaw twitched. His gaze followed the brisk point of the scalpel as if attached to it by a thread. His biceps bulged and a vein beat-beat in his forehead. But the bonds only creaked.

Wisps of sulphurous vapour drifted between me and the tableau. I strained my eyes but the smoke shrouded them. I could only guess what I'd see when the drift cleared. My throat throbbed as the strangling smoke caught it.

From another corner of the laboratory came a hoarse sound. A rusty croupy cough which seemed to have been dragged from a throat of gravel, lungs volcanic with pain.

The vapour moved on across my vision. But the captain of the Guard still strained against his chains. The scalpel dangled. The old man paused, his masked head turned.

Again the cough erupted from the far corner.

I swallowed. I found I could speak.

'You must believe that we have an Army here,' I said. 'Harm us, you destroy yourself. Find a window and look out of it. You'll see the busy stables, the teeming fields.'

The far cough died in a gurgle, a trailing gurgle like the groan of an unconscious man.

Someone is suffering a fit, I thought. There's an epileptic prisoned in this foul place.

The old man bounded across the room. The smoke shimmied aside from his skirts. He trundled aside the screen, which unfolded in segments like a monstrous caterpillar, but at such an angle we couldn't see what it had enfolded.

'Oh, Gods!' he cried. 'Oh, Gods, already! My little ectogene, quiet, oh, quiet! Have I set you off? Don't hurt your raw throat, rawest of all rawnesses! I'll disperse the smoke, only don't choke before ever speaking to me – you're alive, alive! The cruel smoke has jolted, pained you into life!'

An uneasy suspicion crawled into my mind. My flesh crept. The hairs on my arms lifted.

'Let us go,' I called. 'Now you're busy, you don't need us, you can't risk an Army's search here.'

There was a crash of splintering wood. Unnoticed in the smoke and melodrama, Scar had strained, kicked and burst the wooden laths of his cage. He leapt to the captain opposite him and snicked open the chain-catch. The scientist had only just turned as the captain had nearly freed me, Scar nearly freed an Atlantean.

Scar seized a broken lath.

'I'll smash all this,' his shadow dimmed the sparkling labyrinth of glass, 'if there's any more trouble from you.'

The old man wrenched off his mask. Immediately he began a wheezing cough. But there were already tears running down his face.

'Hush, hush,' he mumbled, as though only half-aware of us. 'Let me disperse the smoke.'

Before Scar could spring to stop him, he had sprinkled more powder from the hollow necklace. But this flashed in the gloom. It sparked at the sulphurous smoke, sent thrills of fire through it, grappled and annihilated the slow drifts. We could breathe again.

The hoarse convulsive sound behind the screen full-stopped. Scar and Atlanteans advanced on our captor.

But the old man, with a couple of dance-steps, disappeared. There was a blinding light and a crack, and we were left looking foolishly at a blank floor.

'He was on a trap-door,' the captain said. 'That blaze of light was just good stage-managering. Look, you can see the lines in the floor. How well-laid it is. But there's no handle.'

Scar kicked on it. The Atlanteans tried to drive their blades between the cracks. But the floor remained solid.

I freed Frellis. I expected her to collapse in my arms. But

181

though she held me, she looked anxiously at my face. 'Are you all right, Highness? Have you been hurt?'

Scar and the soldiers smashed the tubes, the instruments poised like predatory mantis. Glass chipped, crepitated. The shuttered beams dulled, went out. Steams rose from protesting liquids, no longer bubbling but thin-screaming as they split.

Shoulder to shoulder, heavy with a curious reluctance, we approached the far screen. The captain hurled it aside. I buried my face on Frellis' shoulder. But I'd seen.

On the slab lay a body, inert, awkward, seeming to be sprawled though it was in fact lying rigidly to attention. It looked patchy, and scabrous, as though it suffered some form of leprosy. At its armpits and its uneven groin great violet weals had been raised. A diseased-looking purple cicatrice wove its sinewy chest to its raw neck. It had no face. Just anatomy – a mass of exposed nerve-endings, and bandages, depressed where the empty sockets must be.

'This never coughed. It was one of us.' The captain gazed at the thing, his own face twisted with pity. 'This poor object is quite dead. I suppose it once served for a ghastly experiment of some kind.'

'Smash it all the same,' Scar interposed. 'Why should the maggots get another nursery?'

But the glass case, that looked so brittle about the thing, made only a ringing sound at the blows of swords and clubs.

'Leave it,' I said. 'Let's get away from here.'

'The Empress can see no more,' Frellis said. 'She is exhausted.'

'I must enlist the Major's aid,' the Atlantean captain said reluctantly. 'We shall comb this wing of the building till we have run the foul madness down. Every door must be kept locked at night. The sentries in the Empress' corridor and before the room of His little Highness must be doubled. Cloths and water must always be kept ready so that at the first sign of choking gas everyone can wrap their nose and mouth in wet cloth to nullify the poison.'

We hastened back through the stifling dust, the blades ready about myself and Frellis. Scar stopped by me. 'Your pardon and my deepest gratitude, Empress –'

'The Empress has been troubled enough by your tongue,' Frellis said.

Scar's eyes became pale slits. He shrugged.

Yes, yes, I courteously admitted as they put him in my arms, yes he is beautiful.

They hovered in case I should drop him. They didn't like to show it, but they didn't quite trust me to hold him the right way.

I scrutinised him, surprised by the truth of my own words. Why, yes, he could be called a pretty child, quite impartially. I would hardly recognise him. His hair is yellow, his eyes have still not lost their first blue. His face is no longer grey, but a healthy pearl-glow with a wild-rose flush on the cheeks. His little bones no longer poke at his skin. There are dimples at his fragile wrists. He twists away from me at first, because I am a stranger and he wants the nurse, but his eyes widen fearlessly as they catch my probably sombre gaze. He stares back at me, touches my mouth, wriggles in my arms and chuckles.

'He is so good,' said the nurse. 'He is teething, but he doesn't cry much. As though he hardly noticed.'

I inserted a finger in the flower of his mouth. Yes, his poor little pink gums pregnant with tooth, itching with thrusting bone. I tried to withdraw my finger. The serrated gums had clamped on it. I worried it out, and it was bleeding. The boy gurgled with merriment.

'Oh, the *naughty* – ' Even Frellis was shocked. They wanted me to see him at his best.

'Yes, smack him.' But he didn't care. They didn't hurt him. He is going to be spoilt. I can't understand how something born out of so much agony, blood, slime and shame can be so exquisite. And already, as I hold him, he is heavy on my curving stomach. There is another being in me.

'Take him,' I told the nurse.

She took him gratefully, like a cat who has watched her kitten in human hands and kept calm only through an effort of will. He turned to consider me.

'Three weeks,' Frellis said, blotting my finger with a lace handkerchief. 'And they've still not found the old man.'

'We can't sleep safe in our beds,' cried the nurse.

'They even set men to wait all night by the laboratory,' said Frellis. 'But he never appeared. And they were grey and trembling with suspense by morning.'

'They are not to stop looking,' I said. 'He must be hunted down.'

'You are pale,' Frellis said. 'You must take care of yourself. You must let us take more care of you.'

'Perhaps it will have scales when it is born,' I couldn't help saying aloud. I couldn't let them see all the doubt in me. I have a loathing of another living like a parasite, month after month, in my flesh. Perhaps because my first pregnancy was a lunatic nightmare from first to last, and because I seem always to be with child though I seem never to be loved, I can't feel any of the conventional exultation that my husband's child is to be born from my spinster's body. Even Zerd's face is dwindling to a dream, an effort to recall bright and all in one piece. I can remember that his hands tingle on me, that it is ecstasy to drown with him, but I can't for the life of me remember clearly what it's like. And I'm *not* glad he's spared seeing me now. I *want* him to see me pregnant. I want him to touch it and say, This is mine. This I set within you to grow.

'Of course the love won't be,' they said. 'Look – Nal's skin is perfect.'

'Nal is different,' I said bitterly.

As the summer solidifies, as the rose-toed doves paddle in the sun and intensify in the high carved cotes, as the coiled fish and its greed grow in my belly, an intestinal worm stealing my strength, as the sea blue-calms and becomes lazy as the lizards lank on our walls, as the foliage as far as the eye can see thickens gold and emerald as living bijouterie and breathes hot perfume to the calm-sea-blue sky, the Castle and its grounds are living.

The fields have been reclaimed. A harvest can be gathered before the season is up. A ready-made orchard glows. The courtyard is a hive of activity. The stables are as fascinating as stables should be. The barracks is a real barracks. There are drill and parades, but I think the busy soldiers are happy, especially with their agriculture – even if this is one of those outposts in the sort of neck of the woods where life and leave and promotion can pass you by for decades. There are seven official whores here, who are always working though each individual soldier sees them very rarely, and an elaborate system of pay-economy and punishment has accumulated round them, so they're an integral part of Camp discipline.

Here, in the Castle, life is infiltrating also. There is even a certain charm in the obstreperous sounds of the child learning to walk in the nursery.

But nothing will grow on the West slope, nothing new, no crops.

Nothing will grow on that side of the hill I think of as the

184

rotting side, though the only thing that *looks* scabrous on it is the glistery weather-bitten epidermis of the statues, and the plants already there, the ilex and the cedars and the laurel and the lush turquoise turf are flourishing.

I find the summer nights hard on sleep.

Hoot-owls, the occasional neigh or whinny, courtship and death on wings in the humid creeper clustering claustrophobic round my window with its teeming stars – these sounds are not what keep me awake. I welcome them. They are reassurance. What throbs against me till my pulses ache is a tension like a ghirza string about to snap, a heavy live-ness in the air which is actively painful, which crushes me like a succubus when I lie stretched still, which makes my heart beat like a runner's labouring uphill.

It's not the threat implicit in the continued freedom of the old man of the secret laboratory. My room is ringed by sentries. I have only to knock a jug to the floor and a taut voice from the corridor inquires whether he's to bash down my door, rush to my aid. No one can get in my window – not even a climber as fine as my little brother.

It's an exhalation of the night that beats on my heart and makes my blood run molten, a slow star-burning rise-fall, the breath of the night's vasty maw, odorous breezes thrill-flickering like fire.

The summer and I are approaching harvest time, slowly, with all the languor of heavying ripeness, yet with great compulsive throbs like the gasping of an air-burned fish.

I feel myself pluralised to more than two things. I move in the night feeling myself some myth, some monster, slow and stately, a hulk with a double soul.

The pitted stone balustrade lay harsh but quiescent under my fingers. The silver sward swept down away under the stars, sprinkled by sparkle, sibilant waterfall of scabrous statue, silver spiralling down-slope to the spiky snake-heads of tense trees.

Something emerged from those trees. I realised like a sleep-walker awakened that I had placed myself outside the surveillance of my guards.

It had seemed only urgently natural, in my restlessness, to place myself in Yula's room on a night I knew she would spend in Scar's room – which is discreetly farther from my suite – on an evening when Frellis had spent hours in her bed with a bad

185

headache and for once had not insisted on coming to tuck me up and bless me good night.

Now as a lean length loped from the trees, my senses returned like a grip of ice.

I was out on the terrace, on the wrong-side of the hill.

Yet I waited to see what the shape was. When I saw it was a wolf of extraordinary size, I was hardly surprised.

Still I did not dash back between walls.

The wolf bounded uphill like something on rubber or springs. It skirted the stone people. Their beckoning fingers, their imperious arms did not stay it.

The waterfall did not stay it.

In a froth, in a spurl, it loped the head of the fall. It paused the other side of the moat, yards from me. Its red tongue lolled, but it hardly panted.

I had the sense not to look at its eyes.

The moat'll keep it away, I thought. I didn't even hurry as I turned back to the inhabited rooms. But the chill plinked from vertebra to vertebra.

The hall was vast, the cobwebs swung in the vaulting. On the far platform was the glow of the sentries' brazier. They had been dicing when I sneaked out, and hadn't noticed me, and I had considered reporting them tomorrow, for negligence. Now, not thirty minutes later, they were snoring.

I reached the far door, and slipped through it. (It was unbolted – the whole sentry-service is as lax as to be expected in a country retreat miles from danger, with peace settling like a pall over the Capital anyway.)

The sentry who should have been the other side of the door wasn't. I'd expected that because when I'd come this way earlier, he'd been in the hall with his mates.

It's only much farther up in the house, where we sleep, that care is taken – because the thought of the old man at large still haunts us.

The warped wood keened under my soles.

My spine had not lost that chill. Something silent is behind me, I quite suddenly decided. I thought, The old man. I whirled around.

In the dark of the deserted corridor the wolf continued to advance.

It seemed twice, three times as big here, no longer kept from me by a stretch of moat. It must have bounded like a gliding thistle-down across that moat, I thought.

186

My first impulse was not to scream. The thing was so near and its gaze had that pale iciness and I didn't think of it as an animal I could disconcert by a scream while aid hurried to me – I thought of it as an intelligence which would silence me, before *it* waited for my aid, or escaped.

I felt the door-knob behind me as I backed against the wall-tapestry.

I never knew there might be a door behind that tapestry. I found the fold where the cloth was loose to lift. In pitch blackness I scrabbled again for the handle. Even when I was through the hidden door – ('Thank my Owngod not locked,' I gabbled religiously, acknowledging my luck in case it gave out) – I was still in blackness.

I pushed with my hands. I knew I'd get panicky in a couple more moments. The chill still thrilled my spine.

My hands met a rough weave of cloth. I understood the other side of the door, too, was hidden by tapestry. That was why no one had known to lock it.

I pushed past the cloth. I stood bathed in a burst of light – a dim starlit room. The furniture's shaping was familiar, though not its shadows and textures at this time of night.

The nurse lay snoring under a hummock of eiderdown. Of course that very small sprawl in an immense white-lace-hung four-poster decorated with blue bows must be my son.

I breathed again. But I must find a way to get the sentries (with spears) along, without myself or the nurse venturing into the corridor.

I pushed my hand through my hair, let my shoulders untense.

The cloth behind me breezed. Behind its breezing, and out into the nursery, strode the wolf.

I did scream. It was quite involuntary. I expected the poor nurse to start upright, even her hair on end, and start gibbering and making signs against evil. But she continued to snore.

But *Wolf not wraith*, my mind leapt. I'm not having hallucinations. I can smell it. This is a wild wolf all right, inches from me, its pads straight from savage forest depressing the nursery carpet.

'Nurse! Nurse!' I said loudly. 'Wake up, wench, for Gods' sakes.'

The sallow woman's snores were unhurried.

The wolf stepped towards me. Its eyes were on a level with my chest. It looked tall and broad. And it looked long. Its whey-grey tail nearly reached the wall.

187

'Get away,' I said.

I held the door and curtain wide for it.

Its tail twitched.

'Get away. Good dog,' I said.

I think it was the wrong approach. Its nostrils flared each triangular scarlet.

It paced towards me. A low growl thrummed its throat.

It reared.

The scream died in my own throat. The nurse's snores continued. Another movement. The child was sitting up in its lace-festooned bed. What a thing to lie among a baby's first memories, I thought. Watching its mother killed. Oh, of course. It won't last much longer. And neither will that security-drunk nurse.

The child scrambled like a soft-shelled crab to the end of its bed. Its nightgown trailed.

'Ulven,' it said.

It reached a hand between myself and the huge animal.

'Back, Nal,' I said in a strangled voice.

The boy's eyes rested on mine. There was a sort of quiet wonder in them. I suppose he remembered having seen me a couple of times before.

The wolf dropped on all fours again. Its tail beat the carpet.

Nal crouched over the bed's precipice-edge.

The brute stretched its belly along the floor. Its forelegs splayed. Its mouth opened, the harsh tongue lolled out amongst the curved fangs.

Saliva drooled to the carpet and steamed.

Nal stretched a hand like an infant starfish, grasped a handful of the rough grey hair.

'God – ' I exclaimed. I waited to see my son rended.

The wolf abased itself. The narrow amber irises dilated.

It turned and paced to the open curtain. Passed through the dark door.

I banged the door shut.

I didn't feel like picking the child up, in spite of my overwhelming relief it was still alive.

Its bare feet dangled out of its nightgown over the bed-edge. It regarded me. A thumb went plp into its rather shapeless mouth.

Its head went over to one side.

'Muvva,' it said laboriously.

The nurse's snore sputtered in her throat and changed its raucous rhythm.

BOOK TWO

THE EXILE

The Children at the Window

I MIGHT as well start the Diary again. The days are dragging as they used to before I was seventeen. I am twenty-two. It was a hectic life but a short one. The fledgling, dizzy with triumph, spun out of the Tower, across mountains and ocean and into another stone age.

I have not seen his face for a year. I can no longer call his image into my mind without an effort, and then I'm sure I sometimes get it wrong.

Equally, he hasn't seen me for a year. Has he forgotten my face? Does he ever try to recall it?

He might like the little girl. She has never seen him, she doesn't know he exists. But he is evident in every line of her, small though every line of her is, and I am not there at all.

She has smooth skin, unscaled. She'll thank my gods for that as she grows older. But it is dusky, with a bluish tinge like an evening sky threatening storm.

Her black hair is already thick and glossy. Her eyes are widely set, very far apart from each other, black, wide when grave but usually narrowed into an almost chronic laughter.

I don't think Zerd would like the boy, though he is fantastically attractive and everybody's pet, in spite of the fact he is older and less sweet-tempered than his little sister.

Skin pale and transparent as a petal, hair like a primrose-clump, eyes blue as some blue flower, but with a sparkle, and capable of showing a thousand expressions in an hour, which I suspect are already no guide to the genuine emotion behind them.

His face, however, is not really pretty.

'A little elf,' the women call him. 'Prince Brat,' the soldiers have nicknamed him when I'm supposed out of earshot. His face is so live it almost defies analysis: but one can concentrate,

189

and discover that one eye is wide and straight, the other slanted a little, a thinner eye with a crease under it as though he had already spent a side of himself in debauchery.

A lot of my time, I am in the nursery. Hardly cut out to be a devoted mother, not quick to take any care of them from the shoulders of their nurse, I have however found out a lot about them because they are the only interesting phenomena in my daily life.

The soldiers, scores and scores of them as there are, are hardly interesting. In fact, I think Zerd picked them out not only for their poor looks but their cretinous qualities. Half-witted morons, the lot, and crudely boring. They even quite like it here.

They have settled down to farming and gardening and hunting and fishing and dicing and the seven prostitutes seem to be plenty for them.

Frellis is much better than I am with the children. She quite idolises them.

'You are marvellous with the children, Frellis,' I said shyly when she'd charmed Nal back into a good mood. I'd just slapped him and then put my hands over my ears.

'You are very kind, Empress.' She calls me Empress as anyone else would call me Cija.

'No, Frellis. You're kind. You're giving them some kind of normal life. They're the children of the Emperor. If they can be kept safe, one day one of them will inherit this oldest of worlds. They're also human children. They have only each other as playmates. No one else *near* their age lives within a radius of many miles, a radius of impossibilities. Their nurse is already unable to understand their games. She bullies them, keeps them clean according to her peasant conception of cleanliness – sees they're well fed and is upset when they refuse more food.'

'She'd like to see them fat.'

'They have enough flesh, haven't they? Seka is all dimples. Thank heavens they run round so much. They're firm and wiry. She tries to keep them sitting still, "being good". I'm impatient with them, though I understand them. You're their only balance.'

'I adore them, Empress.' Frellis paused.

Amazing in someone so gravely dignified, so cool of voice, from those cool features those warm navy glances beam out, a level straight gaze, none of the side-glances and flirting of the

190

eyes that is so natural to most women in conversation. But such a warmth.

She never lets the smallest untruth spoil her mouth. 'I adore Seka. I love Nal, and I revere him as the future Emperor of my land.'

'Almost everyone adores him.'

'That's because he's so beautiful. And so lively. There's no shyness in him at all.'

'I'm glad his hunted, undernourished infancy with all its perils, the long times he was nearly abandoned or nearly died –' I began, my old guilts rising up.

'No, Empress. Those months seem to have left no mark in his subconscious, that's what you're glad of? They are there. They have contributed to all this ebullience, all this brashness –'

Again she paused. The last word seemed a harsh one for Frellis to apply to a little boy. Most brats are obstreperous when they're nearly three. Nal has far more grace and charm than most.

The Major saluted when he noticed me coming down the steps towards him. He faltered in his own stiff-booted ascent. A crumbling of loose stone showered the steps and his gleaming creaky leather.

'Empress! Empress.'

I flipped my fingers past my untidy hair in the answering salute I'm so inexpert at, all I can do is to pretend it's casual because I hardly bother.

'Major. I'd like to talk to you.'

As though I'd touched a clockwork switch, his boots clicked together. A spark spat off his spurs.

'Empress! I am at your command.'

I leaned against the hot balustrade and traced an ancient griffin with a royal forefinger.

(It used to be a divine forefinger. But I've almost forgotten my god-ancestors now I'm with people who haven't heard of them. I felt freer when I was recognised as a little divinity: Less responsibility than a monarch, even an exiled crowned-consort.)

'A delicate matter, Major –' I felt it would offend his sensibilities if I came straight out with it.

His bulging eyes reverently followed my meandering finger. 'If Your Majestic Highness would care to honour my office with Your Majestic –'

'No, it's hardly private. But could one of your Army's women

191

be asked if bearing a child would be too terribly inconvenient?'

'One of our seven young ladies? But who – who has bothered Your Majestic Highness with stories –'

'Oh, I know they exist. Major, this is not a Royal Command.' (I knew it would be one.) 'I don't want any of your young ladies to feel they must go to all the trouble of becoming mothers simply to please their Empress. But if one or two of them –'

'*No* trouble, Empress, I can vouch *for* them, it will not be difficult for them –' The Major stopped himself. A puce blush clashed with his bristling ginger moustache.

'You see,' I honoured him with an explanation, 'I feel that some more children about the castle would be a very good thing for Their Highnesses. As things are, it may be years, and years again, before they even see other children. They may have ceased to be children before they ever meet people who aren't adults.'

The Major pulled at his moustache. Shrill laughter drew our eyes simultaneously. Nal passed the balustrade, his head almost on a level with ours. He was astride Scar's neck. Scar looked up, flicked the Major and myself with a sardonic glance and myself with a glance I couldn't quite make out.

'I thought at first it was one of our soldiers –' the Major rumbled. He had made a brusque movement, then checked himself.

'But it often is. I have no objection, Major, to the interest your men show in my son. But children make better playmates. I think he will learn more from them than from his future subjects who are so much older and eager to spoil him –'

'They are a little rough for a young Prince,' the Major apologised.

'No, Major,' I said solemnly. I let my gaze go dewy to reassure him. Real soldiers would in fact be fine. But these clodhoppers here . . .

'The children of our – of those young women – will *hardly* be fit companions for Prince Nal, little Princess Seka –'

'They'll be *young*,' I stated.

'I shall see that Your Majestic Highness' instructions are carried out,' the Major's heels banged each other again. He'd tactlessly forgotten already that I wanted to sound as if I weren't giving orders at all.

Oh, well, it'll be added interest for them in this godforsaken hole, whether the poor bitches like it or not, I thought defensively. The Major and I once more exchanged our personality-plus salutes.

I do hope Frellis was just being sentimental about Nal. Yet now I come to think of it, there is a haunted sort of look on his face.

Frellis was not in the nursery when, in my usual desperation at finding nothing else to do, I drifted at noon to see if my offspring could possibly amuse me.

'Where is Frellis?' I asked. 'She didn't come in to see me again last night.'

'The Lady has not been here for three days,' the Nurse said on a bright note. She had been getting fed-up with Frellis.

Seka clambered on to my knee. My beads banged her poor little nose and she gurgled in merriment.

'Don't *break* them,' I said crossly.

Dimples appeared in all sorts of unexpected parts of her face and she crowed.

Nal had run to me with outstretched arms but when Seka got there first he stopped. He wandered away again. Now he watched me from behind a table leg. His thumb wavered to his mouth but didn't go in, his expression drooped but wasn't a pout. He looked irresolute. I wondered if he knew I could still see him from the corner of my eye. I wasn't too touched by the outstretched arms bit. He welcomes everyone like that.

'Lady coming,' Seka said happily.

'Soon,' I agreed. 'She's coming soon.'

'Seka misses the Lady,' Nal said past the table leg.

'She'll be along again soon, I expect. Perhaps she has one of her headaches.'

'I don't care,' Nal said.

Instead of reproving his downright rudeness, the Nurse laughed loudly. I almost said a lot to *her*, but don't want to undermine her authority in front of them. 'That's nonsense and naughty,' I said to Nal. 'Don't you ever get headaches?'

'I get toothache,' Nal said. 'Toothache is much worse.'

'Don't be stupid,' I said sharply. 'Look, it's very warm in here. It's nice outside. Shall I take you out for a picnic on the rocks?'

'Is Seka coming?'

'Of course.'

'May we paddle?'

'If you don't mind the long walk to the safe beach. You

mustn't grizzle if your legs ache – unless you want to turn back. I'm not carrying you as well as Seka.'

'Scar can come and I can ride him. I'll go and get him.'

'Oh no you won't,' I said in the Empress voice I don't use on adults. One word from me and Nal does exactly as he likes. He dashed out of the nursery like an albino hare. I tried to trip him. He pretended not to see my maternal foot even as he leapt it.

'Nal, come back this instant,' I clichéd urgently. He pretended not to hear.

'That Scar is no good,' the Nurse sounded surly.

Though I agreed completely, I wondered why she was so sour. His morals (Yula), his popularity with her charges (whom she jealously spoils and bullies like her own possessions – she's not a good nurse like mine were, though I did ungratefully detest them), or the fact she hadn't been invited on the picnic?

I put Seka in a little cotton shift grit and seawater couldn't soil permanently. The nurse sniffed in a I-*might*-have-a-bad-cold-for-all-you-know way when I stumbled with tape-fastenings.

A wicker hamper appeared in the doorway with Nal's legs underneath it and his two white-knuckled hands gripping the sides.

'Food,' he said briskly. 'Chef gave me hardboiled eggs'n wine'n so on.'

Scar wavered into sight behind the walking hamper.

'I'll carry His Highness for you, Empress.' He switched on a smile as soon as I caught his eye.

'I *distinctly* told Nal not to bother you,' I said distinctly.

'That's all right. Little Prince *no* trouble,' he heartily reassured us, flashing the grin about.

We had hardly sighted the beach when the storm broke. The children flinched – mostly, I think, because of the shock of the electric downpour after the calm glorious morning.

Seka began to sob. Nal bounded more than leaped off Scar's back. He began to climb up the cliff we'd just rounded.

'Nal! Come back, where do you think you're going – ?' I cried.

'There's a cave up here.' His voice was shrill beneath the bellowing thunder. 'You'd better sit Seka in it. Seka goes crazy at lightning.'

The rain tried to bash us down again. I gave Seka to Scar.

Nal leaped up above us, hardly using minute finger- and toe-holds so that he was no use as a guide and often so much ahead of us he was invisible in the rain screen. I followed Scar quite easily, though. It wasn't a very steep cliff. Over Scar's shoulder Seka's face stared into mine. Her eyes looked almost blind with terror, rain and tears.

'Silly little baby,' I said. 'It's all right, baby. It's only a storm. That's only sky light.'

'Want Lady,' she moaned.

Nal's head poked out from the rainfall above us.

'Here it is,' he said. 'Here's my cave.'

Scar deposited Seka and the hamper in the musty light-slit murk. He reached an arm to help me. His fingers slid in my necklace. The thread broke, the agates scattered, skidding down the wet way we'd just climbed.

'My beads – ' I clutched the suddenly empty air at my throat.

'Were they valuable?' Scar asked as he hauled me through a drape of ivy.

'Semi-precious – ' It was less the loss of the agates than his casual tone which made me feel quite ulcerous.

We crouched in the cave. Seka was quite genuinely exhausted with fear. She jumped at each thunder-roar, but otherwise only whimpered quietly as if she couldn't turn it off.

'Here, little Highness,' Scar said in a jolly-uncle voice. 'What have we here? Fruit and salad, eh? Let's poke our fingers in the cream-skin. It must be over an inch thick. It goes right over our Highness's knuckles, doesn't it?'

Seka's eyes quavered sideways with a gleam of innocently feverish hope. But before the picnic could interest her, another burst of *everything* – rain, lightning, thunder – did its best to shatter all our senses.

'Where in heaven's name is Nal?' I shouted.

My son's head visited us, lambent, his flaxen hair a halo lifted by electricity into a wild spiral.

'Come in here out of the storm –'

'I like the storm,' Nal said, evading my hand with a careless movement like a snake's. '*You're* more likely to be struck by lightning in there and be buried under a tumble of ceiling-rocks all round your ears, all round and round your ears.'

'That is selfish,' I said. 'If you think we may be struck by lightning in here, you should be begging us to come out to you.'

'It would drive Seka insane to be out in storm,' he said with a sort of matter-of-fact contempt.

195

'Don't use such strong language, Nal. Your little sister is only a baby.'

'Only Lady Frellis could shut her up.'

The waves were just visible through rain when they swashed up and hammered on the cliff, thundering below the thunder. The fume rose outside the cave mouth.

'Nal, come in out of the spray.'

'I can't be wetter than I am.'

'You'll be washed away.'

'He won't, Nal won't, Nal won't be washed away.' Seka started drumming her feet on Scar's lap. She stopped talking because she was making choking sounds.

'She's hysterical,' I felt really alarmed. 'Slap her, Scar –'

'She'd never get over it,' he said.

'This is no time for insincere sentimentality.' I tried to ease Seka out of his arms. She howled and hid her face. 'Lady, Lady!'

I discovered Scar's hand when it was already at my breast. I found this so totally unexpected that I shuddered, as if it were not a hand but a tarantula.

'Gods!' I cried under the thunder and a dramatic slash of lightning stage-lit my words and showed me Seka's tears, Scar's grim smile. 'You're perverted, man.'

'No better way of whiling the time, is there?' he inquired politely. 'This storm won't let up for a few hours at least, maybe all the night.'

'We have food to last us –'

'Empress, I want more than food.' His smile was just as greedy as his statement.

'You can wait till you see Yula tomorrow.' I was so amazed and shocked that I was still trying to be reasonable.

'Yula wouldn't be the same. I'd never forgive myself if I missed this chance.'

He reached around me and I couldn't untangle his arms.

'Please, Scar, remember yourself. I don't want to struggle with you in front of the children.'

'Why, Empress, you're trembling. Scared of the lightning? Or me?' He didn't add any of the usual half-reassurances about promising to be gentle.

'This is your revenge, an expression of the long dislike you've had for me.'

'Hush, Your Majestic Highness, you sound overwrought. You'll set the little Princess off again.'

196

'How can you contemplate an act like this in front of the children?' I had to keep moving and wriggling to check his hands. But though he was not exactly exerting himself, he was effortlessly three times my full strength. He had started to chuckle quietly in the pit of his throat.

'They won't understand what I'm doing to you – '

'If you forget all this now, Scar, it shall stay forgotten.' I tried to gain control of my chattering teeth. 'Otherwise, once we're back at the Castle you'll be sorry you were ever born.'

'I don't need to go back to your Castle, do I? What keeps me there? What has kept me there a year? Food I needn't trouble to find for myself, a roof with only a few leaks. Easy things to find elsewhere. I've been too long in one place. No, Empress, I think I'll please myself. And then take to the wild.'

'You'll be hunted.'

'With the country – and your husband's present rulership – in its present state, I don't think I need be afraid of being hounded out of the million and one bolt-holes available to me in this green and pleasant land of yours.'

And on this flippant note, having settled the matter, he suddenly got deadly serious and I had to fight so hard my heart hurt.

'Seka – Seka's crying – for pity's sake – '

It's a confused memory now. I still have bruises, scratches that have changed to scabs, and I feel his fingers must have punctured me here and there.

Apart from physical reminders, all I can remember of the struggle is my fierce determination that the children should not see – or should not see anything they might understand when they're older.

Technically, he did not quite have me. But I had almost sooner it was the other way. I pulled at my dress folds to hide him but they weren't very full. I wasn't even wearing a cloak, as it had been so hot when we started for the cliffs.

Scar stood up quite calmly.

I stood too, at once. I was between him and the still sobbing little Seka as he refastened his breeches, snapped shut his big brass belt buckle.

'Still undefiled, Empress,' he said quite pleasantly.

I laughed, at least he wouldn't know why. That adjective is the last I can lay claim to.

'Don't show yourself,' I ordered. 'Their Highnesses are watching.'

197

'Is that all that bothered you?' No, he was not feeling pleasant. His smile almost scraped his teeth tight behind it.

'You might have troubled not to puzzle them, not to show them anything they may remember later on,' I said, bitter enough to speak to him.

'Then you shouldn't have fought me, Empress.'

That had actually riled him. There was a rent in the jerkin he now had to face the wild in. Perhaps he hadn't expected the deep blood-bruises from my nails on his arms, either.

Nal had wandered in from his storm. I hated to guess when. As usual, his thumb was pushing his pout out further.

'Mother. When are we eating?' he asked.

From his wide rain-colour eyes I could not tell what he thought, what he wondered, what he knew.

'We aren't eating, little Prince.' Scar's lip lifted from his teeth. 'I am.'

He approached and bowed to me.

'With your Majestic permission, Empress.' I was sitting on the food-hamper. I rose. He hefted it, shouldered it and strode out. The silver sheets struck him in the cave mouth. He disappeared into the storm.

I picked my little girl up and tried to shush her.

'Scar can't take our pincic.' Nal's eyes darkened to violet. They filled his face like pools of ink, and suddenly the flower-like face narrowed and sharpened, took on a look like a mean ferret's.

The child was out of the cave mouth again before I realised what he was at. I ran out after him, my arms still cradling Seka whose arms were round my neck, her sobbing and gasping damping and tickling my throat. The creeper half-over the cave opening – more like tentacles than tendrils – juddered and shuddered at my head, though they had not touched the child as he slipped out.

I didn't want to call to Nal to come back. I was afraid Scar would realise Nal was behind him for some purpose.

I could see an intensification of the rain-driving, vanishing down the cliff. Scar was striding sturdily, the hamper on his well-bruised shoulder, keeping himself at a backwards angle so the storm shouldn't blow him forward into the foam.

At first I couldn't see my son.

Then I saw the little shape, practically on hands and splayed knees, toad-worming its agile way after Scar.

Nal's hand lifted.

198

At first Scar hardly noticed the easing, very gradual, of the load from off his shoulder. But unfortunately that man is no fool.

Scar's arm caught Nal a swinging backhander. My son spun away across the scree.

I sped downslope. I arrived beside Scar in a precipitous spume of storm-wet gravel. Even though I was burdened by Seka, I was in time to save Nal from another punch as the reckless brat again came for Scar's hamper.

'It's ours, our picnic!' Nal was screaming. He was in a furious tantrum. The boy is unstable, I registered. What looked like foam flecked the rosebud snarl.

Scar again lifted his fist to bash away the tugging on the basket.

'Dare strike your Prince!' I cried.

Scar sneered.

'There's no Royal blood, Majestic usurper. Your husband is a general's bastard, mis-fathered by a good man on a female brute. You are a jumped-up camp follower, if the rumours are even half-true. What's the blood in your son then, even if he does ever live to sit Atlan's throne?'

'The Dragon-Emperor shall have *your* blood, Scar. You have said and done enough since the day he left us in your guard.'

'Spiteful, are we?' Scar unsheathed his pale knife. It was just the colour of his sneer. I held myself from flinching. Seka's wet arms slid on my neck.

'I've always disliked you, Empress. Always.' In a position of power, Scar sounded remarkably pompous. 'I just don't like milk-and-water little girls trying their airs and graces on me. I'm no rat, no slave to be trodden underfoot by some fancy bit no better than myself. I've had enough.'

'Are you going to kill my mother?' Nal asked.

'The penalty might come home to roost. I shall just make certain your clutch of royal tongues stays silenced for a while. Give me time to perfect a get-away.'

Scar again shouldered the basket and seized my arm with his free hand.

I suppose he took it for granted Nal would simply follow me.

But as he dragged myself, with Seka, off down the scree, Nal flung himself at what he could reach of Scar, scratching and shaking and boxing his knees and wrist.

Nal was mouthing but quite incoherent.

I didn't know which had infuriated him, his mother's abduction or the picnic's.

Our feet met the level beach-shingle.

When Scar let go my arm, I could feel the dark bruises swell up like bands on the normal flesh.

He flung Seka and me into the half-decked fishing-smack in which a couple of Atlan guards have so often taken Frellis and the children and I rowing on a glassy sea. Now, though it was moored, it was straining and bucking on the big waves. Nal was picked up and tossed in after us. He landed asprawl like a young squid.

Scar hurled me back against Seka when I tried to stop him cutting our mooring-rope. The pale blade sliced the straining strands.

The boat heaved and a wave-back gulped it.

We surged into the surge and roar and surge of the sea-storm.

'Sca-ar!' I heard the thin stretch of my own voice. The wind teased it like a big cat pulling wool.

'Bon voyage and fair breezes to our Royal Family!' I heard his roar, jovial again.

Before the storm-swept shore receded behind spray and black-silver wind, something else landed with a thud amongst us.

Nal swooped on it.

'Scar has chucked our picnic at us!'

I narrowed my eyes against the whistling winds. Salt lashed my face. I felt as if my nostrils had been cut.

The red smudge that was the head of the man Scar climbed to trees and trees swallowed him.

Spume swallowed the shore.

The Children in the World

BUT we have not been drowned, the storm has not devoured us.

Of course, I was certain we'd be overturned immediately.

Obviously the oars were useless – they'd been in the rowlocks at the mooring, and I left them that way – partly because I wasn't prepared for the struggle of hauling them in, partly because I hoped they'd impede the waves' gigantic maws.

She had a canvas sail and I'd an idea I could turn some of the wind, too, if I could run the sail up the right way. But that too was beyond me, so I left our sail alone.

She wasn't a bad little smack, for all her lack of a skipper. In spite, in fact, of the yawning gap where there should have been a skipper.

She rode the rolling breakers that seemed so immense – she raced right up the towering water-walls I thought would crush us – she sped out of the troughs instead of wallowing in them. She had all the right instincts, and knew what she was doing without having to stop and think about it. Gradually my tension relaxed just enough for me to ungrit my teeth and withdraw my fingernails from my palms. It was like being lost while riding, and then finding your steed knows the way even if you don't.

Luckily, the wind and seas were now less terrifying, less immediately dangerous I mean. The worst was the torrential downpour and the switchback lurching I was afraid would make the children sea-sick while they were in the process of catching pneumonia.

Again and again I cursed the fact I'd casually decided not to bring a cloak on the cliff-walk. A sturdy cloak would have been far more use than my Diary.

Seka clung to me as though her arms had been welded into their clutch. She was calling me Muffa now and not calling for her Lady. Indeed, I wished intensely for Frellis now. If only

201

she'd happened to be with us! But then nothing would have happened anyway. Scar might not mind attempting rape in front of two infants of rank – but somehow the idea couldn't have crossed his mind with Frellis there.

Seagulls mewing in the upper reaches of the storm were not comforting. They didn't seem companionship, rational beings like ourselves yet unmenaced by the elements. The winds played too many tricks with their screams. They were too ear-piercing, too wild. They sounded over-excited, like elementals exulting in chaos.

I couldn't tell when night fell, I couldn't tell if there were any stars above the lurch and murk.

I can't remember how I slept, nor what I told Nal when he clambered across my knee and inquired why Scar had sent us out here and when were we going home.

But I could tell when it was morning.

It was no longer a storm. Simply rough seas under rain.

The gulls could be seen now. Slim white arches, flipping lively here and there, diving yawn-billed and coming up with a fish flapping grimly for its wave and losing the fight.

'Where's our land?' Nal asked.

'I can't see it anywhere,' I said.

'How long will we be out here?' he asked. I was about to say something in a light careless voice when I found there was a choke clogging my throat and I couldn't get a single sound past it. I pressed Seka to my breast. I looked down at the long lashes curving peaceful at last on the round cheek on which a snail-smear of tears ended in one glistening roundel, a perfect little grief-drop.

'I like the smell of the water. Can we have something to eat?' Nal asked.

I opened the wicker basket which had washed us up here. 'Not too much,' I said. 'We may need to make it last, for a while.'

I found that because I'd left the oars out, one had snapped. The broken jagged wood looked very fresh beside the rest of its slimy length but was already crusted with salt.

'Still, we couldn't have rowed on our own anyway, could we?' I said.

'We can brain sharks with the broken end and eat them raw,' suggested Nal.

The food, I thought, might last three days if I impress on the children the fact it is necessary they starve.

It lasted, in fact, for two.

Several times I had to stop Nal dipping his mug in the brine.

'No, Nal, for godsakes I've told you no. Sea water is poison.'

'I'm thirsty.'

'So are we.'

'Seka is getting skinny. Isn't she, mother?'

I knew it was no good attempting to steer. I had no idea where I was. I might have been steering for the end of the world.

Under another sky I am able to navigate, though sketchily. I do know constellations, but not constellations over this continent.

'Will we see a sail? Will a ship come and find us?'

'Perhaps.'

There are no sails on this ocean.

Skies bluer. Breezes could almost be called balmy. But I hope we don't get so-called halcyon weather – we'll be horribly thirsty, and if I know anything at all, we'll also get cruel burn and blisters and/or sunstroke.

Silver flanks twisting amongst the crests of which at first I thought they were part. Thin water-spouts. Jets of argent aimed for the low cloud-balls.

'Nal! Seka! Those must be dolphins.'

I got a shock when a lean head the length of a horse's shot out in a nimbus of spray. The marbled jaws gripped on a fish that seemed even larger than the head. Another head sped up. The jaws wrestled. The fish parted in a blood-burst. The two profiles glared. One body looped away, coiling a yard out of the water at each bound. What I had taken for a school of dolphin were the barnacle-studded flanks of one sea-serpent – and there were more than one.

I seized the steering oar this time. I got us away as quick as I could.

That night rain began pouring down again. I huddled the babies in my arms, one to either side of me. Seka no longer wailed. I feel she is no calmer for that, it's simply that she has been beaten to the submissive silence of chronic terror. I put her thumb in her mouth. It is a habit she has never needed, and I can almost hear the nurse lecturing about pushing teeth and features awry and growing crooked. But it may give her some comfort to hang on to.

'Mother! Mother! Lights!'

Nal was right. Pushing the rain-streams aside, transmuting water-drops to prisms and even reflecting rays of rainbow off my eyelashes – lights beyond the night-gusts, little lights, yet they seemed blazing.

'Is it a ship coming for us?'

'No. They're not moving, it's only us moving. Nal! That's the shore!'

The steering-oar was harsh under my hand. My wrists seemed to have become fragile, almost brittle enough to snap at a careless movement. I could feel the emptiness gurning in my stomach.

The little lights came nearer.

'They're not a light-house, not beacon lights. They must be building-lights. Houses on the cliffs.'

'Or a robbers' camp,' Nal said succinctly.

'What a nice idea,' I agreed tartly. 'We'll be careful when we land, but at least they show us where land is. What lucky drifting our boat has done for us.'

'We're on land! Hurrah!' cried Nal. The boat grounded with a grinding sound, a juddering halt.

'This is not land! Oh Gods, we're on a rock!' I yelled. I grabbed my children as the timbers split. Quivering foam received the planks of our fine little boat. The rock seemed to be heaving. I flung myself and the children flat as though I were in an earthquake, gripping the unsolid ground.

The rock steadied as my head cleared. I found Seka had vomited. I wiped her nostrils and mouth with my dress. Her mouth wouldn't shut, she breathed stertorously, her eyes wouldn't open and tears oozed from between the long sticky lashes.

Dawn trickled across the scape. It was a reef or rocks. Odd planks still eddied on rollers among aureoles and areolas of foam. Shore-cliffs towered just a child's paddle away. But they were hardly the cliffs we knew. Black as basalt, strong as sin.

Clasping Seka, Nal's fingers twined in mine, we waded ashore.

We followed the line of cliffs for what must have been three miles. Nal pointed. 'Look, there's a way up there. We could climb there.' Exhausted, I leaned my head against the black slime before we began to tunnel our way up through it. The little girl seemed a ton weight sagging on my pelvis, breaking the bone at my elbows.

I was so tired and weak that it was no effort to stop myself from looking down. There was no pull, no fascination in the knowledge of the precipice slide to the breakers below. Hundreds of feet under us, straight down under my foot-soles – yet the breakers roaring and soughing and sobbing inside my ear-drums as though we were still floating within their swell and surge. What I did find hard was not looking up. The cliffs rose so straight up there they actually seemed to be slanting over me, about to tumble on top of us. The colossal black stretch spun my head, my six senses reeled, nausea bubbled in my windpipe, my fingers slid on the rock and on Seka, my eyes blacked out and I still crawled up the wall of the continent.

'Mother! Mother, don't climb any more. We're on the top. Stay on your belly or you'll lose your balance. Inch over to me.'

Nal's urgent voice interrupted the senses-swim. The urgency of the bile in my mouth eased.

I looked up.

A sky bigger than anything I have ever seen or ever will see crashed and banged about above us, giddily horizonless.

Rain fell.

We slept.

Going by the steelier grey of the sky, it must have been hours later, almost evening, that we woke.

I stared in horror at the little ones.

'Wake up! Nal, Seka! We're drenched! We'll catch some illness and rot away. Come on, little babies, wake up. We must find some place that's dry.'

Rain blew about our ears as we staggered on.

Now Seka couldn't stop moaning. Her voice was weak.

'Muffa, my tummy's coming out.' I thought she was suffering diarrhoea till I realised she felt she was being turned inside out by hunger gnawing on itself. I stared at her with a new sense of blankness. The dimples in her face had melted. Her flesh, usually dusky and rosy, was chill and bloodless. The happy laughing little girl has less stamina than the boy who was born into the rigours of a hunted winter.

If we had not found berries on the little bushes amongst the flats of keening grass, I think we would have blacked out again.

They were large berries with the consistency of bread. They tasted nourishing. If I'd been told they were delayed-action poison, I'd still have fed them to Seka to stay her heart-breaking moaning.

We were on a ridge only a few hundred yards wide. To one side, the black drop, the breakers avid as ourselves. On the other side, we found, a drop nearly as straight, just as immensely deep – to a plain almost as wide as that blowing sky – a grey green limitless plain, a wallow of mist and unguessable points which might be hills or spires or anything at all – and a great disturbance across it all.

'They're like spinning-tops, aren't they,' said Nal, gazing out.

'They're spinning, yes, spinning at a hundred miles an hour across that country down there. They're storm-funnels, maelstroms of gale whirling across the land.'

'We shan't climb down, mother. Let's stay up here and keep on walking and walking along till we come to something.'

We came to night, and a hollow tree in which the children and I nested, enclosed within the dry bark-smell of the trunk, while insects rattled above us, bats whirred past our heads, swiftly silhouetted in the opening, and roosted upside down dangling by their little toes above us, and the winds howled in the branches outside.

'Safe now,' Seka murmured in a drowsy ecstasy. It was the loveliest phrase I'd ever delighted to hear from her.

'Unless the tree crashes,' Nal told her.

'Hush, hush, Nal.'

'Aren't you glad they aren't vampire bats, mother? Perhaps they are. Mother, perhaps they are vampires.'

'So what?'

Sunbeams laden with dancing motes, sunbeams that were in fact positive ballrooms of glinting motes, shafted into the trunk, travelled across Seka's face.

Nal stirred and woke as I woke. He stretched like a miniature of Smahil, arching his chest till I thought his shoulder-blades would meet. He was about to give a cracking yawn when I caught his eye and laid my finger to my lips.

We stayed quiet, Nal restlessly so, till the little girl's eyes opened clear.

Nal had crawled away out of the opening and now came back laden with nuts and berries and even fruit. His mouth was already red and purple with juice like bruises.

'It's warm, mother. Everything's sparkling.'

'Where did you find the fruit?'

'Squirrels gave it to me.'

I let the fantasy rest. We emerged and walked into the forest whose outskirts we'd reached last night at the hollow tree.

This forest was a kaleidoscope. It was all smells and colours and textures. The rain had left globules glittering at the tip of every leaf. The sun sent rainbows whizzing off in all directions.

The undergrowth, ferns and feather-headed grass, was soggy and shimmered iridescent, at times almost blinding. Leggy insects struggled through it all, effing and blinding.

But higher, among the branches, the colours were softer. Rose and turquoise. Huge flowers heavy on creeper-tangles, their petals glowing, their glowing hearts moist. Butterflies like wafted petals, yet with whiplash antennae. Flashy flies big as humming-birds, their gaudy gauze wings humming like clockwork.

Gurgles and splashing led us to water wimpling-dimpling over a tumble of quartz rock that was honestly crystal in places.

Nal scooped water in the earthenware jug, daubed with dragons for him by a soldier, that he has carried all this way slung by his belt through its handle. Like a courtier, or a good host, he offered it first to Seka and me.

As I was helping Seka tip the mug to drink, Nal came up beside me.

'Shall we cook it or have it raw, mother?'

A little red fish pulsed panting on his palm.

'Nal! How on earth did you get that?'

'It swam into my hand.'

'You'd make an extraordinarily good poacher.'

He really can tickle fish. In no time at all (well, about 35 minutes) he had four little fish which we had to eat raw, but they were nice.

'You don't mind if I give the extra one to Seka, do you, love? I know she's only little, but she's awfully hungry.'

'Can't leave corpses littering the forest, I spose,' he grumbled, all witty, and was at once in a proud good temper.

The fish and nuts and things really did save Seka's life, I felt. We walked on (where, we'd not the slightest idea) feeling stronger. When one has to exist a while on very little food, I'm sure one's stomach gets used to the idea and closes up a bit.

Seka slid out of my arms and down me. 'Walk,' she demanded.

Even though they were now gambolling like infants in a paradise or something, I really felt tense as we wandered. At any moment some beast might leap out on us. We might be kingdoms away from the Castle that was well and truly my home now, being the only place my children had ever known. We might be walking in the opposite direction anyway, thus slowly adding even more miles to the many.

'Why aren't you all happy?'

'It's all right, Nal. I just hope that my guard-god, my private Cousin, is with us, stronger than the Atlan landscape gods.'

'Aren't the Atlan gods your friends, mother?'

'Don't worry, Nal. I'm sure they are.'

'Because my father is their Emperor. Isn't he?'

'No Emperor may govern gods.'

'My father is a great Emperor. Isn't he? I can remember him. I can remember when he came to see us just before Seka got born. He came twice. Didn't he? I liked those men with him, they taught me that song. I liked him.'

I wondered if it might touch Zerd to hear the little boy say that. In both the separate weeks my husband stayed with us while I was big with Seka, and still he was more tender than perhaps he has ever in his life been, staying with me in spite of the cries for him in the Capital, in spite of the tactical dangers, the error in politics involved in his absence from the Capital – yet in those weeks he had ignored my first child, his heir; he had not spoken to Nal except when the child prattled to him. I think he had been repelled by the child's transparency, his flaxen hair, his violet veins. But I think his suspicions had also recurred. I suppose he could hardly believe that a son of his should be so unlike him. Perhaps it's a bit much to swallow, that our son would have inherited his appearance only from me. Zerd was wonderful to me. I have never felt so blissful, so enfolded. His tenderness was a blessing, like a god's. But to Nal, if not to me, the doubt slanted still. And perhaps in that ancient Atlan castle the image of Juzd the ex-regent rose, with his eyes like skies, his hair a summer wind.

'I shall be Emperor. When my father is dead. Shan't I, Mother? Nurse says so. The Lady says I shall.'

'Lady where,' Seka toddled like a reflex echo.

'The Nurse says my father is a dragon. My grandmother was a purple demon-lady. My mother is Empress, that's you. What was my other grandmother?'

'Your ancestors are gods.'

'Bad gods?'

It had never occurred to me to ask myself that.

208

'No, Nal, bright gods.'

'Is Seka from them too?'

'Of course Seka is.'

'So are we special?'

'We are a race apart.'

'So other people are here for us to do just what we like with.'

'You must not think like that.'

'It's true even if I don't think it.'

Sun hurled itself on something behind the jungle. Sun was thrown back again. From just behind the horizon thrust something that stood exposed as the morning mist unrolled.

We stood with our heads tipped back but we could not see to the head of this distant thing. There was quite a strain on my vertebrae by the time I picked out its attenuated tip spiking sky.

'What's that?' Nal whispered. 'Is it a tower?'

I shuddered. 'Oh, I hope not. A tower? That height? Why, it must be miles and miles away – it must have a pretty hefty solid circumference, even though it looks like a needle from where we are.'

'It's all shiny.'

'It's metal. Brazen? Burnished iron?'

'It's an iron rod.'

'It must touch stars at night.'

We keep walking and must have covered fair distances each day. As we have no means of knowing in which direction we are making, except in a general way from the sun, we are simply gathering foot-blisters for nothing. Still, it keeps me from thinking *too* much, and keeps the children quite happy, with an illusion of being busy and getting somewhere. Even Seka is getting into the swing.

Seka can toddle quite happily for a longish time – we don't feel she's delaying us. Where are we making for anyway?

When I carry her my arms ache less than they did. Myself, I am harder and stronger. I am again the lithe girl who adventured the Southern mainland disguised as a boy. But still the landscape itself will not acknowledge me.

The sun fights my eyes, roots snake before my feet, breezes chafe me, the massed colours are simply too *splendid*.

I do not feel at *home* in this countryside.

Odd things happen as one nears twilight. In the day nothing eldritch, nothing uncanny has a chance to get its claws into the atmosphere. Everything is too alive, the foliage too vivid, bird-song too multitudinous, water rippling too joyously, the whole of the day's passage too intense.

We emerge from an hour-thick jungle, brush the creeper-loops from their stranglehold on our shoulders, pick the eager-quivering hairy blossoms from our own hair, and find that suddenly we are on the point of a bare hill with all its grass flowing up towards us in throes of wind.

Over there where the horizon rolls and wallows, jagged forest jigsaws jagged hill-lands.

A herd of milky mares canter from one undulation to the next, gliding their impetuosity, a brief spume cresting the dark hills' long roll forward, and behind them, after a pause in which all the land pulses tranquil fragrance, gallop a herd of gilt-glitter stallions, their streaming manes and their flashing hooves a glint on the edge of distance.

Nal rolls himself into a ball like a defensive hedgehog and bounds down and down the hill.

I cradle Seka and carefully tread the hollows and dips of the steep. The grass flows on my ankles. From below, Nal's chortles and squeals guide us. Seka's dark curls whipping my gaze, I can't see much more than the poppy-petals scampering recklessly on the sky-deeps as the wind rips them from the grass below.

The winds themselves buck like stallions. The rains are brief maelstroms. The land emerges soaked. The sun whirls back in place and blazes from every tip, every point becomes a dagger point flashing a sharp star. The undergrowth steams purple mists. The colours are resurgent, shouting glorious.

But at night the land closes in on itself.

Dusk shushes the nests. Reeds sough. Boughs lament softly. Pallid eyes slit the root-convolutions.

The stars have not come yet. The land is poised, waiting in a pit, under a net. It is breathing fast and shallow. It knows what it is waiting for, and will not tell, by any clue given, and is half-shamed by its eagerness.

We enter a gloam-glowing glade and at the far end a shape glimmers. It is an upright shape, a slender shape, one would almost swear a human shape. I hang back, hugging Seka harder than she hugs me. Nal starts forward, his eyes reflecting that shape. The shape shimmers and melts away beneath branch-bones, among black boles. Perhaps it was never there at all.

Night. Stars splash into the sky. The light is white and blue. Shadows writhe away even from each other.

The land is breathing faster and faster. I push the children into the nearest hiding-hole I can discover. We munch big berries, scenty mushrooms. They squabble contentedly. I can no longer identify the other sounds all around outside.

The last day alone in the wilderness. This was a sagging day to kick off with.

'Mother, what's up?'

'Nal, don't worry, love. I'm fine.'

'Seka's too heavy for you.'

He hit his sister's small bare dangle of a foot.

'Seka, down and walk. You're heavy.'

'Nyaah.'

'Nal, don't bully. Leave the baby alone.'

'Why are you fed up?'

I smiled at him, relaxed by his genuine wonder at me. Hasn't it occurred to him that we are in an extremely sorry predicament?

'I think all this wildness and wideness depresses me, that's all.'

'Don't you love it?'

'No,' I said shortly.

'You would love it if it let you,' Nal muttered.

We climbed. The land dizzied me. As though these were natural grazing-grounds for wild herds, each meadow was a different grain, a different shade. The shades clashed. The meadows all slid at angles from one another. Kaleidoscopic planes, menacing perspectives. Countryside so undulatory it was like walking on an enormously billowy ocean, moving at its own gigantic pace. Rhythms slow as that of the mountains growing.

A single roll of cloud, the size of a clenched fist, scowled in the sky.

'Nal, we must rest. Sit on this slope. If it'll hold us.'

'I'm not tired.'

'I'm deathly tired.'

Grasses crushed yet still visible under its clear crystal hooves, a unicorn picked its way up the slope. Seka crowed. She held out her arms. The beast's rose nostrils flared as it bent to nuzzle her wrists in which the dimples are reappearing. A jut of crystal spiked erect between its tremble-haired ears. It liked my little

211

Seka. She could probably have tamed it (they don't breed in captivity and can only be captured). It shied away from me when I tried to pet it and it and Nal looked askance at each other.

It trotted off, swishing its silver-thread tail against its gentle flanks.

Nal had forgotten the unicorn already. He tensed, he stared into the horizon. Something was making towards us, absolutely belting along. It seemed to bound and bounce across valleys and hills.

'What on earth is that, Nal?'

'It's a dragon.'

'Oh, what fun,' I said tartly, wishing the child would give a straight answer for once, and then the thing appeared over the very nearest hill of all and lo and behold a dragon it was.

It caracoled to a stop beside us. Its rider, leaning backwards to yank on the reins, looked down at us from well above our heads.

I had only time to leap to my feet and tug Seka up too. Nal went close and fingered the brilliant tassels swaying from the studded leather harness. The dinosaur's lean nostrils snorted scorching carbon dioxide.

Still at a slant above us, the rider regarded us. She was quite a little girl, about nine years old. She wore dusty traveller's-gear, leather decoratively slashed to let in the speed-breeze. There was a garland of withered flowers awry over her flaxen plaits.

'How near is civilisation, rider?' I asked.

'You want civilisation?'

'Do you know – a castle?' I found I could only finish lamely.

'The statues' hill with a castle on?'

'It has statues, yes.'

'It's not too far from here.'

'By not too far, do you mean at the rate your beast can travel?' I asked wryly.

'I suppose so.' She looked at me searchingly, without impertinence. This must be part of the aristocracy of the inner continent, a part of Ancient Atlan I'd not met.

I hoped the child would offer us a lift – her steed had plenty of room for us, the saddle was a cumbrous bucket-thing and she took up hardly any of it. 'Nal, don't fiddle with the harness,' I said.

'You go ahead and fiddle, lord,' she said, smiling at each of us. She was a poised, well-brought-up little girl, with clear eyes, green though not spectacularly so.

'Your spurs are nice,' Nal told her.

'Filigree, lord,' the little girl said.

'Can you direct us to the castle?' I inquired.

'I'll take you there,' she said. 'You hold your baby pillion. I'll make my dinosaur kneel and you can easily mount behind me. Lift the Emperor up to me first.'

I nearly stuttered in surprise. Then I said, 'No, he is not the Emperor – his father is the Emperor. But how did you know who we – ?'

'The present occupant of the Throne we do not acknowledge,' she said politely.

'Yet you accept my son – ?' I asked as we grouped ourselves round her on the big saddle.

'Your son has the wild blood, the gods' blood, the darkness-divinity,' she said, settling Nal before her so he could comfortably finger the harness that fascinated him.

'How did you find this out? How did you know us?' I felt distinctly ill at ease.

'Juzd said to expect you.'

'*Juzd?*'

The name was a tranquilliser. I remembered at once the ex-regent, the man whom Zerd suspects fathered my son. Through Juzd, yes, I *had* already been introduced to this aristocracy of ancient Atlan. I wondered how he'd fared after I'd let him out of my husband's dungeon, how easily he'd traversed the black under-Canal tunnel with the faint miraculous glimmer around his bare feet warning away the toads, bats, etc.

'Juzd knows we have lost our castle?'

'You were seen the other sunset.'

'The shape in the glade – ?'

'Many shapes, many glades.'

The big saurian bounded hills. Seka gulped wind and laughter at once and began hiccupping, quite happily.

'Why does Juzd say my son is the right ruler for Atlan?' I probed presently. 'Is it the divine blood from my side of the family?'

She turned and regarded me, the eyes child-clear – on the surface.

'From both his mother and father, is it not?' she said. 'And there is a double blossoming in him, he is a single twin.' Double rotting, I added to myself.

213

How much had Juzd guessed years ago? How much has Juzd told Atlan?

'When did Juzd say this?' I asked the flaxen plaits.

'The mark is on our Emperor's face,' she replied as Nal picked flowers from her hair.

The iron rod, which had been always in sight rising from beyond the world's edge, except when blanked by heat-haze or cloud, now jogged away, getting smaller and smaller.

'How incredible to see that rod diminish,' I said.

She took a deep breath, biting the air off between her teeth, milk-teeth still.

'What is it, a tower?' I asked.

'It is not mentioned ever,' she said, quick and toneless.

The saurian's claws gripped and rejected earth, gripped and rejected hills, gripped and rejected valleys. We moved at a fantastic speed. Still the breeze burned. Still the colours smiled. Birds passed like a streak of bright fire. I stilled Seka's hiccups. Still my son-nephew, beloved by this oldest and newest of worlds, picked petals from the flaxen plaits.

The little girl's knees gripped the deep saddle-sides. The reins slapped the saurian-steed's coruscated hide. The little girl's hands controlled the reins lightly, her small filbert fingernails marked by white flecks like those which hit children's nails after mumps or measels, scabs on her thin wrists indicative of an active life, her heel-scuffed boots jogging easily in front of my own blister-weary feet.

It was night when Sedili's men ambushed us.

The girl had at last slid the ten feet to the ground, then made her monster kneel to help us down. She had not bothered to tether it. It galumphed, presumably happy, in a copse which must have seemed shrubs to it. The girl produced from her hip-slung wallet a flask of sour cider and some cakes of coagulated grain and honey, as if we wouldn't have given our eye-teeth for real genuine food earlier in the day.

She offered first to her Emperor.

'No, pour it in my cup or I shan't drink,' Nal demanded as if he were doing her a favour taking her drink – though he croaked dry as a dune.

'See, it's got dragons on. See?'

The young lady bent to admire the daubs.

I ate quietly, crosslegged. I wasn't even eager to ask her

name, or who she was, how she fits into the scheme of things, what scheme of things. This Atlan is a far, far bigger place than I thought when I first occupied its fabulous Throne. Then I thought I sat at the hub of things: now I realise I had hardly scratched the surface of a new world, I have yet hardly touched it.

'We are beholden to you,' I said with great sincerity.

A definite few moments passed before she smiled.

'You've got gappy teeth. Haven't you?' Nal said. I frowned at him. The girl giggled.

A series of pathetic little squeaks sounded from the trees behind us. I thought fate had overtaken some field-mouse. The girl leapt to her feet. 'Not to worry, love,' I said.

'It's my dinosaur –' she said wildly.

She ran to the trees.

'It never makes a sound except when it's worried.'

Abruptly the little squeaks stopped. As she was about to disappear among the trees, I caught her arm.

'Careful – go quietly. I'll go first.'

At first I couldn't locate the creature's bulk and felt oddly blind. After all, its back was the height and length of a king's tomb. Then I saw it – sagged on the ground – and saw the soldiers beside it, hauling out their spears hand-over-hand, and heard the soldiers guffawing.

In spite of my warning to our little girl, I myself had not advanced cautiously. The poor monster's little squeals for help had led me to expect some trouble like a gadfly or a thorn in an awkward place.

Now there it wallowed in its own red pond, and the men noticed my movement. A hand fell heavy on each of my shoulders.

I said as loudly as I could, 'Leave me alone', and hoped to heaven the children would get the message.

But there was rustling in the undergrowth and Nal appeared by my knees – 'Mother, are you all right, mother?' – tugging his little sister who was crying.

The men seized them too. They laughed louder as Nal threshed and bit.

Of the girl who'd looked after us, whose great steed was dead, there was no sign. I wished she'd been able to drag my babies with her.

Other men were stripping the soiled harness of its huge gilt tassels, its fine-quality straps and old wrought-orialc buckles.

'Why did you kill it?' I asked the men marching us off.

'Wanted to see if we could,' he said simply. 'Thought there was enough of us.'

'It was harmless – can't even have struggled –'

'It snorted a scorch right through my mate's uniform.'

'Pity it didn't singe his scalp off.'

'Now, now.'

'We'll provide you with substitute transport,' said another stupid swashbuckler, tossing me like a sack of spuds into a saddle, and then giving a courtly flourish to make his comrades hoot before he leaped up to join me.

'Not taking her back to camp, are you?'

'Course I am. Any objections?'

'Why not share her here? We're all entitled to a go. You didn't capture her single-handed.'

'No, I used both hands.'

'Hur hur hur.'

'Whose men, may I ask, are these?' I interposed (I felt it was *time* to assert myself) in a disdainful drawl to offset my travel-ragged clothes. I already knew they weren't Zerd's men – not as far from the Capital as this, unless they were bandits which they weren't, and not wearing the red insignia which distinguish Zerd's Northerners from the originals.

'Princess Sedili's.'

'So Princess Sedili's army has nothing better to do than set on neutral travellers – like common footpads?' I sneered.

'She's no anonymous wench,' stated a shifty-eyed corporal. 'We should've known by her transport. There'll be a full-scale search out for her if she don't turn up soon where she's expected.'

'Can't tote her to camp, then, Slicer. Court-martial if we upset the natives. Settles the matter, eh?'

'Share and share alike right here, and then – ' a nasty little trooper drew a grubby hand across his throat with a very nasty little sound.

I tried to speak, couldn't manage it.

'Nobody'll ever be the wiser, even if her mates do find her before she rots,' someone said. Slicer shoved me down out of his saddle and they all advanced at once.

Slicer roared.

'Keep your buttons on, lads. I've staked my claim. Wait your dirty turn, the dirty lot of yer.'

I hoped the corporal grasping the wailing Seka and the

febrile Nal would let them go in order to join the queue and they'd be able to crawl and scramble away. I thought that the Atlan wild might be kind to them.

Slicer thrust me behind him. He brandished a knife.

'In order of seniority – out of our way, Slicer,' said the other corporal.

'I've only to talk back at camp,' Slicer said snidely. 'Then you'd lose them pretty stripes.'

The corporal with my children interposed, thoughtfully chewing a reflective fingernail, obviously an intellectual.

'Take her back with us, boys. There may be a ransom.'

Everybody stopped frozen in their delightful attitudes.

'Might be quite a help – if your pay's as much in arrears as mine.' The reflective corporal spat black nail-rind on the turquoise turf.

Slicer tossed me back in his saddle. Nal and Seka were lifted to me even before I could call for them.

The troopers all mounted their big birds, and we made noisily off into the gathering night, whose sinister aura chock-full of pulsing hostility was quite lost on this gallant little band of intrepid hooligans.

The camp was much larger than I'd expected, and somebody'd had the sense to order it pitched on all sides of a bare hill – surrounded by other wooded hills which screened it, so obviously this one had had to be cleared of timber first.

Discipline unflagging out here in the rolling backwoods, we were challenged by sentry after sentry as we panted our arduous way up the hill, and had to give a succession of passwords.

'There must be thousands and thousands of troops under tentage here,' I breathed.

'Our main Army,' answered Slicer.

I gave a start. My breathing became jerky.

By a stream's clean source, and not target-exposed on the crown of the hill, a very long silky tent rustled sibilant in the star-struck air.

A corporal told Slicer to help us dismount. We were passed in by a burly sentry. 'Returning reconnaissance party, sir,' he announced, coming to attention.

'What are you doing here, corporal?' demanded one of the COs dicing on a rug-covered chest. 'Where's your officer?'

'He didn't bother to come with us, sir,' said the innocent-eyed corporal. 'I've a report to make.'

'Who are these?' the CO barked.

'Captives, sir.'

'*Captives?* Atlanteans? Did they attack you? You know effing blind well, corporal, you're under orders not to antagonise the locals. There'll be quite a little penalty for this.'

'I don't think so, sir.' The corporal permitted himself a yellow grin. 'Isn't our beloved Princess on the look-out for a lady with a little boy and even littler girl?'

The CO sucked in a breath. He looked at me, narrowing his eyes. 'But this lady is hardly dressed in state.'

'Only done me duty, sir. Hard enough trying to keep her safe from the men, sir.'

'You told them?'

'No, sir, kept me mouth tight, sir. Didn't want rumours spread around. Eh, sir?'

The CO paused, then said expressionlessly, 'Right, corporal. I've taken your number. Dismiss.'

'Yessir. Thank you, sir. Happy to be of assistance, sir.'

The corporal saluted and stamped out in the silence. The COs at the chest had stilled the click of dice. The candles crepitated wax over the bottles in which they'd been transfixed, they could even be heard.

'Madam.' The CO showed me to a leather footstool, his own vacated seat. 'Please be comfortable.'

I drew the children to my lap. I hoped they wouldn't catch fear from my clammy palms.

The CO disappeared past an inner curtain guarded by an ivory fretwork screen.

The remaining officers started to drink again, and made a couple of throws, but the atmosphere was very watchful.

The big CO returned. He bowed to me.

'Madam, may I ask you to come with me?'

The children tugging on my skirts, we trailed through that silence.

Beyond the screen, the curtain was pulled smartly aside by a well-polished sentry.

I could smell my own sharp sweat.

The room beyond was hard to assimilate, it was full of the florid flicker of candles of a ridiculously wide circumference stood in sconces as high as Nal from the floor. The flames were going like blowlamps under shades of green and blue transparent silk, so all the shifting colour confused the eye.

Stretched slanted on a pyramid of cushions at the room's far

218

end, a big fair woman extended a foot to a maid diligently applying paint to the oiled toenails. Two COs sat beside the woman, who was studying sheaves of papers. The atmosphere was further complicated by the redolent smoke from the long thin cheroot right-angled from her mouth.

Big eyes, I decided their nearest colour was amber, slid sideways under the lids as I entered.

'I want you to tell me who you are,' Sedili said at once over the roar of the candles.

Useless and humiliating to hedge.

'My name is Cija.'

'Empress!' Sedili bowed gracefully from the waist.

'Please be seated, Empress.'

I would have preferred to stand. She loomed over me when we were both on floor-cushions.

'The little ones too. General, could you find us some refreshment?'

A General's sword clanked against his boots as he strode obediently out.

I said to the left boot as it passed, 'Light refreshments are no use to us. There's not much sense in your bringing anything unless it's a nourishing meal each.'

The uniform halted. He wavered his eyebrows at Sedili. She inclined her head. The candlefleer made prisms of her teeth. Her teeth are so even they seem to be waiting in a queue.

She pretended not to look at me as we waited for our meal, but her eye corners were intent.

'You were expecting me?' I asked, keeping the bewilderment well out of my voice.

'No, Empress,' Sedili said at once. 'Not for definite.'

'Then how for indefinite?' Suspicions of treachery right, left and centre flashed through my brain but I couldn't pin down one of them, surely not even the little girl on the dumb dragon would have been able to send word in time that I was on my way.

The Northern King's daughter merely looked away from me and began to give directions to her maid. 'I want the big nail puce, and don't forget to make it appear as though the half-moon is scimitar-curved –'

Again the corners of her eyes had a sort of tension. She was avidly summing me up, in spite of her pose of haughty indifference.

She was making me feel as small as she could, in spite of the

219

punctilious use of my title in our husband's realm.

Without any pretence of not being interested, I sat with my children and gave her the once-over.

I couldn't see enough of this warrior-princess in this confused light. I am afraid I couldn't get much of a real impression, I was too nervily summing up how many good points she had beside how many less attractive. Then again, what I'd call bad points, would other people (men) call those good points?

This big fair royal woman has known more, probably, of Zerd than I ever will. She has known him as a man, and I hardly have. She even knows what he was like when he was becoming the Zerd I was fated to meet.

How did she stir him, how intoxicating to him was the idea of making her his own wife? How often have his electric hands, his vital body been inextricably love to all of this superb big female? She must have extraordinary talents, a splendid organising ability. She has led her father's Army here, she has kept it here on a full-scale campaign, and yet she looks most female. She's built on an ample scale – all curves as well as muscles, with a chest like a figure-head's, like a hill-range folded on itself – yet she's tall enough to look all proud, no suggestion of squatness, yet she's not as tall as the man who married us both, she doesn't look an amazon. Why can't I find something wrong with her?

She certainly brings all the refinements of femininity to this campaign which no doubt she is perpetuating with all the courage and fortitude of any male commander (from what I've heard, she's no play-actor, she knows what she's doing as far as war-making is concerned) yet not many male commanders would make the time to keep up appearances as she does. And her inner tent is all sumptuous, all little knick-knacks which must be carefully packed up and trundled wherever her men go, just because she cares about the decencies of living.

The General came back, followed by a batman juggling a couple of trays. The aroma of our real food, really before us at last, was absolutely delicious. I could hardly wait while the servant, with maddening deliberation, set out the knives and spoons and skewers and then finickingly set them more symmetrically and I held my dignity with an effort that made me almost tremble, willing my example to prevent the round-nostrilled children from grabbing.

'These plates are extremely fine porcelain, Princess,' I said.

'Your perception does me honour, Empress.'

220

She batted her shapely plump strong hand in front of a wide yawn.

At last we could start. I felt like wolfing it down. It was such a strain even to sprinkle condiments in a relaxed manner.

'How daintily your little Prince and Princess eat,' Sedili said suddenly. 'They must be ravenous, yet they are graceful with their table manners. They've been well trained.'

Though her last remark tempted me to think she was on about puppies, her goodwill seems spontaneous. She has every reason to be wary of me, to dislike me with real venom, yet now she was genuinely interested in the babies. She has a generous heart as well as a generous appearance, I thought miserably.

It is probably as hard for a man not to love her as not to admire her.

She waved the toe-tender to a stop, and started to walk to us across the soft carpets, past her commanders. Then she stopped, returned to her cushions a moment, and slipped her feet into her tilt-toed spangled slippers, before coming to us. This too bowed my head. I suppose we were both brought up strictly, both of us destined to head nations. Yet, though no one could accuse Sedili of being lily-livered or finicking, she is in control of her environment, her background is her backdrop, and she won't even be sloppy enough to walk barefoot in her tent before her men. I really have degenerated, haven't I? What was the use of the loving discipline my nurses tried so hard to form me with? It takes nobility like Sedili to make me realise my every gesture is lazy and scruffy. I can't claim that my adventures have necessarily hardened me. Sedili has had adventures too, but has always been woman enough to remain at the helm of hers.

Sedili hunkered on her spangly heels. I hoped they hurt just where she hunkers. She reached a finger and flicked Nal's nose.

I looked quickly for Nal's reaction. He smiled angelically up at our – well, what was she? Hostess? Captor?

'I'll have a bath, Sedili,' I said. 'Then we'll talk. I want you to put me in the picture in so far as your plans include us.'

'Whenever you wish, Empress. I'll have batmen see to washing Their Highnesses and your back.'

'No. I'll see to that myself.'

'As Your Majestic Highness wishes,' Sedili said after a pause long enough to show me she was amused but respected my caution.

Her personal bath-tent is rigged up of layers of cloth-of-gold on gilded poles festooned with gold and scarlet silk tassels. The bath is the sort you sit in, on a sort of hollowed step I consider unhygienic, and it's all of thick glassy porcelain painted with pink flowers and humming-birds with flagellant turquoise tails. A maid in attendance poured an endless supply of hot water and loofahed my back. The maid had bluish skin, and I realised that just as Southern slaves are recruited from the gold-skinned race, in the North the slave-race is that from which Zerd was spawned.

In view of the fact the maid was present to do the work, I felt stupid when I insisted on staying while the children were washed. But I'm not leaving them alone one instant if I can help it.

As they splashed in the water-gushes, and squabbled, and mendaciously howled they'd blinded each other with soap spray, the tassels swished and two more blue slaves accompanied Sedili into the bath-tent.

The blue slave with us withdrew a twist of towel from the interior whorls of my son's ear and neatly prostrated herself.

'I'm sure you'll forgive the informality, Empress,' Sedili smiled at me. 'The children are so pretty, gambolling at their ablutions.'

I nodded. I willed my nervy hand not to push back the wisps of hair steamed to my forehead.

The steam didn't seem to affect the Princess. It didn't even bead on her robes (shimmery pearl-colour, but unpatterned and plain, of course the best of taste). I was wrapped in a towelling gown. At least she was just too late to see me bare and compare me with herself.

'I see my women did not offer you slippers.' Sedili raised pained brows.

'They did. I prefer to go barefoot.'

It sounded defiantly self-conscious, 'unconventional' or something. It was simply that my feet hurt after the gruelling time they've had.

'Tell me, Princess Sedili,' I said as I leaned nonchalantly against a gilded pole (unfortunately it swayed and I had to redistribute my weight) 'just what *you* are going to get out of this kind hospitality.'

Acutely conscious that the man I suppose I certainly seem to love either did love, or does love, this big blonde, every nuance of my own actions in comparison to hers seemed contemptible. I would have liked to erase the callow brashness from my tone the instant I'd spoken. It was as though, unable to match her courtesy and polish, I concentrated on being as boorish as possible.

She restrained any show of the annoyance she must have felt.

'Please regard yourself simply as a guest, Empress. Most certainly the fact that you are a guest in my entourage means that I myself as hostess am in possession of a trump card.'

'Are you holding me to ransom?'

'I do not need ransom, Empress.'

'I know you're not hard up for cash, Sedili. What else do you want me for? I must be of use bargain-wise.'

Sedili retrieved the soap. Nal received it with another dazzling smile, which Sedili returned. A slave darted to dry Sedili's sloshy wrist.

'I don't believe,' Sedili enunciated as tactfully as possible, choosing words ejected from between a deprecating smile, 'that the Emp – shall we call him Zerd, we both know him well – will sacrifice any military rigging, and hard-schemed footholds he's gained in this War, simply to regain a wife he has left to – well, shall we say to rusticate – for quite a few years now, isn't it?'

His name, bared of the titles, sounds very naked from her mouth.

'Perhaps in that fact lies my security,' I said, but we knew I was talking emptily to fill my silence.

'I cannot believe,' Sedili said kindly, 'that you are of any tactical value in our War. Perhaps I should simply return you and the dear little babes to your country-house.'

'That would be sweet of you, such an end to these horrid troubles,' I gushed.

Her smile broadened.

'You are furious, Empress, aren't you? You don't condescend to much pretence of believing me, do you? Very well, I *am* considering whether or not simply to rid Zerd of his Empress.'

Dangerous, I registered, always dangerous, people who don't laugh when amused in a tense situation, but are so in control of it that they can simply widen a smile.

'I advise you to try capturing the Forest Princess Lara, if you murder me. When I am gone,' I said, 'Lara will remain your biggest obstacle – and she has a doting parent.' Something I never had.

'You and I, Empress,' Sedili flicked Nal's nose, 'are in no need of doting parents. We can fend for ourselves. Little Lara, whom I met back on the Mainland when the catastrophic suddenness of Zerd's surprise attack from Atlan had confused both the

223

Southern kingdoms and my father's kingdom, little Lara is hardly to be considered as more than a pawn. It is her father, that gentleman indubitably to be reckoned with, who is the mover of monarchies.'

'I've forgotten what indubitably means . . . ' I sat on the edge of the squealing hilarious bathtub. I felt dead tired. I felt already dead.

'Lara is not the sort of female either you or I could be expected to like,' Sedili smoothly ignored my emotional disintegration. 'I would dispose of Lara without a qualm. But the consequences, just yet, would be too far-reaching – whereas I am really quite sorry that you, a rival of my own calibre, should be so easily disposable – '

Double depressing deepening to desperate melancholia. I'm going to die – I'm unimportant enough to be got rid of –

It's a big bluff, my mind suddenly said. A big blonde bluff.

She'd say the same thing to Lara.

She knows we all three hate each other. She knows we must all three be played off against each other – only she's making sure she's the one to do the manipulating.

And I dislike her. It's no good pretending I admire and respect her. There's a way out somewhere. I despise her, don't I, only I haven't the guts to admit it in case I'm the only person in the world who could feel so.

'You must sleep in state,' said this perfect hostess. 'And though the infants are welcome to a tent of their own, I am quite sure I need not ask you whether you would prefer them to stay with you.'

'Our sheets will need laundering again,' I pointed out. 'Wouldn't it be neater all round to order the assassination immediately?'

'Please, Empress – ' Sedili limply waggled a pained hand-wave. 'I shall be most sorry if we cannot, perhaps, resolve this entire embarrassment in a very much more civilised way.'

Our pauper belongings had been placed in the sumptuous bed-tent.

'Where's my dragon-mug?' Nal asked.

'Oh – that got broken, dearie, as we moved tents – ' a slave answered.

Nal's pupils dilated. Tears sluiced from his diamond-dot eye-corners. He howled. Hectic flush-blotches sprang to his cheeks.

Alarmed, the slave went to soothe him.

'It was all a mistake – we'll find another mug – '

Nal refused solace. The slave tried to pick him up. Nal went rigid and drummed his heels into the rugs.

Seka and I, too tired to say much, too used to his tantrums to be perturbed at all, prepared for bed.

'Highness – ' the slave tried a firm voice of reason and retreated sucking a bitten finger.

'Blow out the lamp. Leave us,' I said.

The slave retired, draperies whispering apologetically.

Nal's sobbing became punctuated with hiccups, drivelled into snotty snivelling.

The big warrior-female would not think him so pretty now, I thought.

The noises of a night-camp percolated the tent walls.

Nal crawled into my bed. Two thin arms insinuated themselves into their usual stranglehold about my neck. The soft smooth wet cheek heaved against mine.

'Mother, I just hate these people. I hate them.'

I refused the ornate silk things they offered me next morning.

'But your own things are quite travel-worn, Empress – '

They were too polite to say worse, but they must have been disgusted by my preference for these salty grimy rags against my now clean body.

'Give new clothes to Their Highnesses,' I said.

Sedili came in without asking and watched the children being dressed.

'What firm, sturdy little mites,' she said. She crouched and held out her arms to Nal who ran into them and cuddled fearlessly on her knee while she stroked his hair. Fickle brat, I noted in amusement.

'Do you like your new mantle?' she asked him.

'It's got a gold edge,' Nal said.

'So it has. That's because you are a Royal Prince.'

Presently slaves were allowed to fold up the bed-tent. We were ready to mount. The Army was making off. The entire hill was on the move.

'Where are we off to?' I asked the groom who presented me with a shaggy bird to share with the children.

'We're off to conduct you to your castle, Empress,' the groom volunteered.

'What, a whole Army – even if it is a bitty one? Sudden, isn't this? You meant to stay here a long while, judging by the trouble that was gone to, clearing this hill.'

'Right you be. Impromptu decision,' pronounced the groom.

Commotion. 'The big lady has fell off her bird,' Nal told me.

Refusing her groom's help, Sedili had nonchalantly leapt up into the saddle. The stirrup hadn't held. Sedili lay in a most embarrassing position, suspended from her restive steed, unable to extricate her foot and spur from the trap-stirrup, her cloth-o'-gold skirts very tumbled. The women of the North don't wear trousers under their dresses, as my mother's people and the Southerners always do.

I remember how I always thought the Beauty very bold, not because she was Zerd's mistress, which after all was an advantageous position I wanted myself, but because when a wind whipped her skirts her legs were revealed all nude except for the sandal-straps twining to her kneecaps.

Now the troopers were in consternation.

'Fools!' I said. 'One of you release her foot.'

'It is forbidden,' one said.

'It is death,' said a sergeant, 'to lay hands on the Princess.'

'The Princess will unmake that rule,' I said, deciding Sedili couldn't speak for herself. Though her face was practically upside-down, I could see its hectic flush.

'The Princess cannot – will not,' said my groom. 'It is an ancient law of the Northern kings. No man whose blood is ignoble may touch the Princess.'

'Nonsense. Her groom was going to help her up.'

'Oh – her *hand* – but not her – her royal leg or foot – nor anything below her royal waist –'

'This is nonsensical – Call an officer of noble blood, or one of the female slaves who wash her –'

'They've gone to find one –'

Meanwhile, Sedili lay still in that humiliating posture. Though her soldiers were red with shame, and no one stood where it might embarrass her further, no one even dared to step forward and pull her skirt down.

'Her bird may trample on her,' Nal said with a certain relish.

I had been about to go and extricate our hostess. But it annoyed me that my action would be construed as an effort to worm my way into her good graces, in case it might put off my execution.

At this moment a man in a striped cloak shouldered a way from amongst the ranks. He calmly pulled down Sedili's hem, slipped her spur clear of the stirrup, helped her to her feet and smoothly into the saddle.

226

'Is he now to be executed for that presence of mind?' I inquired.

'Oh no. He is a native travelling with us as a hired scout. Our laws will not rule him.'

The man turned, the turn of his head caught at my breath, I knew him before I saw his profile.

We all gangled off, a Northern Army on the march, assassination round the next corner – my first real home, my element – except the assassination would be mine.

An unusually sophisticated campfire meal.

In a tent, of course, not in the open under crude foliage and naked stars. Blue slaves to serve us, gold plate on laundered napery.

'You dine in style, Princess.'

'It is my pleasure to entertain my guests, Empress, in the manner to which they are accustomed.' In that case you're making quite a *faux pas* with all this, I answered her in my head.

We ate the redolent roasts with Sedili's COs, but when the cream and ale trifle was served, Sedili waved a few fingers and the COs bowed themselves out.

The tall glasses, teardrops of air caught in them when they'd been blown, were replenished. The Northern wine sparkled glacier-shiny under the Northern candlelight.

'I am glad you are enjoying your stay with our tents, Empress, humbly though we must live thus out in the wilds of a new world.'

'I didn't say I was enjoying your style, Princess.'

'We have not attended properly to your comfort?' Her raised brows were all that showed me how uncouth I was being.

'A little obtuse, Princess, surely. I don't know whys and wherefores of anything, do I now?'

'Then let me explain. Please feel free to ask any questions of me.'

The children were drowsy after the big food, leaning one each side of me. I caressed Seka's curls, letting them run like black sand through my fingers.

'When are you going to kill me?'

'Oh, really, Empress. Must we harp on this? It is quite possible – '

'I know, I know. That everything may be nicely sorted out in a civilised manner. Then tell me, how did your trooper know so

227

specifically to look out for a woman journeying with a little boy and girl?'

'We had our information from a scout.'

'A spy?'

'Not a *spy*, Empress. Surely the native Atlanteans must be allowed to choose for themselves to whom they owe their allegiance?'

'They have already chosen Zerd as Emperor.'

'But to serve me is not necessarily to harm Zerd,' Sedili pointed out. 'After all, I may soon be sharing his throne with him.'

'Does he know this?'

'He has received my messengers.'

'You plan to desert your father's cause, your father's determination to overset Zerd? You plan to use your father's Army for your own ends – ?'

'Or even,' she agreed, 'for Zerd's. If Zerd co-operates with me.'

As she glinted across at me, her smile became much deeper.

'You are young,' she said gently. 'You don't understand, not wisely. Everything which stands between myself and Zerd must be swept away, even you whom I respect, even that greatest of kings my father.'

'Even Zerd?' I questioned wryly.

'I know him,' she said softly yet strongly. The sound was something like the beginning of a purr in the breast of a lioness. 'He is power-lust, he will sacrifice anything but that ultimate intimate lust. I know how to work on Zerd. He will want me still.'

I wanted more than anything, more than *anything*, to know how much he had wanted her once. Yet I could not ask outright. I was afraid of asking, terrified of being answered.

'I suppose,' I suggested, 'you want this throne for your child – ?' I had never heard of any child being born to Sedili. But I couldn't ask outright whether one exists.

'My child – ?' she looked thunderstruck. 'Zerd never gave me a child,' she said bitterly. Her eyes, though some distance opposite to us, ran like a close touch over the sleepy heads of my children. Does she think she can see Zerd in Nal when she goes over him, I wondered.

'Zerd didn't?' I said innocently. 'Oh, I must have been misinformed. I was sure I'd heard you have a son.'

Sedili sat upright. Her bosom was hidden by the gold folds.

But the revealed cleft quivered like a canyon sensing eruption.

'Are you trying to insinuate,' she throbbed huskily, 'that I have ever been unfaithful to Zerd? I have no children by him, I said. Therefore I have no children. I have never been touched by another man, not since I was joined to Zerd in the sight of the gods. I haven't seen Zerd since my father sent him on that "wild goose chase" which turned to my father's ruin instead of Zerd's – I have not spoken to my husband since he set out on that immense journey in the course of which he gathered you among the other little hostages.'

No wonder she hates me, I registered.

'How came you heard of that?' I asked. 'I wasn't aware that's a well-known story.'

'I should imagine I heard it from an exclusive source – from Smahil.'

When the Princess's voice said my brother's name, Smahil hit my heart – the blizzard-blond hair, the narrow mocking eyes with their blue-tinged whites, the lips that have known every part of me in every mood.

'He's still alive?' My own voice felt tight.

'Perhaps not now. I met him about three years ago, in my father's Northkingdom, after our husband, yours and mine, had used his bandits to drive our loyal men to death in the Tunnel.'

'He was one of the handful who escaped?'

'Escaped with a couple of sword-scratches.'

'He's not with your Army now?'

'He is a Major now. But not with me. I don't know what happened when they had to disband his regiment because it had suffered such ravages at Zerd's hands – he may be here, or with my father.'

'He – he told you – ?'

'He told me you were hostages together, five years ago. I'd asked him if, in Atlan, he had seen the new Empress. He described you well.'

I don't know why this annoyed me.

'Oh, he did, did he?' I said.

Sedili pulled blandly on her cheroot.

'And my friend Madfist,' I went on, 'must have described me even better?'

'It was due to the scout Madfist's information that we were able to meet you,' she admitted.

'I don't know how he found out about my youngest child,' I mused. 'When I knew him, there was only my son.'

'Shall we say, he is simply a good scout?'

Sedili rose. The audience was at an end – in the most cordial possible way. I thought of some comment on how useful Madfist had been to her this morning. But it might not have seemed ladylike. It might even have seemed catty.

I am sorry that the Golds 18th Foot has been disbanded. But of course ours, the twin regiment, the alter-ego Golds that split off to march under Zerd, that still exists. The Northern King has lost, but the Golds still exist. I wonder what regiment he is in now? What uniform? He was all textures in the Golds, all leather and corduroy, flashes of gilt, and all smells, sweat-impregnated leather. I shan't think of him again, there's no reason to think of him.

Like all little girls, Seka brightens up like mad when she's with men. Her eyelashes flirt, her dimples dash about. I like to see this. She's been so quiet lately, all beaten-down and grey-natured, and I know she's been through too much for a nervy toddler.

I hit Nal quite a wallop the other night when I found him terrifying her with bedtime stories of haunts and horrors after they'd been left in the dark. The little thing was trembling for ages after I picked her up to comfort her, and when she went to sleep in my arms she started gibbering. But though I've done my best to put a stop to this, and shall keep a watch on Nal, I'm afraid the harm's done. For his age, he has a loathsome imagination. His stories quite scared me. All this time he's been scaring her without my knowing, and she's a thoroughly upset mite.

So I was happy to notice her looking coquettish and shyly playing peekaboo over my shoulder.

'Who's she flirting with?' I asked Nal. (He's now good at riding beside me on a young gelding, a milky-colour bird who doesn't give trouble, so I've only Seka to hold.)

'Some soldier,' Nal said. 'I don't know what she sees in him. He's stripey.'

My heart flew up behind my tongue. I glanced behind very cautiously. I didn't want him to see me look.

Just the same, Madfist. Unshaven and bold-eyed, vivid with health. Those eyes, well, I could never imagine them flinching or being out-stared. Yes, yes, I have seen that power-charged gleam of a gaze fall, yes. I liked him best, embarrassed.

Hard to tell, being so careful to pretend I hadn't noticed him, but I think he was considering my backview as he laughed with Seka. I didn't turn. But my backbone was just about broken to bits from the effort.

'That man knew you when you were still at the breast,' I said in a low voice. 'But you wouldn't remember him.'

'Wouldn't want to.' Nal flipped the reins.

Tonight, what a meeting of the ways, what savaging of preconceptions. All holes and rents now, my outlook, with great cold winds swooping through.

I was looking forward like the rest of the camp to the promised evening's entertainment.

'Tumblers, native tumblers hoping for a bit of baksheesh,' said the CO with the cauliflower ear. 'But it'll make a change, won't it?'

'I feel as excited as a child at the prospect,' Princess Sedili replied without coyness, and the CO stopped pulling at his supercilious nostril and looked at her fondly, suddenly avuncular.

It was a gusty evening. The COs and Sedili and myself sat at a very decent repast on long tables before the tents, and leaders etc. sat on stools balancing plates on their laps and juggling tankards on their knees, and the rank and file, like an ocean, pressed obtrusively round about. Anonymous-looking animals, all the own work of Sedili's foraging-parties, as she is now economising in a most housewifely way with what's left of her kine and poultry, sizzled on slow creaking spits. The roasting smokes strained on the wind like bucking broncos.

'This is like a picnic,' Sedili said to me. 'What a shame you think your little ones can't stay up for it after bedtime.'

'They get excited up late,' I said wearily. I am finding Nal harder and harder to control, now that he's far beyond the familiar castle-nursery routine, but I'm not telling Sedili that. Let her think I'm a fussing rule-bound Mum.

Quite a princely cabaret the troupe put on for us.

There were even dancing girls.

But I don't think the Army appreciated them much. I've not seen much Atlan dancing. I'm used to the Forest belly-bumpers, the Northern somersaulters or the savage artistry of top Southern dancers like Terez. The Atlan dance is graceful but controlled. Half a dozen girls, delicate little fair wisps, all snow and primrose shades, skimmed around on the grass, their professional dance-draperies indistinguishable at times from the long ferns. Though the dance was wild enough, it was shy too. It was the dance of fauns, not of satyrs.

There was some hooting. But not while the men watched the juggler. The juggler was also a conjuror. I recognised him at once. So I wasn't surprised when he pulled out his pipe.

So far the COs had been paying more attention to their dinner. Sedili was staring at it all wide-eyed as a big child, but her staff officers looked all blasé. Though the meal was exquisitely set, a different fork and knife for everything, attentive slaves rebrimming your goblet as soon as you took a sip, finger-bowls, the lot – the food itself was pretty mediocre. But the officers were more interested in indifferent food than indifferent floor-show.

Yet at the appearance of the piper the aromatic air startled electric.

Each time I hear that devil man pipe, he hurts more insides of me.

He blisters my ear-innards, my blood runs bright.

Very dark now, grease seething on the spitted corpses, cold breezes belching among foliage and around shoulder blades. The pipe, or the winds, ran gooseflesh up my arms. I looked across into the rank'n file and a torch-flare showed me right into Madfist's eyes.

I smiled. Madfist glowered recognition back at me. Hard feelings *still*?

The Northern soldiery must envy this native his acquaintance, not to mention his familiarity, with the local talent. Fauna and flora at once, these. One side of him clung an off-duty dancer, already wearing a collar of lovebites as proudly as if it were a necklet of rubies. The other side of him jutted Goat's Gran, dandling a toddler, perhaps one I knew or a new one, and she sneered across at me as she casually slapped away a Northern fumbler.

I've friends over there, haven't I?

Beside Gran bent a shape more rags than female, the crone who helped hurry Nal into a world hardly cleaner than my diseased womb. They all know each other. Ancient Atlan's underworld. The freemasonry of murder and magic.

The sylph with Madfist waved greeting at another who emerged from the undergrowth back under the trees, trailing after a Red-cape sgt-major she'd just been with. She tried to slip her hand in the crook of his arm. He shrugged her off. She followed him meekly to the ranks where he shoved a corporal off a

232

molehill and squatted down, also taking over the corporal's ale tankard, and interrupting a story being told to tell one of his own the other'd reminded him of.

The little dancer attempted to perch on his knee and twine an affectionate arm round his neck.

He elbowed her.

'Off you eff, slut. This is regimental ground, a grand occasion. Can't you see Royalty's present? Trying to put me to public shame with your smarming up to me?'

The edge of his tankard had caught her cheek. She backed away, blue eyes wide and bewildered. Her hand went up to her face. Blood beaded between her fingers.

The crone and Goat's Gran rose as one.

'You call the poor little cow a slut once more and I'll have your guts for garters,' Gran roared. 'How does she deserve such insult then? Not nicked y'earring then, has she, making out she's nibbling y'ear, has she then?'

'I said slut and slut I meant,' said the sgt-major with a righteous look. 'She's no call to try acting my social equal at a banquet. I've had her. That's that.'

The dancer ran to the crone in a headlong scurry, as though the crone's ragged odorous mantle were a wing to fold her away from the scene.

'He begged me,' she choked, her eyes still bewildered. 'He said he really needed it. He said he thought he'd die of desire if he couldn't tonight. I only let him to help.'

I could hear all this because I was near them. Well, I was straining my ears too. But Sedili was still staring at the piper, hypnotised as though she were an overgrown rabbit and his pipe a snake.

The sgt-major, thankful the Princess hadn't noticed the ruckus, spat into the fire so it sizzled, and drank deep. Either side of his tankard his ring-hung ears were bright as plums. His men nudged each other. They sniggered. The sgt-major felt that spitting had not been a nonchalant enough gesture to show his apartness from the native rabble. Madfist's girl had come over to fill Madfist's mead-mug. The sgt-major slapped her behind as she bent to the huge earthware mead-tap. He guffawed, and smiled as his men laughed too.

The girl didn't look too wildly thrilled, but Madfist just lounged back where he sat.

The sgt-major, still clearing himself, remarked to his men, 'All they're good for, these local bitches,' and tried to pull the girl on his burly thigh – not for sociability of course, his contemptuous probing hand immediately strained to make that publicly plain.

Madfist wandered over.

'This one's with me,' he said behind the plum-ears.

'And who are *you* when you're at home?' the sgt-major turned. He enjoyed the sound of his audience's appreciation. 'More native riff-raff, eh?' he said.

Madfist's ringed knuckles caught him under the belt. The big sgt-major doubled up. He wheezed. Then, silently and efficiently, so as not to disrupt the piping for his Princess, he stayed doubled up, grasped Madfist's legs behind the knees, pulled him down, booted him in the groin while an officious corporal chopped across the side of his neck below the jaw.

I felt the shock quite physically, as if part of the pain were mine. I found I'd groaned aloud.

Sedili looked round.

'They're mobbing your scout,' I said.

'Which?' She saw Madfist, rolled up in himself and his agony. 'But he's the man who behaved so excellently the other morning –'

She spoke a few words in the cauliflower ear, and the CO went across the clearing. He passed the piper whose glance slanted over the bladders of his busy cheeks.

But before the CO reached Madfist, the tumblers and drummers and strummers who'd accompanied the dancing troupe had bounded to his vengeance. Northern troopers sprang to defend themselves.

The CO reached a full-scale brawl. The Atlan daggers were out, troopers unsheathed their swords. A Gold clutched his hand in his armpit. 'Some c . . . 's cut me finger off! Who's had it away? Where's me finger?' 'Don't step on his finger, mates,' besought Madfist, gingerly unfolding himself from the ground and lunging at parts of uniform.

'This is – This is – ' Sedili couldn't find an adjective. She looked flushed and distressed, not angry. Officers waded in to settle the incident, but though the troopers were willing to obey orders to give over, they still had to defend themselves from the enraged Atlantean brotherhood of the road, and the officers didn't want to hurt these natives of the Continent they're trying to conciliate.

The girls stood wringing lily-limp hands, chewing rosebud finger-nails.

Goat's Gran held her baby straddled over one poke of her pelvis, while she bashed a meat-spit over the sgt-major's skull. The crone crouched gibbering. Blood slimed the turf. The piper had done a vanishing act.

Sedili held hands over ears. '*Oh*,' was all she said, but with what disdain.

The children will be woken, I thought. I picked up a whole roast partridge wrapped in spice and made for our tent.

A joggy journey. Zigzag to avoid this, then that. Blood on one's sandals, a stray cut on the shoulder. Deafening yelling, curses gurgled in adjacent throats, men sobbing rage. I lost direction, over and over again, then found I was under the trees and sat on a stump covered in creeper, fairly cosy till I heard someone retching nearby.

I started up. Madfist stumbled out of the gloom.

'Madfist!' I said. He clutched his belly and lolled his head against a tree trunk, his closed eyelids swollen and his mouth open groaning. I wiped the traces of unsuccessful vomit from his jaw on my wrist, which I hoped was comforting and cool in spite of the hot partridge I'd cradled. His groans sounded like snores, they just kept coming out of the open mouth, but he opened his eyes and they glinted shrewd through the puffy lids.

'What are you after, Empress?' he asked thickly.

'Simply don't like to see you set on, old times' sake,' I said.

'Set on, f . . . ,' he remarked. 'I did for a few of them myself, don't you fret.'

'OK?'

'I'm laughing now. Give us some of that.'

He picked oozy fruit-rind and herbs off the partridge.

'Go on. Have a chunk.'

'Too rich.' But he took some, and sat beside me to chew, going 'p-p-p' regularly as he spat grease.

'Didn't expect to meet *you* here in the invaders' train,' I said. 'But then, if it weren't for you I wouldn't be here either. I hope you collected a nice reward.'

'Fair.' He wiped his fingers down the side of his boot, leather nearly velvet with age.

'Whatever you get, I'm sure you should demand more,' I said. 'After all, it is blood-money.'

'What are you on about?' Madfist broke off a twig and started to pick his teeth with it.

'She didn't want me for ransom, you know. You've handed me over to be got rid of – permanently, if not painlessly.'

'She's bluffing – or you are.'

'Or you are,' I snapped.

Madfist stiffened. I could sense beside me his old urge to shake or bash me. Quite nostalgic, it felt.

'Why hasn't she got rid of you yet,' he inquired, 'if she means to?'

'I think she's keeping me for company a while. To gloat.'

'If she was merely making use of you that way, why hasn't she handed you over to us in the rank'n file? Sure she'd find that gloat-worthy. Very frustrating, her bastards are finding it, forbidden to assault our Atlan chicks because it'll put us off voting Sedili for Queen.'

'I should think Sedili's so used to frustration she'd hardly notice it in her soldiery – she must breathe it by now.'

'How come?'

'She's still faithful to her husband. She hasn't seen him for just on seven years.'

'Don't you believe it.' Madfist expertly unwound gristle among his molars. 'For one thing, it's common knowledge she and the foreign Emperor – your lord, eh – met up together for the parley after the Christening and the break of the siege – before you were sent off secret to safety. And very friendly they were then.' I saw the whites of his eyes swivel slyly. 'Only for old times' sake, of course.'

'So?' My heart hammered. I didn't feel emotionally grieved, just as though I'd been sledge-hammered.

'Then, she's no screwed-up grass-widow.'

'She told me very sincerely she's not been touched by another man since marriage – '

'There's touch and touch, isn't there.' Madfist kissed his fingertips lyrically into the dark. 'Ah, it's all woman that one is.'

'Madfist – you mean, you – '

'I'll not boast and bandy her high name around. She's all woman, and all Princess too. She's taken care of me.'

'And even Goat's Gran too?'

'Someone had to, didn't they, since you got old Goat murdered?'

'Madfist – I *didn't* – '

'If it hadn't been for the fuss over you, your thundercloud-stranger would never have stuck old Goat – clink and crash, and blood over his waistcoat of helpful little bottles, and no more Goat. I'd have got that black-jawed champion through his stink of a heart if I'd been able.'

236

'That man was your Emperor.'

Madfist whistled.

'Your husband – Sedili's foreign obsession? Well, well, to think I nearly committed regicide.'

'You weren't very near murdering *him*, don't worry.'

'Don't you kid yourself. Only days ago, I could have tickled his ribs with the barb of me dagger.'

'*Days* ago – ?'

'Just before Sedili picked us up, bless her high wide and handsome heart. Shall I bore you with the whole story?'

'Please.'

'A fortnight ago, maybe less,' Madfist said in a once-upon-a-time voice, 'a nasty storm broke over our heads, that's the Gran's and mine and her brats'. It was pissing down with rain. And thunder doing its pieces, and lightning setting the kids off sure they're blinded. So we bolt for the nearest byre, it belongs to the old ruined castle on the haunted hill. We're wakened in the morning by soldiery with rakes and pitchforks and suchlike wild weapons of war.

'Off they take us to their garrison, which is minding the old ruin. And their Major bumbles at us through his ginger bristles. Till he sets eyes on Gran's two older brats, that is. Then he says, We're keeping these and you can eff off.

'Keeping them? Gran bellows out weeping like the thunderstorm all over again.

'No, says the Major, kind and stately. *Adopting* them. They'll be companions, playmates to a little Prince and Princess. A great honour to you and them he says. Honour my arse, says Gran, you give me my brats. But they're marched away and we're thrown out in the sodden morning.

'Going mad, Gran is. Goat would have broke his mushy heart to see it. It even gets on my nerves, and I can stand plenty of wailing and gnashing of.

'If it's not mine.

'She's got to be kept happy, up to a point, and now she's a long way off that point, making my life unsettled, can tell she'll be no good at cooking, nor purse-slitting, nor company in the furze on a rainy night, till she's got her rag-tag-and-bobtail back. So up we go, up the hill ahint the statues again, to see if we can snatch the children back.

'Stealth, we take a lot of care, tippy toes. But the castle's in uproar, not thinking of childer-snatchers at all.

'The Empress is gone, and Their Teeny Highnesses too,

237

everyone's saying. And everyone's searching under floor-boards and blaming everyone else.

'Then even more confusion, they're all half round the bend by now, as a little band of bird-riders comes caracoling up. And *they* ask for the Major, and when he comes they ask for the Empress. And Gran and me, roosting in the ilex across the extremely stagnant moat, recognise their leader under his shabby hood, as that dark stranger, snaky line of beard and all, that made off with our little Empress and her son quite a while ago now, from the Red Inn.

'If, as you tell me now, he was the Emperor, it beats me why his Major didn't twig. Ah, I suppose he'd not seen him years, and not ever never close to, and the hood and the beard (not generally bearded, is he?) and the general shabbiness and most of all the lawlessness, the air of a dangerous adventurer, would put him off the scent.'

'Wasn't the Nurse there?'

'Sallow hag, breasts to her belly? – yes, but very haughty with him she was, didn't know him at all.'

'A tall woman with very blue eyes?'

'Didn't see one like that. Only a coppernob, a cosy armful. She was carrying on. Don't know what you desire audience with the Empress for, stutters the nerve-wracked Major, but she can't see you. And the copper bit breaks in: She's gone, her and the little Prince and Princess, gone off with my man Scar, there's witnesses and proofs and a pretty scandal.

'The hooded dark one was interested as I was to hear of a baby Princess's existence. He was grim, He asked details. Only the abandoned armful would deign to tell him much – she was full of it. Descriptions of a small red-haired man with sinews up his arms, supposed to be kidnapped by the rapacious Empress.

'The bird-band galloped off.

'Gran and I looked at each other in the ilex. That's more pother about our servant-girl at the Red Inn, turned out to be an Empress and saleable, I said. Where's my sweetlings, Gran said.

'We glimpsed their little faces at a window. Oh, very jolly they looked, new clothes all clean and noshing a fair old meal. Poor babas, growls Gran, we'll rescue you yet.

'But the drawbridge is up and there are sentries everywhere, sharpening spears and polishing fingernails. After a couple of hours, I pull Gran away by the scruff of her neck.

'When we scent the foreign Northern horde, I'm for lying

low, making off with a couple of their chooks by night and leaving no prints in the dew. But Gran, as soon as she hears they be on their way to storm the Castle and take the Empress, offers herself and myself – information valuable, scouting-service invaluable.

'Have you gone crazy? I say, shaking her big teeth down her bigger throat.

'The Army'll feed and roof us, she says. And it'll break into the Castle for us. No one else could do that for us. Get the children back.

'This girl Sedili. She's done a lot for us. Meals, tent. Respect. She knows how to treat a man, whether she's a Princess or not. Why did your husband ever leave her?'

I rose.

The sound of the brawl had long since died. The night itself was dying. The winds were about as warm as a dog's nose. The partridge was congealed.

'So have you any idea *why* she wanted us, Madfist?'

'Some, Empress. What are *you* going to pay me for all this information?'

'I've nothing to pay you with, Madfist.'

'Maybe not. But you could give what Sedili gives, apart from pay. Wouldn't hurt you. Doesn't hurt her. There's touch and touch, you see.'

'I mean to be completely faithful, not just technically,' I said haughtily.

'To the same man, eh?' Madfist chuckled. 'Then, begging your pardon, Empress, how about the last night we met?'

'That would have been gratitude – honest sincerity, gratitude for what I mistakenly thought was your disinterested befriending of a waif – and despair. I thought you and Goat were my only friends.'

'We were your friends.'

'You plotted to sell me.'

'No. Goat thought you'd fetch a pretty price – He looked on you as an *objet d'art*, fond of you Goat was, never harm a fly that lad. And look what happened to him because of you. *I* plotted to keep you.'

'Oh well.'

'So you no longer feel any gratitude?'

'I'm drained of such sentiment, Madfist. All relationships are a hollow pretence, we're all out for what we can get – aren't we, Madfist?'

239

'I don't know, Empress dearie. There's Gran,' Madfist said, seeming serious, 'and her hunger to get the brats back. Perhaps she only wants them to bully but then again I don't think so. It's mother love, that's a sacred bond. How about you and your own little ones?'

'They are stones weighting my neck. One day they'll drown me.'

'But you don't sling them off, do you?'

'Don't try to get me sloppy, Madfist. Most of it's duty.'

Madfist's arm folded me against him. I leaned back with a tremendous sense of luxury. His fingers stroked my forehead and twined in my hair.

I *will* go too far, I thought. Even if Madfist kisses me, I'll lose all my self-protection. I'm so lonely. My mind tells me what seems like companionship to me is only the other thing to him. My pride tells me he'll hang another scalp on his bandit belt, both wives of the foreign Emperor have given him under camp-ment starshine what they give the foreign Emperor in his carved gold bed. But my loneliness tells me Madfist's strong gentle fingers are a talisman against loneliness.

Madfist's tongue slicked across my gritted teeth.

Madfist walked me back to the tent. Drowsily I leaned to one side against him, let him take my weight. The whole of the inside of my mouth was still thrumming, like a ghirza string twanged to too much vibrato. In fact, the whole of the inside of me was still thrumming. I felt profoundly shaken, shaken so hard – as though by an earthquake or interior volcano, brutality of molten lava – that I was completely relaxed. Ready to sleep my heart out.

'How about inviting me in for a quick nightcap?' Madfist suggested.

'The children –'

'I shan't worry them. I'm interested to see how the little snow-babe turned out.'

'What's that – music?'

There was a dim light already soft in the tent. The children were sitting up in their beds. The piper, saffron back to us, pro-longed a lilt for them. Nal's curls were bed-tossed, his eyes fixed staring in an ecstasy glazed as a little corpse's. Seka looked quite vacant, her mouth hanging happy, eyes almost crossed.

'He's bewitched my children!' I sprang forward.

The piper turned. He looked at me, at the relaxation easing

every line of me, at Madfist's arm all about me. His pupils dilated disdain.

'He came and played music to us when we woke and cried because of noises in the camp and you never came,' said Nal.

'Doesn't talk. Man play,' Seka said. 'Man only all play.'

The piper sheathed his instrument in the waist-scabbard from which a dagger hilt already protruded. He passed Madfist and myself. As he left the tent, the glow of colourless light faded.

I have never felt so shamed, no not even after I had welcomed incest with Smahil, not even after the Governor. The Governor was so terribly far from being my fault, I fought that till my soul was tattered and my body only a new kind of pain that lasted for weeks. If you think about it coldly, I could have refused the sin with Smahil. But I love him, perhaps because he *is* my little big brother, and I shall never be rid of the repercussion of the single dark.

There will be no repercussion from the Madfist incident, I mean I shan't find I've conceived. But I wasn't in love with him. I don't even like him. He has used me since I first brought him breakfast at the Red Inn. I deserve every atom, every ounce of the shame I feel.

I thought, when I was a Tower-fresh child, that I'd never know shame more corrosive than after the Governor. But now I know fully, as I didn't fully know after Smahil, the self-*invited* shame heavy as filth, of which one will never feel clean.

Back to the tent with Madfist's strength supporting me, for five minutes pretending to enjoy an illusion that I was no longer lonely, falsely uplifted by a silly gladness that at last I had tasted Madfist's vigour I'd always wondered about – thoroughly *used*, in fact.

But the glance of the Ancient Atlan piper, looking after my children while I was out tumbled by the bandit in the bracken, made me see myself as I am. I am lower than I have ever been, lower than any girl I have ever felt smugly able to despise, lower than the big Princess with her golden largesses of 'fidelity'.

Oh, well, now that I come to think of it two days later, it wasn't too bad was it.

Yellow dawn, we reached my Castle.

Sedili waited another day, determined to fall on the meagre

garrison, lulled by years of inactivity, after lights out.

A man was flogged for making too much row singing as he darned his chain mail with steel thread and possibly betrayed our presence. Rag was stuffed in his mouth so his shrieks would do no harm. Sedili is a fine commander. She boxes clever and makes double sure. No chivalry from our big Princess when it comes to war. Or love.

Nightfall, we slunk up the hill.

'Now we settle to the long business of starving them out, do we?' I said. 'No, take the poor buggers by storm,' said the groom. 'What, Sedili's birds can fly, can they? It's a wide moat for them to skim,' I said.

Sedili deployed her entire Army out of sight just below the steep hill-crest, except for a hundred or so of the advance cunningly concealed amongst the jetty ilex. She set me on my bird, Seka in my arms, Nal to the side. 'This scout, being the only man out of uniform, will ride just behind you, only just behind,' Sedili murmured at me.

Madfist's dagger pressed under my left shoulder blade.

'He will stick you, Empress, with a total lack of ceremony,' said Sedili, who must be familiar with Madfist's lack of ceremony, 'if you make any sign to your garrison that you are not alone.'

We moved to the moat-edge. I could smell the stagnance. 'Don't press so firm, Madfist,' I said. 'The point's already cold through my shift. A jog of the birds, and I'll be bleeding down the hill.'

'I like the contact with your shoulder blade,' Madfist remarked.

I call to the gate-tower.

'Open up! This is myself.'

Black silence. Then a scrambling, a light leapt in the black window jutting over the moat and a ruddy reflection oozed across the water stiff as brocade with lily-pads.

Sentries out on the battlements. Flambeaux flowering. Lantern flashed at my face – again, and lingering unbelievingly on the children, on the man who was not Scar but only a single vagabond.

'Empress!'

The drawbridge's underside, all moss and decaying planks, creaked down. The chains squealed their enormous pig-squeal. The portcullis heaved up, slid down, and was reeled successfully up into darkness among the owls' nests.

'Empress, Empress!' The Major led his sentries and night-dress-billowy women and wakened sight-seeing soldiery across the bridge as though it were a red carpet he'd unrolled at me.

Sedili's men glided from the high untamed shrubberies. Knives pressed on the Major's men's adamsapples, shifting slightly to allow for the nervous swallowing, and the Major stopped buckling on his cuirass so that the straps swung loose in their owner's bewilderment.

More of Zerd's garrison gaped on the bridge and battlements, and throwing-spears lifted at aim.

Sedili rode forward, her white bird's claws pocking the frost-feathered ferns and grass. Her pale silver leather mantle fell in folds chilly as the waterfall whose near spray beaded it, her hood of black jet cast a faint filigree of shadow on her face.

'Shoot,' she invited the spearsmen on the walls, 'and your Major, your Empress and the Royal infants die. You are surrendering to Sedili, Princess of the North.'

The dark Army surged up till the hill was all one surge. The ancient drawbridge groaned under the continuous tons of weight. Sedili, in her own name and not her father's, made her entrance to my old Castle.

'Hardly a storming, this conquest,' I observed wryly, later.

'Ha,' said Sedili, 'you would have preferred me to take a few lives if only your garrison could have taken a few of mine?'

'Zerd's garrison,' I corrected.

'We shall soon see whether he still wishes to claim it. I have just despatched my latest message to him.'

'You've had no reply from the others?'

'You are always *interrogating* me, Empress.'

Sedili signalled that the Major's cup and mine should be re-filled. Madfist touched-up the slave as she obeyed. Sedili twitched a frown.

'We may none of us be long here,' she seemed unable to stop talking. 'And though it's the first siege I've stormed for myself, I can't really say I'm proud of it. Those cobwebs! Like great swathes of curtaining! There must be generations, tribes of spiders scuttling and peering down at us from those swinging mazes up under the rafters! I'll order those broomed down. There has certainly been stupendous lack of cleanliness here in your – short absence, Empress.'

'I've always preferred those left, Sedili. They are somethings' *homes* and don't trouble us.'

'They don't?' Sedili wafted smoke-rings from her cheroot.

243

'Do you enjoy the toadstools pushing up between the flagstones of your passages? Leprous-looking. And stag-beetles indulging in pitched battles in the fungus on the cellar walls? It seems quite an incarceration you'll be occupying down there, Major – I didn't *mean* it to be so like putting you in a dungeon, merely keeping you away from incitement of your men, under lock and key below stairs.'

'Below stairs here is also below moat.'

I peeled a fruit for Nal who trustingly spat the pips out in my palm. He would keep trying to hook Sedili's smoke-rings on his finger. Sedili noticed and navigated them towards him.

Madfist hunched by the fire on the giant hearth. He snatched yams from Gran's toasting-trident and sizzled them into his mouth. The reunited brats tumbled nearly into the flames, wrestling and tugging each other by the matted hair.

The Major, partaking of his last meal with us above moat-level, though as Sedili points out he'll be most honourably in custody down in the cellars and it's more his fault than hers that they're pretty vile, looked pensively at the brats and then across at me. 'I hoped you'd be happily surprised on your return, Highness, to find I'd adopted some ready-made companions for Their Highnesses and so obviated such immediate necessity for home-grown ones – It has all turned out so different.'

'It would have been a lovely surprise, Major.'

Juzd, I thought, must be the only person in Atlan who could have made himself quite at home in the poor ginger-Major's position. Just twiddle your toes and generate a few beams of light. . . .

'When are you returning to civilisation, Sedili, as obviously you are beginning to pine for its niceties?'

'I try to take its niceties wherever I go. Living hard on campaign holds no terrors for me,' the Northern Princess exchanged creased-eyed smiles with the child on my lap.

She means her camp is nicer than my Castle.

I don't think anybody is happy here, except Gran who can bash her hand across her brats' faces and backsides again, and the Nurse who is excited at being reunited with Seka and Nal.

Nal and Seka screw up their noses and wriggle away from the Nurse's pendulous-bosomed embraces. 'You smell of armpit,' said Nal for which I promised him two nights without supper. 'Want Lady,' said Seka.

The Nurse looked blank and hurt to the point of misery.

Then she tried to smile brightly round at us all. She has lost another tooth since we left.

'Frellis should be here,' I said severely, hoping to hear Frellis' whereabouts without making the Nurse feel her presence unimportant beside Frellis' absence.

'No one has seen Frellis for a long time,' the Nurse said. She spoke hesitantly. For once she added no Castle gossip, offered no explanation. Seeking comfort, as though Seka were a little furry kitten or puppy or warm muff, she scooped her up and cuddled her close. I willed the child to be too sleepy to try wriggling away.

'No one has *seen* her? Ridiculous,' I said.

'No one – No one at all – ' Nurse's voice wobbled like a turkey's. 'We don't know a thing – not even if one of them soldiers have cut her up – '

The Major stirred protestingly.

'The little ones are asleep,' and though Nal and Seka were wide awake, Sedili yawned so a smoke-ring did a blue belly-flop. 'We shall retire.'

So everyone stood up in the middle of their conversations, except Gran who continued to glower contentedly by the hob.

Sedili relieved the Nurse of Seka. At first the Nurse didn't realise the foreign Princess was taking the baby from her. Then, instead of that involuntary clinging-on, she released her into Sedili's arms and simultaneously, as if it seemed a very real surrender and defeat to her, she dissolved into sobs, burying her tears in Seka's dark ringlets.

'You are overwrought, Nurse,' I said conventionally. I meant to pat her on the shoulder but I found her clinging to me, shaking and crying. I clasped her and smoothed her hair and she was so shocked that she shot away as though I'd stung her, gulping apologies.

'The woman is incapable. You and I must bed the babies,' Sedili said to me. She was itching to get unbuttoning little buttons and directing incompetent chubby fingers with dimples instead of knuckles, bed-time-storying and mug-of-warm-milking, tucking up and 'Sleep tight, watch the bugs don't bite' and kissing bye-byes. She is kinky about kids.

The big Princess has a maternal instinct the size of a bear-hug. Probably she's postponing my death till Nal has time to make a painless transference to her as mother-image, and probably she wouldn't resent me so much if it weren't that she thinks I have done what she couldn't, borne Zerd an heir.

We each shouldered an infant and set off through the Castle corridors. I had the candlestick and a little dripping of tallow accompanied our steps like an echo softer than that from the stone, or like a pattering companion.

'Were you *comfortable* here?' Sedili presently asked with a sound of awe.

'I passed my days in a melancholy so heavy and fecund it was almost tangible, so tangible I now feel nostalgia for it so it must almost have been pleasant.'

'I think I would have wasted away here.' Sedili's voice held horror. The dank stone, the dark and decay all seemed loathsome to her.

'We have been brought up differently, Sedili. I know little of the Northern Court, but weren't you reared to gold splendour, shining spaces, saluting soldiery all gleaming, jewels set in everything you touched?'

'Every Royal house is so.'

'No, Princess, I was brought up in that Royal shabbiness that only the most ancient dynasties can evolve, accumulate and evolve.'

'Sooner the hard life here,' she said vigorously, 'than the splendour there with every man whose voice is broken, unless it's cracked again in senility, away here – and the women left with only each other and birds for company. I hear half the Northern babies born now are beaked and feathered.'

Two figures cannoned into us from a side passage. What terrified us was not this collision in the dark, but the bigger newcomer whose instant reaction was to fling himself forward down. He got a flying tackle on Sedili's legs below the knees, bore her to the stone.

'Nal – !' I cried, sickened by visions of his head splashing on pavings as Sedili loosed her hold on him. But he had sprung clear and stood beside me, with the strangers, regarding Sedili. Some of her hair was down. Her bosom heaved. She looked frightened, and younger than usual.

No wonder we had been given enemy treatment even before our faces were glimpsed. I recognised the smaller figure. That old man.

'Scientist –' I said, not knowing how to address him.

'Upstart-empress,' he crackled salivatory.

'Oh, you are acquainted –' Sedili looked happier. She glared at the bigger figure. 'I will accept an apology for your clumsiness. No bones broken – even more fortunately for you than myself. You may hand me up.'

The tall young man, whom I'd never seen before, made no move to help her off the ground.

He didn't even look at her, not once. He kept his eyes fixed on the old man. Seka stirred convulsively in my arms. 'Oh, *Lady*!' she cried.

The boy – or young man, hard to assess the age of such a hefty yet shambling, concentratedly servile yet agile figure in such dark – did not take his eyes from his master. Yet something about his gaze tugged my memory.

'What have you there, old sneak-thief?' I asked. The scientist cradled a collection of bottles much as I cradled my daughter.

'Don't take a high hand with me, little alienity,' the old man mouthed. 'I may have been foraging in your pantries and chests, not tonight but plenty nights, but you're in no position to play righteous.'

'You can set your hired tough on us. We'll have our guards called to us within moments.'

'You haven't tried it yet, I notice.'

The old man tapped his assistant on the arm.

'If I ordered, you'd kill her for me, wouldn't you?'

Still the younger did not shift his gaze from the master. He didn't *glance* our way.

'He hasn't even nodded, old thief,' I said. 'He is more aware of our soldiers' danger-potential than you are.'

'Nod.' This time the old man accompanied his command with a vicious rap of his cane on the big boy's wrist-bone. That must ache, I thought. Slowly, stiff, the boy's neck-muscles tightened and a violet vein throbbed in his throat. He is repressing his anger, I thought. But the throbbing intensified till his head had gone up once, back down, then stopped. It had been an effort to nod. This accorded ill with the panther movement he'd used on Sedili.

'Are you blank of any instinct whatsoever? Co-ordinate, think constructively!' the old man barked, robes quivering pregnant.

The young man didn't apologise, but he drooped like an enormous flower wilting, dejection and shame in every line of him.

'The lady wants you to nod. Therefore nod *to* the lady the information you would willingly kill her.'

The young oaf, or idiot, or whatever he is, turned sham-

247

blingly to me. He repeated his nod. And he was thinking the kill. Obviously one of the few words that meant anything to him. His hands, out of proportion, very large indeed even on the ends of his big rag-sleeved arms, clenched up and then the fingers opened out and worked through the air towards me.

Seka gave one shriek. 'Lady!' Then she fell to gibbering and gasping.

The idiot's eyes, glowing direct on us from the mildewy gloom, were the fine unforgettable intellectual gaze of Lady Frellis. Even the dusting of mascara on the lashes was hers. Seka had the horrors. She was impossible to soothe. Her sobs came one on top of another till they seemed two or three at a time, and shook her entire shocked body. She gulped for air like a drowner given up hope.

The old man, still cuddling the bottle of acids and poisons in glass bubbles, suddenly tittered. He set briskly off into the maze of stone. The boy lurched after him, the sinews of his body still rippling murderously where his stinking rags revealed them.

'Friends of yours?' Sedili leaned on Nal's shoulder to rise weakly.

'I knew of the old monster. He laired here before our arrival.'

'The young one (if he is younger) is more the monster,' Sedili shuddered.

'Then you don't know the old one. No, the boy is merely his slave, his animal, something feeble-witted he has press-ganged to his service since I last knew of him.'

'Did you notice that – boy's – arms?' Sedili said.

'The hairs were black on one, red on the other,' Nal said.

Autumn again. The leaves pour down. Big falling saffron leaves looping over and between anything that moves beyond the old walls. Drifts of russet piling the crumbling terraces. Corpses of summer foliage.

Seka hasn't spoken since we encountered the two madmen in the dark. The dumb piper (I believe he must be dumb) had some effect on her, linked effectively with the trauma of being glared at by her Frellis' eyes from the twitching murderer's face.

Each dank day finds me, so far, still alive.

I can't officially go farther than the terrace. Sentries (Sedili's, now) stand armed at every cracked corner, leaning against every accordion-pleated pillar.

But I know this labyrinth better than they ever can. When I

am sure snide eyes are not watching me from behind, or from peep-holes in the walls so thin, so honeycombed with decay made respectable by a cover of plaster like net that slugs find it easy to seep in and out of the rain, leaving oozy shimmery slime-trails over things, I can scurry to the hole in the ceiling and lever myself up on to my roof.

Up here the wind flaps the sky. Wind bubbles in the chimneys. Wind scatters the clouds and they dash about. Turrets are lassooed by light.

I can't come up here too often till my escape with Nal and my silent little Seka is properly planned. I don't want to rouse Sedili's suspicions by being missing frequently.

A magnificent cavalcade cavalcading up the steeps. All at windows and arrow-slits.

'Flags flappy like smoke,' Nal says. Seka's nose flattens to pug-shape, stuck to the window-glass like a rubber suction sticker.

'All old gold and high-stepping claws,' says the Nurse.

'My messenger returning from Zerd – with far greater honour than I sent him with,' says Sedili.

But once the cavalcade has high-stepped across our drawbridge, it is discovered to be far, far more than a returned messenger.

The rightful Emperor of Atlan (I shall always think of the golden boy who abdicated for Zerd as the rightful ruler) is seventeen now. We haven't seen each other for long years. But he recognised me at once, before Sedili could introduce us at that night's banquet.

'I hope I see you well, Empress?' It is very odd to be called Empress by the ex-Emperor.

I don't like to ask about Zerd's health. The boy's manner is so poised, so calm and cool. He has grown up, but like a forced hothouse flower, a sophisticated diplomat before his time.

Not a bad banquet, though improvised all hasty. And then Sedili's tame fiddle players in the gallery are shushed and the ex-Emperor stands up to make a speech. He thanks us all for our kind welcome. But he is not here merely to visit us, nor to fraternise with the enemy, charming though the enemy is – this is a very bold pleasantry, but the enemy Princess smiles.

'I am among you now,' says the boy whose clear high voice still seems to linger before any 'I' as though it should be a 'we', 'to make a Proclamation.'

Stillness throughout the hall, even mastication stills in case it covers the boy's voice in individual eardrums.

'As you doubtless all know, Her Northern Highness Princess Sedili was expecting a messenger from our Majestic Emperor the great war-lord Zerd. Princess Sedili had informed the Emperor that his Empress Queen Cija was no longer lost in the wilderness, but safe again in this Castle in which he long ago placed her – owing to Princess Sedili's safe-conducting of her here under Princess Sedili's own personal escort.

'I am come in the messenger's place. I am come to assure you all of what you might have disbelieved from any lesser messenger. I shall ride about our land calling this Proclamation, telling it in inns and noble halls, and it shall be posted in gold letters throughout the land for those that can read it, sealed with the Emperor's own seal.

'There have reached our Majestic Emperor's ears two accusations concerning his Queen Cija, which accusations no one can sit our ancient Throne if accused of. Witchcraft and unlawful fornication.'

The hall broke into a buzzing like a gigantic wasp-hive.

'Therefore, from this moment, the woman Cija is no longer Empress in this land, and no man shall call her Empress nor keep her unlawfully. Tomorrow she shall be taken to the Emperor.'

It was hard not to pitch forward and vomit.

They might have told me before the hall was told, if only five minutes before, I thought. I might have been able to control myself better. Now everyone, every trooper and scullery-scrubber and camp prostitute has seen me go white. Thousands of eyes have watched me to see the bile rise up to choke me, and have seen it.

Sedili herself filled my goblet.

'Ah, Empress – but no, I must call you Cija now, mustn't I – this decision of Zerd's grieves me even while I must confess I worked for it. Now that I know you, I cannot but feel for you.'

So you arranged public humiliation on a grand scale.

The banquet broke up when the torches guttered. 'I shall see you tomorrow, Cija, to bid you a fond farewell.' Sedili picked her way between drunken sprawlers, finicking with her skirts so that they shouldn't be seen up by any prostrate snorers.

Madfist rose to follow her. But as he reached her, Sedili glanced at the boy ex-Emperor and brushed Madfist haughtily aside.

'I have no use for you tonight, Atlantean,' she said quite clearly. 'Sentry the woman Cija to her room and make sure her door is locked from outside, her key removed.'

Madfist helped me as we scrambled down the rocks. The salt air soughed stiff in our nostrils.

We crouched beneath an overhang. The sea screamed under the rain. Waves roared in their own hollows and canyons out there. They banged the boulders just below us. Every now and then spume shot high in a spout of a pillar, blanched and very sudden in the starlight.

'She is a bitch, that fat foreign whore,' Madfist growled under the beat of rain and night-sea. He felt his humiliation as I felt mine, he who had adored Sedili, he's quite celebrity-conscious.

'Now for our friendship's sake, Madfist, tell me how all this came about.'

'I'll tell you because you're neat at clambering through little secret roof-holes and I'm sorry about the way things have gone for you.'

He picked up a hula-legged crab I'd almost sat on. It tried a savage little nip. But his blunt fingers pinioned behind its head. It spun in the spume-light as he hurled it down the cliff.

'Simply, as I could have told you before, Sedili was afraid to bump you off. She didn't want Zerd's anger and vengeance, just at a time when she's hoping to call off hostilities and crawl back into the marital bed – and on to the marital throne.

'Back at the Capital, the forest-lord who I believe is father of Zerd's second wife Lara, is getting fed to the back fangs with Zerd saying *Maybe* I'll divorce Cija and remarry Lara. So this Lara's father delivered an ultimatum: Are you, or are you not, going to sanction our riding out right now to this here Castle, killing Cija, so she's definitely out of the running and no reprisals, and you marry Lara all fair and square – she's Empress and I'm the Emperor's father-in-law (and a power behind the throne)?

'Zerd refused point-blank to have you killed. He cut out the tongues of anyone who knew which Castle he's put you in.

'Sedili's spies told her he was in trouble with Lara's father because of this.'

Smash wallop bang bang bang went the waves on the precipice.

'Sedili sent a message from here, to say that she would call off the war, turn traitor to her own father, desert the cause of the

North eventually to serve it by a merger – give her father's Army over to Zerd's use against Lara's father – if only Zerd would take her on as his concubine, second only to yourself. Tact, eh? *She* knew better than to demand the crown right away.

'She added that she was with you here, having taken the Castle without taking one of its lives. And she gently added that you had been unfaithful to Zerd with a man called Scar (witnesses available, including a girl called Yula) and that you are well in with a known magician resident, secretly, in this Castle.'

So he is tired of me. Too much trouble, no returns. He certainly believes tales that I'm unfaithful. He may even believe I'm sticking pins in wax images of him. Perhaps I should. He has a chance not just to avail himself of Sedili's Army, but to have again this dazzling woman to whom he dared to raise his eyes in her father's gold-paved Court. The first love is always the true love.

'But I was hanging about,' said Madfist, 'when the little boy arrived this afternoon with his big news for her. And she was amazed that Zerd was actually deposing you before giving you a trial.'

'Do you suppose that's why I'm being taken back to the Capital tomorrow?'

'Of course, little ex-Empress. Stand a fair trial.'

I looked aside and up. Madfist's profile was dramatic, all dark with silver highlights, grainy skin. His arm encircled me, all lovely and warm and strong, and pulled me against the wide straight shoulder.

'I wonder how things will turn out. I wonder how things will go for the babies. I need a tutor, especially for Seka. This is when I most miss Frellis – when it becomes obvious that if Seka's dumbness lasts, she'll need above all else someone loving and patient to teach her to read and write. Or she'll never be able to communicate with the rest of the world.'

'She did used to be just beginning to chatter, didn't she?'

'Oh, yes, it's psychological of course that she can't make a sound now. But happening at such an early age – I doubt if she'll know how to speak ever again. Even if the block in her mind lifts, she won't ever have learnt to talk. She won't know what to do.'

'Don't you fret a deal? And don't be frightened about getting back to the Capital. *He'll* take care of you.'

'Not if there are political pressures, he won't . . . Sedili says, he's all power-lust. And Sedili is all Zerd-lust.'

As so often, I tried to conjure Zerd's image in my head. It wouldn't come. The eyes came, but nothing else. Then the eyes turned into inky whirlpools out in the sea, and they whirled as if they would suck my gaze and down and down.

'I want to kiss you,' Madfist said in a humble tone I knew must be part of his arsenal.

Sedili's leavings, I said to myself. But so what? *I* didn't want to leave him.

He lay me on the rocks. 'They're all slippery – I'm scared of sliding –' 'I'll look after you.'

Madfist was different. He was violent yet tender in little unexpected ways, each a little surprise that made me want to cry.

'Cija,' he said presently, not moving his mouth from my ear so that his first use of my name tickled like a feather boring into my brain, 'I don't trust Sedili nor your Emperor. I'll help you escape.'

I tried to sit bolt upright, but found he was too far across me.

'Stay still,' he murmured. 'No need to jump about. Do you want to escape? Or do you want to risk the Capital? Are you longing to see him again?'

'Oh, yes – No – What's in meeting him for me? I'd like to get out of it all. This political maelstrom pulling tighter and tighter – I've been in it for five years. But I never chose it at all. I've a right to a life of my own, doing something I want to do. Not just playing a forgotten wife, a wife-in-waiting, a forsaken Queen all palely loitering – till I am pulled into the pit of the maelstrom just because I married someone famous. And I am executed. I have collected children along the way. But I'll look after them with my life if I am allowed a life for myself.'

'I'll take on the little ones too. I'll ditch Gran and hers. I swear to you – Cija – I'll guard you and save you and make you happy. It'll be the life of the road, but that's not bad. Oh, I swear to you, there's no double-dealing this time. I'm not planning any plans to sell you or hurt you in any way. I'll always keep you safe and happy.'

'There'll be a dragnet for us out over the land. You'll be dragged into it –'

'You're naïve, not knowing this land. Who'll be after us? The combined Northern Army, together again at last under Zerd and Sedili? This is a *continent*, this Atlan. Not a big kingdom. They haven't a chance of knowing its reaches. Huge wildernesses, whole countries are still unmapped, inland seas uncharted. But I know the road, that unboundaried road that winds and wanders all over. I know its fellowships and its secret bolt-holes, where to hide up and where to go underground and where to fly free as whooping herons. Will you come with me? I would be terribly glad. I would, little exile. But it means you decide to leave your Emperor.'

'My husband . . . '

'Decide tonight. Decide now. There's not too many hours till dawn.'

'I'm with you, Madfist.'

'We'll go back and get your children.'

I made to rise but he groaned and said, 'Stay. Five more minutes here. Little fast minutes. Oh, even the faint wax in your ears is like honey.'

It seemed the most miserably shattering thing anyone had yet said to me. Smahil said that once to me, and at first it shocked me – especially as it implies I don't wash as often as I do – and then I treasured it. But it must be a sort of accepted phrase. Smahil had not coined it after all. Neither had Madfist, who must have heard it from the same Northern troopers Smahil picked it up amongst.

A heavy depression emptied my heart. Red skeleton leaves blew down on us. Madfist made some suggestions, since we weren't risking my pregnancy. I agreed to the mildest, and listlessly let him bare my breast. It hardened instantly in the biting storm-swirled air so that it hurt when his tongue and teeth touched it, though the inside of his mouth was as hot as the spray was cold. Madfist's saliva was gentle as Nal's and Seka's had been. I hoped he'd finish soon, when I could get the children.

Torches flashed across my face. Madfist sprang up, an automatic reflex, and pushed me further under the overhang.

Sedili and the boy ex-Emperor were helped by torch-waving slaves, down the wet rocks towards us.

'See,' was all Sedili said. Madfist was too late to snatch my dress back over my breast.

Sedili's troopers stared impassive, none letting me off the hook of their stares. Some of my own sentries were sallow with anger, I supposed at Sedili's interference, till I realised they might be bitterly ashamed of me.

'I expected this,' Sedili said silkily. 'She has been missing several times recently. I knew she must have a secret hole out of

254

her rotting home. I knew that if I sent the Atlan scout with her, she would corrupt him as she has corrupted others. This must be added to the report.'

The golden youth nodded. Two men with him scribbled on pads hung at their belts.

'Seize them,' Sedili ordered casually.

Madfist's sword parried at first. But there were too many of them on the slimy cliff. We were seized.

A seagull dashed mewling shrilly, piercingly, before Sedili's face. The breakers boomed and swashed.

'The man who has dared to use the body of his Emperor's wife will be tortured tomorrow,' Sedili said. 'If he lives after nightfall, he shall go free. But he will never be able to dishonour another woman's body. And he will never be able to boast of his crime.'

Clever, competent Sedili, I thought. Cut out his tongue and he can't tell anyone about Sedili and her technical fidelity.

'I shall set out tomorrow with the woman,' said Sedili. 'Let her lord judge her. Now throw her into some locked room high on the walls.'

The stars were spinning. The stars were whizzing white wheels.

Still it was not dawn when the lock creaked and three figures skulked in. I pretended to be asleep and didn't move. Someone with garlic breath bent over me. I shot my nails into the face.

The figure started back with a curse. It was the old scientist. Sedili swung a dark-lantern. It had not got his eyes, but big scratches grew scarlet and pulsed on his face as I watched, though the skin hadn't been broken.

'Hush, hush,' Sedili said to me. 'Here, Empress, it's courteous to name you so, we come bearing gifts. You are Royal after all, you shall choose the manner of your death. Drink of this cup here. Or test the blade of this fine antique dagger, honed so sharp the edge of the blade is nearly transparent.'

'Or my assistant will strangle her with a twitch of his capable hands,' offered the old man helpfully.

'What have you done with my children?'

'The little speechless one can be smothered with her little pillow, tossed down the cliff. Pity, but she'd only complicate the succession. But the heir rides with me to Zerd, since I can't give Zerd one of our own. He's a fine child, that one. One of my generals has been trying to jolly him out of asking for you. *I*

255

have a little boy at home, just like you, my general beamed. I doubt it, the child replied polite but icy.'

'How will you explain my non-appearance at my trial?'

'On the way to the Capital, we were set on by bandits and lost you. I suppose you mean to choose the poison? A more feminine way to die. In fact, the dagger or the – er – hands are only in case you struggle at the cup-brim. You see, the poison takes some hours to work. You will set off with us tomorrow before all these Castle witnesses. Not till we're under way will you collapse.'

'Is it painful?'

'Not unreasonably so.'

'I hope you have trouble burying me. If I'm found, even in decades' time, it'll be obvious I died of poison – and by whose hand.'

'I have given this gentleman here a fine supply of chemicals and in return he has provided *me* with a handsome bottle of something in which you'll dissolve as soon as it's poured over you.'

I looked at the three of them.

'You make nice friends, Sedili. Do you know what this boy is? An ectogene, a homunculus. I last saw him stretched stitched together on a laboratory slab. All he lacked then was eyes. He is an amalgam of all the old man's victims.'

'I should have given you the drink at the banquet without telling you,' Sedili mused. 'But it wasn't quite ready. Also, I didn't want you to die before you had played farther into my hands – as you did play, most effectively.'

The homunculus, throughout our conversation, stood like a rag doll at rest. Except that it was upright on its feet, it was as limp. Its great uneven shoulders hunched. Its patchwork hands dangled, fingers now and then giving a jerk like the reflex of a cut-up conger.

Yet it was not a robot, not a machine out of use till switched on again.

Its eyes – Frellis' beautiful dark brilliant blue eyes, now so unnerving – were fixed for the most part on its creator. But as the conversation veered, every now and then its gaze shifted. I think it was trying to co-ordinate as he had jeered at it. Often it looked at someone who was not talking, but I could see it beginning to note that people who opened and shut their mouths were talking people. It opened and shut its own mouth, silently, which till then had hung slack as an adenoidal child's.

256

Horrified as I was, up against the barrier of death, I was awed and shaken by the scientist's feat. Truly, Atlan has fostered great esoteric knowledge. I had read in my Tower of man's urge to copy the gods and produce life. But I knew it as an impossible dream, like alchemy, a Fata Morgana darkly bright on man's horizon. Now here in a morass of stone crumbling like a mouldering cheese, a foul old man had stitched and seamed together who knows how many murders, and by some means breathed life into the unmatched nostrils. And the thing *lived*. It walked. It perceived. It struggled to understand. And it closed up its slack mouth as it saw that real people did so.

Now the homunculus made its first independent action since that lightning-speed tackle with which it had brought Sedili down in the passage as soon as it saw people other than its master. It moved over to the window-slit. Its body, that was now one body but had been dozens, all stiffened together. The hairs on the back of its neck raised up.

The scientist, alert to every move of his creation, turned from Sedili and said, 'What do you see?'

The thing struggled to explain. But its vocabulary wouldn't supply even the first noun and verb. It was obviously disturbed – or perhaps stirred. It seemed excited, yet pleasurably so, without yet knowing what pleasure was.

The scientist shrugged and began to explain to me and Sedili the subtle workings of the poison which might be the last taste I'd ever know. My tongue dried to a leather consistency. I tried to swallow, couldn't.

A long howl reverberated through the room. Sedili looked round, staring. She'd jumped – we'd all jumped. The thing at the window still held its head thrown back. Saliva flecked its sharp teeth.

'*You must never howl*,' the scientist said.

The thing's rolled-back eyes, Frellis' blue eyes blazing feral as a wild dog's, flashed. This time it did not hang its big patchwork head.

'Fool!' the scientist's hand slapped across the big jaw. 'Learn, learn! There are things in yourself you must control, and remember, use your memory, you have one, I shall make you wish I'd never raised you out of the blood and slime unless you learn to control those things in you.'

The big hands, that had belonged to two separate victims of the scientist, lifted and jerked of their own volition.

17   257

Storeys below, blows shook walls. There was a hudden hub-bub. Yells, a bell clanged alarm.

At last my two assassins hurried to the window. The thing there was loth to move aside. The scientist's cane struck it across the shins. 'Let us see!'

Seeing, they drew deep breaths. Sedili seized my wrist. 'Drink, at once.' I bent to the cup till the liquid fragrance dizzied my nostrils. The drink was the colour of syruped straw-berries, smelt wholesome, nourishing. I dashed it from Sedili's solicitous hand. It hissed across the rug, not soaking into the wool. A fly alighted in it and sizzled.

'Strangle her,' Sedili ordered homunculus. It hung its mouth again and waited for the order to be confirmed by the voice it was trained to obey, its creator's. The scientist had forgotten me. 'They will harm my laboratory!' he shrilled.

He flung open the door and dashed up the passage. His creation rushed after him. Sedili said, 'This is *ridiculous*', and clamped my wrist in her big hand and pulled me in her gloomy wake.

'What *was* outside the window?'

But she wouldn't answer. Meanwhile the din from below rose swiftly, storey by storey, towards us.

'Surely a brawl would be quelled by now? Are we being attacked? Who would have got past the moat and defences, who could be troubling your vast garrison?'

The way to the lab wound, like a long stone corkscrew.

Sedili began calling the scientist.

'Wait! Finish my work first, have him kill her, it'll take a few moments and then I can leave you and attend to the threat below.'

But the shape ahead squealed back, 'They'll fire my labora-tory! I must save my precious work!'

Sedili forced me to spurt ahead and we caught up the other two. The scientist had just reached his big studded door. I stumbled. The thing reached a hand and pulled me up. 'Oh – thank you – ' I said. One of its ears pricked.

'Thank you,' it repeated.

Inside the lab the retorts and tubes were all asparkle and aquiver, everything ticking busily away, all mended. I had not been here since the red man Scar and I had been captured.

The cacophony from below at last caught up with us. The door was burst in.

I expected soldiers, friend or foe. But huge wolves leaped

through the door as though they were flying. And with them ran a handful of men, that could hardly be called men. Striplings, garlands of something or other acockahoop on their heads and round the waists of their skins – garments, not tunics, just pelts with the hair still on, slung from one shoulder.

'Hold. Explain yourselves,' Sedili barked.

The wolves were better at barking. Before they could bury fangs in our throats, the scientist had shoved us through into a smaller room. This time he did not forget to lock the door.

'What are they – ?' Sedili babbled. 'Ancient Atlan,' said the scientist. 'It won't hurt me. It's you, Empress – ' he meant Sedili – 'it is after. But even now it is destroying my laboratory – those forest predators, careering around, wanton destruction of what they can never understand – listen to them, listen.'

He was almost beside himself. Tear-spheres rose up in his rheumy eyes.

'How did those wolves and apemen get in?' Sedili demanded.

'Bounding across the moat – '

Suddenly he whirled on homunculus. 'My maps! The oldest things in Atlan! Probably the most precious of everything precious in there! Get in there and save them!'

'Where are they?' the thing's rusty voice issued from the un-dead throat.

'In the marqueterie cupboard. Break open the door.'

'What do they look like?'

'Don't you know yet what *maps* look like?' the creator screamed. 'I took you a round of everything in there and made you repeat the names. *Use your memory, what were you given a memory for!* Get in there.'

'The wolves will make an end of him,' Sedili said.

The scientist unlocked the door. The howls and crashes from the lab increased. The thing gave its own howl. It rushed into the pandemonium. The scientist locked the door, with difficulty for there was pressure from outside, and leaned against it gasping.

'What is happening, old fool?' Sedili cried.

'Ancient Atlan has been aroused. I don't know by what, but I know it is against you.'

'Why against me?'

'You are the alien.'

'Those wild monsters out there had opportunity to attack me the long while I've been in their forests.'

259

'Something has aroused them all together. They are usually never together.'

Something scraped the door, three times. The scientist yelled 'Is that you?'

'I've got the maps,' announced the rusty voice.

The scientist slid the door-bolt. The homunculus squeezed in.

'Give them to me, give them.' The knuckly old hands grabbed the scrawled parchments, then brought them in a backhander across the thing's mouth, squashing the superfluous would-be helpful statement, 'Here they are.'

'There is one missing! You didn't pick it up, did you? Did you? You left it there! And there's one mangled, mangled and torn! *When will you learn?*'

Frellis' eyes were bewildered.

In spite of the fact I knew how Frellis must have died to give sight to this monster, how the last thing her eyes looked out on was a vivisection-knife, and how their last expression as hers was helpless agony – I stopped hating this thing. It hadn't asked to be patched together.

'I must get down to my Army – it can't get up to me, having no idea where to find me,' Sedili determined. 'My men should have crushed this odd intrusion by now. A wolf-pack and several berry-crowned boys against an organised, disciplined *Army* . . . '

'Leave the door locked now till they've done their worst,' the scientist warned bitterly. 'You don't know what you'd be facing.'

'At least, now tell your assistant to finish off this usurper,' Sedili indicated myself.

The old man considered me. He lifted a lip and cackled.

'May I die a death more horrible than I deserve,' he remarked, 'if she at least isn't out of the way for you –'

He had hardly finished the first part of the sentence when a low growl bounced off the walls. I thought a wolf had got in. But his creation, gladly obedient to the last, was arching forward, fingers flexing. As those victim-fingers hooked in the scraggy old windpipe, the taker and giver of this life tried to scream – 'I didn't mean – fool – fool –'

I'd never seen anyone strangled like that. This was not a tightening round a throat, not a final constricting of breath. This was a frenzied but unstoppable scrabbling, the literal tearing-apart of a throat. Sedili could hardly believe it. She ran for the door, preferring the animal wolves. But on the way she doubled up sick. I had an impulse to hold her head. As always when out of control of a situation, she looked intensely young and vulnerable. I could see the splendid child Zerd had dared to covet. And I can't when she's being splendid.

I tugged at the bolt. The lab was a sparkling debris. I was afraid to step forward on that unsteady sharp ice-rink of shattered glass. But otherwise it was empty. The stuffed old woman lay with her rockers in the air. The stuffed alligator twitched lack-lustre scales. Ancient Atlan had gone.

I hurried down the stairs. I knew Sedili, to whom the thing was accustomed, would urge it to follow and finish me.

Outside the arrow-slits the dawn was paling. Stars started somersaults. Gods, no, they were sparks – red, white, blood-orange. We had indeed been fired. Old wood, all this Castle that was not older stone – that must keep the Army busy, quenching that.

Lower. I could hear the roaring flames. Shadows swung past corners before I could see what cast them. Running men. Soldiery frantic. Water relayed in buckets from the well and scummy moat was not enough. Acrid smoke. Men coughing even as the wolves got them.

My men and Sedili's combining forces to fight fire and forest. Ancient Atlan attacking men whether mine or Sedili's.

The wail of the pipe froze my blood.

I grabbed Goat's Gran as she pulled her knife from a Northern throat.

'What happened – ?'

'She were going to cut my Madfist about. I called the Forest. I called the piper and he called they great wolven – '

Ancient Atlan, now that it had been called together, had indeed taken a hand. This was far from a desperate revolt by a handful of wild youths leading a wolf-pack against a garrison. In fact, I even saw a couple of the boys – or what were they? It was hard at times to tell their sex, unbearded as they were and maned – lounging back on the stairs, plucking the herbs and berries from their hair and waists for a snack before rejoining the battle. Of course, the fire now raging was a decisive factor. But it seemed that the Castle itself was against the intruders now that the Ancient Atlan had wakened all at once. The pipe whirled like the smoke. Atlanteans ran to safety across galleries but the pursuing soldiery hurtled in dust haze and crashing timber as the balustrading filigreed with rot-growths, suddenly caved in. The flames were little tongues licking every limb of a soldier who had raced through a burning arch, but the wolf who leaped through it after him was unscathed. The wolf caught him. His flames were extinguished.

I stepped across a swathe of fallen velvet. I stumbled. 'Gods – there's a body under this –'

'The curtain fell on him and suffocated him,' Goat's Gran said. I wondered if she knew she made it sound as though the curtain itself had been part of the Castle's sentient hate.

'Where are my children, Gran?'

'How should I know? Mine were got safe to the byre when this started. Perhaps he thought to save yours too.'

I tried to find the piper, to make my way to him. He would know. But the wails of the diabolical instrument came from every side by turn.

Then I saw Juzd! Oh my grey-eyed pedlar, calm and wisdom and safety in this weirdest nastiest of confusions! I pushed my way. Up the stairs, past a doorway that was a sheet of fire. Dodge a man waving a javelin, on to the beacon of the blond head – and it's not Juzd, not Juzd at all. Somehow I was so sure that Juzd was really behind all this, that Juzd would know why Ancient Atlan had been set to ruin Sedili's stronghold when the call went out that a bandit was to lose his manhood, that three times I was so certain I saw Juzd I made my painful way to his side and found someone quite different.

I thought I was going mad. I rubbed my eyes. As I opened them, once more I thought I saw that particular profile looking coolly over the glorious flames. I shook my head and made myself sit on the creaking wood of the nearest staircase. Fighters swayed past me, up and down the treads. Black specks floated around. There were smells one tried not to identify. Everything was burning and crumbling. But I must go into every room. I must not leave the Castle before I am sure I can't find my children, now left by Sedili's guards, alone, whimpering for me or perhaps for Frellis not me, hope already lost and *yet* hanging on, on, to that last . . .

Gods. Help me find my deserted babies. I've never been any good to them. Now I'm letting them die. I'm letting them *burn* . . .

I started crying their two names, which were soon running into each other. My throat seemed to crack. From every side, above the howls, the grunts, yells, roaring flames and collapsing timber, high frantic children's voices answered, still not quite believing they had heard me – and they hadn't, I hadn't, it was only the pipe, terror-panicky little Seka unable to answer anyway, call again, they're *somewhere*, or already – no, they're alive still, my heart and my hope and the beating of my blood tell me that if I can find them in the next few minutes they'll be still *safe*, but the few minutes are passing and my throat won't call and the Castle is redder than any tomb of an inn and is collapsing about our ears.

Madfist bounding towards me. Sedili emerged from some flame-gusty corridor, the tendrils of hair still damped to her brow.

'Madfist! Give me *any* idea where my babies would be – '

But the hate-tenderness Madfist felt for me was nothing beside the hate-adoration the Princess had hurting in him. His face was set, glowing scarlet. He knocked Sedili against a wall with one sweep of his arm when she tried to elude him. Sedili shrieked. The froth from his mouth flecked her robe. He had been in her before two of her COs, incredulous with horror at his blasphemy, sheared his head off. They dared not help Sedili up. She lolled against the wall. 'Zerd, forgive me, my Zerd, forgive me.'

I had to go to her. I so much hated to, that I nearly walked past her. I knelt.

'Sedili, let me smoothe your dress.' My own clothes still smelt of Madfist. 'Oh gods. They've killed him, did you know?'

'I've betrayed Zerd – ' She wouldn't lift her eyelids. Tears ran from under them, rubies in the light. I wondered if she knew who I was.

'No, Sedili, less than ever you did – They killed him for you, the scout is dead – all this is going on, but it began just because you were going to castrate him – Sedili, oh Sedili, tell me where my children are.'

'They are safe.'

'Not if they're in this Castle. Which room?'

Staff-officers converged on me. Blades glinted, red in blood and fire. As Sedili continued to moan with closed eyes, I dashed up and ran.

Up against a gusting tapestry, the ex-Emperor of Atlan stood at bay among a half-moon of wolves. But none would lead and leap first. The boy was afraid of Ancient Atlan. I remembered all Juzd had told me of Ancient Atlan's respect for his equally ancient straight-lined dynasty, yet simultaneously contempt for the simplicity into which the safe centuries had lulled the gold citizens by the coast.

'Emperor – ' I'd forgotten the boy's name. 'Where are my children?'

'Call off your devils.'

'They are not mine. They are the piper's.'

'What piper?'

He knew nothing of the Ancient. 'But you must know where my children are.'

'Sedili knows,' he said.

'Are they in the Castle?'

'Sedili will see the heir at least is safe.'

'Sedili is incapable of seeing to anything.' I flung away from the boy. An oak beam crashed down where I'd just stood. The spiders-webs flared up, a sequined shroud, an evanescent net briefly ablaze, sparks spattering. The boy who had denounced me leaped desperately into the main hall, but he was all right: the wolves kept their distance still.

'Nal! Seka!'

I was too weak to dodge when I saw the big shape of the homunculus staggering down stairs that were half not there.

Its head moved aimlessly, side to side, and as the flamelight caught its teeth it was obvious these were at least part of the wolf in it. This explains some of the odd *wrong* look of its large head – even the jaw and the rest of the skull were not meant to go together.

It saw me. It shambled up to me. It handed me something. I saw it had faithfully clutched to this moment the old man's maps.

'Thank you,' I said. I smiled at it, and looked at the maps, and put them in my cloak pocket with this Diary, as I would try to show pleasure in the gift of a feeble-wit child.

But I don't think this quintessence of all hybrids understood even the idea of a gift.

'Thank you,' it repeated, as once before. I hated standing looking into Frellis' eyes, yet I was afraid to turn and go on searching for my lost babies, in case it remembered its old orders to kill me, though they'd been Sedili's orders, not its master's.

I tried a sickly smile.

The thing copied me – or rather, it stretched its lips. But there was no smile in its eyes – I suppose not much in mine, either – and its gaze was beseeching. I'd never seen such a pathetic look.

'You are very very lost, aren't you?' I said.

It did not know to nod to agree with me.

'I tell you what to do,' I said. 'Your master is gone. Now I am your master.'

I wondered if it knew the word master. I said everything slowly and as clearly as I could for the row round about.

'We must get out of here. It is dangerous. We may burn,' I said pointing earnestly at the flames. Could it sense danger in the heat and noise and sparks? 'People may try to stop us going. You must stop them.'

I moved forward. It moved after me.

It dragged its foot through a pyre that had been chairs and two men. A low growl told me it was angry at the pain it hadn't had the know-how to avoid. Its ragged cross-gartered legging was on fire. I must beat it out, but would it construe that as attack? Still, I need this thing's strength with me, I thought. Can't let it burn.

I said, 'Your leg is hurting. I shall stop it.'

I bent carefully above the huge foot. Oh, I don't know what foot that was. All hairy toes and curved talons, veins like map-rivers. I beat the sparks out of the legging. It let me.

We came to the main courtyard. It was hardly recognisable. The drawbridge was down.

Sedili's top COs raced at me. 'You! Stop. You are under arrest.'

Swords surrounded me. 'Stop them, they are *bad*,' I said. The homunculus lifted one above his head and dashed him to the paving. Flames were reflected in puddles of every sort of liquid, rain, brains, blood. Another CO had a sword at the thing's belly. The sword was twisted out of his grasp, and the metal too was twisted.

An entire wall heaved and crashed down.

For moments I thought I had been deafened as I limped away over the candy cobbles. The thing thought, then gravely presented me with an arm to cling on to for assistance.

I said Thank you and it said Thank you.

The moat smelt treacly. Dawn crept pallid on the hill. We followed it down among the shards. The statues were hardly any of them upright. 'Has there been an earthquake?' I wondered. Statue after statue lay toppled. Many of them had fallen on members of Sedili's soldiery. They had fallen sprawled. I didn't like the way they had fallen. The marble arms seemed to hold the soldiers in scabrous embrace.

Just over the drawbridge we paused. My long home tumbled behind us. Spires and turrets spiking the dawn suddenly disintegrated. Fire shot out in sheets over the drawbridge. Stones bounced in a fiery avalanche. The homunculus stooped. It had picked something from the debris.

'He is another me,' it said.

I saw what it had picked up. It was Madfist's head. I ran. The thing ran. I wished the world would end. It was ending. The world was all over.

Everything was not all over. The byre had caught alight. The hay was aflame. Straws whirled everywhere. The faces of the prostrate statues glowed, no longer marble but bronze. And from the byre the children ran, scurrying, scampering, rolling down the hill, clutching at the ilex but laughing. Goat's Gran's brats, all hair and grin. And Seka.

I swooped on Seka. I cradled her. I would never, never let her go again.

'Little one, little tiny Seka. You're all right. Where is your brother?'

But she could not tell me.

Seka is warm as toast, cosy as a largish potato baked in its skin. Sleeping with all the organic enthusiasm of babyhood – every breath a whuffle like a badger with flu, her soft saliva gathering on my skin – she fits me where she curls against me. But though I am equally dog-tired, I can't sleep. I can't.

Back in the wild again, and by now I am good at snatching its sustenance. Berries, roots – we are more used now to empty insides and also better at hunting out this meagre diet. Autumn, too, though colder and bleaker in the wild, is almost easier to eat in than the turn of summer. Scrogg-apples, and big ripe juice-dark berries everywhere.

But this time there can be no more aimless wandering. This time every minute, every instant is a danger and I dare hardly sleep.

Now I know for certain what kind of threats the Wild does hold. Mad beasts and madder men. Beings of every kind. I had to step, carrying Seka, over men, many of them mine, parts of whose poor bodies had been purposely pulped by the toppled weather-scarred statue bodies. I *know* I saw an entire Castle which, once ignited, burned out of sheer malice. I know I saw a swathe of curtain suffocate the breath out of a man.

Every tree I lean against for shelter may feel malignant about it.

Atlan's Wild is no home for myself and the little girl, who

266

deserves life if I don't. In other continents, living wild means some rough refuge for the hunted. But not here. All sorts of things are abroad here.

I can't get the homunculus, hand-toting Madfist's head, out of my own head.

Where is the man-made misfit now? Is Madfist still with it? It might be behind this tree even now. It might have discovered stealth. Who knows what weird suggestions for sport or 'duty' can enter its mind from all the unliving ingredients there?

I have noticed a definite pattern in lives I've watched. My own pattern appears clear to fate. The tower and the flight and then the tower again. And Kond's head bounding across the cave floor. I felt about Kond exactly as I felt about Madfist . . .

Is it unlucky to love me?

I suppose unlucky women always ask themselves this. It's almost conceit. Making one's myth, a secret bitter-tasting yet gratifying image for oneself. The fatal femininity, the praying mantis deadly to the male who is nevertheless fascinated, irrevocably . . . But mainly I am unluckier in love than those whom I interest. And the two people who really have got excited about me, have led meteoric lives.

Smahil, unless he has by now died gloriously in battle somewhere or other, is a nonchalantly-martinet Major in some uniform which no doubt suits him fine though it may also look flamboyant on him. Zerd is Emperor.

You never loved me, Zerd, did you? There was passion, and even tenderness too.

But I was something between a toy and a suspicious animal that, once tamed, lost its savour.

I still miss you. My very guts hurt. I can hardly recall your face, yet the void you've left in me aches like an abyss, my whole body and all my memory and all my emotions, my humour and my pity and my anger and my understanding and my confusion weep from the inside like weeping life-blood, a peculiar tearing wound that can't be stopped.

But it has dulled. I am used to it. The shocks of losing you and being cast aside by you have begun to cancel each other out by their very keenness.

My whole life, I mean in the big world, has been pivoted on you. But for you I would still be bored to tears, a caged half-individual with a horizon fixed for ever.

I had to kill you. I had to escape you. I had to understand you. I had to keep you.

Nothing succeeded.

I don't even really want you any more, not really. You were not my friend. Not as my brother was. You are no good to me when you are with me. You are a tiger devouring me, the night comes out of your eyes and my love for you makes me fear you and myself.

I don't want your fierce body. Let her have that. I want never to embrace you again. It would be like embracing the big blonde battle-maid, all flesh and splendour. She has been all over you in her concentration and reality, your skin must have been tainted by hers, she would fold you up and keep you in her womb if she could.

I shall get away.

I don't care what to.

But my life shall be no longer Zerd. If anyone kills me, it will be because I am me, not because I am involved in Zerd's wars and hatreds.

I would have died for Atlan's purity. But that was all different. Atlan has a purity the rest of the world is too ordinary to compass – but it's purity gone rotten too long enclosed, it's a rife fervid purity fermenting itself like a hermaphrodite.

And the Long Snow is coming.

The Long Dark

GOOD old civilisation, here we come. The earth smells dunged round here, that's how I can tell we're getting near normal or near-normal mankind. They use a lot of human manure out this way, I know. And dead rabbits hung from boughs twist and decay in the grey winds. They're scarecrows but the crows flap and gather to caw on the crops just the same.

I bathed this afternoon in a high-banked pool. But I didn't go right in, too freezing thank you. Just washed myself and the child from the bank. I recognised the overhang where Madfist jeered down at me, keeping a proud grip on my rags. It was that unfriendly pool that was thick with petals: it is still unfriendly, *brrrr*, but now crackly brittle leaves lilt on the surface.

My back still hurts – that big blister where flames must have seared the flesh – the sort of accident you don't notice at the time, in the heat of the moment as I'd say if I were in the mood for sickish puns, but gosh that blister certainly came up later – all the liquid in it hung towards the bottom of the blister, at my waist, and I couldn't lie flat but I can actually bear the touch of my necessary clothes on it now so it must be healing up. About time.

It was lemming-instinct that passed me as close as possible to the inn. I was longing to go in. I would have been quite glad in a morbid sort of way if Seka had suddenly been taken ill and I'd had *no* choice but to take her to the inn.

Then I remembered that's how it all started with Laran having to get to a doctor. My mind clams up with guilt every time I think of poor, poor Laran.

Yet this long dull red building in its cow-soiled yard in its withy fencing fascinates me. It's like that urge when one stands near a cliff-edge – almost irresistible, one step forward, only one

269

little step, and one could have the unique experience of hurtling down to that hugest of all adventures, death. One little step – and one's leg moves forward for it and one has to run like mad in the opposite direction.

I am now in the same plight as three years ago. I have no money, hardly any clothes, not even a fur hood this time. I have no name, no servants. Now not Sedili only is hunting me. I have no name, Zerd himself has stripped me of my rank and I am outcast.

I have another baby with me. And the first baby is gone.

I suffered so hopelessly in this place, at times believing I'd never get out, that it means Home to me – Home being the ultimate cage, when all is said and done. The squalor draws me, and the bullying. Once bullied, always a victim. It's a temptation to step past the withy gate, one little step, and give up all my responsibilities, except that of jumping to orders someone else has had to think up for a change.

Oh so what? The inn is behind me. I'm facing to the coast. The leaves scud and skirl. The rains beat on the holly bush under which we crouch. Each little red berry, round and glacé-wet, each multipointy shiny leaf is sliding with never-ending raindrops. Every time one plinks from a point, another plops down. Seka moaned when I was pulling her under the bush and the holly pricked her. But most of the time, dumb and numb from weather and the upheaval of her small life, she is like no company at all, just something heavy to lug around with a breaking back.

Is she longing for me to explain to her what has happened to her brother? Or does she know?

Since she can't ask, I won't mention him. It is useless to surmise. Something has had him – either Sedili, or the fire, or the wild things to whom he with his double blood is chosen Emperor.

Stepping carefully, I climbed over the stile. The little field was absolutely chock-full of gorgeous turnips.

I tucked my skirt-hem up in my belt to form a large loose pocket, slung my shoes round my neck by their thongs, tucked Seka under the hedge – 'Don't worry, sweetheart, your Mother is just going to steal some gorgeous turnips' – and waded into the mud.

270

A hand on my shoulder. I am so weak the touch spun me round.

I'd been stooping only five minutes, and had hardly a skirtful, but I'd been too busy to notice the approach of the girl and the little man.

I stared at them, so furious at being discovered pathetically (and muddily) pilfering like this that I considered whether I could make a get-away after pelting them with vegetables – not from fear or self-defence, but annoyance.

Reenah burst out laughing.

'Ah, Cija, my ducky! You're always at something, aren't you?'

'Do you know her?' Scar asked Reenah.

'Course I know her.'

'So do I,' said Scar.

'Oh, do you?' Reenah was surprised.

I distributed the heavy mud-humped things more securely in my skirt. Impatiently I wiggled my toes in the soft mud till Reenah and Scar finished their mutual discoveries.

'I might have expected *you* to get to know each other,' I remarked.

'How's Yula?' Scar asked, swaggering slightly.

'I'm sure you're not interested,' I said.

'Not, I must confess, to the point of burning curiosity.'

'Is Madfist with you?' Reenah asked me. 'He stopped off on his summer wandering, stayed some days at the inn, and told me he meant to journey to the Dyke Road beyond the haunted hill-castle. And so rumour says, that's where the Empress lives – or lived.'

'How do *you* know this is the Empress?' Scar asked.

'An old boy-friend of mine was helping me sell her once,' she said with a saucy look at me.

The last I saw her, Reenah had one of those pretty paper-pale faces, all eyes. But that was winter and this is just after the fall of summer.

Now her cheeks retain spots of wild-rose, like pink fruits drowning in cream. She's not yet in her thick woollen winter shift, she has two that she uses alternately, sewn into them week and week about to keep the draughts out, and I never before saw how expressive her breasts are. They jiggle all the time as she talks, because she can't stand still at all. She can almost gesture with them. They seem to move independently of each other at times.

'I suppose you want to know why I'm here,' I said, liking Reen (in spite of the threat she constitutes) simply because she's so cheerful to look at.

'We know,' Scar said blandly. 'Let us head you back to the inn. I large notice is posted on the barn door, informing all and sundry and those interested by money in particular, that you are not to be harboured, but that you are worth more alive than dead.'

'Are you going to sell me again then, Reen?' I asked, rather looking forward to giving myself up and being brought before Zerd through no fault of my own, I could still tell myself it was not my decision.

'No,' little Reenah said at once. 'This is a different matter, eh? Not ransom, it wouldn't be, not ransom at all this time. Blood money it would be. I'll not take that for you.'

'Why? Have you heard rumours of what they mean to do to me in the Capital?'

'Try you for witchcraft and defiling the Royal bed.'

Some bed, I thought. Bird-spotted cliffs above an angry sea.

'I might be acquitted.'

'If there were thoughts of acquitting you in high heads, they'd not have brought you to public trial and taken your title in the first place. They'd have hushed it all up.'

'Remember a story I told you on a roof?' Scar's leer was toothy. I could see his gums as his lip curled back. There were gaps in his conversation where once he would have called me Empress.

His gaze should have fallen under mine. I was just remembering properly our last meeting. The spiteful, in fact murderous little beast had set his Empress and her two infants adrift – in a storm – in a tiny boat he didn't even know was sea-worthy.

'You, Scar,' I said. 'Doubtless you'd be glad of the reward. My death won't send you red-eyed, will it now?'

'No, but mine would,' he ha-ha'd.

'Shush then,' Reenah said at once. 'Don't go talking death-talk. You'll get well away.'

'You're not thinking,' I inquired, 'that at my own trial I'd bring up something about all that attempted rape and marooning you tried on the occasion of our last meeting? Apart from the fact my evidence will suddenly be worthless, don't think a trifle like that will stick in my gullet when I'll have so much else to consider.'

'Don't try sharpening your tongue on me,' Scar warned.

272

'I've nothing to lose. Have I?'

'Yes, as a matter of fact I think perhaps you have.' Scar looked important and mysterious, which might have worked better if he'd been taller.

'Well, don't keep me dangling.'

'I can't trust anyone else, a feeblewit from Reeney's inn for instance, to tote you to the Capital. I'd never get the reward for myself that way. I can't take you myself either.'

'So I shan't have the pleasure of your company on the long trek? Shame.'

'I can't appear in the Capital,' Scar said. 'Some three years ago I committed a pretty petty crime – which is why I deserted from the Coast base. That was just before I met yourself.' Scar bowed his bow.

'So?'

'Well, I've since heard – there's a great grapevine at this inn, I'm glad I turned up here – that they're still after me. There was a top brigadier died in very suspicious circumstances at the time I scarpered. Nothing to do with me. But they're still angry about it. He was valuable and popular. The Emperor trusted him. They've decided his death might have had a deal to do with the disappeared medals – which merchants in the Capital must still remember giving me a good price for.'

'So no Capital for Scar. No capital gain.'

'Know what I'm going to do, Empress?' He caught himself at the slip of the tongue. If you didn't know him, you'd've thought he'd been rude by mistake, he was so annoyed with himself for giving me my ex-title.

'I'm going to take ship,' he informed us, unable to make any statement without striking a bit of an attitude. 'Travel to the Coast. Get on something sailing for the Mainland. I'm sick of this Continent – ' he slapped Reenah's small behind. 'I came here for a bit of prosperity. All I've had is squalid old troubles. I'm moving back, to the squalid troubles I'm at home with!'

'Quite a rolling stone. Aren't you?'

'Want me to safe-escort you?' he asked abruptly.

I dropped several turnips in shock. Then I had to bite my lip not to cry, they bounced so heavy on my bare toes in the ooze, but at the same time I was laughing and laughing.

'I've had so many offers like this recently,' I said. 'In fact, I've begun to regard myself as so much merchandise. Travel-baggage. What's wrong with you, Scar? Losing your grip aren't you?'

'*Lovely* travelling companion *you'd* make,' Scar said with distaste. 'Can't believe in a little disinterested kindness, can you?'

'Since when have I ever been shown any?' I demanded, forgetting to laugh. 'You'd find some way to claim that reward if I travelled with you. I'd be crazy to trust you and I'm not crazy yet.'

'At one time I thought the Capital was the centre of Atlan. I had some idea that it was an island more than a continent – '

'You'd heard that Atlan goes all in rings and circles?'

Scar replied, 'Yes, I've heard that one. I wonder what *is* in the very middle?'

'The smallest circular-walled canal of all, perhaps,' I said.

'Then we must be a vast way off the heart of Atlan,' Scar said.' This Canal's a big'un by its look.'

We leaned on its carved stone wall. You could tell how old the stone was – pretty old. I sat Seka on it and she dangled her legs. She pointed at the enwalled water. It still flowed briskly. She looked happy. She gurgled as she sometimes does with laughter.

Does she notice she has lost the power of speech? Perhaps when she's older I'll have the courage to talk to her about an effort to get her speech back.

'These traces of all sorts of different colours in the bricks – ' I said. 'I don't admire the Ancients' taste much. Must've looked awfully gaudy.'

'You're not thinking,' Scar told me, impatient. 'It would've been just a bright break in the colossal green landscape. Now it's dingy.'

'No. Pale, mellowed.'

'Come on eh. We'll never hit the ruddy gold coast at this rate.'

I lifted my daughter and followed him meekly.

I shall not have much time or affection for this Diary from now on. I think I shall bring it up to date, then either lob the whole lot overboard, or keep it as my only souvenir of my marriage – this, and Seka.

Autumn as such has not reached the marsh-jungle. But chill winds riffled through the vast ferns which grow here instead of trees, and all the indigestible tropic colours were muted by mists.

274

'*Must* we make our way through this?' I niggled Scar, whose journey-craft I didn't trust. 'Can't there be another way round? We'll sink.' 'Too big to pass except by crossing it,' he'd say, and then I'd complain again till his mouth tightened and his eyes took on that look like an ill-tempered mule's.

We had to balance on fallen logs. Luckily the ferns are so immense that when one falls its stem forms a log. I trod as light as I could, holding the baby. Sometimes the logs, under our pressure, floated – or dipped – but none sank till we had time to hop to the next.

'What's that?' Scar halted in front of us, his hand up. I had to stop so suddenly my foot went through the rotten wood and a holocaust of pink ants poured out and began exploring.

'A bird yelping,' I said. 'Do get on.'

'It's a human voice,' Scar muttered.

'These ants are crawling up my skirt.'

'It's a man calling out.'

I listened through the mist swirls. 'He's in anguish,' I said. 'He's been yelling *Help* so hard he can only gurgle it now.'

'Quick.' Scar made a move.

'You're going the opposite direction.'

'Don't want to involve ourselves in his bother, do we?'

Well, the drift-logs themselves decided that. We could only step on what was there, and short of going backwards, we could be led only (in a roundabout way) to the scene of the cries.

Seka clung. Her hands were trembling limpets on me. Through the fern fronds and the stinking hazes coiling off the swamp, we saw the huge long lizard, patterned so like a log we might have stepped on it had it been still, sinuously half-swim half-thrust through the marsh. And in its jaws struggled a miniscule man.

Scar seemed to choke.

I started forward. He savagely pulled me back. 'There's nothing we can do. Pray your high-nosed gods it doesn't see or scent us.'

'Where did the poor man *come* from?' I said. 'This is hardly a residential area. Is it the travelling season? The man looks very small.'

'He'd be your size close to,' Scar said. 'You'd look small too in jaws like that.'

Night closed a fist on the swamp. We crawled into the centre of a bunch of fronds. I tried to touch not even Scar's cloak. The exhalations of the marsh rose about us, visible even at midnight.

Insects ticked the night away.

Seka was not with us when I woke at dawn.

'Gods! Scar – the baby –'

'She must have climbed out of the fern while you were snoring,' Scar said.

There were the signs. A log had been swayed in the ooze. Tiny bare toesteps could be made out on the mud marking the stemskin. But the tracks disappeared.

'She's sunk – or fell prey to some overgrown worm,' Scar said.

'She may have tried to call –'

'Made a bad job of it, didn't she? Get on. We've done our level best to trace the mite. If we don't think of ourselves now, it'll be another night here for us.'

'I can't leave – she may be lost – she'll never see me again –'

Scar pushed me so I staggered. The log we were on rolled us nearly over. 'You're hysterical.'

'I'll show you what hysteria is if you don't let me search properly. I'm not going till I see some sign –'

'Then you can traipse your own way out.'

'You were wrong, Scar, I know you were. I know there was a way round this swamp. We shouldn't have come here –'

'And if we hadn't, something else would have nobbled us. Ah, come on with you.'

I think even Scar was stabbed by nausea as we saw the deep, deep pits and the immense slither marks which could have been left only by one of the dinosaurs.

And now I said to Scar, 'It's my child, or it was. Don't come with me now. We'll be both done for.'

'Then leave it,' he said.

'I can't, Scar.'

'Then I'll come with you.'

I needed company so much I couldn't make myself beg him any more to leave me. It must be obvious to him anyway that this trail was unlikely to lead us to anything but an end to things. Yet the picture of the tiny girl, after the life which has been nearly all horror and bewilderment, carried off in the foetid jaws and struggling with every muscle and nerve to make some sound to call me – the picture would hurt my mind's

276

eye for ever unless I destroyed it, even if in doing so I also destroyed my mind's eye and mind.

'Look.' I bent from our log.

'I see it. Her bangle.'

'But no carcase, no blood even. It's got her, the thing's got her all right.'

The ferns met over our heads. Scar breathed very hoarse.

The trail of the monster, which was alternately steps and slither, became now slither only, which led under the mud.

'Tunnel,' Scar said.

'I'm going in, Scar. Don't you come.'

'You're mad, you can't go in that. Pearly gods. The filthy tunnel will collapse on you. And can you imagine what you'll be trapped in with?'

'It won't collapse,' I answered his first argument. 'It's bastioned with roots.'

'The squelch underfoot won't support you.'

'I'll take down a floating log-stem that I can propel like a raft. I'll come back if anything looks like going wrong.'

'You won't be able to.'

Scar leaned into the dark to say, 'So long – if you're not changing your mind.' He added, 'Please.' Then he said with a deep breath and in a hurry in case he changed his mind, and with an air of selfless nobility, 'Think what life could still offer you. Don't throw the lot away, because you think you've lost the lot already. But you haven't quite. You could be a wife again, you know. Listen, if you don't go in there I'll even marry you.'

Overwhelmed by this unexpected honour, I didn't speak.

'No? Well, I'll be on me way.'

But he hung around behind me as I floated down the squelch. At last the murk became impenetrable – as far as vision was concerned. Up in the hole mouth, the small man's silhouette left me.

The stench reminded me of everything horrible I have ever, ever smelt – and that rotting. I could see how this hybrid element – not fire, water, nor air – but mud and stink must be home, womb-cosy, to a primeval serpent. In places the rot was so virulent it was bubbling. At others, it was so far gone it glowed with the phosphorescence self-generated by extreme decay.

I tried not to breathe. But the stench beat on my head as though it were crushing my skull from every side. I knew Seka was down there. I knew she had not been mangled up in the swamp. In case I could find her alive – even in case she could glimpse my face, know that I hadn't forgotten her, be together once more in this last deepest of horrors, before the end of us both – I must go on, in and down.

At a point of absolutely pitch blackness, how could I go farther? My nerve went. And I wished I'd lost it farther up the tunnel behind me, when I could have gone back while there was time.

Now I couldn't feel the wall any more. I'd been able, all this while, to keep my fingertips on either wall *and* stop them going in when the decay got too soft and bubbly. But, dearest God, now the log revolved a little under my feet, so I had to keep treading, and there was no wall to touch. I had no way of knowing whether the walls were just inches farther from me than my fingertips could stretch, or whether the tunnel had widened right out below the swamp. There was still ooze low above me, so low I had to keep my neck bent and my knees stooped. Drips of slime fell. My hair, face, neck and arms must be spotted with filth and sores.

Before I give up and die in this hell my life has led me to, I will flail about and try to find walls, try to get back up to the light of the swamp which now seems paradise. I will go panicky, see lights before my eyes in the black, try to touch the tunnel (though, only now, it occurs to me that if I did find it again, I'd be extremely hard put to it to push myself on my raft *up*, though it was comparatively easy to float *down*). But I will not find it, for that's the way fate goes in dark holes, where there's room for despair only. I'll moan, I'll pray. The perilous narrow log will roll. My breath will not be breath but gurgles, which feel to myself the intensest of all pains and prayers. I'll drown in bottomless decay.

But first I'll call her.

My voice might attract some lurking shape now coiled in invisibility. Anyway, my child won't be able to answer me. But if she's there, my baby, she'll know I didn't forget her.

I opened my mouth. I summoned the call from my throat.

No sound. My tongue is too heavy to move.

I don't know how long I stood there on the gently playful log, my toes gripping numb. I willed and willed and willed that my tongue lift and a sound come.

An hour later, maybe, I croaked.

'Seka!'

Violent chills raped my spine, my waist sank and my belly quivered. Terror of my own voice beat me up.

I *knew* I'd attract something's notice. I was *sure* the serpent, the vast slug, the swamp-spawned saurian would come inexorably and slime its coils around me and swallow me now.

Sound.

'*Who's there?*'

I thought it was my own voice. Then I realised I hadn't said that. Then I realised I must have heard it as an hallucination. Then I just screamed out.

'*Seka, Seka!*'

But how could Seka have spoken? Seka can't speak.

Anyway, I think that was a man's voice.

I wasn't concentrating. Perhaps I am mad.

'Who's there – ?' asked a man's voice again, thinking the same things I was thinking about hallucinations and minds playing tricks in this pit.

'Oh, *I* am,' I said, remembering I had an identity.

'Gods,' the man's voice said in acceptance of my statement. 'Scar? Is that you? Have they got you too?'

I had no idea whom I meant by 'they'.

'My name is Jaleril,' the man's voice said with an effort. 'Have you come for me?'

I have gone mad after all. I would have to fish my heart off my toe-nails, it had sunk so. Jaleril is *my* name, or *was*. I said my name was Jaleril when I was dressed as a boy in Southern-city on the Mainland leagues and worlds outside this filthy promised-land.

I stayed silent. I would not bandy words with my alter-ego. I might be mad, but I need not make a show of myself. Fate had had enough of a laugh at me already.

'Is anyone there?' the voice asked presently, hopeless.

'I am Cija,' I told Jaleril.

'That's a Mainland-name!' Jaleril-out-of-blackness said. 'Are you alive?'

'Help me out.'

I trod my log towards the faint voice, which I could tell was nearer than it sounded, half the faintness being despair.

I came up against something. It stirred.

My fingers probed. I found they were on the outline of a body, human at that. It was cased in an envelope of slime. Its arms were pinioned to its sides. Quite easily, with my nails which I haven't cut for ages, I pierced the slime-film. I ripped

279

at it. The man in it groaned. He had been pocketed in the mud wall and filmed in, positioned like a foetus, and a couple of tiny holes were all he'd been able to breath the foul air of the under-swamp through. It was strong of him, weak as he was, to have lived since last night when we'd seen the monster carry him away.

He fell out, probably numb. I grasped him on to my log and managed to steady it.

'We're on a log, floating on the rot,' I explained. 'Please try not to overturn it.'

'Smart,' he wheezed.

'Is the thing here?' I asked.

'Can't tell. If so, it must be asleep else we'd have attracted its notice by now.'

'Is there a baby here?'

'A baby?'

'Help me propel the log. We'll go right round the walls. Now I've found them, I shan't lose them again.'

'Can't we just get away quick? Gods' Gums, to be captured again after this miracle!'

'I came here, and worked Gods' miracle for you, only because I'm looking for my daughter.'

Something little stirred in the wall under my hand. I thought it was more bubbling ooze, it was so slight.

Then I tore and scrabbled the film apart. What if she'd *not* been given air-holes? What if the movement had been the reflex of a corpse buried in the shifty mud? I even bit at the slime.

I caught her into my arms.

'I've got her! I've got her! Seka, it's me!'

Two incredulous arms, skeleton-slim, had strength to come up against my neck and lie still unbelieving.

'You're not dreaming. I'm not dreaming. We're not, we're not. Or if we are, let us die before we wake up.'

'Come,' the Jaleril said.

'We must feel round all the walls, first. Make sure no other wretch is being left here while we live our miracle.'

'Our miracle may be cut very short,' he pointed out. But we could have been murderers, I think, and still not have left any-one else to that horror now we had known it.

Bones, pitiful bones, some still with flesh or hair, was all we found. With a long shin-bone as oar, the man I'd rescued pro-pelled us back up the tunnel. Till we saw the light, I thought it was all a trick and we were sliding up the serpent's throat. When we saw that faint light that dazzled and bit our eyeballs, I kept expecting it to darken as the monster came down to us.

Of course, it darkened. Of course.

Seka began to whimper and move in my arms. She had sensed what we could not yet see.

Slithering towards us, filling the entire tunnel formed by and for its coils alone, down came the serpent.

Of course it could see us. This was its element. Its eyes would already be fixed on us. Its yards of tongue flickering vaguely in the anticipatory deeps of its gullet.

'We *are* done for after all,' I remarked.

I looked aside at Jaleril's movement. In the shine of the rapidly approaching twin eyes, I could see the limned outlines of his fingers and the knife he was pulling out.

'Lucky that serpents, unlike most captors, don't take care to disarm one,' he grunted, looking green.

Incredulously, I heard that I'd laughed. 'A knife that size is enough to scare any dinosaur,' I said.

We could feel a blast of its breath as the jaws opened, wide enough to strain the tunnel. Its breath stopped us breathing. It was filth itself, almost solid. Behind the cave-yawn of the jaws, the eyes, titanic wagon wheels of pallidity, cast enough eager light to highlight the gums, on which fungus grew, and the flicker of the tongue.

Swoosh and, in sucking motions of the tunnel walls and roof, it slithered on us.

Jaleril poised the knife, hefting it in his hand.

'It's hopeless – ' I took breath to tell him as the thing's rush made mud-waves and our raft started bucking.

'Those eyes are so big – I can't miss – ' he moaned.

He threw. We were hurled backward as the onslaught sent our log hurtling down the mud up which we'd just pushed and climbed.

I fell into the mud. But I managed to grasp the edge of the raft-log. It slid past, burning my fingers with friction, but I held on. I blessed Seka's hold on me, developed by all our adventuring through which I've carried her.

I didn't know what had happened to the man.

The tunnel seemed almost a maelstrom. The log was going round and round in its descent. Currents had happened in the mud. I hung grimly on. I won't give up till the last instant, I thought. I'll force fate to kick me again and again while I'm down. The mud roared.

Look up. The tunnel is scintillatory in the glare of the eyes up there. A tiny black dart quivering in one, jerking as it jerks – and it's not the pupil. It's the clever Jaleril's knife.

It's sent the thing crazy. It's most upset. The light of that eye is fading. There's a spurt of blood. It sprinkles myself and Seka, warm.

Furious, the coils thresh so, mud is being chucked down all around us, upon us. The tunnel seems taking on the same spasm-coils as its inmate.

Seka in my arms actually gives a scream.

The tunnel collapses. Mud rains on us. The serpent, unbearably close, like a scaly wall, whooshes past into the depths as the whole unnatural structure gives.

Arms grasp us from the mud-holocaust.

'Up – up to the air – we've that chance – '

The bastion roots hold up here a moment or two longer, out of the way of the blinded serpent's threshing.

In the swamp, we clambered into the nearest fronds. We collapsed. I could not stop shaking for long ages. The man, after the dire effort and his experience being kept as saurian's fodder in the subterranean pantry, alive and fresh till he was needed, was too numb to shake.

With ferns, we brushed a little of the filth off us. Seka could not take her eyes off my face. That was a great scream she managed without realising it as the tunnel caved in. I hoped she had stayed sane through all this.

'Here is your bangle, sweetheart,' I said to her.

'Where do you come from?' I asked the mud-black man.

'We are based just beyond the swamp,' he said. 'I am one of the men of a non-Atlan chief called Ael.'

We came into Ael's camp. It was well disguised. I'd never have known it was there if Jaleril hadn't known.

The vegetation was still monster ferns. But the ground was no longer queasy. We had passed beyond the swamp.

Hard, till right among them, to tell which is giant fernery and which leather tents. Behind mounts the sheer cliffs, towering. Waterfalls on it are blown backwards, up instead of down, because there's a hard wind. The waterfalls look more like smoke than water. The cliffs appear to be smouldering.

There were the smokes of Ael's bandit fires as well. They were the pyres of victory-victims. Ael's bandits were roasting their meat on spits stuck into the burning bodies, the mounds of their defeated enemies. 'Kill two birds with one stone,' they joked. 'Burn the buggers and roast our dinner.' They'd just had a brush with Sedili's coast-guard force.

'We are at peace now with Sedili,' I said.

'They attacked us first,' they said as they gave Jaleril, Seka and myself food and wash-water. 'That's our story and we're sticking to it. *They* can't tell different, can they?'

A moss-green wooden tub, so warped the water trickled out through the slats of the sides before I'd got myself cleaned free of the horror of the pit we'd been in. Sand instead of soap, but it was fine white sand, and didn't scrape or scratch, only tickled.

A bandit-female took Seka from me. She was asleep, the first time in ages. A good sign.

'The Lord will see you now,' the woman said.

I followed her across the campment. I hardly felt their stares which ordinarily would make me shrink.

Ael's portable kingdom again, that nothing has been able to uproot though he never lets it put down roots in one place for long. Stronger, in its own compact way, than Zerd's. I shall no longer call him my husband.

I will sleep with Ael when he repeats what he said years ago. Then I kneed my steed and I left Ael behind me and I made off into the horizon-haze. Now I have more sense. I need haven.

Ael, who never calls himself a king, is stronger than most kings. And he has wanted me a long time. Not obsessively – but a long time.

He is not afraid of offending Zerd. He is afraid of no one. He and his strictly lawless cut-throats fight for whom they choose.

Step by step, I approached Ael in the leathern tent. It smelt like Smahil – much stronger, but the same way. The half-dozen of Ael's personal bodyguard – though really every last one of his bandits is his bodyguard – diced in a corner. Boar-hounds, massive hackles and beastly crowded teeth and legs too powerful to have grace, gurned on bones already chewed dry. The rusty tent-poles, once 'gilt', turned too as the winds outside grew strident. The carpets, deep piles on the ground inches beneath us, had been chucked carelessly – a dozen deep in places, only

283

three deep in others, and it was like climbing on the flat. The raggy fringes sprawled and caught at the heels of my new sandals.

Ael's eyes watched ahead of me. His arms were each as thick as the chair-arms along which they stretched rested. His skin gleamed in the gloom – not the exotic reptilian look Zerd's has. Ael's arms are all heavy un-polished armlets and chains often indistiguishible from the cuts and scars of various ages that coruscate the flesh.

Dark blue, his eyes stopped me.

'Thank you, Ael.'

'No thanks due to us, Empress. You saved the life of our poor blighter in the worm's larder.'

It was in my mind to say, Had that atoned for the loss of the other life Ael's men have always blamed me for – Kond's? But it would have been hypocritical to mention Kond now. Time has soothed the guilt and the odd ache, so that it is now just odd enough to be pleasant, and I quite enjoy remembering Kond instead of feeling awful about it. It really would have been making use of his name to use it now.

'I wish I had never left the bourne you once offered me, Ael,' I said instead, feeling the years roll aside and myself back again facing the dark blue eyes and the light voice.

'You would have been safe, yes. But not Empress.'

'Is that a higher fate than safety?'

'Fate plays us all off against each other, Empress – safety against nobility, health against wealth. We each think we are the loser to the next man.'

'No need to call me Empress, Ael. You've heard the proclamation?'

The big man nods.

'So now you're Sedili's allies,' I said.

'That's official, more or less,' Ael agreed.

'No less about it.'

Ael's mouth stretched in his mirthless grin. 'Oh, yes, it's gone out over the length and breadth of the land – or the length and breadth of this neck of the land. But even now Zerd is quashing it.'

'*What!*' I had to lean against a pole. 'Zerd – changed his mind – He changed his mind, did he – ?'

'It wasn't Zerd's proclamation,' Ael said placidly.

'But – the Emperor's seal – '

'Easy to get hold of that,' the bandit chief said with contempt.
'No, it was the boy's proclamation.'

'The Atlantean ex-Emperor?'

'Nitwit hothead.'

'But – how did he dare?'

'Did it for Zerd's own good.' Ael stretched. The chains on his arms clanged. 'He's blindly partisan to Zerd. Would do anything he judged helpful to Zerd – whether Zerd wishes it or not. He knew if Zerd wanted to shout him down later, he'd have to be careful not to do it *brutally* – can't antagonise Atlan.'

'Was any of this Zerd's idea?'

'He wanted you back at the Capital – and taken back there under safe conduct. He soft-soaped Princess Sedili into letting you go by telling her you must be tried for your alleged crimes of witchcraft and fornication – alleged by her. At least, that's what he told the boy to tell her. The boy wilfully misunderstood. And he said, as you know, that no one accused of such crimes could sit the ancient throne of Atlan. And Zerd can't dispute that too hard – after all, must keep the Atlanteans sweet.'

'Zerd has to keep everyone sweet.'

'So Zerd is just tactfully oversetting clauses of Atlan law here and there. Telling the people he'll give you a particularly fair trial and if you're proved innocent, you'll be considered not even accused.'

'How did the boy think my dethronement could benefit Zerd? Wasn't it just spite?'

'From your view, just spite,' agreed Ael. 'He's blindly partisan to Zerd. I don't think he realises that's the only pattern his mind could have followed after he gave up his throne and his crown and his all to Zerd in his childhood – blind adoration, or blind resentment. Now he's sure you've endangered Zerd's cause all along simply by being alive. You're in Sedili's way, and Lara's. He wants more than anything to ally his beloved Atlan, under his beloved war-lord Zerd, with the might of Sedili's Northmen and Lara's father's junglemen.'

'But now Zerd's telling people I'm *not* to be hunted down dead or alive?'

'He wants you in the Capital. But not dead.'

'He must know the boy made the mistake on purpose! You don't mix messages like that by *mistake* –'

'He must pay attention to the boy. Can't flatten him. The boy's war-hero-mad and is forming Atlan's Army after all.'

'Does Zerd still think I'm on my way to him with the ex-Emperor and Sedili – and our heir and daughter?'

'Zerd has heard of the fire and Ancients' carnage at your Castle,' Ael said sombrely. He giggled. 'Zerd doesn't know who's on his way to him and who's lying about in mangled bits.'

'Is he worried?'

'He'll get over it.'

I left the pole, loose gilt now flaking my dress, and paced up and down.

'That's true,' I said violently. 'He'll get over it. No one but you knows I'm not dead now, Ael. Sedili, if she survived, and everyone else thinks I died in the Castle incident. Zerd will think I didn't manage to survive that. A man called Scar, if he ever turns up anywhere and talks to anyone, thinks I died in the larder-lair under that swamp there. You won't tell anyone different, will you?'

Ael is not the man to be in the power of. He is a sadist. If I am untraceable, I am not dangerous to hurt. But I must offer something he'll appreciate in return for the safety I must have.

'Ael, I'm pleading for the safety I didn't accept once from you. It's the only important thing in the world, security. A roof for myself and my child, food, warmth in the coming Snow.'

Ael gazed through me.

'You can do with me as you will,' I half-whispered.

'I don't want you,' Ael said.

He gave no sign that he enjoyed my humiliation. His sadism is physical, he is not cruel to mentality. Nevertheless, I have never offered myself to anyone and been refused.

'I've no place for a woman with a mind and will and whims of her own,' Ael said, refraining from referring to me as a bitch, a remnant of his studied courtesy to me at Court. 'This is War. I wanted you at the start of this war. Now I'm fighting against time. I have to squash Sedili while I can still claim that as *my* mistake. Zerd can forgive me doing what he wants me to do, just so long as I can claim I didn't *know* I was supposed to do the opposite.

'I know you're not the woman to be a drag on campaign. But I don't want anyone with any personality, any wants, any needs. A mare would be enough for me now – or any tongueless bint who doesn't even trouble me with her name.'

'What are you going to do with me then?' I asked, rejected.

'What do you want me to do with you?'

'I still have a choice? I've told you, I want safety. For myself and the child.'

'Zerd's child.' Ael reached up and grasped a bluebottle buzzing too near him, and proceeded to pinion it to his chair-arm with his knife-point.

'She's just mine now. He's never even been to see her. She was born after his last visit to me.'

'So.'

'I want to get away. No one'll know, only your bandits who never talk out of turn. I'm officially dead now. Let me get out of Atlan. Let me get out of Zerd's War.'

'He misses you,' the bandit said suddenly.

'You said he'll get over it. War – and Sedili – and Lara – will help him. He'll enjoy the process of forgetting me – and only wish it could have lasted longer! No, it won't take him long to forget me.'

'I'll give you a pony and escort to the beach a few miles off – and one of our boats. You'll be out of here, shaking the leaf-mould off your heels, before the Long Snow immobilises the Continent.'

All the gunge-globules on the muddy road were glowing. Clop clop the ponies' hooves pocked it.

The sun led in the tide.

Harbour. Dawn. Sky all shades of rose and primrose. Masts and rigging. Sails albatross-full. Seka sucking a contemplative thumb.

Ael's bandits actually dismount from their ponies a moment to see me aboard.

The ship's leaving (illegally – though Zerd ordered it, he who made the law no shipping) to trade with the Mainland. 'And we're not to trade *her*, eh?' The captain pulls his ear till Seka and I think it'll never regain its natural shape. 'Can't sell her the other side of the ocean?'

'Not unless you can be sure Ael and the Dragon-Emperor never come to hear of it,' say my trustworthy escort.

'Too risky.' The captain thumbs me to my berth. 'Back there you'll be. Anchor away. Make sail!'

The golden coast hazes down the purling wind. The spray and the dolphins leap and shimmer. Albino dolphins, Atlan creatures. I spent a lifetime yearning for Atlan, the great good stronghold, the last purity, before ever I heard its name. I curse

287

the day I first set foot on it (as Atlan too curses that day when storm and war broke loose) and I hope never to see Atlan again.

I hope never to see my husband again.

'Look, Seka! Silver dolphin.'

The rose clouds darken.